DMITRI

By Briana Michaels

COPYRIGHT

All names, characters and events in this publication are fictitious and any resemblance to actual places, events, or real persons, living or dead, is entirely coincidental.

All rights reserved. No part of this publication may be reproduced, stored, or transmitted, in any form or by any means, without the prior permission, in writing, of the author.

www.BrianaMichaels.com

COPYRIGHT © 2024 Briana Michaels

Author Note

    Please don't use this, or any other book of mine, as an educational tool. It might be inspiring, but always play responsibly and do your research. I take creative liberties because this is a work of fiction and I'm a chaotic creature in all aspects of my life.

    This book contains very heavy themes, so please visit my website, www.BrianaMichaels.com, for a list.

    Thank you for reading!

Dedication

To the ones who want the big,
bad monster to protect you.
Here he is.

Chapter 1

Daelyn

Murder is wrong. I'd never survive prison. I need to take care of Addie.

I remind myself of these three simple facts while I stare at the asshole sitting on my front stoop. "What are you doing here, Ace?"

"Watching the sunset."

My little sister is sitting next to him, her smile way too similar to the one I used to wear at her age, and I don't like it. My stomach twists. "Get inside, Addie."

"Relax, Dae. I'm not going to bite her." Ace stares down at Addie with a flirtatious smile. "Unless she wants me to."

Addie's smile gets bigger.

I drop my grocery bags on the sidewalk and take a step forward. "Addie. Get inside. *Now.*"

"Why? It's not like Ace is a stranger." She has the nerve to roll her eyes.

My sister is the most defiant sixteen-year-old I've ever known. She's worse than I was at her age. I'm sure a lot of it is my fault, because she doesn't ever have to suffer consequences for her actions. I usually like that she's not intimidated by anyone, including me, but right now, I hate it. Especially when she digs down and doesn't do what I ask in times like this.

"Hey." Ace gently rests his finger under her chin and makes her look at him. "I really appreciate you keeping me company out here today. How about next time I come, I bring you a present?"

Addie arches her brow. "What kind of present?"

"Be a good girl and go inside, then you'll find out." He has the audacity to stare at her mouth.

I stomp forward, grab him by the collar of his shirt, and rip him back from her, breaking the spell between them. Addie glowers at me for a hot second before storming towards our front door, the chains on her Doc Martens clinking as she goes, and then she slams the door shut.

Ace laughs and shakes his head. "She's such a spicy black cat."

"Stay the fuck away from her, Ace. She's off limits and you know it."

"Says who?"

"Says *me*. She's sixteen." Which he's well aware of. Ace has been coming around for a couple years now. He's twenty, the youngest member of the crew I'm involved with, and is great at being bad. Just Addie's type, I fear.

"She's legal," he counters. "Finally." When my hands ball into fists, his smile morphs into a sneer. "Don't even *think* of swinging, Dae. You'll regret it."

He's right. But it could be worth the price I'd pay just to feel the brief satisfaction of knocking his teeth out. Letting out an exasperated breath, I relax my stance a fraction. "Why are you here?"

He pulls out a vape and takes a pull, letting orange cream scented smoke billow around us. I hope he didn't vape around Addie.

All humor and sarcasm is gone from him when

he says, "Kaleb wants to talk with you."

Fuck. Not again.

Crossing my arms over my chest, I grind my molars together. I can't say no. "When?"

"Now." He stands and pulls his keys out his pocket.

Double fuck.

Ace glances at the groceries scattered all over the front walkway. "Pick your shit up off the ground first. I'll wait."

Shame heats my face as I pluck the apples that fell out and stuff them back in one of my reusable bags. "Just give me five minutes."

"Two." Ace takes another puff of his vape. "I've been here a while already, and I got shit to do."

Biting back a snarky response, I bring my groceries inside and drop them on the counter. "Fucking asshole," I whisper to myself.

Addie's sitting on the couch, watching me like a hawk. "He's not as bad as you think, Daelyn. Ace is actually really sweet."

Her defending him makes me queasy. "That's what he wants you to think, Addie. Stay away from him."

"God, you're such a hypocrite." She pushes up and heads for the front door.

"Don't—"

She slams the door so loud it shakes the walls. *Brat.*

I rush over to the window and see her stuff her hands in the back pockets of her tight black cutoff shorts as she talks with Ace again. He says something that makes her laugh and my heart trips on itself. Skipping putting the food in the fridge, I run back outside to break them up again.

It's futile. I can't keep my sister away from Ace and the other guys any more than I can escape the Hell I signed up for.

But I have to try.

"Addie, come inside and put the groceries away."

She ignores me.

We got into a fight last night, and I wanted so badly to make up with her today. I'd gone out to buy all the ingredients to make her favorite dinner, but at this rate, it's a lost cause. If I have to talk with Kaleb now, he'll likely keep me out late, and Addie will be home alone again.

I hate this.

"I'm going to Tasha's," she says, turning to face me.

Good. This at least takes the guilt of me not being home tonight a little more bearable. "Okay," I say in a lighter tone. "Have fun." I hope my smile looks easy-going and real. I hate when there's tension between us. I don't like fighting with her. And I don't like being the bossy bitch in the house. But sometimes I have to be the bad guy, damnit. It's a necessary evil.

Ace takes another puff of his vape and stuffs it back in his pocket as he heads to his car. "Come on, Dae."

Walking forward, I mentally tick through my responsibilities, rearranging their order of priority. *Kaleb. Ace. Bills. Apology dinner for Addie.*

My sister stares at me while I do this, and after a few heartbeats, she shakes her head. "I'm sorry, Dae."

I want to cry. I want to scream. "I'm so sorry,

too. I shouldn't have yelled at you last night. That wasn't fair."

"No, I shouldn't have taken cash out of your purse without asking. It's my fault."

We hug and I want to say a million other things. *Do better than me. Stay away from danger. Put the groceries away before the milk sours on the counter and our money is wasted.* "Have fun at Tasha's, okay? Be home by noon tomorrow."

"Okay." Addie hugs me tight. "Love you."

"Love you more."

And just like that, I can breathe easier.

Ace lays on the horn, and we both jump back from each other, startled.

Asshole.

Addie flips him the bird but he doesn't let up on the noise.

"He's such a dick," she says, but there's humor in her tone.

I change the subject before we get into another fight again. "Can you put the groceries away for me before you go? I bought the ingredients to make your favorite."

Addie's eyes brighten. "Sweet! Yeah, no problem. I gotta work from two to ten tomorrow night, but maybe we can make the lasagna together the day after?"

"Perfect." I tuck stray blue hair strands behind her ear.

Ace doesn't stop honking even after I get in his car, buckle up, and stare at him with my brow arched. Unfazed, he keeps pressing the horn and glowers at me with this silent threat that says wasting his time will cost me.

He's just like Kaleb. Heartless, cold, and charismatic only when he wants to drain his prey of something.

Nausea hits me soon after we turn off my road and I take shallow breaths. In through the nose, out through the mouth. His car smells like grease, weed, and cologne, which doesn't help my fight against the bile rising in my throat. Meeting Kaleb like this always makes me feel sick. I never know what he's going to ask of me.

And I can never say no to it.

"Do you know what he wants?"

"Above my paygrade." Ace blows through a red light.

My palms sweat. "How long were you waiting for me?" I need to figure out how much time he spent with Addie.

"Long enough to piss me off."

My mouth runs dry. There's a new tattoo on his forearm, just above the scar that marks him as a possession. I know because I have the same scar on my wrist. It makes me wonder if Ace is in this shitshow because he wants to be, or because he has to be. Not that I'll ever ask.

"Stop staring at me." Ace speeds up. "Put your focus where it belongs, Daelyn."

Right. Any hope I ever get of cracking this guy open and seeing the truth of him always dies fast. Maybe Addie isn't the only one who slips under his spell. Only she's a naïve fool who finds bad boys hot. I'm older than Ace and find this particular bad boy a potential ally.

At least, sometimes I do.

Stop it. Ace is not like you. He has choices and you

don't.

But is that even true? Kaleb is brutal and owns a lot of things, especially people. Ace only started working with him a couple years ago. Maybe he didn't have a choice either. Regardless of how he ended up in our crew, he still works for the same monster as me, and that makes him a bad guy. I can't fuck with anymore bad guys, and I know damn well none of them can be trusted. Me included.

We finally pull up to a strip club and confusion has me balking. We usually meet at a hotel. "He's in *here*?"

Ace turns to face me and arches his brow like I just asked a really stupid question. His eyes are bright green and bloodshot. Is that from lack of sleep or something worse?

Why do I even care?

When I don't budge, Ace leans over and unbuckles my seat belt, then shoves my car door open. "Get out."

"Fuck you too, Ace." I climb out and slam the door hard, hoping it'll shatter his window. He slams into reverse, and I have to jump back so he doesn't hit me with his car. Gravel dust flies in my face as he leaves the lot in a hurry. "Asshole!"

Sucking in a deep breath, I tap my pocket, seeking comfort in the knife I—

Shit, I left my knife at home. In my purse. On the counter with the groceries.

I'm an idiot.

Looking back at the road, I debate on running. But I learned a long time ago that running gets you chased. Chased gets you caught. Caught gets you disciplined.

I don't have the strength to go through Kaleb's punishments again.

Rolling my shoulders back, I swing open the door and am smacked in the face with the scents of stale beer and cheap perfume. Kaleb sits at the bar, alone, staring into an empty glass. He doesn't look at me when I approach. Doesn't acknowledge me when I sit on the stool next to him either.

This is bad.

The bartender wipes her hands with a towel and offers me a tired smile. "Hey sugar, what can I get you?"

"Water, please." I don't drink alcohol around Kaleb. I need every brain cell in perfect working order in case shit goes sideways.

She sets a glass of water in front of me and immediately grabs the bottle of tequila for Kaleb. He places his hand over the top of his glass, shaking his head once. Without a word, she turns away and puts the bottle back, leaving us alone.

"What do you want, Kaleb?"

He keeps quiet, staring at the selection of top shelf liquor, until I'm positively squirming.

I hold my breath. Blow it out. Take a sip of my water.

"How have you been, babygirl?"

Is he for real? "Oh, you know. Living the dream."

"Still working from home?"

I hate that he's playing with me. He knows exactly what I do all day, every day.

"Yup." I take another sip of my water and stare at the bottles of liquor like he is. The trick to dealing with Kaleb is matching his energy without taking the upper hand.

He'll likely cut your arms off if you try.

"That's good. Gives you more time with Addie."

The worst part about Kaleb is I can never tell when he's being sincere or not. That unreadability got me in this mess to begin with. Kaleb can come off as the most charming man on the planet and his looks only reinforce that he might be a great time for someone who loves herself a big red flag.

The man's a wolf with an entire Prince Charming wardrobe.

"What do you want, Kaleb?"

"I just wanted to see you. It's been a while."

Not long enough. But he's right. We haven't met for several months. I think the worst part about this is that I had a break, and it made me delusional enough to believe he'd forgotten about me. I actually started thinking that maybe I was out, and he was going to leave me alone for good.

Wow. When did I get so stupid?

Kaleb turns to me and rests one of his big, inked hands on my thigh.

The heat of his palm, the weight of it, and the massive size all remind me what he's capable of. He can bring pleasure as swiftly as he can bring pain.

Kaleb used to be my boyfriend. Sometimes his touch stirs old, familiar feelings that blur and confuse me. My body melts and recoils at the same time. My brain sighs and freezes. My heart stops and stutters. There was a time when I would have given this man the world and he knew it.

Now, I only give him my time because I'm forced to.

His eyes lock onto mine, and the monster finally comes out to play. "I need you to fuck someone for me tonight, babygirl."

"Fuck them how? Like slash their tires or slip something in their drink?"

"No. Fuck them. Spread your legs and open your mouth."

My blood runs cold. "Who?"

"No one you know."

That's not helpful, but at least it's not *him* I'll have to spread my legs for. I'm ashamed to admit that it took me a long time to get over Kaleb. He fucks like a beast and was so protective and possessive of me when we first met. I fell hard for him.

But he never cared about me. I was a temporary toy turned possession. Once his claws sank into me deep enough, I couldn't do anything without him knowing about it. Then his control morphed until I could no longer survive without his help.

Now, I depend on him.

"Why do I have to fuck this guy?"

"Because I told you to."

"But *why*?"

Kaleb's fingers dig into my thigh, making me cry out. "You will do what you're told."

"I'm only asking why!" Anger spikes in my veins and I smack his arm hard enough to make his grip slip.

In a flash, Kaleb's out of his seat and has me pinned against the bar with his hand around my throat. My back is bent at a harsh angle and tears spring to my eyes, but I won't let them fall. Crying only makes him happier.

His voice stays controlled and steady when he

says, "Make it good for him. Make him want you again. Then when you're done…" He swallows hard, like he's the one getting choked here. "I'll let you go."

I'm not sure if I'm floating from the hope of his promise, the adrenaline spiking in my system, or if he's lifted me clean off my feet with his hand around my throat, but I'm getting dizzy.

"Okay," I say, as stars dance in my blackening vision. "Okay, I'll do it."

Kaleb drops me immediately. "I wasn't asking."

I know, but pretending I have a choice makes me feel stronger. Coughing, I grip the edge of the bar and try to take in a full breath. "Who is it I'm fucking?"

"The winner of a fight tonight. Ace will take you." Kaleb slaps a hundred-dollar bill on the bar. "When you've finished this job, we'll be even."

It sounds too good to be true. I don't trust it. "How do I know you'll keep your word?"

Kaleb tilts his head and the man I once fell for almost peeks out. It makes me feel too stupid to live because I'm always looking for a glimpse of the good in people who have no such thing left in them.

"Have I ever lied to you, babygirl?"

No. He hasn't. That's what pisses me off most. Kaleb's a twisted bastard with an honesty streak. It's how he got me to trust every toxic word he's ever told me.

"Answer me, Daelyn."

"No," I whisper. "You've never lied to me."

He tips my chin up with his finger, his voice softening when he says, "And I *never* will."

As Kaleb leaves me stranded at the strip club, I trick myself into believing this is the last time I'll have to put myself in the line of fire.

Even if the scar on my wrist says otherwise.

Fuck the winner. That's all I have to do. One night, one man, one last job, and it's over.

That's not too hard, right?

Chapter 2

Dmitri

Violence pumps in my veins and if I don't exorcise it, I fear I'll become a mindless animal. I've put off going back in the cage for months, but the aggression riding me lately has become unbearable.

I get it from my mother. She was a nasty bitch whose temper could have made Satan piss his pants. I also got my dad's patience and precision.

Which means I'm a deadly combo of my parents and it terrifies me.

Waiting two weeks for this night has been pure Hell. Every second that ticks by is slower than the last. I can't sleep. I can't eat. I can't fuck.

Hopping on my Ducati, I slither through city traffic like a snake. The fights have already started. I'd have been there earlier but couldn't leave work until I was sure it was safe to. As head of security at the Monarch Club, the most elite sex club in the tri-state area, my job is to make sure our guests play safely. Tonight, we had an incident. Some dumb fuck thought coercion was the same as consent.

I taught him otherwise.

I'd allowed myself one hit.

One.

Fortunately, that's all it took to knock the bastard out. And now that I've had a taste of fresh blood, I'm a shark circling, desperate for more. If I don't get this aggression out of me fast, I'm scared I'll lose my head.

Violence is like a drug to me. A high. A release. A poison I've suffered from since I was a kid and now have a craving for.

After I took care of the now blacklisted member, I quickly rushed down to my dungeon and busted my knuckles on a punching bag. When that didn't come close to taking the edge off, I cut my thigh with a knife. Still didn't help. But I knew better than to go back and be around the club's offender. I'd kill him. So Ryker and Vault hauled his unconscious ass out of the club while I tried reeling in my control to no avail.

And going to a cage fight tonight is going to open pandora's box again. If Ryker and the other's find out I'm doing this... *Shit*. If only the shame I should feel for my actions was strong enough to make me turn around.

But that's not going to happen.

I have no shame.

Look, I know Ryker would fight me if I asked. We've thrown a lot of punches over the years, for various therapeutic reasons, but this isn't one of those times where a split lip or concussion can fix me. I need more.

I need blood to pour and bones to crack. Even if it's my own.

Ryker, Vault, or even Knox would never take it that far. Trust me, I've begged.

Cage fighting in an underground club I've belonged to since I was sixteen is the only way to get what I need right now.

Pulling up to the abandoned warehouse dubbed the Scrapyard, I turn the engine off and immediately hear the riotous hollers from inside. Storming in, I head straight for the cage in the center, tearing my shirt off as I go. It smells the same as it always has in this run-down joint. The coppery scent of blood, musky sweat, cold metal, and wet concrete—along with booze and smokes—it's the smell of my extremely short childhood.

I'm home.

Jerking the cage door open, not giving a flying fuck about the two fighters already swinging, I lock onto the first man I reach, and smash my head against his. He stumbles, dazed. The other guy jumps on my back and punches my side.

Cute.

I spin around and smash him against the fence. He barks a bunch of nonsense in my ear, and I pry him off my back, flipping him over my shoulder before slamming him against the floor. While he's busy trying to catch his breath, I punch his face over and over and over and over and ov—

Someone peels me off the poor, limp bastard.

I rip out of their hold and go for the second guy in the cage again. I can't hear the crowd. I can't feel my legs. I can't think straight. Everything's a red haze and I'm getting tunnel vision.

I square up and stare at my opponent. "Hit me."

He doesn't need to be told twice. His left hook lands square in my jaw, snapping my head to the side. Fuuuuck that felt good. "Again."

He hits me in the gut this time.

"Again!"

Roaring with anger, fear, or, for all I know, frustration, he barrels into me and drives me backwards until my spine hits our enclosure. The cold steel does nothing to soothe my burn. He jabs me in the ribs, the gut, the face, and kicks my thigh. It hurts.

It also awakens.

"My turn," I growl, sucking in ragged breaths. My opponent doesn't stand a chance against me. It doesn't matter if we're a match in weight and height. It doesn't matter that I've given him plenty of free shots. *He* doesn't matter.

Fury blooms in my veins. I jab him in the kidneys, the face, the head, his spine. We're a tornado in the ring and I don't let up until several men peel me off his limp body. They back off me once I go willingly, and they leave the cage in a hurry.

"Who else?" I look around the Scrapyard for another willing opponent. I'm sure I look like a lunatic. I definitely feel like one. Finally, after so long, I feel alive again. I'm myself.

And I'm not done yet.

"Who else will fight me?"

A bulky man steps up to the challenge. The crowd roars and blood swishes in my ears. We circle each other, and he gives me a run for my money. The numbness and detachment I've lived with for years starts subsiding as my red-hazed world comes into crystal clear focus. I drive him back. Land a few jabs. He spins out and puts me in a headlock, his fist making my face its only target. He hits the bullseye several times. Each blow echoes in my skull.

We tear into each other until I finally wrestle him to the ground and put him in a body lock that forces him to tap out.

They have to peel me off him, too.

"Who else?" I stumble back onto my feet and blood pours from my mouth. My ribs hurt. I can't see out of my left eye. "*Who else?*"

No one rises to my challenge.

No one else enters the cage.

"There's none left," Old Man Silas says. "Dmitri, you took them all out."

"How many?"

"Seven."

I just fought *seven* men? I only counted three. Dread consumes me as reality sinks in. *I lost time.* Half this fight has fallen into the black hole of my mind.

"You did well, son. Real well." Silas has been running these underground fights since before I was born, and he knows praise doesn't do shit for me. Never has. He points at the boarded-up office that was converted to a bedroom when I was seventeen. "She's upstairs."

"*She?*"

"I know how you are, Dmitri. When you said you were coming tonight, I made arrangements for you."

Just like old times.

Swiping the blood from my nose and mouth, I storm out of the cage with a new target to take my aggression out on.

My prize.

"It's good to have you back!" Silas yells as I beeline through the crowd of wannabe fighters and heavy gamblers. A few motherfuckers try to pat my back, but I smack their hands off. No one touches me without consent.

Taking the stairs a little slower than I prefer, I hold my side and spit blood on the steps.

Silas knows that after a hard fight, I like a harder fuck. He's always found a willing, consensual partner for me. I guess I should be grateful he went to the trouble tonight, but I know it's likely just a ploy to get me back in the ring as a regular. I've made him a lot of money over the years. He probably thinks taking care of me tonight will lead to more of the same energy from me later.

It won't.

It can't.

Tonight's fight is a one-time thing.

Aw fuck, why am I lying to myself? I'll be back again, and Silas and I both know it. No matter how hard I try to give this up, I can't do it. I'm too weak. Too hooked. Too broken.

My dick is hard as steel, and I haven't even seen my prize yet. Opening the door, I'm nothing more than a hot-blooded feral animal as I prowl over to the woman chained against the wall. I'm too mindless to take note of her beauty, and her chains are a given.

I have a type, and Silas knows it.

Looming over her, I suck in heavy, labored breaths. "Are you here of your own volition?" Blood drips from a cut in my cheek as I wait for her to speak. "Answer me."

"Yes."

Her tone strikes a chord I don't care to consider.

"Call red if I'm too much." I yank my belt off first and shove it in her mouth. "Bite down."

Her pearly whites clamp onto the leather strap, and I barely make out what she looks like as I tug my jeans down and snag a condom from the pile on the floor by her feet. Sheathing myself, I lift her thighs and drive into her.

No introductions. No foreplay.

I'm not in the mindset of good manners, which makes me so fucking dangerous.

She grunts in my ear. I bleed all over her tits. Her thighs quiver under my grip. My dick rams into her hot cunt. Every thrust brings my crazed mind more peace.

"You're doing so good," I manage to grit out.

She doesn't respond because she's still biting down on my leather belt. And as long as she keeps that thing in her mouth, she's not calling red, which means I can keep going.

Her body takes what I give it. My brutality. My length. My frenzied thrusts.

Her pussy makes a lot of wet noises while I drive into her, and I focus on that while chasing my release. It hurts to breathe. I can't see out of my left eye. The other one is blurry. My face throbs. My muscles scream. My bones ache.

I come hard, filling the condom.

The woman dangles from her chained wrists and when I let go of her, I finally notice her legs have been wrapped around me this whole time. Her hazel eyes blaze with wild desperation. Her nostrils flare with each ragged breath she takes.

I try pulling away, but her thighs tighten around me, keeping me right where I am. This girl is an anaconda. My ribs and bruised torso scream in protest under her pressure. It makes me want to fuck her more. I don't think she came yet, and damn me for not giving her pleasure before stealing my own. I never would have done that if my head was on straight.

Then again, I wouldn't be here at all if my fucking head was on straight.

"I got you." Rubbing her clit with the pad of my thumb, I rock back and forth inside her, praying the condom doesn't bust while I do this.

The woman spits out my belt and says, "Harder."

She has the voice of an angel.

My hips turn to pistons, and I rub her clit more. The chains clanking from her shackles sound loud in my ears, and my gaze lifts to her wrists. Shit, her skin is red and cut up from the cuffs.

"Hang onto me, babygirl."

Her legs tighten around me more, robbing me of breath. Grunting, half in pain, half in arousal, I press her flush against the wall for stability and flick the safety locks on the cuffs to free her.

She immediately wraps her arms around my neck. "Harder," she begs again, but her eyes shine with unshed tears.

This woman's a dark beauty.

"Please." Her fat bottom lip is cracked and dry. "Please give me more."

How can I say no to that?

With my dick still buried balls deep inside her, I shuffle us over to the bed. My blood is all over us. We both look down at the mess I've made on her sweet skin at the same time.

Unfazed, she swipes her fingers over her tits, smearing my blood, and then shoves them in my mouth.

Where did this woman come from?

My dick jerks in her cunt. Her eyes roll back when I suck on her fingers and drive into her again. I move slower, with better precision, to hit her deeper pleasure points. She's stunning, all bloody and pale and perfectly limp under me. I want to taste her.

Pulling out, I sink to my knees and eat her sweet pussy like a victory meal.

"Oh my god." She runs her hand over my buzzed hair. It makes me want to grow it out so she can pull it by the roots.

Sinking two fingers inside her, I hit her g-spot and let my Dom side out to play. "Don't come until I tell you, babygirl."

"Daelyn," she pants. "My names is Dae...*fuck*...Daelyn." Her head tips and back arches as she succumbs to the pleasure.

I relentlessly hit her g-spot until she screams with her release. Her voice cracks. Her body shakes. Her pussy clamps down on my fingers like she doesn't want to let me go.

"That's a good girl." Happy to have given her a little release, I place a soft kiss on her swollen clit. Her cheeks are pink and flushed. There are dark circles under her eyes that I can see even with my blurry vision and the concealer she's wearing. "Do you want more, Daelyn?"

"No."

I shove inside her, hooking my finger to hit her g-spot again. "You sure?"

Her eyes flutter. She likes what I'm doing. I do too.

Daelyn gyrates against my hand and opens her pretty little mouth. "Red."

I pull out immediately. There's blood on my hand and I have no idea if it's hers or mine.

"Shit." I spread her thighs to make sure she didn't tear.

"Stop."

I back off and put my hands up. "Sorry, I was just making sure you're not bleeding."

"If I am, it's fine." She clamps her legs shut and

covers her tits with her arms.

My cell goes off in my pants that are still down around my fucking ankles. Whatever bubble of pleasure I thought we were in pops. Ripping the condom off, I toss it on the floor and yank my jeans up.

My cell won't stop ringing, damnit. Digging it out of my pocket, I see why. It's Ryker. "What?"

"Where are you?"

"I'll be back soon."

"That's not what I asked."

I know. But I'm not ready to tell him I've gone back to the cage. "What do you need?"

"For my fucking security to get back to work. Unless you're…"

"I'll be back at the Monarch in twenty. Just stepped out for some fresh air."

There's a long pause. Ryker can always tell when something's up with me. He's been on my ass for weeks because he senses I'm not doing well anymore but hasn't pushed me for answers.

"Okay," he says cautiously, then hangs up.

Turning around to find where the girl went, I catch her over by a chair in the far corner of the room. Something close to guilt has me opening my mouth and saying, "I can give you a ride home."

"I already have one, but thanks." She snags her dress and pulls it on, then drops into the chair and slips her feet into a pair of well-worn black combat boots.

Realizing I've come full circle and am right back to my old ways, in this room, with a random woman to use for my pleasure, makes me feel sick.

As she hurries to get dressed and likely hightail

it out of here, I sit on the edge of the squeaky bed and stare at the puddle of blood on the floor over by the chains dangling from the wall.

    I don't notice until the door slams shut that she's left.

    Good. At least one of us can escape me.

Chapter 3

Daelyn

"Don't let the sauce stick."

"I'm not!" Addie quickly grabs a wooden spoon and stirs. "Okay, it stuck a little but that's just extra flavor. You're welcome."

Making lasagna has us both ridiculously happy. Who doesn't love pasta? It's also a great distraction from the thoughts that haven't stopped racing through my mind since I did my last job for Kaleb two nights ago. As far as going out with a bang, I have zero regrets. And now, my debt is paid and I'm *free*.

"You've been in a good mood, Dae." Addie taste tests the sauce and smacks her lips. "You get laid or something?"

Snatching the spoon from her, I lick the back of it. *Ohhh that's good.* "Can't I just be happy because I'm with you?"

"Oh pah-lease." She dips her finger into the ricotta mixture and wipes it on the tip of my nose. "You're a horrible bullshitter."

True, but I'll keep practicing. "I'm just in a good mood, that's all."

There's no way I can tell Addie that I fucked a stranger two nights ago as my last job for Kaleb. She doesn't even know I've been in debt to him all this time.

There's a lot Addie doesn't know about, actually. I envy her ignorance. Sometimes I want to tell her stuff, but she's had to grow up fast enough and dragging her deeper into my shitshow won't help her. It'll kill her spirit or worse, make her think my actions are acceptable.

"Preheat that oven, baby." Addie rubs her hands together and stares at the assembly line of noodles, filling, cheese, and sauce. "It's time to put this bad boy together."

My stomach flip-flops as I hit the digits on the oven and get it going. As great as it is to be out of Kaleb's debt, I still can't shake the feeling that it's too good to be true. I've done a lot of shady shit for him. A lot of illegal shit, too. Fucking that fighter the other night was the easiest job he's ever given me, and I don't trust it. So, I check my cell for the hundred-billionth time today.

No missed calls. No messages.

Nothing.

My heart stirs restlessly in my chest. I haven't been able to stop thinking about that guy since I left him in the warehouse bedroom.

Ace dropped me off at that shithole on the edge of town with direct orders to find a man named Silas and do what he says. I had no clue what I was getting into honestly, and the rundown building was scary.

Even so, I went in.

If that doesn't tell you the level of desperation I've reached, nothing will.

I risked the very real possibility of being kidnapped, raped, or murdered, and walked into it with no fear.

I need therapy.

Lots and lots of it.

It's just that I'm completely numb. If Addie had

to grow up fast, then I've had to grow up at lightning speed. I'm twenty-five and have lived through more nightmares than a fucking horror movie convention. Hence my detachment to life and desperation to survive.

Hell, Addie's not even my real sister. We're trauma bonded foster kids. But I'd die for her without hesitation. She's been my motivator for a very long time.

"Beautiful." Addie sprinkles the final layer of cheese on the dish. "We should have made two, so we don't have to share."

She can eat this whole thing because I don't have an appetite anymore. Especially not when I hear the sound of a particular engine pull up to the front of our house.

Addie hears it too, only her eyes light up. "Ace is here."

Glancing cautiously out my front window, I watch him park, get out, and lean against his car. He crosses his arms over his chest and stares directly at me.

Fuck.

"Stay," I order, jabbing my finger at Addie. "And don't forget to set the timer for the lasagna." Then I turn up the volume to the music playing on our little Bluetooth speaker so it will drown out the conversation I'm about to have outside with Ace.

Numbness runs up my body, starting at my feet and reaching my cheeks by the time I step onto my tiny lawn. "What are you doing here?"

"What do you think?"

"Kaleb and I are done. I did my last job for him two nights ago."

Ace opens the passenger door. "Get in the car."

"No." I step back. "I'm serious, Ace. We're done. I'm *out*."

He huffs a laugh and shakes his head. "Dae, you know that's bullshit. You don't get out."

"Yes, I did. I'm done. Kaleb said—"

"Kaleb said to come get you. So here I am. Get in the fucking car, Daelyn."

"No." I backup more.

He advances. "Don't make this ugly."

"I'm not going." My heart runs in panicked circles like a headless chicken. "I'm out!" Spinning on my heels, I race across the lawn and up my front steps.

Ace is on me before I can reach the door.

"Let go of me," I snap.

"We've got an audience," he warns in my ear. To my horror, a neighbor two doors down is watching us while she waters her roses. "We don't want anyone here knowing you're a drug dealing whore, now do we? Think what CPS would do about that." Ace lets go of me and flashes her a smile. "Nice roses."

Mrs. Rainey shakes her head and turns to water her other flowers.

Ace grips my arm. "Are you going to behave now, Dae?"

Shaking the hair from my eyes, I turn around and give him my best fake smile. "Of course."

Going into survival mode, my body relaxes, and a stillness takes over my organs. Like a zombie, I head to Ace's car.

After dropping into the passenger seat, I look at the window to my living room to see Addie's watching us. She looks annoyed as she mouths, "What the *fuck*?"

"I'll be back soon!" I call out, hoping she didn't see what Mrs. Rainey did. "Don't forget the garlic bread in the freezer!"

Ace waves at her and if her smile is any sign, he probably winked or made some other flirtatious gesture I can't see. That means she didn't see the exchange between us when he stopped me from getting back into the house.

Thank God.

After Ace gets in the car, we both buckle up and he starts the engine. Mentally preparing for the worst, I stare at the burn scar on his arm from Kaleb's signet ring that matches the one on my wrist. If I had a knife, I'd cut it off me right now.

And I wouldn't pull up the blade until I sliced my arm from wrist to elbow.

…

I have no clue where Kaleb currently lives — probably the seventh circle of Hell since he's the goddamn devil — so it's no surprise when I'm brought to a hotel. We've met here tons of times and I'm pretty sure he owns the building.

Dread tries clawing its way up my back, but my psychological walls won't let it find purchase. Keeping my head down, I let Ace escort me through the lobby and into an elevator. I hit the fifth-floor button before he can.

Silence fills my ears until they're ringing.

When the doors open, Ace slips out first and keeps his gaze straight ahead. We pass a guard standing outside Kaleb's room. His name is Casey, and he's a sweetheart some days and a fucking animal on others.

Ace knocks twice and the door opens. I step inside first, like always.

"Did she give you any trouble?" Kaleb asks without looking up at us. His fingers fly across his cell as he types something.

"None."

My breath nearly catches. Ace just lied. Why?

"Good." Kaleb jerks his head, silently dismissing Ace, and the door shuts. It's just me and Kaleb now.

In the beginning, he and I would be on each other in an instant, tearing each other's clothes off. He'd push me against the wall and kiss down my neck, suck on my tits. I'd beg for his cock. He'd fuck me for hours, making me come so many times I'd sob. Then he'd fuck me some more.

Those days are long gone.

"Did you have fun at the fight?" He still hasn't looked up at me.

"Sure." What else am I supposed to say?

He chuckles and slips his phone in his pocket, then settles on the foldaway couch, stretching his arms across the back of it. Our gazes lock and, once again, I try to find what kindness I swore used to be there. But his eyes are so cold they send shivers down my back.

"Did you fuck him?"

"Yes."

"And?"

"And then I left."

He shakes his head and leans forward, resting his forearms on his knees. Dressed in a black button-down, with the sleeves rolled up, and black dress pants, Kaleb looks like sex on a stick. Especially with his dark hair freshly cut and face clean shaven to accent his sharp jaw.

The ink on his arms and hands has always mesmerized me. L-O-V-E is tatted on the fingers of his right hand. H-U-R-T is tatted on the other. When we first met, he was a charmer. A leader. He promised to always take care of me, and I believed him. I depended on it.

Once, a man at a club grabbed my ass and Kaleb marched right over and snapped his arm like a twig. The bone stuck out and blood dripped all over the floor. I loved him for that.

As a girl who grew up in broken homes, danger became my love language. You either cower from it or crave it.

Guess which one I do.

For a long ass time, Kaleb was my protector. My provider. The man who cared about me when the world didn't even know I existed. And then, little by little, the dream I had of being with this perfect guy turned into a nightmare. His tone changed. His affection hardened. The promises he made twisted into more than I bargained for. He didn't give me anything for free, even if it seemed that way at first.

"What was he like?"

Kaleb's question knocks around in my head like a pinball. "Rough."

He smiles, knowing that's how I like it. "Did he scare you?"

"No."

"What else?"

I don't know what he wants to hear. "You said I was done. That after I fucked him, I was free."

"You will be."

Will be? What the hell? "I already fucked him, Kaleb. I did it. I'm done."

"You're not even close to done." He stands up and saunters over to me. "I said fuck him."

"Yeah. Spread my legs. I did."

"There are other ways to fuck him. You only did the bare minimum at the fight, which is a good start, babygirl."

I can't believe this. Rage eats away my fear until I'm left shaking with anger. "I'm not going to be some rent-a-whore."

"You're going to be exactly what I fucking tell you to be." He wraps his hand around my throat. "I need you to fuck him."

"How?" Damn my voice for shaking. "What more do you want from me, Kaleb?" Tears fill my eyes so fast I can't control the way they fall.

"You're so pretty when you cry, Dae." He leans in and licks the traitorous tears from my cheek.

It makes me sick. "Please don't."

He swallows hard before letting go of me. Taking a step back, he shoves his hands in his pockets and pulls out a pack of cigarettes and a lighter. "I promised you this was the last job, and I don't break my promises. You know me."

I do. Which means I have to decode what he's asking of me now. "How am I supposed to fuck him?" Because Kaleb said to spread my legs and open my mouth, which I did, goddamnit, and just like always, it's not enough for him. "Just tell me exactly what I have to do."

"I need you to get close to this guy. Figure out what makes him tick. What makes him break. What matters to him."

There's no way. It'll take me forever.

"You can do this for me, Dae." He pulls a cigarette out with his teeth. "You're good at making a man feel like he can tell you anything."

My heart collapses. Memories fall from the dark hole in the top of my brain, and splatter behind my eyes, playing out in scenes I don't like dwelling over…

Kaleb and I laughing in bed as the sun comes up. Kaleb sending over a thousand roses to my house for my birthday. The way he stared at me from across a bonfire we had to celebrate Ace's initiation. How he would kiss me like I gave him life. How he told me about his father dying, and the way his voice trembled as he broke down about it.

I can look at us now and admit Kaleb is not the man I thought I loved, but he is still raw and vulnerable when I am the only one looking. We've been through so much together, it's hard to remember my life before he came into it.

Addie isn't the only person I've trauma bonded with. Kaleb and I share things, too.

Until he turned my vulnerabilities into his strengths and used me all up.

He lights his cigarette and takes a long drag, blowing it out through his nose.

Running his thumb across his bottom lip, his voice stays low and soft when he asks, "How bad do you want to be free from me, Daelyn?" To make it worse, he closes the space between us again and grabs my hand, running his thumb over the signet he burned into me. "Tell me."

"I…"

There's no answer that won't get me in hot water. If I say I want out badly, he'll do something to break my heart because on some level I'll have broken his too. If I say not badly, then he'll keep using me for his illegal businesses and I'll end up in prison.

Then where will Addie be?

I'll have to redirect this conversation to take the focus off me. "Why do you want to fuck him?"

Because if I'm going to bring that fighter into Kaleb's world, don't I deserve to know why?

"Don't worry about it." Kaleb takes another drag of his cigarette. "I should have known better than to lean on you for this."

Hold up. What? "I can do it."

"No. It's fine. He's a lunatic, anyway. I don't want you around that."

I see the game he's playing with me and still I engage. "I just want to know *why*, Kaleb."

"He…" Kaleb looks away from me and runs his hand through his hair. It's the only sign I've ever picked up on that tells me when he's truly upset. "He killed my father."

The little bit of me that still cares about Kaleb flares back to life. Everyone has a reason for being the way they are. Kaleb's father getting murdered is the reason Kaleb's an angry, cutthroat sonofabitch. He's a wounded animal that lashes out and handles everything with violence. He keeps his guard up because he feels like no one understands him. He has no one. Nothing.

Except me.

A memory of him telling me his sad story creeps into my brain, rewiring my cells again. I cling to the way his soft voice spoke of his heartbroken mother, that at thirteen years old he lost his hero, and how hard life's been for him ever since. He told me I was the only one who had ever dug their way into his heart, and he wanted to bury me in there forever.

Then a few years later, he heated his signet ring and branded me his.

I wasn't the love of his life. I was a pawn in his game.

And I still am.

It's terrifying to realize that death might be my only way out of Kaleb's world for good.

"What did you learn about him the other night?" he asks, studying me.

"Nothing. He just came in and fucked me."

"Did he speak?"

"Only a little."

"What did he say?"

"Just to call Red if he got too rough."

"Anything else?"

"He put a belt in my mouth to bite down on."

Kaleb's brow arches. "Did you like it?"

"Yes." No point in lying. Kaleb knows better than anyone how rough I like it in bed. "I was chained to a wall." Showing him the red marks that haven't faded on my wrists makes my belly twist. He holds my hands and presses a gentle kiss on each one.

Locking eyes with mine again, he keeps his mouth close to my hand and asks, "Did you come?"

"Not at first. But afterwards."

Kaleb swallows hard. I think there's jealousy in him somewhere, not that he'd ever admit it since he made me do this. It's his fault I fucked that guy. Besides, he doesn't care about me like that anymore. I'm not sure he ever really did.

"Afterwards?" He runs his thumb over the signet scar. "Tell me more."

"He..." I hate this so much. "He came first and

then made me come."

"How?"

"Fuck, Kaleb, why does it matter?"

Anger morphs his face as he grabs my wrist harder and yanks it, spinning me while twisting my arm behind my back. "Everything. Matters. Daelyn." Keeping the pressure painful, he asks again. "How did he make you come?"

Shit, this hurts! "He ate me out, okay?"

"He tasted you." Kaleb lets me go and backs away. "Good."

I rub my aching arm and swallow the bile rising in my throat. "Good? What the hell does that mean?"

"It means he's already addicted to you." Kaleb walks through the open glass French doors that lead to a balcony and flicks his cigarette over the railing. "Trust me. I know *exactly* how it feels."

My mouth runs dry. I'm not that special and Kaleb's out of his damn mind.

"Anything else?" he asks with his back to me.

I almost tell him about the fighter mentioning a place called the Monarch, but something stops me. After I got home that night, I'd looked it up and discovered it's an elite sex club on the ritzy side of town. It's a simple piece of information to give, but instinct tells me to keep it to myself for now. And if Kaleb isn't looking at me, he can't catch me lying.

"No. Like I said, he was a mindless animal. He just fucked and bled all over me. Then it was done."

"Except he also made you come."

Thanks for the reminder. "So what?"

"That means he cared."

"Doubtful."

"He came first and still took care of you, Dae.

That means something."

"It means he has decent fucking etiquette."

"No." He turns around and clasps his hands behind his back. "It means he wanted to give you pleasure. And he told you to call Red if he was too much. That means he might have seemed like a crazed animal to you, but he was in his right mind and remained cautious of your wellbeing. Did he take the cuffs off you without you asking?"

"Yes."

He smiles like he's figuring it all out. "He has a conscience, then. Otherwise, he would have left you dangling until someone else freed you, hours, maybe even a day later."

My throat closes. Kaleb's too smart for his own good. Too perceptive. Too devious.

"Did you like it?" he asks, crooking his finger for me to come closer.

"Yes." I hope it hurts his black heart to know that. I hope he knows it wasn't a punishment for me to fuck a stranger in a warehouse.

"Good. Because you're going to do it again and again until he cracks." Kaleb smirks. "He hasn't been in the ring for a long time, but I'm working on a plan to lure him there again."

"How?"

"Don't worry about it."

I step closer. "If it's not something to worry about, then why involve me anymore?"

"Your part isn't over, Dae."

"How much information can you possibly want about this guy that you can't find on the internet?"

Kaleb doesn't answer. Instead, he pulls out another cigarette and lights it up. "Don't disappoint me." He takes a long drag again and blows the smoke into my face. "You know what will happen if you do."

His warning starts my panic. I can't go through that again. I barely survived it last time. "How am I supposed to find him again?"

Kaleb arches his brow and flicks his cigarette at me. "Figure it out."

Chapter 4

Dmitri

It's been two weeks since I was in the cage. Feels like a lifetime. Since that night, I've worked relentlessly at the club, just to keep myself occupied.

"Will you help me tonight?" Sophie asks from the other end of the sauna.

"Absolutely."

Sophie's one of our Femme Dommes. Splitting her time between the Monarch Club and her day job has left practically no time for herself, which Ryker and I have been trying to help her understand. The woman needs rest. Friends. A life.

I said I'd be her assistant tonight with a BDSM class we're teaching on impact play. Guess she was afraid I'd back out. Not surprising, considering I've flaked on her twice in the past month because I cannot get my shit together and haven't been in a good headspace to flog someone.

"Your bruises are nearly gone." She doesn't tear her eyes off me as we sit across from each other in the sauna. "That's good."

"Mmm hmm."

I'm sure a lot of people assume she's got a thing for me, but I know better. No one can be in love with a monster like me.

I'm fuckable, not lovable.

And I'm not really Sophie's type.

We sit in comfortable silence for a while and I

almost nod off when she startles me by saying, "Well, time's up. Back to work I go."

I should probably get back to work, too. After hitting the shower, I stop in front of the large wall-to-wall mirror in the dressing room and stare at my reflection. Christ, I look like shit. All my bruises are fading and I...

I want them back.

Shame hits me hard, and I try to understand how the fuck I got this way...

My mother flicks her cigarette ashes into a dish. "Where are you going?" Her Russian accent is always stronger when she drinks.

I keep my head down and pretend like I didn't hear her.

A drinking glass flies across the living room and smashes against the wall. My fight-or-flight response kicks in and I freeze.

"Answer me, Dmitri."

"T-to my friend's house."

"Where is friend's house?"

"Up the street a little."

Mom stares at me from her chair, the silence spreading down my spine like ice. Finally, she says, "Be home before your father."

"I will."

Scurrying outside, I book it to the playground that's further out of my neighborhood because the one close by is for littler kids. I don't have any friends. I just needed to get out of my house because Mom's on her third glass already this morning and she gets meaner as the day goes by, even though she'll be sober by the time my dad comes home from work.

Out of breath from running the entire way to the better playground, I drop into a swing, panting. The rusty chains squeak, grinding my nerves. Mad that I'm stuck and lonely, I kick the mulch under my feet. Great, my shoe has another hole in it. My big toe is showing.

In the fenced off grass ahead of me, there's a bunch of kids playing soccer. Their parents obnoxiously cheer for them and there's even a snack stand because spoiled kids can't do shit without French fries, hot dogs, and candy.

My stomach growls.

Hopping off the swing, I make my way over to the fence and climb it, then head to the back of the line for the snack stand.

Fishing a crumpled dollar from my pocket, I straighten it out as best I can while waiting for my turn. I took it from my mom's purse when she passed out yesterday. Scanning the price list on the board, I pick an affordable option.

"What can I get you, honey?" the woman asks from behind the counter.

"Chips."

"That's seventy-five cents."

I hand her the money and get my change, thrilled to have something to put in my empty belly this early in the morning. As I head back to the swings, I look over my shoulder and see two kids about my age laughing and pushing each other around.

"Can I spend the night tonight?" the shorter one asks.

"Yeah, sure," says the other.

Three little kids squeal from the slide at the playground, and one hops on my swing.

Great, there goes my peace and quiet around here.

Bypassing them, I detour towards the basketball hoops. My stomach growls, as if sensing I have food in my hands and demands I open the bag immediately. Which I do. People say you can't eat just one chip, and I agree. I'd eat a dump truck full if I could. The salt and vinegar chips make my mouth pucker, but I can't stop shoveling them in. But now I'm a little thirsty. A quarter won't buy me a drink.

My spit is free. That'll work.

Sitting against the fence, I dump the rest of the chips into my mouth and stuff the empty bag into my pocket.

The two older boys start playing basketball together. The court is a wreck; the ground is all torn up with weeds growing out of the cracks, and the netless basketball rims have broken backboards too.

"Shit," one of the kids says when the ball rolls over to where I'm sitting. I glance at it and don't move.

"You gonna throw that back or what?" the taller one asks.

Getting up hurts. My mom kicked me in the ribs pretty hard yesterday. Without saying a word, I grab the ball and throw it as hard as I can.

In the opposite direction of these two assholes.

"Motherfucker." The taller one storms off after it.

The shorter one looks furious. "What's your fucking problem, dickhead?"

I have too many to count.

They both look like they're my age — maybe thirteen or something.

"I'm talking to you," the shorter one stalks over. "The fuck is your problem?"

I square up, spoiling for a fight. I'm tired. I hurt. And I'm angry that no one sees me. Not even these two shitheads can see me. I'm just a weirdo in their way who pulled a dick move.

He pushes me against the fence.

My back hurts because I slept in my closet last night.

"Knox, leave him alone." The taller kid makes his

way over to us with the basketball resting on his hip. "He's not worth it."

"He needs a fucking lesson in manners."

I roll my shoulders back. "You think you can give me one?"

"Fuck right I can." Knox swings out and I block him.

Putting all my weight into it, I barrel into the kid and tackle him to the ground. I don't even know why I'm picking this fight. I don't understand why I want to smash someone up when I know how much it sucks to get beat on.

But I swing fists anyway.

Knox doesn't stay down long. We toss and tumble, punching and kicking, until the tall kid breaks us apart. "You two done now?" he asks like he's in fucking charge.

I wipe my bloody mouth with the back of my hand. Tears fill my eyes and I have no clue why. I'm just so fucking angry and all these emotions rise to the surface and need a way out.

"Yeah. We're done." Knox swipes his nose. I clocked him pretty good and he's bleeding like me.

"Good. Come on. Let's play ball." The tall kid walks away from both of us, and that's when I notice Knox has an old bruise on his arm. It looks like a handprint.

Without thinking, I lift my shirt up to my wipe face off with it.

Knox looks down and sees the big bruise on my ribs.

We stare at each other for a long time. Long enough for the tall kid to holler, "You two numbnuts playing ball or what?"

Knox glares at me a little longer and I stare at him with what I'm sure are soulless eyes. I don't know how to feel anything besides the short bursts of rage I sometimes get.

"Yeah," he says and walks off.

I watch, still trying to catch my breath. My hands

shake. I want to throw up my chips. I'm still thirsty.

Knox calls out over his shoulder, "Are your legs broke, asshole? Come on. Time to play ball."

I trip on his words. I just beat him up, and now he wants me to play basketball with them? These two assholes must be more fucked in the head than I am.

"What's your name?" *the tall one asks once I make my way over to the court.*

"Dmitri."

"I'm Ryker, this is Knox." *He bounces the ball to me.* "Winner has to get the losers slushies from the gas station. Deal?"

I bounce the ball to Knox, prepared to walk away. "I don't have any money."

"Neither do we," *Knox says, and bounces it right back to me.*

We smile at each other, and the rage I keep siphoning from fades a little. Ryker smacks the ball out of my hand and makes a layup. Knox grabs the rebound and we're suddenly playing like we've been friends forever.

A little while later, a third kid shows up on a bicycle with a Bluetooth speaker and cell phone. His name's Vault, but I don't get why they call him that and I'm not asking. He blasts music I like, and we team up on the court.

When it's over, I'm tired and dizzy from starvation and dehydration.

"Hey." *Ryker looks over at me as he, Knox, and Vault head in the opposite direction from where I live.* "Wanna spend the night at my house tonight?"

I'm not sure I should. But I don't want to go home if I don't have to. "Don't you have to ask your parents for permission first?"

Ryker shrugs. "My mom won't mind." *He tips his head towards the street.* "Come on. Knox owes us slushies, then we'll head to my place. Bet my mom's got dinner *already waiting. Hope you like spaghetti."*

I stall out, suddenly realizing how late it is. We've been playing ball all day. The sun's almost set.

My dad is home.

Fear spikes in my system and I beat feet across the playground and back to my house without saying anything to Ryker or the others. My cheeks are numb by the time I push open the door and am smacked in the face with the scent of dinner.

"There he is!" My dad chimes in the kitchen. "You're just in time, son. I almost ate your dinner, too." His big smile suddenly drops and brow furrows. "What happened to your face, Dmitri?"

Oh. Right. My face. "Got into a fight."

"Did you start it?"

Yes. "No."

"Did you finish it?"

No. "Yes."

"Atta boy." Dad points at the empty seat between him and my mom, and I pull out my chair and fall into it.

She glares at me with a fork and knife in her hands. "You're late."

"Sorry." I stuff a slice of bread with butter into my mouth.

Her expression is as cold as her voice. "Maybe you need a lesson on how to tell time."

"Aww, leave the kid alone, Anya. He's just having fun."

"Fun. Getting into fights is fun*?" She drops her silverware with a clank. "He will be just like you."*

My dad's brow arches. "You say that like it's a bad thing."

"Always fighting. Always out late." She snags her plate and mine before I get a chance to eat any of what's on it. "He needs discipline." She tosses my food in the trash

and drops my plate in the sink.

"Anya." Dad's voice drops in a pleading tone. "He didn't even get to eat his dinner."

"If he wanted to eat it, he should have been home when I told him to be. Which was before dinner." She smacks the faucet and pours water all over my empty plate as she washes it.

Dad looks down at his plate and I know he'd slide it over to me if there was anything left on it to eat. But there isn't. My mom doesn't make enough for leftovers or second helpings. She controls all the portions because she controls all the grocery money.

I don't understand why we can't afford a decent amount of food every week when my dad makes good money as a mechanic and also fights for cash on the side. If we can afford her alcohol, why can't we afford extra apples or even a bigger box of cereal?

"Go to your room," Mom barks.

"I was actually going to spend the night at a friend's house."

Dad's eyes widen with joy. "Hear that, Anya? He has friends!" The smile on his face embarrasses me. "Go on." He points at the door. "Get out of here, kid!"

I'm out of my chair before my mom can object.

"Be home by ten tomorrow morning," my dad hollers. "I'll take you to the gym with me."

"Okay!" Finally free, I fly out of the house so fast it's like I grew wings.

Except I have no clue where Ryker lives or if I'll ever see him and the others again...

"What's going on, Dmitri?" Ryker asks from against the doorjamb. Christ, I didn't even hear him come in. How long have I been standing in the

Monarch Club Member's bathroom, staring at myself in the mirror?

"Nothing."

He saunters closer, concern darkening his stormy grey eyes. "The cage fight didn't quiet your monster. It awakened it."

He's right. Pretending otherwise is insulting to us both.

"I need this." The confession shreds my black heart. I'm hard-wired for pain and rage. And we both know what gets me off because I'm a masochist.

"Is…" Ryker clears his throat. "Sophie helping you with that?"

"No." And I won't ask her to. She's too precious for me. Too *good*.

"She would if you wanted her to."

"I know, which is why I'm not going there."

"Do you want *me* to help you?"

Sweet offer, but hard pass. I'm too far gone for even Ryker's form of abuse. I need…

Fuck, I don't know what I need. I just know I haven't found it yet.

Ryker comes closer. "What were you just thinking about that had you oblivious to the fact that I was in here with you, D?"

It's not like me to let anything slip under my radar. We both know that. So for him to have startled me in the bathroom isn't a good sign.

"I was thinking about the day we met."

Ryker relaxes a little. "That was a fun summer."

I never found out where Ryker lived that night, so I slept on a bench at the playground and was back home before breakfast the next day. I went to the gym with my dad, then he headed to work for a double shift, and my mom beat the shit out of me before locking me in the closet until a half hour before my dad got home that night.

Desperate for friends, I returned to the playground every day for the next week and a half, until Ryker, Knox, and Vault showed up again. We've been inseparable ever since.

I know where I'd be by now if I hadn't met them all those years ago. I'd have followed my dad's footsteps, which has me scared now because I'm pretty sure I've followed them anyway. "Going back in the cage was a onetime thing."

"Don't lie, D." Ryker's tone grounds me. "It doesn't help anyone. Especially you."

He's right, I think to myself while splashing cold water on my face. The agony I live with barely registers. I'm too used to it. "I can't feel anything anymore, Ry. I don't know what's wrong with me."

"Nothing's wrong with you, D."

"Now who's lying?" I step back and look away from my reflection. "I won't go back to the cage again."

"Maybe you should."

I tense, shocked by what he's said. "What?"

Ryker shrugs. "Look, I'm not a fan of you cage fighting the way you do, but I also know you've always been this way."

My hackles raise. "What way?"

"You need an outlet. Everyone does, D."

"Sex works, too."

Ryker shakes his head. "Not for you."

"I don't appreciate getting called out like this."

"No offense, man, but we both know sex only works *after* you've released tension in other ways."

Ryker's tone softens before he adds, "I see you, D. You've been hurting for a while. I just wish there was a way I could help."

Shame heats my back and slides around my neck like a noose. "I lost time in the ring." My confession lands like a boulder between us. "I put down seven men. Only counted three. I blacked out in the middle of the fight and can't remember most of it."

"Jesus."

Now he understands what my real problem is. I've turned into the deadliest combo of my parents. "Silas and a few others pulled me back."

"I can't believe that old man's still running the ring."

I can. Those cage fights make him a lot of money. What happens at the Scrapyard, stays at the Scrapyard. He's got all the right people on payroll and can wipe evidence faster than most businessmen can wipe their asses after a morning shit. Silas is also on no one's side but his own. He'll do anything for anyone at the right price and never say a word about it ever again.

It makes him equal parts an ally and enemy for most. To me, he was a second father.

Ryker crosses his arms. "What happened after Silas pulled you off?"

"I went up to my old room and fucked my prize." Again, that's not a new mode of operation for me. Ryker knows I get off on my pain. He's been to plenty of cage fights back in the day too, so he's seen my set up there.

"Silas had someone waiting for you?"

"Yeah." And now he knows that I didn't just happen to show up on the night of a fight. My arrival was prearranged. What kills me most right now is the concern in Ryker's gaze. It's not because I'd made arrangements to fight, either. I know this look on him too well. He's worried I went too far with the prize chained up for me. "I didn't hurt her. I was right enough in my head by the time I got there."

I can't read his next expression, but there's definitely relief in there somewhere. It makes me feel like an unpredictable animal Ryker can't decide if he should train or put down.

"She was beautiful," I ramble for no good reason. "Fierce and feisty. Like a black alley cat."

"Does the alley cat have a name?"

I'm ashamed to admit I don't remember. Some of that night is still hazy and I think it's because I'm concussed. "Dae… something. Maybe."

Wow, I'm an asshole. Shouldn't I remember the name of the woman who I've thought about non-stop for the past two weeks? I don't even know why I keep thinking about her, honestly. She was just a prize. I've had plenty before her that didn't stick with me.

Still, every night, as I lay on my cot in the dark cold room in the basement of the Monarch Club, I jack off to the memory of that woman. Her scent. Her sounds. Her sopping wet pussy.

My cell goes off and the number on the screen drains the blood from my head. It's Silas. "I gotta take this," I say quietly. Ryker leaves without saying another word, but I sense his disapproval. My hands shake when I answer because I know better than to take this call. "Yeah?"

Part of me hopes the old man has a new fight set up. Another part of me is annoyed I don't have the strength to block his number.

"We got a slight problem, Dmitri."

My protective instincts kick in. He might be the devil who rules my Hell, but he was also the angel who saved me when no one else could. I owe him. "Are you okay?"

"Yeah, yeah, I'm fine. But do you remember that woman you enjoyed after the fight?"

My entire body locks. "What about her?"

"She's been at the Scrapyard every night since. I think she's looking for you."

Chapter 5

Daelyn

I swear this stupid warehouse is gaslighting me. I know damn well this is where that cage fight was two weeks ago. Ace drove me here, so I never got the actual address, but I distinctly remember the faded sign propped on the edge of the roof with the words worn off it. The atrocity looms over me now, taunting me.

That night still feels like a fever dream. The fighter I fucked being nothing more than a fantasy I'd made up in my warped little mind. But I remember, with perfect, clarity how his strong hands grazed my body. How his lush mouth pressed against mine. The scent of his blood while it dripped all over the floor and my chest. His deep voice rumbling against my ear when he asked if I'd come there of my own volition.

All because I can't figure out how to find this man doesn't mean he was a figment of my imagination, damnit.

Marching around the building, I look through one of the filthy windows like I have every single time I've been here in the past two weeks. And just like every other time I've looked, the inside is still completely empty. Not a trace of that night remains. It shouldn't be possible. I saw the lights and all the equipment the other night. It was all *here*. That man was fucking *here*. Larger than life. Unforgettable. But now the cage is gone. The chairs aren't here. No bars loaded with booze line the back nor are there projector screens covering the four walls. No trashcans, or lights, or people, either. The entire place looks like an abandoned hollow shell.

Frustration makes me want to scream.

Okay. Chill. It's not like I was in my right state of mind when Ace dropped me off that night. And it was super dark out. There aren't any lights in the parking lot either, so maybe I'm not in the right place after all.

Shit.

"Can I help you, darlin'?"

Startled, I spin around, clutching my heart. "Oh! Sorry." The old man coming closer doesn't look happy to see me, but I am very, very happy to see him. He's the one who chained me against the wall in the bedroom upstairs. "I'm... um. I was here a couple weeks ago. Do you remember?"

His expression is unreadable.

"For the fight?" I add, hoping I don't sound delusional.

"I don't know what you're talking about, but this is private property. I suggest you move along. It's getting late and nothing good happens around here at night. Especially to pretty women like yourself."

I'm not scared. I've faced worse than whatever could come get me here. "I know you remember me. I was the woman you brought upstairs."

He doesn't respond.

"I was there for the winner," I press, starting to second-guess myself again. "There was a cage in there. And hundreds of people."

The old man purses his lips and shakes his head. "You got the wrong place, darlin'. This building's been closed for over a decade. And I've never seen you before. I'd for damn sure remember a pretty little pussy cat like you."

"I'm telling you, I—" Forget it. He's either suffering from memory loss, lying, or I'm certifiably crazy. "Sorry, I'll leave."

My heart clammers in my chest as I walk around the side of the building towards the front again. I had to take the bus here, and it's a long way back home. For the past two weeks, I've come here every night, expecting to find that fighter only to leave empty-handed.

He's not here.

Nothing is here.

Kaleb's going to be furious that I've failed him, but this isn't the place and I don't have a name to search. I don't have anything except the phantom sensation of that fighter's huge cock between my thighs and the red skin on my wrists from the cuffs, which have already disappeared like they never existed in the first place.

Ace won't help me either, even though he's the one who drove me here that night. It's like everyone's making my mission more difficult on purpose, and I hate it.

Fuck all these assholes.

Leaving the parking lot, I sense that old man's gaze burning into my back. Anger spikes in my veins and I ball my hands into fists, relishing the bite of my nails digging into my palms. I want to punch something. Someone. Anyone.

I'm not crazy. This *is* the right place.

And I'm coming back every fucking night until I find what I'm looking for.

What other choice do I have? The Monarch Club requires a membership, and I can't afford one, so that's not an option. Besides, I don't even know the name of the fighter or if he's a member or employee there. And I'm not about to bang on the door of that ritzy place because I'm too paranoid that I'm being followed, and I can't let Kaleb know I withheld any information from him about this guy. There's no way I could explain showing up at a random fancy sex club for no reason. He'd see right through that lie and knock my teeth out.

Constantly vigilant, I scan the street over and over while making my way back to the bus stop. I'm tired, hungry, and fed up.

Addie's spending the night at her friend's house tonight, which is the only good thing that's happened today. Work was exhausting. I'm flat broke, thanks to all the bills that came in through the week, and I'm sexually frustrated beyond belief.

Headlights shine from behind me, and my paranoia kicks into third gear. I'm sure it's one of Kaleb's cronies tailing me. Holding my head high, I don't dare look back to check. The bus stop is just up ahead, and by the time I reach it, the bus is already pulling over.

The ride home takes forever.

My eyes are burning when I finally make it to my destination. Cars pass by every so often, but I'm not nearly as scared in my neighborhood as I am in others. The streetlights keep things illuminated well, and there are two women jogging on the other side of the road together.

Shoving my key in, I unlock my front door, step inside, and take in a deep breath. Safe at home, I can finally let my guard down again.

Tonight was another bust, but I'm not giving up

until I find that guy. I can't. Kaleb doesn't make empty threats and there's no way I'll risk his wrath. Not when I'm so close to getting out of his circle of Hell.

"There is no getting out," the darkness in my mind whispers.

I tell it to shut up.

Kaleb doesn't lie. What he says, he means. He promised I'd be out after this mission, so I have to believe it's the truth. If it's not, I'll die… either mentally, spiritually, or physically. Likely all three, knowing how thorough Kaleb is.

In the dark, I slip upstairs, and stop at Addie's bedroom. Pushing her door open, I inhale the scent of her perfume and remind myself why I'm doing all of this. Her room's a mess. I love it. To me, it shows that she's comfortable and safe. Before she came to live with me, Addie stayed with a foster mom who had severe OCDs and was a neat freak to the nth degree. One sock out of order, or a shirt not hung up correctly in the closet, and she'd beat your ass for it, and the dad was just as strict.

I'm so glad Addie's away from that foster family, but I've dragged her into another bad situation. One she doesn't even realize she's in the middle of.

My stomach drops as I close her door and head to my bedroom down the hall.

Clicking on the light at my bedside table, I sit down and kick off my shoes. Too tired to cry, too numb to care, I strip out of my clothes and set my alarm for work in the morning. Five a.m. is going to come way too fast, especially considering it's already two.

What was I thinking, hunting down a stranger

in the middle of the night? I must be insane.

Dragging my sorry ass into the bathroom, I wash my face, brush my teeth, and stare at my reflection for a long time. I barely recognize myself anymore. The dark circles under my eyes make me look like a drugged racoon. I haven't washed my hair in four days and it's so greasy that not even a messy bun can help it anymore.

You know what? Enough is enough.

I start the shower and hook my phone up to my little speaker so I can blast screamy music while I reset my life—starting with a shampoo, shave, and sugar scrub. By the time I'm done, I feel worlds better. Now to snag a couple hours of sleep before work.

Sauntering back into my bedroom naked, terror clutches my throat when I see I'm not alone.

It's him.

Sitting on my bed is the man I fucked two weeks ago. Only he looks completely different from that night. No more busted, swollen face and blood dripping everywhere. In fact, this guy doesn't look anything like the man I slept with in the warehouse. That one looked dangerous.

This one looks devastatingly dangerous.

The night we fucked, I didn't get a good look at him, considering one of his eyes was completely swollen shut, and the other was close to the same condition. Not to mention the poor lighting in the room and the fact that I'd shut my mind down and went into autopilot for most of it.

This guy—the way he's built, the grace with which he moves, the breadth of his shoulders, the clothes, the energy he exudes—he's the perfect villain for any story.

No wonder I'm attracted to him.

He remains sitting on my bed with his hands clasped and elbows resting on his knees. "What do you want?" he asks in a gruff tone.

My mouth runs dry. I've been searching for him for two weeks with no success and he's found me instead. This should bring me some semblance of relief, but it doesn't. "How did you get into my house?"

He looks up at me with eyes that are the palest ice blue I've ever seen. They almost look silver. "Answer my question first."

I don't want to. There's nothing I can say that will help me. I look like a psycho either way. *Stick to the truth. Keep it simple and short.* "I wanted to find you."

"Why?"

He's not flattered. He's terrifying.

And my pussy purrs like I'm in heat.

His gaze doesn't sail lower than my chin, so he can't see how my nipples are hardening or that my thighs are pressed tighter together. Water drips from my hair, trickling down my back and onto the floor. I can't budge to grab something to cover myself with. Hell, I can't even grab my gun, considering he's sitting on top of where it's stashed.

"I don't like repeating myself, but I will just this once." He rolls his shoulders back and deadlocks his gaze on me. "*Why* did you want to find me?"

I don't have an answer that will save me. "*How* did you find *me*?"

"I followed you home."

He's what I felt watching me, not Kaleb's cronies. Holy crap. "Why?"

He stands up and must be at least six-four. His black t-shirt stretches tightly across his bulky chest and his arms bulge with muscle. I know he has scars on his chest.

I know the size of his dick. The way it feels inside me.

I know the heat of his touch when he wraps his hands around me.

The stroke of his tongue.

Bite of his teeth.

A breath shudders out of me as I cautiously step back.

"I'm not here to hurt you," he says.

Bullshit. I'm in the middle of a dangerous game with Kaleb and his enemy. The only one who will get hurt *is* me.

"What do you want?" I take another step back.

"I want to know why you're so fucking desperate."

I stall out and lie. "I'm not desperate."

"Yes, you are." He closes in on me. "You've been looking for me."

Lying will get me into worse trouble, but I want to deny the truth. "I was only looking for another cage fight." There. That's not technically a lie. If I found another cage fight, I might have also found him. Win-win.

"You got a thing for fighters, little Firefly?"

Firefly? That's a weird one.

"Not really." But the way my body's reacting to this man says otherwise. "I mean, not *all* fighters."

"So, just me, then?" His cocky grin shoots heat to my core.

Is he flirting with me right now? Maybe flirting

back will help me out of the hole I've dug myself into. I soften my expression and offer a coy smile. "Maybe."

He prowls closer. My room is small, so it doesn't take more than three steps before he's nearly on me with my back against the wall. He could eat me alive and leave no trace behind.

I *hate* how much that turns me on.

His tone is dark when he asks, "Why me?"

My mouth is so dry, I can't swallow. "I…"

His frosted gaze roams over my face as if he's noting every little detail. Then his eyes drop to my mouth. "Answer me."

Lie, Daelyn. Say whatever you have to. "I want to get to know you."

He chuckles, amused at my feeble attempt to flatter him. "Why?"

"Why not?"

He twirls a long chunk of my wet hair between his fingers. "I'm not the one for you, Firefly. Don't mistake the other night for something more than it was."

"And what was that?"

"You were a prize. A hole to fuck. That's all, babygirl."

I *hate* that nickname so much. "Daelyn," I correct. "My name is Daelyn, *not* babygirl."

"Daelyn," he repeats like he's decoding an ancient language.

"Do you have a name?"

"Yes." He flashes another smile and tilts his head, studying me.

"Are you going to tell me what it is?"

"No." He tilts his head the other way. It makes me squirm even if I'm not afraid of him as much as I was two minutes ago. If he was here to hurt me, he would have at least touched me by now. "Not until you tell me why you've been to that old warehouse every night for the past two weeks."

How does he know that? Heat fills my cheeks. "I told you. I wanted to get to know you."

"Why?"

Because it's the only way out of the trouble I'm in. "Because you... you're..." Words fail me when he licks his lips, staring at my mouth like he wants to kiss me. It makes all my brain cells flicker and die.

"You're what?" He continues twirling my hair in his fingers.

"Desperate." The confession slams down like an axe between us, severing the tension.

His brow crinkles and eyes harden. "Dmitri," he says darkly, letting go of my hair. "My name is Dmitri."

Then he kisses me so hard, he lifts me off the motherfucking ground.

Chapter 6

Dmitri

Call me a fool. Call me a psycho. Call me a monster.

"My name is Dmitri." The instant my hands are on her, I know I'm incapable of letting go. Slamming my mouth to hers, I kiss her like I'm just as desperate as she is for a repeat of the other night. I don't know where Silas found this woman, but goddamn, am I so grateful he did.

She's even more gorgeous than I remember. And crazier, considering she wasn't all that freaked out to find me in her bedroom like a fucking stalker.

I'll analyze that later. Right now, I just need to *feel* something.

I need to feel…

"Daelyn," I growl before biting her fat bottom lip.

She hooks her arms around my neck and kisses me back. The woman tastes like mint and strawberries. I'm an idiot to believe I've found someone who matches my level of fuckery, but that Daelyn not only stalked my stomping grounds for two weeks, in the middle of the night mind you, and wasn't even freaked to find me in her bedroom just now, has me so hard I could snap.

This woman isn't easily intimidated.

That's a red flag.

I love red.

It's the color of rage. Blood.

Her pretty little mouth.

Having an entire conversation while she was naked, and not peeking once below her chin, is a lost battle now. My hands graze, grab, and grope every inch of her body. She lets me. Begs me. Opens her thighs and invites me.

"So fucking wet," I groan after slipping a finger into her pussy.

Daelyn sucks in a harsh breath and leans against the wall, hooking one leg around my middle. She's not nearly as desperate for me as I think I am for her. The fact that I broke into her house like a creeper and am about to fuck her proves that I still haven't regained my control like I originally hoped.

But it would be safer to fuck her than to fight someone else.

And I *need* safety.

Please, God, if you exist, help me. Let me get this rage out of my system. Fix me.

Keeping her flush against the wall, I relentlessly hit one of the many pleasure points I know women have deep inside their cunts. Her thighs shake when she comes. She's so pretty. So breakable.

"Give me a taste." Dropping to my knees is my downfall. One lick of her sweetness and I'm addicted. This woman's orgasms might as well be ambrosia for the gods to feast on.

"Fuck me," she pleads. Her eyes are glassy and words breathless. "Please. I want to feel you inside me again, Dmitri."

The hairs on the back of my neck stand on end.

I ignore the way goosebumps ripple down my arms as I tug on my belt. Standing up, I shove my jeans down to my knees. Aaaand stop just a moment before I make a huge fucking mistake. "Condom."

"In the top drawer." She smacks the side of her dresser we're standing next to. "Hurry."

I reach in and snag a package, ripping it open with my teeth and sliding it over my throbbing length. When I lift her up, she hooks her ankles together and I impale her in one thrust.

Again, no foreplay. No games. No nothing.

If I was at the Monarch with a sub, I'd play with her for half the night before getting inside her like this. I'd make her so swollen and needy for my dick that she'd have fat tears sliding down her rosy cheeks. But desperation has many faces. Needy whimpering is just one of them.

Ugly rough is another one.

When I fight, I lose all sense of time and touch. I feel nothing. Adrenaline pumps hard enough to send me into autopilot, and my muscle memory does most of the work. But afterwards, the endorphins wear off and I have no clue which of my injuries will hurt first, worst, or last longest. My body awakens when nerve endings fire off left and right, shooting pain through me, and I come alive all over again while buried balls deep in a woman.

Tilting my head to the side, desperate for pain now, I offer her my throat. "Bite me."

I like how quickly she obeys. Her teeth graze my skin and then she chomps down so hard I wouldn't be surprised if she drew blood. The instant, sharp pain sends happy signals straight to my dick. I fuck her harder.

I like that she didn't run when she found me in her bedroom.

I like how her house smells.

I like how brutal she kisses.

I like how her pussy grips my dick.

I like how she grunts each time I thrust.

I like that my chaos is growing quiet.

I do *not* like how my instincts keep screaming that this is a problem.

No one in their right mind likes the real me. This woman is a trick. Or she's a mental case. Either way, she's dangerous.

And so am I.

Daelyn's nails dig into the back of my neck as she holds on for dear life. "How… do you feel… so fucking… *good*?"

My Prince Albert piercing probably has something to do with that.

Hooking my arms under her legs, I bounce Daelyn on my dick and fuck her deeper. It's got to hurt her cervix. I make her come two more times, because I'm still a motherfucking gentleman, before I decide to end the fun.

Pulling out, I rip the condom off and toss it on the floor. "Suck my dick."

This woman doesn't need to be told twice. She slams onto her knees and chokes on the top half of my cock.

"Bite down."

Daelyn's eyelashes flutter as she looks up at me with a mouthful of cock. Her brow crinkles.

"Bite. Down." I hold her head and grab a handful of her hair.

The instant her teeth dig into my shaft, I feel the first stirs of an orgasm.

Finally.

"Pull on my balls."

Sweat blooms down my back. Daelyn sinks her claws into my ball sac and tugs like she's going to rip my nuts out. She bites down on me a second time, much harder, and fresh pain shoots to my groin and down my legs, making them lock.

I fuck her face, letting her teeth scrape my sensitive flesh. She tugs my balls again and my release rushes out of me almost instantly.

"Fuuuuuck." Tipping my head back in ecstasy, I blow my load. "Don't... swallow." Dizziness makes me sway on boneless legs. Every orgasm I've had for the past two weeks were pathetic compared to this one. Cum drips down her chin because it's more than she can hold in her mouth. Especially with my dick still in there, too. Damn, she obeys me so well.

"Good girl." I slide my cock out from between her lips. "Spit it out." Holding my hand under her chin, I wait.

She opens her mouth and lets my jizz pour into my palm.

"Such a good fucking girl." I swipe it all over her gorgeous face and feel like a god.

She looks mortified. Turned on. Confused.

I want to lick it off her. Fuck her more. Clean her up. Tuck her into bed and kiss her goodnight. Instead, I yank up my pants and tuck my dick away.

"Thanks for that." I back up before I reconsider my next move. "See you around, Firefly."

"Wait." She stands up slowly. "Where are you going?"

"Back where I belong," I say, swinging open her bedroom door.

"Where is that?"

"Not with you." And that cold, hard truth makes me shiver.

I leave her house faster than I broke into it, but not without leaving her a parting gift first.

Chapter 7

Daelyn

At five in the morning, I'm not logged into my computer like I should be. Instead, I'm lying in bed, with a delicious ache between my thighs, and enough confusion in my brain to make me feel hungover.

Dmitri.

That crazy, sexy stranger broke into my house last night and fucked me so good I'm still reeling with the pleasure.

Look, I've been in a lot of dangerous situations where I've done some shit, seen some shit, and had to clean up some shit. Last night should have scared me more than it did, which speaks volumes as to how desensitized I've become.

I blame Kaleb for a lot of it.

Pulling the covers over my head, I close my eyes and sigh.

Dmitri.

His soulless, glacial blue eyes will haunt me forever. To think last night I'd nearly convinced myself that I was delusional and had made him up, only to have the ache between my thighs, and the condom wrapper still on my floor to prove that he is very much real.

And he must very much like me.

They say it's better to work with the devil you know than the devil you don't. What kind of devil is Dmitri? Better than Kaleb, or worse?

I didn't get to see him fight in the cage that night, but there was an obvious shift in the crowd when he arrived. That much I could hear from my position on the wall in the room with a bed and small closet.

Ugh, speaking of that room. I can't believe that old man lied to me about the building. He totally gaslighted me! And the worse thing is, even with all the proof I had, his stonewall nonsense still almost worked on me. I was doubting myself left and right, and he added to it.

Kaleb's cronies are the same way. They act like they don't know what you're talking about, even though they know everything. They play stupid. Lie. Ignore. Deflect. It's the only game they can play and win. Losing could get them killed.

Is Dmitri playing the same game, or a different one? A worse one?

How on earth did he know I was there looking for him? The only security cameras I saw were busted and hanging off the sides of the building as if someone had knocked them with a baseball bat or something. But he knew I was there looking for Dmitri, or last night would have never happened. That old man must have told him I was there.

"I'm not here to hurt you," Dmitri had said last night. *"I want to know why you're so fucking desperate."*

"I'm not desperate."

"Yes, you are. You've been looking for me."

He's right. And I'll be back at the warehouse tonight to find him again.

Kaleb told me Dmitri killed his father. Simple math puts them at the same age or close to it. Not that I can really tell how old Dmitri is, but he doesn't look much older than Kaleb. Can a kid kill a grown man and get away with it, especially if that man was a convicted felon with a rap sheet a mile long?

I met Kaleb when he was sixteen, and I was twelve. Six months after I moved in with my foster family, he and I became two peas in a pod. He lived down the road from my school, but I never knew where exactly. He always either came to my house or made me meet him out in public somewhere.

Dmitri's kind of playing that same game. He came to me last night and I have no clue where to find him still.

Jeez, my head hurts. This is too much braining before sunrise. Time to start the day and make some money.

Rolling out of bed, I throw away the condom and wrapper still on my floor, then head into my bathroom. Twisting my hair into a messy bun, I wash up, remembering what it was like to do this last night after Dmitri smeared his cum all over my face. It was disgusting. Degrading.

I loved it.

Just one more surprise I wasn't prepared for, honestly. I'm usually a slut for praise. Call me a good girl, and I'll do just about anything you want me to. Kaleb knows that and uses it to his advantage.

Dmitri just stormed in, railed me, degraded me, and left.

But there was something about it that made me feel, I don't know... appreciated? Respected?

Wowwww. I need to get a grip.

Tell that to my pussy. It's already whining that Dmitri's not here to do it all again.

Okay. Shower, coffee, and work. No more dirty

thoughts of the enemy of my enemy.

Twenty minutes later, I'm in comfy shorts, a ripped, oversized t-shirt, and at my desk, logging into the portal so I can get started on my day. I'm a medical coder. It's not the greatest job, but it's interesting and I get to do it from home, which is perfect since I don't like the idea of Addie being home alone. It's not safe here anymore.

Which is entirely my fault.

Three hours later, the front door opens and Addie steps in, looking rough.

"Good morning."

"Hey." She drops her bag on the floor and kicks her flip-flops off. "Coffee still on?"

"Yeah." I open the next patient case and start working on it. Stacks of books with colored tabs poking out of the pages line both sides of my laptop. I've scribbled all over a notepad, making reminders for myself. Sticky notes are everywhere. It looks messier than it is. I have a system.

"How are you working on a Saturday?" Addie asks from the kitchen.

"Money don't make itself, babe." I rub my tired eyes. "I fell behind this week and need to catch up." The money isn't great yet, but the flexibility makes up for it. I get paid per chart I complete, but as the newest member of the private company I'm working for, I somehow always end up with the charts that are long and take me hours to finish, which means others have already snagged the shorter cases they can complete quickly and get more done in a day than me, thus making more money than me.

It is what it is.

"Want to go to the movies later?"

"Can't," I say with a sigh. "I'll probably be at this all day."

"Girl, you work harder than an ugly stripper." Addie trudges past me and into the living room, plopping down on the couch. "You need to take breaks."

"Taking breaks is why I'm behind." Finding where I left off, I start my project again. It's tedious work, but I get to learn new things each day and that's kind of cool. The chart I'm on now is for a one-hundred-and-fifty-five-day hospital stay. Poor dude.

I grow quiet while concentrating again. Addie eventually turns on the TV and settles on the couch like she has no intention of getting up for the day. Ah, to be sixteen again. "Do you have work later?"

"Nope. Thank God." She stretches out on the sofa. "I'm exhausted."

"When did you go to sleep?"

"I haven't yet. We stayed up all night binging anime with some friends and then I just decided to come home early."

Worry makes me lose my place on the chart I'm in. I thought it was just Addie and Tasha hanging out last night. "Who were the other friends?"

Addie doesn't respond.

"Who were the other friends?" Tasha rarely has more than one person over at a time, and her parents don't allow big slumber parties. "*Addie.*"

She's passed out on the couch already.

Tip toeing over, I grab a blanket from a stack we keep on a chair in the corner and cover her with it. There's a new thick leather bracelet on her wrist. Guess she added to her collection. My girl has bracelets going halfway up both arms. I don't know how she sleeps with all of them on. Her makeup's smudgy and hair is falling out of her messy bun. The nail polish on her fingers has almost worn completely off, too.

While Addie sleeps peacefully on the couch, I won't allow myself to sink into the depressing thoughts that always harp on the fact that I've failed her. I'm not equipped to take care of a teenager, but here I am doing it. I'm not even qualified to take care of myself half the time. But here I am.

Here… I still… am.

Fighting back the crushing weight of being the world's biggest disaster, I walk over to a window so I can open it. Fresh air will do us both some good. Then I head to the sliding glass door in the kitchen and open that one, too.

Hang on. What is that?

A small, folded piece of paper is tucked beneath the handle of the sliding door. With shaky hands, I open it and read the message.

Put a bat on the slider as a stopper next time, Firefly.
Unless you want me to come back and mess that pretty face up again.
- D

So, this was how he broke in. Last night I'd checked the front door and didn't see a single mark on the lock or doorjamb. None of my windows had been broken, either.

Kaleb used to sneak into my bedroom back in the day. He now has a key.

Dmitri made his own entrance and left no trace of his existence behind.

One was my god. The other is a ghost.

Okay, I need to stop comparing the two of them. It's not helping, and I need to concentrate on my work so I can get a fatter paycheck. But even as I sit down and stare at the laptop screen, my mind is already elsewhere…

"What are you doing?" I spring up from my bed and gawk at Kaleb. "If the Brenner's find out you're in here, they're going to be furious!"

"So?" He slips into my bedroom like a demon.

"They'll beat me."

"I'll kill them before they touch you, Dae."

Kaleb's disregard for authority isn't scary, it's inspiring. He sneaks in through my window all the time, and I never know when he'll visit, so it's always a terrifyingly fun surprise. But I keep my window unlocked all the time for him, just to make it easy.

Dressed in black chucks, dark jeans, and a grey hoodie, he sits on my bed and reaches into his pocket, pulling out a bracelet. "Happy birthday, babygirl."

I gawk at the pink threads strung together with a little knife charm dangling off the end. My stomach gets a bunch of butterflies in it. "Thank you."

His smile is spectacular as he slides it onto my wrist and makes it snug. Then he brings my hand up and kisses my palm. Kaleb does little things like this all the time. It makes me feel special.

He makes me feel special.

"Were you my good girl today?" he asks in a low, quiet, sexy voice.

My belly flip flops because… it always does with him.

"Yes." Reaching under my pillow, I pull out the fat envelope of money given to me in exchange for the package I handed over this afternoon. Dropping the brick of cash into

his waiting palm, I chew on my bottom lip, wondering how long it'll take for the Brenner's to find out about me and Kaleb and kick me out of their house. If that happens, Kaleb said I can live with him. He has the money to take care of us, obviously, but as bad as I want to pack up and move in with him now, I can't. There's a damn good reason for my staying as long as possible, which he understands.

"You're incredible, Daelyn." Kaleb cups my cheek and runs his thumb along the sore spot under my eye. I'd been in a fight with another kid in the house two days ago and it still hurts. "Did they give you any trouble?"

"No." I lie. They scared the shit out of me, but I'm not going to tell Kaleb that. I need to be strong, so he'll keep me. "They wanted to know where you were, though."

His right eye twitches a little. "What did you tell them?"

"I said it was none of their business and that if they didn't want the product, I had another buyer lined up."

"Clever girl." His features soften as his gaze lowers to my mouth. "You're always looking out for me, aren't you?"

"We look out for each other," I whisper with hope in my tone.

"That's right. And do you know why?" He leans in, our mouths super close to each other now. "Because that's what love is."

All the butterflies in my belly crash into each other and fall to the pit of my stomach, flopping on the ground.

"You love me?" I'm too caught up in his proximity that I no longer care about the light turning on in the hallway.

"Of course, I love you. Would I be here if I didn't?"

No. He was going to move away but talked his mom into staying here. For me.

He works hard every day and returns night after

night. To me.

And everything he has me do makes me a better partner for him.

"I have to go away for a few days," he says. "But I'll come back with a present for you."

I don't want a present. I want him. He's always running off for days and days and I hate it. I hate that he never tells me where he goes. I hate that he doesn't call while he's gone. I hate that I have no power in our relationship.

"Take me with you this time," I beg in a whisper.

The light in the hallway turns off again. I hold my breath as we listen to the soft footfalls of my foster father disappearing back into his room and his bedroom door clicks shut.

"You know I can't." Kaleb swipes the hair from my face. "I'm still getting everything ready for us."

Us. *There's an* us. *I cling to it like the love-sick fool I am.*

"But you getting this," he says, shaking the envelope, "helps me a lot. Thank you, babygirl."

I love when he calls me that. I feel like I can do anything, be anything, endure anything.

"You're welcome." *My bravery fortifies because I'm Kaleb's good girl. His babygirl. He only calls me that. He only sneaks in, risking his life every time, just to see me.* Only me.

"Can you be quiet?" he asks, tugging the strap of my tank top down my shoulder.

I nod, wondering how far we'll go this time. He loves to eat me out. Does it a lot. And I try to reciprocate the favor, but he acts like it's an honor to go down on me and never wants anything back in return. He's such a giver.

"That's my good girl." Kaleb gently presses me down on the bed and pulls his hoodie off.

Blood rushes to parts of my body that make me hot,

shaky, and ooey-gooey all at once. He unfastens his fly. My gaze flicks to the door and I pray no one hears whatever we're about to do.

He pulls my sleep shorts down, taking my underwear with them. My heart kicks like a wild animal in a cage.

"I don't have a condom," he says. "But I'll pull out, okay? Do you trust me?"

My mouth goes dry. I can't swallow. This is scary and dangerous and exciting and stupid. "Yes, I trust you."

"I'm clean." He shoves his jeans down, and his dick juts out, long and hard, as he crawls on top of me. I spread my legs to make more room for him. "You're clean too, right? I have to be able to trust you, Daelyn."

"Y-yes. I'm clean." Of course, I am. I've been saving myself for Kaleb. And now everything I've been wishing for is about to happen. He has more money, he has me, he has what he needs to build us a future together, and I helped him get there. All I have to do now is wait until he gives me permission to run, and I'll be on my way. Straight into his arms. Into the life I've helped him build. We're so close.

He's... so close.

I stare into his eyes, falling under a spell as he aligns us. Then he spits on his fingers and reaches between my legs, swiping my pussy to wet it. My heart kicks wildly in my chest and the butterflies fluttering in my belly turn into hornets buzzing through my bloodstream. I'm scared, but I want this. Every time I face something terrifying, I think he likes me more.

"Happy sweet sixteen, babygirl." Kaleb holds me down and shoves into me...

"—starving."

I rub my eyes for the umpteenth time and finally log out of the system for the day.

"Hello. Earth to Daelyn." Addie waves her hand in my face. "Did you hear a word I just said?"

"Sorry. I was in a zone. Repeat it."

"I said I'm *starving*."

"Then make yourself something to eat."

"Ugh, we don't have anything."

"Yes, we do!" I close my laptop. "We have so much food, it's crazy."

"No. We have ingredients. This isn't a food house. It's an ingredients house."

"Good thing you know how to put ingredients together to make a meal, boo."

Someone knocks on the door, making me jump.

Addie peers out the window and smiles. "It's Ace." She opens the door for him before I can stop her.

Ace steps in like he lives here too and holds up two pizza boxes and a paper bag. "Who's hungry?"

"We ate already," I lie, hoping he'll leave.

Addie rolls her eyes. "She's full of shit." She snags the bag from him and squeals. "Burgers too? You're my hero."

No. He's a villain.

"We were just leaving," I say, standing up. Ouch, my knees hurt from sitting for so long. Geez, what time is it?

"Where are you two going?" Ace asks, shoving a slice of pizza in his face.

"Yeah, Daelyn. Where are we going?"

Addie is so unhelpful. And that's because I've kept way too much from her. She has no clue Ace is a snake. She has no clue that I've been roped into criminal activities just to keep this house and put food on our table. Her ignorance is causing me more misery than I can handle lately.

"The movies."

Addie's brow arches. "But you said—"

"Well, guess what? I changed my mind. Let's go."

Ace watches our exchange like a wolf studying its prey's behavior.

"I can't, Dae. I'm going to Tasha's tonight."

My heart falls. "Again?"

"Well, yeah. It's summer. That means midnight swims and sleeping in."

"But you didn't sleep at all there last night."

Ace stays quiet, chewing his food. I don't like him hearing anything we talk about. He'll read into it or report it to Kaleb. Nosy snitch.

"Sorry, babe. I made plans with her already and I'm not flaking." Addie chomps down on a burger. And now I'm taking in her outfit. She's showered and painted her nails a fresh bright blue. Jesus, how long did I ignore her today? Checking the time on my phone, I can't believe seven hours passed by and I didn't say a word to her.

I've neglected her.

Guilt makes me nauseous. I took this job so I could be here for her, but I'm not present like I need to be. Guilt makes my shoulders sag. "Okay. I'm sorry. Time got away from me and I…"

What can I say? She's sixteen and I'm not about to burden her with grown up shit. I took her in to help give her a better life. That means letting her go to her friend's house, midnight swims, and anime all-nighters.

When living with the Brenner family, it was lights out at eight and we couldn't make a peep, or we'd risk the belt. There were no sleepovers or friends hanging out at the house, and our rooms had to be spotless at all times. We had surprise inspections.

Addie has the opposite of that now. Whenever I feel like I'm being difficult or strict, I remind myself that it's okay to ease up. My life is not hers. I can't blur the lines or our childhoods.

"What time are you supposed to be there?"

"Whenever I get there." Addie inhales more of her burger.

"Who else will be there this time?"

"Just me and Tash." Addie grabs the soda Ace holds out for her. I don't like that he's so attentive. Or that he brought burgers from her favorite restaurant. "She got overwhelmed with having more than me there last night. Said she's not doing that ever again. But I'm super proud of her for trying to step out of her comfort zone, you know?"

I almost suggest Tasha spend the night at our house tonight, but we don't have a pool. And my house isn't safe if strange men are sneaking into it in the middle of the night to fuck me.

Dread lands like a brick in my belly.

Maybe the more Addie stays away, the safer she'll be.

I've royally fucked up. Even though this last job for Kaleb will set both me and Addie free, she doesn't know about any of it, and the further I can keep her out of the hole I've dug myself into, the better off she'll be.

Addie is my *only* priority.

"Okay. Well… let's finish eating first." I shake off the tension that has my shoulders cramping and head over to the kitchen table with them. "What are you even doing here, Ace?"

"Gee, Dae." He folds another slice of pizza in half and takes a big bite. "You're shit at being appreciative."

Addie chuckles from across the table. "She's just hangry. This is awesome of you."

No. It's sneaky of him. I glance at the new bracelet on Addie's wrist and suddenly want to throw up my one bite of pizza. "Where did you get that bracelet?"

She glances at it and shrugs. "Me and Tash got matching ones. Her mom ordered them online for us."

Addie doesn't lie to me. She's never had to. It's just a friendship bracelet. Nothing more. It's not like the one Kaleb gave me for my birthday all those years ago. It's not the same.

I need to get a grip.

"Let me see it." Ace reaches forward and the way he takes her hand makes my skin crawl. "Sweet."

He's not Kaleb. Addie's not you. Chill, Daelyn.

Addie pulls away from him and takes several big gulps of her drink before polishing off her burger. Her cell goes off and she checks it under the table. Wiping her mouth with a paper napkin, she kicks into action. "Well, bye, guys. Behave yourselves. Thanks for dinner, Ace." Addie puts her flip-flops on and grabs the bag she'd packed while I was engrossed in my work and not paying attention to her earlier.

Ace leans back to watch her. "Need a ride there?"

"Nope." She heads out, and the front door slams shut.

Unfazed, Ace grabs another slice of pizza.

Am I supposed to just eat with him like we're friends? I chew slowly, watching him like a hawk.

"What are you really doing here?"

His jaw clicks as he chews. He looks tired and annoyed. "Can we just eat in peace, Daelyn?"

Fine.

We silently polish off one whole pizza and he eats the other two burgers in the bag while I pick at the fries. Then he leaves without saying a word.

My gut sinks with more worry.

Something else is going on here.

I don't know what it is, and I don't fucking like it.

Chapter 8

Dmitri

Despite giving Daelyn plenty of time to heed my warning, every night I've come to her house, the sliding glass door has *not* been reinforced. This is the fifth night in a row that I've checked. However, this is the first time I've entered her home since my original break in. Every other time, I only tested the door, disappointed to find it unsecured, and left to take my aggression out on my punching bag in the Monarch's dungeon instead.

I thought I could work her out of my system that way.

I can't.

Something about this woman calls to my demons and I'm certain it's going to end badly for me. That's fine. I'm used to it.

Lifting her flimsy sliding glass door off the tracks, I slide it over and make a space big enough for me to squeeze through. Her house smells so fucking good. It reminds me of a florist shop, but I don't see flowers anywhere. She's had her windows open lately, too. There's a freshness in the air that wasn't here the first time I came into her space.

Creeping through her home, I love all the comforts she's got scattered all over the place, like pillows and blankets and candles. This rundown house needs a lot of upgrades, but it feels good in here. Homey. Sweet. The stairs creak as I climb them. I cautiously peek in the first bedroom and find it empty, just like last time. Whoever her roommate is, they must not stay here often.

Good.

Making my way down the hall, I pass the bathroom and crack open Daelyn's bedroom door. She's sleeping in a tank top and her right leg rests on top of the covers.

She looks so little in her bed.

Innocent.

She's anything but, I remind myself.

I'd taken pictures of her driver's license the other night when I broke in here and had Vault run a background check on her. She was a foster kid and graduated from a local high school. Two years ago, she got her associate degree from a community college and works as a medical coder. My girl is tough and smart. What a turn on, right?

Standing at the foot of her bed, I'm captivated by how precious she looks.

Like a viper sleeping in its nest.

How did you get roped into Silas's cage fights, little firefly?

I asked him where he found her, but he refused say. Not that I thought he would. Silas never tells me where he gets the women I fuck after a fight. Only that they're clean, willing, and ready for me. He wouldn't lie to me about that. I trust him implicitly. Besides, the less I know about my prize, the better, because it's not like we're dating or anything. I've had several repeats over the years, especially when I first started fighting for money in the cage, but over time, I've gone less and less. If I want to fuck, there are plenty of Monarch Club members willing to join me.

Maybe that's why I'm so fascinated with Daelyn. It's not that she's someone special, it's that she's the first step back into the world I've secretly missed with the most toxic fiber of my being. She's that first spring breeze that blows into an abandoned house. The rekindled flame after the fire nearly dies out and it radiates a wave of much-needed warmth to your frozen fingers. She's the very first bite of a favorite home-cooked meal you haven't been able to eat in years.

"Don't." Daelyn says, stirring in her sleep. "Please. Don't." Her face scrunches up. "Wait." Her back arches, head pressing harder against the pillow. Then she flops flat on her back again. "I'm sorry. I'll be good." She flinches and curls up on her side. "Stop." Her breathing changes. "Stop!"

My protective instincts kick into high gear.

Who terrorizes her in nightmares?

What has she been through that's brought her into my world?

What's going on in her mind?

"No!" She kicks her feet as if fighting off a monster. "Stop it!"

"Daelyn," I say loudly to wake her. I will not touch her. I know firsthand how that can be a big mistake because I accidentally gave Ryker a concussion once when he tried to wake me up from a nightmare. I don't like being touched unless I consent first and am prepared for it. "Daelyn, wake up."

She whimpers.

"Daelyn. Wake. Up." Fuck it, I'm going in. If she knocks my teeth out, so be it. "Hey," I say loudly, sitting on the edge of the bed, shaking her. "Wake up, Firefly."

"Help." She cries in her sleep and actual tears slide down her cheeks. "Oh my god. Help."

I will once I know what's wrong.

"Babyg—" Shit, she didn't like being called that last night. "Daelyn, come on, sweetness." I tug her arms and lift her up. Then I slide her into my lap. "Shh, I got you." I rock her gently, running my hand through her damp hair. "Wake up for me, Daelyn. Come on. Open your eyes."

She doesn't.

How the hell can she sleep through someone yelling her name and manhandling her like this?

My gaze lands on a bottle of sleeping pills sitting on the side table. Fuck. How many did she take?

"Dmitri," she mumbles against my chest.

My heart skids to a stop.

She hooks her arms around my back and clutches my t-shirt. I stiffen immediately. Daelyn inhales a long, deep breath against my chest and her body relaxes instantly.

Holy shit. I'm not sure what to do. No way did my scent just comfort her. She doesn't know me like that. And she hasn't been around enough for any part of me to be familiar to her.

"Daelyn." I don't like that I can't wake her up. I don't like that I can't shake the feeling that something bad is going on and I can't see it happening. I don't like that I'm suddenly insanely protective of a woman I do not know.

It doesn't stop me from taking care of her, though.

Repositioning her back into bed, I crawl in with her and become the big spoon. Hooking my arm around her side, I pull her in close, like I'm protecting her from an army of sleep paralysis demons.

This settles it. I'm certifiably out of my fucking mind.

I've never held a woman like this before. Even the Butterflies I've been a Dom for at the club didn't get this much from me. I hold them until they fell asleep, then bolt back to my dungeon for a little space.

I'm not bolting from Daelyn.

Holding her against me, I count her breaths, memorize her bedroom. I inhale the floral scent of her hair and rub little circles on her belly with my fingers. I whisper things in her ear, hoping they'll penetrate her dreams and keep the nightmares at bay.

Something I do must work because she doesn't flinch or cry out for the rest of the night. She stays motionless in my arms until it's after ten in the morning. Birds chirp loudly from her open bedroom window. Cars are annoyingly loud on the street, reminding me why I love my silent dungeon so much.

She didn't let go of my shirt all night. Tucked into my chest, she breathes deeply, slowly, and her hair tickles my nose, making me sneeze. *Shit!* I sneeze again. *Double shit!* Trying to keep the noise down, I end up making my ears pop with the third sneeze.

Daelyn stops breathing. Her body stiffens.

"Sorry," I say, before sneezing a fourth time. *Fucking hell*.

She cautiously pulls back and lets go of my shirt. *Of me*. Her sleepy eyes grow wide as she stares at me with confusion and horror warring on her sweet face. "What are you doing here?"

"You didn't reinforce the glass door."

She scoots away from me, not realizing how close she is to the edge of the bed, and almost tips off it. I snag her arm and pull her close to me again before she falls on the floor. "You should have blocked my way in if you didn't want me here, Daelyn."

Flustered, she presses her palms on my chest and pushes back a little. I could be a gentleman and give her space. If she shoves me any harder, she'll slide herself off the bed and onto the floor, because I'm not catching her a second time.

At least that's what I tell myself.

"When did you get here?"

I casually glance at the clock on her bedside table. "About ten hours ago."

Shock blasts across her face. Then she winces and rolls over to stretch her fingers out. "Ow."

"You had a tight grip on me most of the night. Your muscles and joints are probably cramped." I reach out to her. "May I?"

She twists to look at me again. "May you what?"

"Give me your hands."

Begrudgingly, she obeys. I massage her palms and fingers, wiggling each one individually. After a few minutes, I let her go. "Better?"

"Mmm hmm." She rolls out of bed, her dark hair a tangled mess with the hairband buried in a knot at the base of her neck. Daelyn rubs her eyes and stands up, giving me a spectacular view of her ass in the little booty shorts she's wearing. "Why didn't you wake me?"

"I tried."

She glances at the bottle of pills on the side table, her shoulders slouching when it dawns on her why she didn't wake up. "Shit."

"You take them often?"

"No." She grabs the container before I do. "Not

that it's any of your business."

With that, Daelyn marches out of her bedroom and slams the bathroom door shut.

Sitting up, I stretch my limbs and pin my morning wood against the waist of my jeans. I'm not touching myself for a while, so it'll have to deflate on its own. I hear the toilet flush and faucet run. Eventually, Daelyn comes back into her bedroom and looks annoyed to find me still here.

It pisses me off.

Instead of saying something nice, I go for the jugular. "You have nightmares often?"

I don't like it when someone asks about mine, because it's a personal issue I don't like sharing, but I've just spent the evening keeping her close and safe, and for her to act like me sticking around while she takes her morning piss is obnoxious, I'll make sure she feels some kind of way too.

"No," she says cautiously.

The pills are no longer in her hand, so I assume she put them somewhere in her bathroom.

"Do you take sleeping pills often?"

"Why are you so fucking nosy?"

"I'm just trying to figure you out." I climb out of the bed and slowly prowl closer to her. "You called out for me in your sleep."

She snorts. "Yeah right."

"You did." I get close enough to smell her minty breath. "I wouldn't make that up, Daelyn. The question is… Why?"

Her cheeks turn crimson. "You're delusional."

"I know what I heard. You whimpered and cried and said my name. You held onto me all night, Firefly."

Her brow furrows as she looks down at her hands. "Well, I don't know why I would have done that," she says defensively. "And I don't know why you stayed here, either."

"Like I said, you were having nightmares."

"So?" She crosses her arms and won't look at me. "That doesn't mean you need to stick around."

True. "Are you hungry?"

"No." Her stomach growls, betraying her with perfect timing.

I tip her chin, forcing her to look up at me. Arching my brow, I hold her gaze for several heartbeats before saying, "Don't ever lie to me, Daelyn."

She swallows hard.

"This won't work if you fucking lie to me."

Her eyebrows knit together. "What won't work?"

"Whatever this is."

Daelyn's stomach rumbles again and she clutches her belly and huffs about it.

"Come on." I nod towards the door. "Let's get you something to eat."

"I—" Her stomach rumbles and she smacks it. "Oh my god, shut up!"

She's adorable.

"You a pancake or waffle girl?"

"I'm not going out to breakfast with you."

"Fine. Brunch it is." I glance at the clock. "Unless you want to waste more time being a difficult little brat, in which case, I'm down for lunch and dinner, too. Whatever you want."

Her shoulders droop. "Why are you doing this?"

"Be more specific." I arch my brow. "This, as in coming to see you again, like I said I would. This, as in holding you all night so you could feel safe while you slept. Or this, as in wanting to take you on a date so I can get to know you better?"

Her jaw slackens. I think I've stunned her.

"Or I can just cook you a meal here." I shrug like it's no big thing. "We don't have to go anywhere if you don't want to."

Suddenly, her eyes widen, and she glances at her clock. "No, no. Out is fine. Out is good."

Interesting.

I step closer to the door, giving her space again. "Then get dressed so we can get out of here."

Chapter 9

Daelyn

I may not have a clue what I'm doing, but I know, without a shadow of a doubt, that it's a mistake. My mind races with a million scenarios with my heart beating fast in my chest, as I put my shoes on while Dmitri leans against the doorjamb, casually watching me.

Am I about to have breakfast with the man who broke into my house twice?

Yes.

I have to get closer to him so I can find out whatever it is Kaleb wants to know.

My stomach twists, my nerves screaming that I'm in over my head, but what choice do I have?

None.

When it comes to Kaleb, I never really have a choice. At least it's always felt that way to me. He owns me. *But not for much longer*, I remind myself. And that's exactly what gets me up on my feet, grabbing my purse, and heading out with a silly smile on my face.

It's already hot out, and there isn't a cloud in the sky. Dressed in cut-off shorts and one of my favorite band tees, standing next to Dmitri, I feel small and frumpy. How can a guy make dark jeans, combat boots, and a black cotton t-shirt look like runway material? It's rude.

He slept fully clothed.

Next to me.

All night.

I can't believe I didn't wake up at all. An enormous man snuck into my house, crawled into my bed, and touched me all night long and I didn't have a fucking clue. Damn those sleeping pills. I only took them because I was so desperate for sleep. For the past week I haven't been able to turn my brain off, and part of that was because I'd been expecting to see Dmitri again. It's why I didn't block the sliding glass door.

But after several nights of waiting, I gave up because I needed sleep so I could do my job, take care of Addie, and get my brain functioning, so I'd be ready for whenever Kaleb or Ace showed up again. Figures the night I drug myself is when Dmitri shows up. Shame tightens my throat, making it hard to swallow. He probably thinks I'm a junkie or something.

"I don't normally take sleeping pills," I blurt out as we walk down the sidewalk. I honestly don't know where we're going for breakfast and am following Dmitri's lead, because he seems to have a plan in mind. Either that, or he's just as good at faking it as I am.

He doesn't look at me when he asks, "Do you normally have nightmares?"

Wow. Of everything that's transpired between us already, this question feels awfully personal. And he keeps asking about it.

What do I have to lose by telling him a truth... or a lie?

I'm too afraid to look at him when I answer. "No." Stuffing my hands in the back pockets of my shorts, I clear my throat. "So, where are we having breakfast?"

"What's your favorite place?"

I don't have one. It's not like I have extra money to go out with, and when I do, I always let Addie choose. "I'm down for wherever."

"In that case." Dmitri casually puts his hand on my lower back and steers me across the street. "I'll pick."

Relief is not what I should feel right now. I should be terrified. This big, intimidating creeper with a violent streak is literally steering me into an alley.

But I'm more relaxed than ever.

Jesus, I'm messed up. And I'm totally dumping those sleeping pills down the drain when I get home. Regardless of whether it was the drugs that let me sleep so deeply last night, or Dmitri holding me without my realizing it, I'm way too relaxed for my own good around this man.

Maybe I'm disassociating?

Wouldn't be the first time. Or the thousandth.

We stop at a sleek black motorcycle.

"Hop on." Dmitri pats the backseat and lifts a helmet off the back.

"This is yours?" I can't understand why he'd park such a beautiful, expensive luxury between two dumpsters in an alley.

"Yes, it's mine. I don't steal."

That's not what I was implying. I'm not even sure what I was trying to get at with my question. He's throwing me off and setting me right, which makes zero sense. Why do I feel safe with a man I should be terrified of? My bad judgement calls are further proof that I need to get out of Kaleb's world before I'm killed.

I know what he did to Kaleb's father, which means I'm about to have breakfast with a murderer. A stalker who broke into my house more than once. A monster who fucked me while we were both covered in his blood.

Even with all those facts staring me straight in the face, I still don't feel scared of him. No matter how hard I try, the emotion doesn't surface. Not even when Dmitri silently puts the helmet over my head and adjusts the strap.

A monster wouldn't hold their prey all night, would they?

A killer wouldn't protect their target by putting a helmet on them, would they?

A stalker wouldn't stick around until they were caught... would they?

I'm so confused. All that good sleep I got last night isn't enough to get me through this. I'm tired of running, of out-maneuvering. I'm tired of fending for myself and protecting Addie from the very life I've dragged her into. I'm tired of working my ass off and having nothing to show for it.

Dmitri climbs onto the bike and looks over his shoulder. "Use me to hop on, Firefly."

Why does he call me that?

And why do I like it?

His shoulder is hard as a rock when I grab it to straddle his bike. I don't like that I'm wearing a helmet and he's not. It means he's putting my safety over his. Like a gentleman.

He's not a gentleman, he's a killer and a fighter and a bad, bad man.

Dmitri starts the engine and slips out of his hidden parking spot, yielding onto the main street effortlessly. I try to guess where we're going, but any spot I come up with, we either pass, or it's in the opposite direction.

Finally, fear sets in. I've willingly gotten onto the back of a bike with a man I do not know or trust and am letting him drag me further and further away from my safety zone.

That's the definition of too stupid to live.

If he kills me, I hope it's quick.

My stomach rolls because I can't believe that's my first thought in a situation like this. I've lost my will to fight. To survive. Kaleb took everything out of me so long ago and demands more and more every time I'm forced to confront him. And this is the result.

Dmitri is my end game.

I've run into the arms of a killer and will finally be at peace if this big brute will just put a bullet in my head. Snap my neck with his big hands. Snuff me out with my own goddamn pillow.

Addie will be better off without me. I've pulled her too close to danger just by being her guardian when I am supposed to save and protect her from all this awful shit.

My brain shuts down, and I retreat into this dark space where I feel nothing. I don't hear or see anything either. I'm a shell with a heartbeat, and that's it.

On the back of the bike, I check out and accept my fate.

...

"Daelyn."

I blink, finally snapping out of my mental retreat.

Dmitri's holding my face, his expression concerned. "Jesus." Only when he swipes my cheeks with his thumbs do I realize he's taken my helmet off. "Why are you crying?"

Am I? Huh. It doesn't feel like I'm crying.

And I don't have an answer to give him. It doesn't matter anyway. Tears don't sway devils. Kaleb taught me that.

"Talk to me," he urges.

I look around to see where we've ended up. I don't recognize the parking lot, but it's packed. The sun is bright in my eyes. People are walking around, and kids are running down the sidewalk. The scent of something delicious wafts in the breeze.

"Daelyn." Dmitri shoves his face into mine. "What's wrong?"

"Nothing," I say, slamming my mask into place. "I… the sun is just really bright, and it made my eyes water."

He sees through my lie immediately. His jaw sets, brows digging down as he glowers at me. But he doesn't press me even though we both know I'm full of shit because his helmet's tinted visor was over my eyes the whole ride.

"Come on." He holds his hand out for me, and I climb off his bike. I'm not even sure how he stabilized it while I was in my head, or for how long.

Whatever. It doesn't matter. "Where are we?"

"My favorite place for breakfast." He clasps my hand like we're a couple out on our weekly date. "Since I didn't know your favorite, I figured we can go to one of mine."

I numbly follow him and when we step inside, I'm suddenly hyperaware of how underdressed I am for a place like this. Embarrassment heats my face. "Do they have a dress code?"

"Why?"

"Because everyone looks so nice."

"So do you." He squeezes my hand and heads towards the hostess.

She smiles up at him. "Good morning. How many?"

"Morning. Two of us."

"Would you like a booth or table?"

"Wherever we'll have privacy," he answers, making my heart gasp.

"Sure thing." She grabs two menus and tips her head. "Follow me."

Dmitri stares straight ahead, still holding my hand, and I keep wondering why on earth I chose this crappy outfit today when I should dress to the nines to lure this man into my web of lies and deceit for Kaleb.

"Perfect. Thank you so much," Dmitri says, as we approach a booth in the back corner of the restaurant. Letting my hand go, he gestures for me to have a seat first. Once I slide in, he sits across from me and steeples his fingers.

I busy myself with the menu. The prices aren't listed, which makes me uneasy. "So… What's good here?"

"Don't know. Never been here before."

I freeze. "But you said that since you didn't know my favorite, we were going to one of yours instead."

He leans forward, looking menacing and sexy at the same time. "You lied to me, so I lied to you."

My stomach drops.

"Lie for a lie, Daelyn."

Oh my god. He's an asshole.

And so am I for doing all of this.

I recover quickly. "Does that mean for every truth I give you'll give me one too?"

He nods, but his jaw ticks like he's grinding his molars. I'm not sure if he's being honest or not, but this could be my opening. My way into this man's life, where I can get information to share with Kaleb.

Do it. Ask him anything. Bare your soul if you have to, because it's your only way out. Do it for Addie!

I lean back and cross my arms. "Can I ask you a personal question?"

He nods.

"And you'll answer it honestly, no matter what it is?"

He nods again.

I'm not buying it, but I'll play along, just in case. Narrowing my gaze at him, I lean in. "No matter how personal it is?"

He arches a dark brow at me and nods again.

"No matter how damning?"

He smirks and nods.

I think I've got his interest now. I *know* I have his attention. He hasn't even blinked, and his steady eye contact has me fighting to hold it instead of breaking away.

Time to fire the first shot.

"Have you ever killed someone, Dmitri?"

Chapter 10

Dmitri

This woman continues to surprise me at every turn. My mind scrambles to figure out why she'd ask such a ridiculous question and I end up settling on the way we first met. She was, after all, my prize for winning a brutal series of cage fights that would have put weaker men into their graves. Lord knows I've beaten plenty of people within an inch of their life, but they either asked for it, or fucking deserved it.

Her sudden question, however, hits way too close to home, and I don't like it. Keeping calm, I say, "Not yet."

That's honest enough.

My stomach twists as I hold Daelyn's gaze a moment longer. She's just stirred up something that's been riding my ass these past couple of months, and it's hard to swallow the guilt lodged in my throat.

Daelyn huffs, and her nose crinkles in this adorable way as she frowns at me. I think she's disappointed with my answer.

"My turn." I tip my head to the side. "Have *you* murdered anyone?"

She cocks her eyebrow and sarcastically responds with, "Not yet."

Brat. God, what I wouldn't give to bend her over my knee and spank her ass until it was cherry red right now. Then I'd make her —

"Welcome to Maggie's. I'm Rory and I'll be

serving you today. What drinks can I start you off with?"

Daelyn breaks our staring match first and fake smiles at our server. "I'll take a black coffee and an orange juice, please."

"No problem. And for you?"

"Water."

"Okay. I'll be right back with those, then I'll take your order." Rory spins around and walks off.

I keep my attention on Daelyn. "Do you know what you want?"

She swallows hard, then plucks the menu back up. "Nothing has a price."

My heart squeezes. I remember when I always had to math out what I could afford to eat each day. I don't like that Daelyn's doing it now.

"This is my treat. Order anything you want."

She doesn't look happy with my offer. Jesus Christ, I'm trying to be a good guy here and she's making it extremely difficult. Between her sleeping pills, leaving the door unsecured so I could break back in, her tears during the bike ride, and now asking me about murder, I'm overwhelmed with the number of red flags red flagging.

A sensible man would walk away immediately.

Too bad I'm not sensible.

I run on intuition and there's a delusional part of me that keeps whispering she's in danger and that I should help her. Time to lighten up a little and see if I can salvage this dismal date.

"What do you do for a living, Daelyn?"

Her eyes dart around the menu. "I'm a medical coder."

I knew that already but can't tell her that. It's

nice to know she told the truth, though.

"What do you do? I mean, besides beat the shit out of people in fight rings at night in the middle of nowhere."

"I'm in security."

She rests the menu on the table. "Really?"

"Lie for a lie, truth for a truth." I nod. "Yeah, really."

She eyes me up and down. "I can totally see it."

"Here you go." Rory sets our drinks down and pulls out her tablet. "Do you know what you'd like to order?"

I tip my head at Daelyn, letting her go first.

"I'll have the shrimp and grits with a side of home fries, and an order of the hushpuppies, please."

Damn. A woman with a big appetite is a hell of a turn on.

"You got it. And for you, Sir?"

"Steak hash, hold the onions."

"Alright, that'll be out shortly."

Once Rory leaves, I dive right into another question. "Do you have a roommate?"

The color instantly drains from Daelyn's face. "What?"

"I saw another bedroom at your house. Do you have a roommate or a kid or something?"

She takes a sip of her orange juice and I notice her hand's trembling. It makes me want to ease whatever fears she has because I've unknowingly pushed a button. "I'm just asking because I want to be careful if you leave your sliding door unsecured again. I don't want to scare someone else by accident."

"I hardly think you need to sneak into my house anymore, Dmitri."

"I disagree."

She sets her drink down. "Why?"

"Because you like it."

Boom. The way her pale cheeks suddenly turn crimson tells me I'm right. My girl has some fun kinks. I can't wait to unlock them all.

"Yes. I have a roommate." Daelyn clears her throat. "And she's off limits."

Fine by me. I'm not interested in anyone but the menacing beauty glowering across from me. She fidgets in her seat, and I can't tell if she's debating on stabbing me with her butter knife or bolting out the door.

"I'll stay clear of her," I promise. "And again, if you don't want me to come back, just put a baseball bat or a large piece of wood on the bottom of your sliding glass door. I won't get in any other way other than that entrance. You have my word."

Scoffing, she crosses her arms. "Words don't mean much where I come from."

I almost ask where that is, but table it, for now.

"Your turn," I say, giving her the control. I don't want this to be an interrogation, but I also want to know as much as I can about her. There's a reason I'm drawn to her, and it's not just her great tits and juicy ass. Nor is it her sparkling personality.

She takes another sip of OJ, and her hands aren't shaking so much anymore. That eases my protective instincts a fraction. "Um. What's your favorite color?"

"Blue green."

"Like the Caribbean?"

"Like your eyes."

She rolls them hard, but her smile pops out even though it's obvious she's not impressed by being flattered. "That is super lame, Dmitri."

"It's also super honest." I chug half my water. "Your eyes look like the Caribbean to me. I was obsessed with seeing those waters when I was a kid. I couldn't fathom there being something that pretty in this world and was convinced all the pictures I saw were photoshopped."

"I've never been there, so I can't confirm or deny if it's true."

"Me either."

Her brow pinches together. "Your turn."

"What's *your* favorite color?"

"Green."

"What shade?"

"All of them." She visibly relaxes. "Beach or Mountains?"

"Don't have a preference." I've never been to either. In fact, I've barely left my hometown. "You?"

"Beach." She gets this dreamy smile on her face. "I went once when I was a kid and I loved it."

"Here you go." Rory pops over with our food. We both lean back as she places dish after dish on the table. "Enjoy!"

Daelyn stabs a shrimp and forkful of grits. "Why do you fight?"

Ah. We're back to personal, serious topics. Fine by me. "It's a way to blow off steam."

"So is going on a run, or fucking, or—"

"I do all those too," I say, cutting her off. "Trust me."

Her cheeks redden again.

I stab into my steak hash and shovel a huge bite into my mouth. It's pretty good, but my boy Knox could make this much better. He's been having me,

Ryker, and Vault hop around to all the fancy spots in town, taste testing random dishes so we can tell him if they're worth reinventing or not. He's a damn good chef, self-taught, and is always eager to put his own twist on things at his club's secret restaurant.

"Have you ever lost a fight?"

"No." It's suddenly hard to swallow my food. "Does it bother you that I fight?"

She stuffs an entire hushpuppy into her mouth. I swear she does it on purpose to give herself extra time to come up with an answer.

"Be honest," I warn.

As I wait for her answer, my body starts coiling tight. My mother hated that my dad fought for side money. She didn't mind spending it on booze every fucking chance she got, though. And for someone who pitched a fit and said his violence was juvenile, she sure knew how to swing a punch herself.

Fuck, I feel sick now.

"No," Daelyn says quietly. "But I would think it's kind of hard to be with a fighter."

Does she want to be with me? It's a little early in the game to be thinking about commitment. But damn my pathetic heart for gasping at the thought of it being a possibility. "Hard, how?"

She shrugs and takes a sip of her coffee. "I'd be pretty upset if you came home busted up all the time."

"You weren't sad when I came to you all busted up the night of the fight."

"I didn't know you then."

And still, she fucked me. "You don't know me now, either."

"True." Daelyn carefully sets her coffee down. "Have you ever hit a woman?"

"Absolutely not." I don't realize my grip is so tight around my fork and knife until Daelyn gawks at it. Shit. I bent the fork handle. "I don't tolerate physical violence against a woman. *Ever*." Then I do one better, because we're all about honesty today, right? "The last time I found a man hitting a woman, I beat him within an inch of his life."

She stares at me for a long moment and then shoves another hushpuppy in her mouth. At least she cut it up this time, so she won't risk choking on it.

"Does my fighting disgust you?" I hold my finger up just as she takes a sip of her OJ. "Let me rephrase. Did the way I fucked you that night disgust you?"

She snarfs her juice.

Laughter blows out of me because it feels nice to catch her off guard. I swear she's been a concrete wall this entire time, and I've finally managed a little foothold.

Daelyn wipes her face with a napkin. "Oh my god, it's in my sinus cavity!"

That makes me laugh harder.

She tosses her napkin at me. "Nice to see my pain brings you pleasure."

I stop laughing immediately. "Are you hurt?"

She sniffs hard and takes another sip of her juice. "Ugh. Not physically, but my pride is likely on life support from it."

Rory comes out of nowhere and asks, "How's everything so far?"

I swear this server is stealthier than a ninja with the way she keeps showing up out of the blue. Either that, or I'm way too entranced by the woman across from me to stay aware of my surroundings. I hope it's not the latter. I can't afford to be lazy in that department. Especially after the news I got a few weeks ago.

Fuck... I don't want to think about that right now. It won't do me any good because I can't go back and change a damned thing.

I can't save him.

Never could.

"—you mean."

Wait. What did she say? I missed it. And where did Rory go? "Repeat that?"

"I said yes, I liked it, in a gory, dangerous, adrenaline rush kind of way, if that's what you mean."

I don't even remember the question I'd asked. Grabbing my water to buy myself time to re-collect my thoughts, I'm fucked because there's no water left in my glass. The ice at the bottom tips and falls into my face.

"I like it rough," Daelyn says casually. "It's usually the only way I can come. I need that extra oomph to penetrate my chaotic brain and dominate it so my body will submit."

Sweet Jesus. I remember what I'd asked now. And her answer has my dick hard as steel. "How do you know it's the only way you can come?"

"Uh, because it's me and I know me."

Not good enough. People make new self-discoveries all the time. "I bet I could show you other ways."

She rolls her eyes so hard I don't know how they haven't detached. "Eat your steak, Dmitri."

"I'd rather eat you."

She leans back and frowns. "We're shit at conversation."

"I disagree. Murder, orgasms, and beaches are perfectly acceptable topics for a first date."

That makes her laugh. God damn, she's beautiful. I'm dying to strip her down, both physically and mentally, to see the real woman hiding beneath the mask she keeps wearing around me.

A terribly brilliant idea hits me. "Have you ever heard of the Monarch Club?"

Chapter 11

Daelyn

I'm out of my motherfucking mind. After we finished breakfast, Dmitri dropped me back off at my house with explicit instructions to, "Wear a nice dress. Hair down. Be at the Monarch Club's front door at seven sharp."

I've been staring at my cell ever since he blazed down the road on his motorcycle, leaving me stunned speechless on the curb. He'd put his number in my contacts list, along with the address to the Monarch Club, and saved both under the name *D*.

D for Dmitri.

D for danger.

D for death.

D for don't go, it's a trap.

As I head inside my house, I check Addie's location and see she's still at Tasha's. *Phew*. Pulling up our text thread, I type with shaking fingers, *I love you*.

Then delete it.

I only reach out like this when I'm stressed, and I don't want to lean on Addie for comfort when I'm the reason for the mess I'm in. Scrubbing my face, I sigh heavily and get a new plan going. Rage cleaning for the rest of the day with heavy metal blasting might fix me.

My life might be a mess, but that doesn't mean my house is too.

By three in the afternoon, the summer breeze

blowing through my open windows doesn't cool the sweat trickling down my back. We don't have air-conditioning and I usually keep the house like a dark cave with the curtains drawn, but I need the sunlight, if only to brighten my darkening mood.

The flurry of possibilities whirring in my head about tonight has me tense. What will Dmitri and I do at the Monarch? What dress should I wear? I'm wet at the thought of fucking him in a swanky sex club. Will there be an audience? Do I want there to be?

My pussy clenches.

Why am I like this?

Why can't I stop putting myself in situations that will only hurt me in the end?

How will D hurt me?

I hate how eager I am to find out.

So, I shut it off. All my fantasies go back into the no-no box, and I shake away the lust wrapping warmth around me and replace it with cold resolve. I'm not going to that club for fun. I'm going to complete a mission and be done.

This is business, not pleasure.

While music blasts in my ears, I scrub my tub until I've completely numbed out again. The lyrics turn to white noise, and the smell of cleaning products fades. I don't notice the ring of soap scum as I scrub, scrub, scrub.

And I don't notice that I'm not alone.

Not until an earbud is ripped from my ear.

"*Boo.*"

I scream and swing out, knocking my assailant in the face with my scrub brush.

"Fuck, Dae!" Kaleb stumbles back, holding his eye.

Oh shit. Oh shit, oh shit, oh shit.

"Kaleb," I squeak, my heart ramming against my ribs. "What the hell!"

He blinks fast, his right eye bright red and watery, while fury laces his tone. "Fucking *Christ*."

"Flush out your eye," I order, steering him by his shoulders towards the sink. "Here." I smack the faucet on, gather cool water in my hand, and pull him by the shirt until he bends down. Then I splash his eye until I think he'll be okay. "Sit down," I say, guiding him until the back of his legs hits my toilet. "Here, put this on your eye."

He takes the cold washcloth from me and slaps it on his face.

"I'm sorry."

"Not your fault, babygirl. I shouldn't have snuck up on you like that."

I bite my lip as a swarm of bees and butterflies battle in my belly. "What are you doing here?"

"Wanted to take you out for lunch."

Yeah, right. I can't even remember the last time we shared a meal together. "Why?"

"Christ, Dae, can't I just take my girl out to eat without having another motive?"

"I'm not your girl."

The look on his face gives the butterflies the upper hand over the bees in me. But the victory doesn't last. "You'll always be my girl," he says.

There was a day when those words would make me melt. Today, they make me want to vomit. "What are you really doing here, Kaleb?"

He tosses the washcloth in my sink and stares at me with one green eye and one slightly swollen red eye. I'm sure it stings, and I wouldn't put it past him to act extra wounded just to get sympathy out of me. Now I feel duped. I should have let the chemicals eat his eyeball until it blinded him.

"I've missed you," he says in a softer tone. "Lately I've just…" He gently grazes my side with the backs of his fingers. Then they curl around my waist in a firm grip, and he brings me in, spreading his legs so I'll stand between them. "I need you, Dae."

My mask almost drops.

My strength nearly wavers.

But I can't fall for his bullshit again. No matter how sincere he sounds, I refuse to allow myself to believe it's the truth. Even if he's never lied to me before, he's manipulated me with his words, which is just as bad.

"If you need comfort, I'm sure Kayla or one of your other girls would be happy to fill that role, Kaleb."

He's got plenty of women begging to bounce on his dick. Trust me. I've seen it.

"They're not you."

I look away from him. He only wants me because he thinks someone else has me. And that someone is who Kaleb himself forced me to be with.

"No one else knows me like you do, Daelyn. I don't want another woman. I want *you*."

Funny, he said those exact words the day I walked in on him railing a girl named Savanah. He said he didn't love her like he loved me. That she was nothing but a hole and I was his everything. He got mad when I wouldn't listen to his bullshit, and he blamed his betrayal on me by saying I wasn't around for him as much as I should be. That he had needs, and it's not his fault that he had to turn to another woman.

Then he got on his knees, cried, and begged me for another chance.

He kissed me like I was his salvation.

He lifted me into his arms and carried me away, promising me a dozen and one things that he was going to do to make it up to me.

Only to cheat on me again a month later.

I was eighteen then. Finally free from the foster system, I'd come to live with Kaleb so we could have a beautiful life together. Instead, I caught him fucking other women in our bed, and I was too deeply involved in a dangerous life with the only guy I'd ever loved, and therefore couldn't run as fast as I wanted away from all of it.

It was complicated then and is even worse now.

Kaleb has kept me on a short leash long after I kicked him out of my heart. And the worst part about it is, I don't think I know how to be unleashed. The collar, invisible but snug, is a comfort to me.

Kaleb wraps his arms around my waist and rests his head against my chest. "You always smell so fucking good," he says quietly. "Like a field of flowers."

My eyes water.

"Remember when we went to that big garden with the orchid house?" His hands splay across my lower back. "Answer me."

"Yes."

"Remember how we fucked under the cherry blossom tree?"

I squeeze my eyes shut, letting a tear escape. "Yes."

"You smell like that right now." He breathes me in, his grip tightening. "Like sex and flowers." He runs his hands over the band of my shorts until he reaches the fly.

I step back. "No."

His eyes darken. "*No*?"

"I'm off limits." He's always respected this one and only boundary I've resurrected between us.

"Off limits," he repeats, as if that's a foreign concept he can't grasp. Standing slowly, he keeps his gaze locked on me. I try to hold my ground even when he calmly grabs my wrist and holds it up. "This mark says you're off limits to everyone *but* me."

Kaleb spins me around and pins my arm behind my back, bending me over the sink.

I don't fight it.

With one hand, he roughly unfastens my shorts and yanks them down. Then he cups my pussy over my panties and shoves me forward until the edge of the sink cuts into my belly. "You're *mine*, Daelyn. Don't you ever fucking forget it."

I don't respond.

Agreeing would be a lie.

Disagreeing will have him do something I'll regret forever.

A stronger woman would fight back. But I'm not strong. And he's right because I am his… for a little while longer.

"Look at me," he growls against my ear.

My body shakes as I look into our reflection.

"You're *mine*," he says, digging his fingers against my pussy with a bruising grip. "Say it."

"I'm yours."

"Good girl."

He lets me go and smooths his hair back, taking a calming breath. I swallow the saliva piling into my mouth, scared I'm going to puke all over the sink I've just cleaned.

"I'm sorry," he says softly. "Fuck, I'm so sorry." He jerks me to him and holds me tight, kissing the top of my head. "I'm a goddamn mess, babygirl. I shouldn't have done that."

My silence makes him more desperate.

"Forgive me?" When I still don't respond, he tips my chin with his finger. "Please say you forgive me. I mean it. I'm sorry. I know your boundaries and I shouldn't have acted like that. It's just that..." His eyes tighten like he's in pain. "I'm so fucked in the head about Dmitri. I can't turn off my rage or my possessiveness. It's driving me crazy that he's touched you."

"You made that happen, Kaleb. Not him. And not me."

"*I know that*!" he screams in my face.

I can feel his heart jack hammering against his chest when I press my palm against him to keep him back. The veins in his temples have popped out, too.

"I'm sorry I put you in this position, Daelyn. But you're the only one I trust. I can't give this job to anyone but you."

Sure, he can. He chose me because he doesn't really care about me. If he did... if he ever loved me even for a day... he would *never* have done the things he's done.

"I've got you, Kaleb."

He makes this distressed little noise that almost breaks me.

Almost.

But my walls are back up and I'm numbing out again. Detaching is second nature to me. I'm too good at it. "Let me get dressed and then we can grab a bite to eat."

"I'm not hungry anymore," he says. Bending down, he pulls my shorts back up and buttons them. "I'm gonna go."

The war of butterflies and bees in my belly amplifies. He wants me to fight him. To tell him to stay. I refuse.

"Okay." I hold my breath, reading his expression.

He doesn't give away a single emotion. Kaleb's gaze locks on mine for a heartbeat, then drifts to my mouth, my tits, my pussy.

His cell goes off and he answers without looking at who the caller is. "What?"

"We gotta problem," I hear Ace say.

"On my way." He shoves his cell into his back pocket and stares at the joining of my thighs for a moment longer before turning and walking out.

It's only when I hear my front door shut, that my knees buckle, and tears fall.

Chapter 12

Dmitri

At seven sharp, I'm glaring at the security cameras. *Where is she?* I hope she hasn't decided to back out of this. Then again, I kind of hope she does.

Finally, Daelyn steps into view of the camera, gracefully gliding up the walkway to the main entrance of the Monarch. She halts at the door and my heart skips a beat when I watch her fluff her dark hair to make it fall on her shoulders in long waves. She squeezes her eyes shut, her hand hovering over the doorknob, and I swear I stop breathing.

Then she opens it.

I keep myself from dashing out to meet her in the lobby. Can't look too eager, right? Calmly leaving Ryker's office, I stroll leisurely through the club, knowing Daelyn needs to sign waivers and an NDA before she can get into the heart of the Monarch.

It's early, so there aren't many guests here yet.

I've spent the day devising a plan to chip away at Daelyn's defenses so I can figure her out. If that makes me a manipulative asshole, so be it. My patience only goes so far, and I've been at the end of my rope with a lot of things lately.

Part of me knows I'm using Daelyn as a distraction from the horrors in my life and I don't care. She brings me peace. For me to admit that says I'm more fucked in the head than ever.

This woman is a stranger and a liar. Her

showing up in my life like this is also too perfectly timed, which is highly suspicious.

Daelyn's got a temporary pass at the Monarch, as my special guest, and I've waived the fees for her. I didn't tell Vault yet, so the background checks will wait because I want to deep dive into Daelyn my own motherfucking way.

The first glimpse of her when I reach the lobby has me slowing my roll. She's arresting. The security feed did not do her justice in that dress. My girl is a motherfucking smoke show.

No. She's not my girl. She's my…

What? My distraction, project, toy?

I'll go with submissive, because if I get my way, that's exactly what she'll be from this day forward.

"Daelyn," I practically purr while making my way towards her. Keeping a warm smile plastered on my face, I drag my gaze down her luscious body. "You look absolutely scrumptious."

Never mind how that just made me sound like a tool. I mean it. She looks good enough to eat, which is exactly what I plan to do. A meal like her should be savored over several hours and we've got all night.

"You're all set," Sophie says with a tight smile. "Please stay with your Dom at all times while exploring the Monarch."

I'd put Sophie on task to greet her, because she's the only female I truly trust on our staff, and I figured a woman greeting Daelyn may be less intimidating than say Ryker, Vault, Bull, or literally anyone else here at the club.

"You're my Dom?" Daelyn asks quietly as I escort her deeper into the Monarch.

"Only if you want me to be." I'll ignore the

kernel of doom growing heavier by the millisecond in my gut. I shouldn't have sprung this on her. I should have told her my intentions ahead of time. "You said you knew what the Monarch Club was when I asked you about it this morning."

"And I said yes, because I do know." Her gaze darts everywhere as I lead her down a wide hallway with doors on each side. "I just didn't realize you were a Dom here. You said you were in security."

"As a good Dom should be." I'm playing games I shouldn't, dashing around truths like this. "I work security at the Monarch and am also a Dom when the occasion calls for it."

"I'm an occasion now?"

Yes, one my dick will rise to every time.

"You're my guest," I say, opening a door and allowing her to enter a large room with several seating arrangements and a few toys placed on tables. "This is a mingling room."

"You mean orgy room."

"A get to know you introduction room," I counter. "Orgies are upstairs. Usually in one of the VIP suites or the penthouse."

Her jaw drops and cheeks grow rosy. "Oh my god, you're serious?"

With an arched brow, I nod. Does she want to see those spaces? I'll take her. Does she want to participate? I'll join her.

Later.

"Want to play another game with me, Firefly?"

I don't bother hiding my wicked smile. It's a miracle I haven't rucked her dress up and eaten her pussy in the hallway with how dynamite she looks tonight. Wearing her hair down was a punishment I set on myself. My hands itch to gather it and tug hard enough to make her lose her breath.

Especially while I rail her from behind.

Focus.

"What's up with you playing games, Dmitri? First, lie for a lie, truth for a truth, and now…"

"A staring contest," I say casually.

Confusion looks adorable on her. "That's it?"

"Did you want more?" Because I'll happily oblige. I find myself eager to give her whatever she craves.

"I…" Daelyn snaps her mouth closed and looks around the room again. "What do I have to do besides stare at you?"

I press my hand against her back, bringing her closer to me so I can whisper in her ear, "*Win.*"

Her breath shudders out of her. "Win," she repeats quietly.

"Keep your eyes on me, Daelyn." I run my fingers up her rib cage. "While I make you come."

She said she needs rough sex to find release. I'm on board with that, but it's likely not the only way she can blast off. I know this because I heard what she *wasn't* saying. She shuts down. Numbs out. Detaches herself in situations just to get through them. I'd recognized that look I saw in her eyes the night of the fight when I fucked her against the wall. I also read her body language when I fucked her at her house.

This is a mistake, the angel on my shoulder reminds me for the dozenth time.

This is going to be fun, argues the devil on my other side.

They can both fuck right off because ultimately, the choice is Daelyn's. What she says, goes. Nothing else matters.

"We don't have to play, if you're not interested." I toss her an easy smile. "I just wanted to have some fun with you."

"Like I'm a toy you can play with?"

Her tone is aggressive, but the way her cheeks blush leads me to think the idea turns her on. "If you want to be a fucktoy, we can negotiate that, too."

"Negotiate." She says it like that's a foreign concept.

I'm starting to see how very new she is to kink.

"As your Dom, my first and only priority is you and your safety, Daelyn. I need to know all your hard and soft limits. What you like and don't like. I'll never coerce you into anything and will stop the instant you tell me your safe word."

She scoffs like that's not really how this works. It's insulting and makes me see red.

"I don't know how things have gone for you in the past, Daelyn, but here, with me, or any other staff member at the Monarch, for that matter, you're in charge. *You* call all the shots."

"If that's true, then I'd be the Dom."

Fuck, she's too new. I'll need to tread much more slowly than I anticipated. That's okay. It'll give me more time to unravel her and learn about the woman who's captivated me all too easily.

"A Dom leads and protects. There's a power exchange between us." I sit her down on one of the chaise lounges. "Everything we do must be consensual. I can guide, encourage, and teach you about yourself through sex, but first we must be one hundred percent honest with each other."

Some of the color drains from her face.

I don't mean to scare her, but this is important. I can't believe I was stupid enough to think that all because she was brought to me that night of the fight, and that she said she was aware of the Monarch Club, that it also meant she's a part of my world already.

Red flag.

"You like rough sex," I say calmly, knowing that much already. I'd also quickly peeked at her paperwork as she signed the bottom of it and handed it to Sophie. "And anal."

Her cheeks blaze scarlet.

"What else?" I lean back, patiently waiting for her response.

"I…" Daelyn breaks eye contact with me. "I like being choked a little. And…spanking is okay."

"That's good to know," I say, encouraging her. "What's something you absolutely do not like?"

The vein in her neck stands out, pulsing rapidly. Her eyes dart away for a second. "I don't like to be gang-banged."

"Okay." I somehow manage to keep my voice even, but my instincts flare with fury because what the fuck has happened to her in the past? Was she assaulted or coercively forced to endure something she didn't want? Maybe I'm reading into things too much. Time to back it up. "Is there anything you've wanted to try and haven't yet?"

She stares at the carpet, thinking. "I'm not sure."

"That's okay." I gently place my hand on her leg, making her flinch a little. Shit, she's jumpy. I'm botching this fun night up before it's even started, which isn't like me at all. Then again, neither is bringing a guest to the Monarch. Or breaking into women's houses.

Daelyn's got me out of fucking character.

Red flag.

I keep my body relaxed so I don't come off too intimidating. "How about a safe word?"

"Crocodile," she says immediately.

I like it.

"Good girl." Kissing the top of her head gives me a chance to smell her shampoo. I have no clue what this woman washes with, but she smells incredible all the time. She's like a field of flowers mixed with arousal. "Tonight, we're just going to get to know each other, okay?"

She nods.

"And you must be honest with me. Always." I cannot stress that enough, and the way she tenses in tiny ways every time I bring it up makes me wary. "If I don't know what's going on, I could end up damaging you and that is the last thing I want to have happen."

"I'm already damaged," she says under her breath.

My rage comes back, full force. "Hey." I grip her chin and make her look at me. "No, you're not. Don't say that about yourself, Daelyn, *ever*."

She knocks my hand away, unfazed. "You don't know me, D."

I like that she's called me D instead of Dmitri. I shouldn't, because that's what only my closest friends call me, but hearing it come from her lips makes the hot rage flowing through my veins cool off a little.

"That's why we're here, Firefly. To get to know each other."

"With a staring contest?"

I shrug and pull out another smile. "I mean, we

already discussed beaches, orgasms, and murder. It's time to bring our relationship to the next level. Besides, staring contests are fun."

That earns me a nervous giggle. "I just have to stare at you while I come."

I nod.

"That's it?"

"That's it." It's harder than it seems, which she'll find out if she agrees to the game.

Her eyes narrow. "What do you get out of it?"

"What do you think?"

Daelyn looks away from me and shakes her head. "I honestly have no idea."

With a gentle nudge of my finger to her cheek, I make her face me again. "I get *you*, Firefly. There's no greater victory prize than that."

…

After some prodding questions, Daelyn tells me she likes both praise and degradation, and also has a thing for danger. As if I hadn't already picked up on that.

No extreme pain but crops and floggers are fine as long as it's not too hard. No golden showers. Yes, to toys. Biting is encouraged. No fire, but she's open to melting wax.

"What about you?" she asks.

"Nah, this is all about you, Firefly. My needs will be met just by watching you come undone."

She rolls her eyes like that's preposterous. "You like pain," Daelyn says, as if trying to throw it in my face.

"I do."

"So I can bite, scratch, and whip you?"

"Like I said, tonight is about your pleasure. Not mine." Goddamn, the thought of her melting hot wax on my balls is really fucking tempting, though. Before I allow myself the fantasy, I pipe up with, "The club is open already, but guests don't usually arrive until…" I glance at my watch. "Five minutes ago."

"Okay."

"Do you want to stay here, or move to a private room?"

"Oh, umm." Daelyn bites her bottom lip. "I think this first time should be private."

"I agree." Lacing our fingers together, I guide Daelyn upstairs to a smaller bedroom. "Would you like the door locked? No one will come in if it's closed, but I can lock it as an extra security measure if that'll help you relax more."

"Yes. Lock it." Her gaze falls to the floor. "Please… Sir."

I hate being called Sir, but we haven't discussed honorifics yet, so she doesn't know that. "I prefer King."

Surprise flashes in her eyes. It's okay. I get that a lot. But here's the thing—I want to be called King because I treat my subs like a fucking queen.

She'll learn.

"Is there a preference for your honorific?" I ask.

"Anything but babygirl."

Yeah, she mentioned that the other day. I'm not asking why because it doesn't matter for our dynamic. "Is Firefly okay?"

I've called her that a few times already, and she didn't seem to mind.

"Yes. That's fine."

"Thank you," I say, cupping her cheek.

"For what?"

"Trusting me. Coming here. Being with me." There's a lot to be grateful for.

She pulls back and bristles. "Umm. So, when does the staring contest begin?"

It's like that, huh? Okay. I'll play. "Would you like to be tied down first?"

She glances around the room. "Yes. Maybe."

"Get on the bed for me."

Daelyn crawls onto it, giving me a spectacular view of her ass in that short dress, and lies on the pillow like she's about to have a pelvic examination. It's hard to keep my laughter buried and the only reason I haven't cracked up yet is because she's truly nervous and that's not funny. "If at any point you want out of the restraints, just say the word. Do *not* hesitate. Understand me?"

She nods, biting her lip again.

"And if you get confused or feel uneasy, use your safe word, Firefly. The scene ends and we can discuss what worked and what didn't, so you're most comfortable with what we're getting into. Understand?"

She nods again.

"Words, Firefly. Use your words."

"Say Crocodile and you stop."

"And?"

"We discuss and regroup."

"Good girl." I kiss her forehead before lifting her right arm up and cuffing her wrist to the built-in restraints on the headboard.

Her breath shudders out of her in a nervous rattle.

"Is that okay, or do you want me to release it?"

"Umm." She looks up at her cuffed wrist. "This is good."

"What do you do if it's not good?"

"Say Crocodile."

"Such a good fucking girl." I kiss her throat column before fastening her other wrist to the headboard and climb off the bed. Christ, it's hot in here. Peeling off my suit jacket, I lay it across the footboard and roll my sleeves up.

Daelyn watches me like a hawk. "You're still overdressed."

"No, I'm not."

"Are you going to use your dick, hand, or mouth on me?"

"None of the above." I pull out a wand, testing the vibration settings. "You okay with this?"

Her cheeks flush. "Yes… King."

Fuuuuck that sounded good coming from her pretty mouth.

Climbing onto the bed like a massive panther, I crawl towards her and lift her dress up over her hips. The black panties she's in are already soaked. I can smell her arousal, which sends my dick into feral mode.

As badly as I want to fuck her brains out, I won't. This is about getting Daelyn to open up to me. It's about chipping away at her walls and eventually cracking her foundation, so I understand her better. That means my dick is staying hidden and my attention will remain solely on the beauty in my bed.

Hooking my fingers into the waistline of her panties, I slowly drag them down. "Goddamn, you smell good enough to eat."

Her thighs quiver.

Just before I can press a kiss on her cunt, she slams her legs shut and, in a rush, blurts, "I lied to you."

Chapter 13

Daelyn

I should have just kept my mouth shut and let him pleasure me, but nooooo, I had to have a conscience.

God, Dmitri's icy eyes get even colder when he asks, "What did you lie to me about?"

Call me stupid. Call me crazy. Call me toxic. I don't care. For whatever reason, I don't want to fuck this up with Dmitri.

"I've never been to the beach," I confess.

Wow. I can't believe I'm suddenly acting this way. I can make lies roll off my tongue sweet as honey, except with Kaleb.

And apparently now with Dmitri.

I need to be careful that I don't get too close to this man because it won't just ruin me, it'll destroy us. Wait. There isn't an *us*. And there never will be because I'm here for one thing, and one thing *only*. To fuck Dmitri so I can earn my and Addie's freedom.

Dmitri pulls back from me and sits on his haunches. His big, muscular body looms like a dark cloud with lightning flashing in his gaze. "Why would you lie about that?"

"I don't know." Now I feel like a trussed up goose in cuffs. "I… breakfast was weird."

"It was *breakfast*." Dmitri runs a hand down his face and sighs. "Did you lie about anything else?"

I shake my head, feeling horrible for having

disappointed him. "No. I swear."

And as long as he doesn't ask me personal questions, I'll continue to tell him only truths. I just need to make sure we keep things at a surface level with our personal information, and only sexual when we're in the Monarch or at my house. That should be easy. No guy gets serious about life when they're fucking. I'm convinced it's an impossibility.

Stealing a glance at him, I hate how Dmitri looks hurt that I've lied about something as stupid as going to the beach. Except I get it. He told me something personal and I shit on it by lying when there was no reason to. I could have easily said I'd never been to the beach either, and we'd have had something in common regarding a trivial matter. Instead, I was dishonest, and that little white lie has me feeling sick with regret now.

"I'm sorry," I squeak out, hating the unshed tears blurring in my vision. "I'm so, so sorry."

"It's okay," he says in a deeper, more exhausted tone.

"No, it's not. I don't even know why I said it."

"Shhhh." Dmitri crawls on top of me and cups my face. "It's okay, Firefly." He swipes the tear that falls down my face. I think I've cried more with him in a week than I have with anyone, collectively, in five years. I have no idea what that means. "But from now on, only truths, okay?"

"Okay." I sniffle, regretting my outburst because the sexual tension between us has broken. He's going to kick me out of the club, and I won't blame him when he does.

If he had any sense, he'd see I'm a big problem and run for the hills. Red flags like me should be avoided at all costs. So why is he caressing me instead?

Is this another game? If so, I'm not sure I want to play.

"Do you want to leave or stay?" He draws back to read my expression. "Answer me, Daelyn."

"Stay," I say with zero confidence, and one hundred percent desperation. "I want to stay."

His jaw ticks while he stares at me. Then he nods and whatever anger he felt about my beach lie seems to fade with his next kiss. His mouth is soft against mine. Strong. Confident. Persuasive. No human should be able to kiss like this. It's unholy.

"Do you think you can win?" he asks against my lips.

"Only one way to find out."

That earns me a genuine smile that makes his icy eyes almost silver. Their color is absolutely mesmerizing. Dmitri is pure seduction, sent to take me straight to Hell.

I can't wait to burn.

"Eyes on me." He lifts off me a little more. "You break eye contact, we start over. Understand?"

"Y-yes."

"Yes, what?"

"Yes, King."

"That's my good girl." He clicks on the vibrating wand and a wicked smile ghosts his face just before he presses the head of it against my pussy. The vibration is strong. So strong. My eyes flutter and he snaps his fingers. "Ah, ah, ah, eyes on me. No closing them."

I don't think I'm going to win this game.

But I'm gonna try.

My orgasm builds immediately. I'm not sure if

it's from the toy or D's gaze, because both are intense, but I already feel my brain sliding into survival mode. The vibration makes me so sensitive, it's brutal. I stare at Dmitri while my body coils until I can't see beyond this dark tunnel encompassing my vision.

My body instinctively builds more invisible survival layers to protect me.

He shifts the vibrator.

I hold my breath.

It's not going to work. I'm not going to come like this. The toy can't make a diff—

Dmitri pulls the vibrator off me, and I gasp, not realizing how close I was to actually orgasming until he took it away. My body suddenly feels like a live wire, desperate for contact so it can go crazy.

"Keep those beautiful ocean eyes locked on me, Firefly."

He presses the head of the toy against me again. My body spasms at the initial contact, intense sensations wreaking havoc on me instantly, and my eyes flutter.

He lifts it off me again.

Desperation makes me scream. "God damnit, King!"

"You lost. Again. So, we're going to start over. *Again*." He cocks his brow and presses the toy on me a third time.

My clit is going to die.

I yank against my restraints like a spitting mad animal. But I don't break eye contact with him again. I refuse. I'll fucking win this game even if it kills me.

"That's my good girl," he growls. "You're doing so well for me."

I'm getting dizzy.

"Keep going, Firefly. Fuuuuck, that's it. Keep your eyes on me. Don't close them. Ride it. Ride. It."

My hips undulate against the toy and my entire body grows tingly. Gaze deadlocked on his, I hang on like it's a fight for life or death. "Please," I beg with a cracked voice, except I don't even know what I'm asking for. "*Please*."

My orgasm hits me like a lightning strike, sending jolts of pleasure coursing through my body. Eyes wide, I don't stop staring at Dmitri as I come harder than I ever have in my life. Every molecule I own blows apart. I'm nothing more than atoms floating in the air. My heels dig into the mattress, and I lift my hips, desperate to keep my climax going. I need more. I need…

"*Please!*" I scream at him, and then squeeze my eyes shut because I cannot stand the look on his face right now. I can't pinpoint what I think I see. Awe? Fury? Passion? Anger? Lust? In my experience, those emotions on a man's face have not boded well for me.

And I'm restrained.

Panic slices my arousal to ribbons. "Crocodile."

The instant I use my safe word, it's like the black tunnel I'm running down blows to smithereens and the bedroom comes back in technicolor. Unfortunately, so does Dmitri.

My blood swishes in my ears. My body is all tingly. My mouth is dry. My clit feels numb and my pussy aches.

Dmitri swiftly unties my wrists. "Talk to me," he says. "What's going on in your head?"

I'm not telling him shit. He doesn't get to know that part of me. This was only supposed to be a game, not a fucking exorcism of my demons.

"Daelyn," he says a little more sternly. "We can't work on it if I don't know what's up."

Work on it?

Work. On. It?

"I'm not a psych project." Kicking him back, I scramble off the bed and my legs give out the second my feet touch the floor.

"Jesus. Come here." Dmitri lifts me up before I have the sense to stop him and he carries me back to the bed, setting me on his lap. "I never said you were a fucking psych project. But as your Dom, I need to know what's happening in your mind so I can make sure you stay in a safe head space. And if you end up in a sub drop, I need to help you with that too."

Sub drop, shmub drop. I'm so out of here. "Let me go."

He drops his arms, giving me freedom, and the instant he does this, I feel even worse. It's like Dmitri giving me what I want makes me even more upset.

Because it's not what I *need*.

Now I feel confused and vulnerable and empty and angry. Instead of running out of the club, like I should for both our sakes, I slap him. Full palm, straight across his motherfucking face.

My hand stings from the contact and a red handprint blooms across his cheek. Dmitri's eyes flash with a very dangerous expression that makes me smack him again. He groans and doesn't stop staring at me.

This man is the king of staring contests, and it pisses me off. So, I slap him again.

"More," he growls at me.

I slap him a fourth time, but it's nowhere near as hard as the others had been.

He still doesn't budge. "Again."

Is he serious?

A sheen of sweat blossoms across his forehead. His pupils have blown wide.

Oh, right, I almost forgot that pain gets him off. I should punish him for making me feel so vulnerable by leaving, so he'll have to get off by himself.

I should. I really, really, *really* should.

But I can't seem to move. It's like his glacial gaze has me frozen in place. I look at his face, the breadth of his shoulders, the way his chest heaves with each controlled breath he takes, the stiffness of his posture, and how his suit pants are tented from his hard dick. God, I want him badly. Every time my mind says to be careful with this man, my body wants to be reckless.

I take a step back. Then another. And another.

The more distance I put between us, the sicker I feel.

Geez, maybe I *should* be someone's psych project because I'm definitely worth studying at this rate. Something in me may be fundamentally broken.

And I'm so sick of doing what I'm told. I'm tired of following orders. I want something for myself. I want something just for me.

Fuck it. I'm in this to win. If only for tonight.

"Do you still want me?" I ask with enough audacity to make my inner demons perk up.

"Yes," Dmitri growls.

"How bad?"

"Bad enough to tear the world apart to get inside you, Firefly."

He won't have to go as far as destroying the world, but I can't say the same for the Monarch Club.

"You want me that fucking bad? Come get me."
 I bolt out the door.

Chapter 14

Dmitri

I give Daelyn a head start. *Ten, nine, eight...* when I reach *one*, I rise to my feet and make it from the bed to the door in a blink. She's already at the end of the hallway, her hair flying behind her as she cuts to the right.

So, I go left.

Daelyn's not leaving the club. She wants a chase. She wants danger.

And I plan to give it to her.

It's not a surprise that she's acting out. I put her in a tight spot—making her connect with me during that staring contest in a way I doubt she's experienced before. It's rattled her. *Good.* That means I'm one step closer to breaking her. This outburst only encourages my actions and solidifies my plan.

Heading straight for Ryker's office, I barge in and find him staring at the surveillance screens with a scowl. "The fuck are you doing, D?"

"Having fun." I storm over to the other side of his desk and quickly scan the monitors.

There she is...

Daelyn weaves through the crowded lobby and heads to the double doors that will take her into an employee only area.

"Make sure no one stops her," I say gruffly to Ryker.

Before he can open his mouth and lecture me, I

dash out of his office and head to the kitchen, where I'll wait. It doesn't take long for Daelyn to bust through the doors.

Standing to the side of a massive fridge, with a chef's knife in my hand, I swear I *feel* her before I see her slip past me, as if Daelyn's presence calls to my inner beast with a soundless cry. Acutely aware of her rapid breathing, the *pat-pat-pat* of her feet on the tile, the swish of her dress brushing across her thighs — it's like all the other noises in the crowded kitchen have faded into nothing and all that exists in my world tonight is this woman.

I sneak up behind her and quickly hold the blade to her throat, pressing the backend of the knife against her skin. Daelyn freezes immediately, her chest rising and falling with each harsh breath that punches out of her.

Leaning in, I catch a whiff of her glorious floral scent and rumble against her ear, "*Found you.*"

Spinning her around, I drop the knife on the counter and toss her over my shoulder like a sack of potatoes. Everyone in the kitchen keeps their head down and stays busy while this happens. They don't even bother to look up as I carry her out.

Daelyn kicks her feet and pounds on my back. "Put me down!"

"Not on your life, brat." I spank her sweet ass twice, which makes her scream.

Unfazed by the club members gawking at us, I carry Daelyn through the entire club like she's my prize. A treasure I now possess. Every time she moves, I spank her again. By the time we make it back up to the bedroom, I dump her unceremoniously onto the bed, letting her bounce on the mattress. Her cheeks are red, hair's a mess, and that dress she's in has ridden high enough to show off her glorious ass.

"Climb back up there," I order. "And hold on to the motherfucking headboard straps."

Daelyn doesn't move.

"One," I count in a deadly tone. "Two."

She slowly scoots up until her back hits the headboard. Then, with a trembling chin, she holds the straps where the cuffs dangle and snaps at me, "You're an asshole."

I know.

"Am I, Daelyn? Why?"

"Because you... you're..." Letting her gaze drop, she doesn't say another word.

Yeah, that's what I thought.

She thinks I'm an asshole because I've put her in a vulnerable position, even if she enjoyed every motherfucking second of it while it happened. What she's not understanding is that she's the one in control, even if I'm calling the shots. She could let go of the straps right now. She didn't have to scoot up the bed.

She could have left the club.

Instead, she challenged me to chase her. Riled me up and set me loose.

I saw the way her eyes lit up when I admitted I would tear the world apart to get inside her. What she fails to realize is that I wasn't talking about her pussy.

This woman is playing a cat-and-mouse game I don't entirely understand.

Standing at the foot of the bed, I stare at her, taking in all the tiny clues her body's giving me. "How do you feel right now, Daelyn?"

She swallows hard and glowers at me. "Like an

idiot."

"Why?"

"Because…" She looks away and I snap my fingers, which makes her eyes lock on mine again. Daelyn bristles, her grip tightening on the straps. "I feel too confused."

Now we're getting somewhere. "May I sit on the corner of the bed?"

She nods, looking surprised I'd ask permission.

The mattress dips from my weight. "What are you confused about?"

She takes several heartbeats to answer. "I don't know why I slapped you. I don't understand how I… what I'm…" She curses under her breath and lets go of the straps. "I'm a bad person."

Agree to disagree. "Nothing you did here with me makes you a bad person, Daelyn. If someone's ever made you feel shameful about what you like, that's a conversation we're going to have too. No one has the right to make you feel—"

"No, I mean I'm a *bad person*, Dmitri." She tucks her legs under her butt and sits up. I can't tell if she's positioning herself to bolt again or curl up and hold herself.

Or pounce on me.

"Tell me how you're bad." If I know her thought process, then maybe I can help her work through it.

"I'm not telling you anything. I've already said too much, and it's got me all messed up." She scrubs her face and sighs. "I need to leave."

I don't want her walking out of here with how things stand between us. "Stay the night with me here in the club."

"I think it's better if I go."

"Why?"

"Jesus, can't you just drop it! I'm a bad person who does bad things and being here… with you… it's only because I—" She sucks back the rest of the sentence. I notice her hands are shaking. "I should check in with someone. Where's my phone?"

"It's safely locked away downstairs. We don't allow cells or cameras of any kind in the club for several reasons. I can't allow you to have it, Daelyn. It's protocol."

She climbs off the bed in a huff. "Then I definitely have to leave."

"Who do you need to check in with?"

"That's none of your fucking business."

"It is when you're under my care."

Her expression softens for a fraction of a second. It happens so fast I almost miss it. But she likes the idea of being under my care and the way she pushed, obeyed, and is currently acting out, has me scratching my original plan and forming a new one.

"As your Dom, in or out of the club, I'll protect you and take care of you, Daelyn."

Her breathing picks up, and I think she's about to cry.

"You hitting me earlier wasn't to spike my lust. Hurt people, hurt people. Is that why you think you're a bad person, Daelyn?"

She stares at me like she loathes me. For someone who wears some kind of mask to hide her emotions, they always end up leaking out of her eyes, anyway. I don't like it when she cries. But sometimes we have to let our emotions out, so they don't eat us alive. I have fighting as my outlet. What does Daelyn have?

Me. She has *me*.

"I hit people all the time," I say cautiously. "Am I a bad person because I fight?"

Risking another slap to the face, I cautiously start closing the distance between us. She doesn't move away like I anticipate. She still hasn't broken eye contact with me either.

Such a good girl.

I love a woman who stands her ground, even when she's scared while doing it.

Soon, I hope Daelyn will learn she doesn't have to fear me. "I'll never hurt you," I say softly. "I don't expect you to believe me tonight, but if you stick around, you'll find out how well I treat people. I don't make promises I can't keep, and I promise I will never, *ever* hurt you."

She doesn't flinch when I slowly reach up and tuck some of her hair behind her ear.

"Stay," I whisper, keeping my gaze locked on hers. "*Please.*" Leaning down, I press my mouth to hers, lingering long enough for her to moan against my lips, then I pull away gracefully.

"I'm so sorry I hit you," she whispers.

"Don't be."

"I shouldn't have done that. It came from a place of anger." She sounds genuinely remorseful.

"You didn't hurt me, Firefly." Even though I'm sure the handprints on my face would suggest otherwise. "I'm good at taking a beating."

She gulps, her brows knitting together with what can only be described as sympathy. If this is what it'll take to get her to open up to me, so be it. It's not like my past is a secret, anyway. I came to peace with my existence a long fucking time ago.

"Who hurt you?" I ask, knowing I'm prying.

"It doesn't matter anymore."

"It does to me."

"You don't know me."

"Which is why I'm asking, *who hurt you*?"

She holds my stare for another few heartbeats, her mouth firmly sealed shut. I almost give up and change the subject when she suddenly blurts out, "Who hurt *you*?"

Lie for a lie. Truth for a truth.

"My mother."

Let the next game begin.

Chapter 15

Daelyn

I was not expecting him to say that. "Your *mother*?"

My heart bleeds for a man I barely know. The enemy of my enemy. The man I'm here to fuck in every way… destroy in every way… for Kaleb. For my freedom.

My brain compartmentalizes every thought racing through my mind while my soul forces my body to step closer to him. "I'm so sorry."

"Don't be," he says with a shrug. "You didn't do it and you didn't control her. Some moms are just bad moms."

And some women are just bad women. *Like me*.

I'd almost caved and told him why I was a bad person earlier. The confessions were on the tip of my tongue. Courage and fear warred in me so violently, I'd detached and let those truths fall into a dark pit in my belly.

If it's a choice between being honest with a near stranger who made me have the best orgasm of my life or staying silent for the safety of Addie's life and mine, there is no question which I'll choose. Dmitri may be a very bad man, or an extremely good one, but none of that matters as far as my deal with Kaleb goes. I have to remember what I'm doing here and why.

Except every time I let myself slip and fall into Dmitri's silvery stare, my resolve melts a little more.

He didn't have to tell me that his mom hurt him. In fact, it could be a bald-faced lie just to get me to open up to him. But it doesn't feel that way. He looks genuine as he backs up to give me some breathing room. All night long, he's been focused on me, my well-being, my pleasure, my safety.

Bad guys don't care about those things.

Kaleb never did. Even when it seemed that way in the moment, I eventually learned it was a trick. Dmitri hasn't shifted his machinations in his favor at all.

Yet.

This might be a good way to find out more information about him, I remind myself. *Pry. Play along.* I should do whatever I have to so I can get this over with. *Think of Addie.*

She's why I freaked earlier about my phone. I hadn't expected to have to give up my cell earlier, but it makes sense for a place like this. However, asking for it back and being denied caused me to panic. I'd only calmed myself down after mentally rehashing that my anxiety is high because I'm out of my depth with a stranger and far from my safe space at home. If I can even call it that, considering Kaleb owns the house I rent.

Wanting to check on Addie is out of habit. I've turned into a helicopter with her, constantly hovering, and we've been in several fights about it lately. She wants me to ease up, which I've tried, but my paranoia always ends up winning and I track her down, call, text, or even show up where she is just to make sure she's doing okay.

It's my inner child needing to be saved, I think. What I would have given to have someone care that much for me when I was a kid living with two parents who didn't want me. Who didn't take care of me. Who gave me up—one for drugs, the other for convenience. When Kaleb came into my life, he always popped up to check on me.

Oh my god, am I turning into a Kaleb?

My stomach plummets.

Wait. No. I do it from a place of love. He does shit from a place of control. We are not the same. And...

Addie is fine. She's safe. She's away from all the bad things.

I need to focus on Dmitri now. He's my priority. He's my way out.

"I have a type," I say, hating how my voice quivers. "My type is dangerous."

Dmitri keeps his mouth shut as he gives me his undivided attention, which is something else he's done from the very beginning.

"I was neglected a lot as a child, and it got bad enough that a teacher made a call to CPS. My parents gave me up without a fight when I was seven. My mom's a junkie. My dad moved on and didn't want me. So, into the foster system, I went."

Dmitri's shoulders slump a little, but he stays silent and gives me time to share without being pushy. I'm not used to that. Kaleb always talked, talked, talked, pushing me for things until I caved or was so tangled in his interrogations that I'd inadvertently spill the beans on something.

Every word, to Kaleb, becomes a weapon he uses against me.

Every word, to Dmitri it seems, becomes the armor he uses to help protect me.

"Any way, I didn't have it as bad as some kids did in foster care. I was beaten if I didn't obey or keep my room spotless, but following their rules wasn't hard. I just had to keep my mouth shut and be good."

He swallows while his jaw muscles flex.

"I've always been into guys who are dangerous. The ones who don't care about authority or getting in trouble. They *are* the trouble." Really, it's only Kaleb, but he's taken up most of my existence, so here I am. "I seem to always be drawn to the bigger, badder monster."

Dmitri's eyebrows twitch.

"I think that's why I'm confused with you," I admit. "You're my type."

"A big, bad monster."

Well, when he says it, it sounds less threatening.

Dmitri calmly approaches me again. My heart kicks at my chest when he wraps his arms around me in an embrace that cocoons me in his body heat. He cradles the back of my head with one hand while the other splays out over my lower back. The top of my head rests perfectly under his chin and I feel so secure here with him. "Thank you, Daelyn."

Why on earth is he thanking me?

"You just gave me a very precious gift," he says, as if reading my mind. "Thank you for trusting me enough to open up like that."

His words swirl around in my head, weaving through the edges of all the broken pieces of me until they join like Frankenstein.

It feels good to say these things out loud. I don't have friends, and I rarely tell Addie things about me because I'd rather she not dwell in the past. Besides, her history is worse than mine. The last thing I'll ever do is traumatize her just to get something off my chest. She doesn't deserve burdens like that.

"Thank you for listening," I finally say, surprising us both. "And if the offer still stands, I think I want to stay the night."

Dmitri pulls back so he can look down at me. "Of course, I still want you to stay." He cups my face with gentle hands that are strong enough to crack bones.

Like I said, I'm always drawn to a bigger, badder monster.

I've gone from Kaleb to Dmitri. From a bad boy to a killer.

Great.

It's just pretend, I remind myself. *This isn't real. He's not actually into you, you're just a temporary toy and you're not really into him, because he's just a means to an end.*

Except it feels real when he holds me in his arms like this. It tastes real when he kisses me. It sounds real when he talks to me.

I'm in so much trouble.

"Are you hungry?" he asks.

"Umm. Maybe a little."

His warm smile makes me relax even more. "How about I call room service?"

"There's room service here?"

"Honey, this is an elite sex club. There is *everything* here." He pulls out his cell and makes a call.

"How come you get your cell, and I don't?"

"Because I work security here and you don't." He winks and goes into commander mode. "Hey, it's D. Can we get a tray of apps brought up to room seven?" Dmitri moves his cell away from his mouth and looks at me. "You want wine or anything?"

I shake my head.

"Burger? Steak? Tofu? What?"

"Ummm, maybe fries?"

He tips his cell closer to his mouth. "Double fries too. Yeah, and a steak, medium rare." He looks at me again. "You want cheesecake?"

I shake my head. "I'm not much on sweets."

He smiles like he can relate. "That's it for now. Thanks, man, I appreciate it." Dmitri hangs up and tosses his phone on the bed. "How about we get you out of that outfit and into something more comfortable?" He points at the hem of my dress. "May I?"

I nod and he lifts my dress up and over my head.

"God damn," he says playfully. "I'm not much for desserts either, but seeing how fucking good you look, I'm suddenly getting one hell of a sweet tooth, Firefly."

"Yeah, well, I'm high in fat."

"Even better."

Damn him for making me blush.

I let him unhook my bra. My panties have been gone since the staring contest.

"Turn around. Let me see my prize."

"Your *prize*?" I burst out in laughter. "You didn't win a damned thing tonight, buddy."

"Agree to disagree." D's gaze grows hungrier as I spin around to show off my ass.

"Stop right there."

I halt.

"Can I touch you?"

Why does he keep asking permission for every little thing? "Yes."

He runs his rough hands over my ass cheeks. "Mmm. Still cherry red from the kitchen."

My heart flutters.

"About that..." I turn around to face him again. "Nice detail with the knife."

D's grin goes a mile wide. "You liked?"

No, I *loved*. "Meh, it was okay."

His laugh shoots adrenaline into my system. "You're a terrible liar, Daelyn."

"I'm not lying."

"You loved it."

"I wouldn't go *that* far."

"Your pussy loved it."

"She's a kinky bitch. Don't shame her."

D puts a hand over his heart. "I would never."

I believe him. And I really liked that when he gave me an element of danger during our cat-and-mouse game, he used the back end of the knife against me instead of the sharp side. The thrill was there, without the threat of injury or death. I've had it the other way around before. One star. Do not recommend.

In fact, Dmitri does a lot of things I've had done to me before, only his way works where the others didn't.

Stop comparing him to people in your past. That's not why you're here, Dae.

I keep dropping into these over-analyzing tailspins and it's got to stop.

Dmitri points at the bathroom door. "How about I start up a bath for you?"

Confusion has my brows scrunching. "Why?"

"Let me take care of you tonight, Firefly." He kisses my forehead, which makes me feel precious.

I... don't know what to say except, "Okay."

"Good girl." Dmitri leaves me standing naked in the bedroom and a few seconds later, I hear water running.

"Do you like bubbles?" he calls out.

"No."

"Oils? Bath salts?"

I quietly enter the bathroom to see him bent over, holding his hand out under the faucet to check the water temp. "Bath salts would be nice."

As he pours a scoopful into the water, someone knocks on the door.

"I got it," Dmitri says. "Now get your fine ass in this tub."

"Yes, King." Oh my god, I can't believe I'm smiling so cheesily right now. My actions are giving me whiplash tonight.

The bathroom smells like lavender. He even lit candles. Towels are stacked neatly on floating shelves, and there's a basket of salts and bath bombs next to the free-standing tub. The Monarch seems more like a swanky hotel than a sex club.

Not that I've ever been to a sex club before.

Or stayed overnight at a swanky hotel.

Dmitri comes back holding a bowl of fresh fruit and clucks his tongue at me. "And here I thought you'd already be wet for me."

I roll my eyes and bite my bottom lip to keep from smiling.

How is it so easy to be with this guy? Maybe it's because I got something off my shoulders earlier telling him a little about my past. The way he just accepted it and listened shouldn't have me feeling so at ease, but it does. He didn't pry or judge or give me some bullshit response.

I saunter over and pluck a grape out of the bowl. "That was fast room service."

"I'm a priority here," he says with a big grin. "Which means you are, too."

I hate how my heart and pussy just swooned.

"If you want me to, I'd love to feed you this fruit while you relax in the bath."

This man is spoiling me rotten. "Are you not going to join me in here? The tub's definitely big enough for two people."

"I will if you want me to."

He's way too accommodating. As much as I want to be suspicious, playfulness takes the reins instead. I pluck a strawberry out of the bowl next and run it between my breasts, over my nipples, down past my belly button, and hold it over my pussy.

Dmitri's gaze traces all my moves until it stops at the joining of my thighs.

"Got a sweet tooth now, big guy?"

He drops to his knees. "Fuck yeah, I do." The man's tongue drags over my fingers, obscenely. Then he licks the sides of my pussy before finally shoving his face into the strawberry so he can lick my sweet spot before eating the fruit out of my hand.

Sweet mother of wild heathens, he's too sexy for his own good.

Dmitri looks up at me, chewing slowly with humor in his eyes. "I'm still hungry," he declares on his knees.

I spread my legs a little more. "Eat some more."

His pupils blow wide. I don't think I've ever noticed this reaction happen before with other men. Dmitri can't hide his attraction. It's visceral. Primal.

And it's all for me.

My breath shudders out of me when he licks my pussy like it's the best thing he's ever tasted. Before I know it, he's lifting me up, hooking my legs under his arms, cradling my ass in his hands, and bracing my back against the tiled wall. I can't care about falling when his tongue fucks me this good.

He nuzzles against me harder, grinding against my clit. Then, with a grunt, he repositions me enough to free one of his hands so he can finger me, too.

I'm dangling on the edge of madness, over six feet off the ground. The tub is going to overflow. Our food is getting cold.

I don't care.

Right now, I don't care about anything other than another release. "Harder."

He fingers me roughly, his tongue sinfully swirling and flicking my clit. A tightness coils deep inside me, pressure building quickly. Slamming one hand on the ceiling, the other holding the top of his head against me, I grow dizzy with need. If I come like this, I'll fly apart.

I need that.

I need—

He sucks on my clit hard enough to make me detonate. My pussy clenches as I scream through an orgasm that has Dmitri digging his fingers into my ass cheeks to keep me from falling and possibly breaking my neck. Adrenaline courses through my system, making my head spin.

Even after the wave of pleasure subsides, Dmitri seems intent on savoring every drop he's wrung out of me. Then he slowly, carefully, lowers me back to the floor.

"Having dessert first is the only way to enjoy a meal." The wicked, satisfied smile on his face is stunning. With a little pull on my arm, he escorts me over to the tub and turns the faucet off before helping me climb inside. "Do you still want me to join you?"

"Yes."

D nods once and unbuttons his shirt. The candlelight flickers all over the room, casting his muscles into shadows and soft light. He's beautiful. Peeling his shirt away, he turns around to hang it on a towel hook and my heart skids to a stop when I see his back.

Oh my god. "What is that?"

Chapter 16

Dmitri

I turn to Daelyn, controlling my tone and play dumb. "What's what?"

Although I assume it's the scars on my back she's referring to, I'm not about to proceed as if that's the case without knowing for certain.

My girl stutters her words out when she says, "I... I'm s-sorry. That was really rude of me."

"No, it wasn't. If you have a question, ask it. If you're concerned, voice it. I can't help if I don't know the context, though."

She sighs and casts her big doe eyes up at me. "You said your mother hurt you."

She's definitely referring to what she sees on my back. "Yes."

"Did she do... that?" Daelyn shakes her head quickly. "I'm sorry. I shouldn't ask such a personal question. You don't have to answer."

I know I don't, but I will anyway. "Not all of it, no. But most." Calmly sliding my pants down, I step out of them and stand before Daelyn naked. I've never had a problem with my body. I don't even mind my scars. What I *do* have an issue with is when someone looks at me with fucking pity. It makes my skin crawl.

"It's okay, Firefly. I'm over it. Have been for a really long time."

So much for being honest...

"Dmitri, get in here, now!" Mom yells from the living room.

I close my algebra textbook and get off the floor. I have no clue what's got her mad this time, but her tone already has me bracing for the worst. "Yes, Mom?"

"Did you tell someone that I neglect you?"

I freeze at the entrance of our living room, my heartbeat kicking up fast enough to make me dizzy. "No, Mom."

Her eyes harden as she holds the iron down on my dad's shirt. "No?"

"No, I swear."

"You would lie to people? Make me out to be a terrible mother? Get me in trouble? What kind of son lies about something so cruel?"

I take a step back, my instincts screaming for me to run. But I can't. I have no place to go, and running to Ryker's is only a temporary solution to my long-term problem. I'd have to come home eventually, and she'll be waiting for me when I do.

"You're a bad boy, Dmitri."

My fear spikes and bile rises in my throat.

"Come over here."

My legs wobble. At almost fifteen years old, I've been reduced to a terrified mouse trapped in a cage with a predator every time I'm home. If anyone suspects I've been neglected, it's my fault. I have no clue how this could have happened, but it must have been one of my teachers at school because my friends keep my secrets. Except, I don't speak to any of my teachers and none of them even seem to notice me. I keep my head down, mouth shut, and do my work. Even though I'm on the honor roll, I'm still labeled as a problem kid because of all the fights I get into outside of school. And I only skip classes on days I'm too sore to sit in a chair.

What if one of my teachers or some nosy parent suspects abuse and has reported it?

Oh my God. *My stomach drops out of my ass. Dad will find out about everything. I'll get taken away. My parent's marriage will be a wreck. It'll all be my fault.*

CPS. Divorce. Punishment. I have no clue what to expect to hit first, but once it does, my life will be over. I'll lose my friends. I'll lose everything.

"Do not make me repeat myself," *she seethes in Russian.*

As the last bit of weakness escapes me in a trembling breath, I shut down and step forward to face the consequences.

I'm not real. I can't feel.

I'm not real. I can't feel.

I'm-not-real-I-can't-feel.

"Take off your shirt."

With trembling hands, I pull my ratty t-shirt off and work hard to keep my expression blank and breaths even. If I show fear, she'll make it worse. If I show courage, she'll still make it worse. There's no winning this game with her.

I'm not real. I can't feel.

Mom looks at my torso with cold, dead eyes that are the same color as my own. It's an artic blast nothing can survive. I'm sure she's admiring the bruises and cuts she put there. But some of the fresher ones are from a fist fight I got into last weekend. Will she ask about them, or assume those are her handiwork too? I'm not sure which is worse.

"Turn around."

Blood drains from my head as I do what I'm told.

It's four o'clock. Dad will be home in three hours. Whatever she does, I'll get over it by then. I have no choice.

The smell of alcohol seeping from her pores grows

stronger as she draws near.

Not seeing what she's about to do terrifies me. It's also probably for the best. I'd rather not know. Squeezing my eyes shut, I shrink inward and tense my entire body like I can somehow morph into a concrete wall.

I never fight her off because even though she's hit me hundreds of times, I can't find the will to hit her back. She's a girl. A girl monster, but a girl. A woman.

My mom.

For some fucked up reason, I protect her by keeping this secret between us, waiting for the day she'll stop and apologize.

Others don't know how good they have it. And I've been spending more and more time at Ryker's house because there I'm safe and fed and have fun. I'm loved. Miss Ashley treats me like her own kid. She even keeps my favorite snack at the house just for me.

Why can't Miss Ashley be my mom? Why did it have to be Anya?

These are the questions that swirl around my head, giving me something to focus on as I wait for the fist that will undoubtedly land on my kidney, or the back of my head, or wherever there's a fresh piece of flesh that doesn't have a mark yet.

"You're a bad boy."

Something presses against my back on the lower left side. The thud swiftly turns into searing, blinding, unholy pain that has me screaming until my voice cracks and quickly gives out.

I fall to the floor, gasping for air. My vision goes white. Saliva pools in my mouth, dribbling onto the carpet as I stay on my hands and knees, blinking back hot tears and trying not to puke.

"Do not go to school looking like you do. Be better. Cleaner. I will not have anyone saying I neglect you, and

you're certainly old enough to wash your hair and put on clean clothes."

"Yes, Mom." I crawl away, biting back my whimpers.

Be better. Cleaner. Wash my hair. Put on clean clothes.

Be better.
Cleaner.
Wash my hair.
Put on clean clothes.

My legs and arms are rubber noodles as I drag myself back to my bedroom. The instant I shut the door, I throw up into a trash can. It takes time for me to pull myself together. The burn from her iron is so agonizing, nothing I can do will relieve the pain. I can't run from it. I can't touch it. And if I go into the bathroom to run cold water over it, I might just take a straight razor off the sink and use it on myself so I can be done with this life called Hell.

So, I embrace it.

I let the pain sink into my motherfucking bones and fortify me. Every blow, every scar, every ounce of agony I've endured strengthens me. Soon, resilience will make me unbreakable.

Sucking in deep breaths, I stare at my nearly empty dresser. I've had a growth spurt lately and most of my clothes don't fit anymore. I haven't washed my hair in three days because we ran out of shampoo and my mom won't let me use hers because she says it's too expensive to waste. My dad's head is shaved most of the time, so I have no clue what he uses on his head, but I'm guessing bar soap. I've tried it but my long hair gets too dry and tangled and conditioner doesn't exist for anyone but my mom in this house.

I'll steal some shampoo at the store later today.

I should have done so last week, but hadn't cared enough. I didn't think anyone would say something about my hygiene. It's not like I smell. I'm just in crap clothes and my hair is getting too long. It's past my shoulders now.

Refusing to look at the damage to my back, I rummage through my drawers to find a better shirt to slip on. The instant the cotton touches fresh burn, I gag and sway, those white dots dancing in my vision all over again.

I need to get out of here. Now.

I need help.

I need...

To be better. Cleaner. Wash my hair. Put on clean clothes.

Stepping out of my room, I wipe the sweat beading on my upper lip and ask, "Can I go to my friend's house? I did all my math homework."

She doesn't look up from her ironing. "Yes, of course."

Because she wants me out before my dad gets home. There have been a few times when her abuse has been bad enough that I need time to heal or we risk Dad finding out, which neither of us wants. She's made it so very clear that if he did, he'll kill her. If he kills her, he'll go to jail.

And then where will I be?

Sometimes I think we'd all be better off if that's what happens. I get angry at my dad for never noticing the things she does to me. Ever hear the expression, love is blind? Well, that's my dad. Mom seems to have some kind of spell on him, and she turns the sweetness all the way up when he's around. And lets it all vanish when he's not.

But I love my dad. I don't want to make things worse for him. He works hard and loves me and that's got to be enough. He's the only good thing I have in my life.

Well, him and my only friends. Ryker and Knox know about my mom, but they've sworn to never tell. So has my friend Vault. Miss Ashley can't find out either, because she'll pity me and then I'll hate her for it. Besides,

Ryker's dad was abusive and honestly so is Knox's, so crying to them about it is like preaching to the choir. We've all got tragedy in our lives. At least Ryker and his mom got away from their monster.

Me and Knox likely never will.

And Vault? Well, he's got his own fucking problems, which just goes to show no one has a happy life in reality.

I think I'll go to the gym on Monday, if my back isn't too sore from this, and ask for boxing lessons. I'll barter to get them. Maybe offer to clean the gym every day to earn it. I could ask my dad to teach me to fight, but if Mom finds out, there would be hell to pay, so that's a no-go.

But I have to do something. *I can't keep getting beat like this. If my mom can reduce me to a crybaby crawling away on his hands and knees, who will be next? There's always someone bigger and worse out there.*

Time to be the biggest, baddest monster in town.

Thank God I've got a high pain tolerance. At least my mom gave me something *good to work with...*

"Come here," Daelyn says softly.

My heart thuds heavily as I step into the tub with her. All my words catch in my throat, and I have this horrible ringing in my ears. After the past few weeks, my world has imploded and I think I'm using Daelyn as a coping mechanism, which isn't fair.

I'm still going to do it, though.

No one's perfect, especially not me.

Chapter 17

Daelyn

When Dmitri lowers himself into the tub, I have this strange urge to hold him between my legs and cage him in false safety. Because, let's face it, I can't do shit to save him. I'm here to fuck him. I'm a liar and a trickster and bad, bad person.

But with D, in this moment, I'm just a woman who's found solace in the arms of a monster I'm quickly adapting to. I blame my past. If I didn't adjust fast to my surroundings, I always feared there would be consequences. The Brenner's were the last foster family I was with, not the first, second, or third. I counted my lucky stars with them because they were the least violent of all my shelters, and I had Kaleb, who eventually taught them a lesson.

My belly twists at the memory of how terrifying that had been.

Stop it, Dae.

I think Kaleb robbing them blind then setting their house on fire, with them still in it, was the pivotal step on my path to damnation. Luckily, they'd escaped with only a few minor burns, but Kaleb didn't want to stop until they were six feet under. I had no clue what he was planning to do to them. He only ever said shit like, *"I'll take everything from them, babygirl. Just for you…"*

I tried convincing him that revenge wasn't

necessary. That it was too much, too wrong. But he only harped on the ways they'd treated me throughout the years, and the things they'd done to other foster kids who lived with them as well. Back then, I thought he was a psychopathic hero. Now, I see he's just a psychopath.

Especially considering arson isn't the worst things he's done "on my behalf."

Letting out a long sigh, I reset my mind and refocus on the present and the better, badder man I'm with now. Dmitri and I face each other in the tub, the hot water rising over my breasts as we settle in.

He leans back, resting his arms on the edge of the porcelain and regards me with a look of indifference. "What's racing through your pretty little head, Firefly?"

I'm not telling him the truth. That's way too much damning information. I also don't want Kaleb in my head anymore. "Why do you call me Firefly?"

"Do you not like it?"

I do, but it's such a weird nickname to give me. "I'm just curious."

Does he call all the women he sleeps with Firefly or just me? I hate how the term makes me feel special and endeared. I don't deserve it.

He smiles and does the same thing I just did by answering my question with another question. "Where did you get that burn scar on your wrist?"

I sink my arms into the water and keep a straight face. "Tell me what burned that triangle in your lower back first."

The corners of his mouth slightly lift. "An iron. It was just the tip, though, so it's not nearly as big as it could have been."

The way he's comparing what is, and what could have been, makes me queasy. I've rationalized my own traumas the same way.

"Your turn, Firefly."

"Mine's from a ring. It was just something stupid I did when I was younger." Not a complete lie. I may not have held myself down and branded my body, but I agreed to it.

Sort of.

Dmitri stares at me until goosebumps erupt down my arms and my nipples harden, even as I'm submerged up to my throat in hot water. The lavender scented bath salts relax me as I mirror Dmitri's posture.

He closes his eyes, and a sigh leaves him.

We drop into a dead silence, and I grow antsy. I can't relax around a killer. It's bad enough I'm in a tub with him. Or that I'm sleeping with him.

Or that I'm "fucking" him.

"When do you fight again?"

D's eyes open into slits. "Why?"

"No reason."

His mouth curves into a devious smile. "You gonna be mad if I fuck some other prize?"

I hadn't thought of that part of it, and I'll never admit that jealousy has the audacity to coil in my gut at the thought of someone else chained up with her legs spread for him.

"You'd have to win to get the prize."

"I don't lose," he says, like it's a well-known fact.

"Not even once?"

"Not since I was a kid."

"Well, aren't you special?" Our legs are tangled,

so I curl up until my kneecaps break the water's surface. "How's it feel to be a legend, Dmitri?"

His rumbly chuckle spreads heat through my body. "I'm not a legend, Firefly. Just a man with nothing to lose."

"Everyone has something to lose." I have Addie. Surely Dmitri has someone he cares about too.

He dips his hands in the tub and leans forward, searching for something under the water. When his hand wraps around my ankle, he gently pulls it towards his chest and massages my foot. "When I cage fight, I go in knowing there's every possibility I will not climb out of it. I'm okay with that."

Nausea makes my belly roll. "That's…"

"The truth of my lifestyle." He flashes a smile that doesn't reach his eyes. "Does my fighting bother you now?"

Yes. The thought of this man dying in an underground cage fight sends panic racing in my bloodstream. I don't want that to happen. I don't want to lose Dmitri.

Kaleb's words from the other day suddenly haunt me… *He hasn't been in the ring for a long time, but I'm working on a plan to lure him there again*… What could Kaleb possibly use to drag Dmitri back to the ring with?

And how can I stop it?

Okay. Whoa. Whose side am I on here?

Shaking the chaos from my brain, I pull my foot out of his grip and wrap my arms around my knees, hugging myself. I don't belong here. I shouldn't be doing this. Everything about this mission is *wrong*.

Even when Kaleb thinks his actions are justified — like setting fire to my former foster home —

it never is. He's just being a criminal, an asshole, and a monster who uses pathetic reasons to excuse his deplorably evil actions.

How am I going to get out of this?

Even if Dmitri is a murderer, Kaleb is no better. I'm standing between a lion and a wolf, and both blood thirsty animals are spoiling for a fight.

"That right there," Dmitri says, leaning forward to run his hands up my legs. "That look on your face is breaking my heart, Daelyn." He slides me closer until I'm caged in his embrace with my head tucked under his chin. "Shhhhh, don't be upset that I fight. I've never gone against anyone who doesn't deserve an ass-whooping anyway, Firefly."

He thinks I'm upset over him fighting. How horrible am I to let this continue?

Whether or not Dmitri is a bad guy, I don't want Kaleb to win the war he's waged between them. "Don't fight anymore," I plead.

"It's not an option for me."

"Yes, it is."

He lets me go and the atmosphere around us shifts. Chills. When this happens between me and Kaleb, I get hurt, so I immediately go into damage control to prevent it from happening this time with Dmitri.

"I'm just scared for you. You say you have nothing to lose, but it's not just about you. Others will care if they lose you, Dmitri. Ever think about that?"

The energy between us warms again.

"Aw hell." He tightens his arms around me and kisses the top of my head. We hold each other for a while before he finally says, "I haven't fought in a long time. But shit's gone sideways for me lately, and throwing fists is my way of dealing with my demons."

I lightly run my fingers down his back. Scars are everywhere on him. There's no way I'm touching the triangular shaped one left by that iron. I'm still sickened to think of how the hell a mother could do that do her own son.

"It's not all bad in the ring," he says lightly. "I met you there."

I pull back, rolling my eyes dramatically. "Lame."

Dmitri laughs. "Lame but true. How else would we have met?"

I'm sure Kaleb would have cooked up some other way to put me in Dmitri's path. "Maybe fate would have shoved us together some other way."

"I don't believe in fate."

"Well, I do."

He chuckles again, like I'm adorable for saying that, and ungracefully spins me around, just to slide my ass against his groin so he can be the big spoon. We stay like this, nestled together, in silence, for a while.

"The water's getting cold," he finally whispers against the shell of my ear.

"So is our food."

He reaches over and tries to grab the bowl of fruit off the counter, but his arms aren't long enough to reach it. "Damnit."

I lean forward and he stands up, making some of the water slosh out of the tub. Dmitri snags the bowl and looks down at me with a devilish grin. His hard dick is right in my face, the piercing gleaming in the candlelight. His legs are so thick and muscular. There's a long cut on one, but it's scabbed over, and I wonder what happened there.

Plucking out a grape, Dmitri rolls it between his thumb and forefinger before placing it between his teeth. Then he squats down, leans into my face, and arches his brow.

Rising on my knees, I gently take it from him with my teeth. We kiss, rolling the firm grape back and forth between our mouths. He growls and lifts me up, unceremoniously taking me out of the tub. He pulls back and eats the grape while saying, "Don't let go of me."

I wrap my arms wrap around his neck, my legs hooking tight at his waist. He saunters out of the bathroom with both of us dripping wet. Goosebumps ripple all over my body as Dmitri storms over to the waiting tray of food and pulls the lid off the first dish.

"Open that pretty mouth for me, Daelyn."

D feeds me a French fry while I cling to him.

"What would you like next?"

I stare down at the tray, waiting patiently as he lifts the lids off each plate. He makes me feel like his little pet that he enjoys taking care of. I hate how much I want it to be true. "I want the burger."

He grabs the hefty sucker and holds it up to me. "Bite."

My god, this shouldn't be so fucking hot, but it is. Wetness drips out of me and it's not from the tub. Flavor bursts on my tongue and I'm suddenly ravenous. I go to take another bite, but Dmitri pulls it back before I can get it. "Patience, Firefly."

He holds my gaze for several seconds before slowly bringing the burger back to my lips. "One more bite."

I chomp down and take a bite that's too big to

chew.

Dmitri laughs as he wipes some of the mayo off the corner of my mouth. "What next, baby?"

My heart sighs as I point at a croissant I don't remember him ordering. In fact, he hadn't asked for the fruit bowl either. Or the roasted asparagus. There's a lot of extra food on this big tray.

He lifts the pastry to my mouth, and I wait for him to give me permission to eat it.

The thrill that shoots through me when he smiles at my obedience is a huge red flag. I don't care. I like that I'm pleasing him. I like the way I feel when I make him happy.

"Bite," he orders gruffly.

I stuff as much of it in my mouth as I can, sending flakes of buttery crust fluttering all over us. I'm like an animal that hasn't eaten a decent meal in forever.

Dmitri roughly runs his hand over my mouth and chin, knocking the crumbs off as I chew and swallow. I'm clinging to him so tightly he doesn't have to hold me at all.

"Christ," he whispers.

"He won't save you."

His gaze lifts from my mouth to meet my eyes. "Can you?"

"I'll try," I reply, not knowing if it's a lie or not.

Our mouths collide and we turn into a tornado of lust and violence. His kisses are punishing. Bruising. I scrape my nails down his arms, leaving red ribbons on his skin.

Abandoning the food, he gets us onto the bed, and I force him to climb in with me, on top of me, because I still haven't let go of him.

"Fuuuuck." He twists out of my locked arms, which makes me pout. "Gotta get a condom."

It's probably the only excuse worth letting him go for.

He snatches a fresh package from a stocked bowl on the end table and rips it open with his teeth, spitting the wrapper onto the rug. As he slides it over his length, I'm annoyed that I can't feel his Prince Albert piercing bare inside me.

Dmitri lifts my legs, hooking them over his shoulders, and grabs one of my ankles. With his gaze locked on me, he sucks on my toes, rolling his tongue over each one. The sensation is so strange, so sensitive, that I squeal and try to twist away from him. But his grip tightens on my thighs, telling me to be still.

He nips my arch, my heel, my ankle and calf, then sets my leg back onto his shoulder. Dmitri's chest heaves with each slow, steady, deep breath he takes as he aligns his cock against my entrance, teasing me by rubbing his tip on my clit.

"Jesus," I groan.

"He can't save you either."

"Can you?"

We hold each other's gaze for several heartbeats. Then Dmitri shakes his head slowly and shoves inside me, inch by motherfucking inch.

At least he's being honest.

And if one of us is going to die by the end of this, we might as well go out with a bang, right?

Chapter 18

Dmitri

I wake up to find Daelyn gone.

It shouldn't surprise me. Her survival instincts must have finally kicked in and she's realized what a damaged piece of fuck I am.

Last night, I took her hard and rough. She screamed my name. She cried. She clung to me and begged for more.

My plan's backfiring spectacularly. I thought she was going to be the distraction I needed to get out of my darkness. I hoped connecting with her would crack her shell and let me see the woman beneath the mask. All I've managed to do is dig my own fucking grave. The hole in my chest, made by her absence, proves it.

After ravaging her body, I kissed every exposed inch, licked every wound, caressed every muscle, worshipped every part of Daelyn she'd let me have. I summoned orgasm after orgasm from her pussy.

And her ass.

Honestly, that she could walk out of here is a miracle. I'd planned to spend the day giving her serious aftercare, and she's robbed me of the privilege.

Laying on my back, I scrub my face and blow out a long breath. Five used condoms are in the trash by the bed. I hadn't even wasted time running to the bathroom between sessions, because I didn't want to be away from her for even that long. The night was a passionate, reckless fever dream, and I was so enthralled, so addicted to the unholy pleasure she brought me, I didn't bother spending longer than a minute out of her body before plunging back into it.

Jesus, I'm an animal.

I'd finally passed out, my last thought being that the moment I turned my back or closed my eyes, she'd vanish like a dream.

Which is exactly what she did, goddamnit.

Rolling out of bed, I stumble into the shower and wash up. The food I ordered yesterday still sits on its tray, wasted. I snag the half-eaten croissant and shove it in my mouth, loving that Daelyn's mouth was on it, too.

Wow. I'm pathetic. Where that woman's lips have been should *not* turn me on like this. Not over a pastry.

I shove a handful of cold, stale fries into my mouth next. They taste like nothing. The younger, starved me would have attacked the half-eaten burger and untouched steak, regardless of how long it sat out. But I don't do that anymore. Risking food poisoning will only keep me away from Daelyn, and that's not happening.

The bowl of fruit is still up for grabs, so I shove handfuls of fruit into my mouth instead. I've spent too much of my childhood going hungry to throw all this food away as an adult. It doesn't matter that I can make something fresh. Deep down, I'm still the deprived kid who lost it all because I couldn't hide my demons like I was supposed to.

After getting dressed, I yank the door open and storm down the hallway, ready for work. Guilt eats at me for taking the night to myself, especially last minute. And I took a room that was likely booked by a member, not giving a fuck that I was using my privilege to do it.

Heading to the kitchen first, I beeline for the espresso machine. Ten minutes later, I'm halfway to Ryker's office, prepared to get my ass handed to me for my recent behavior.

Ry's at his desk, his woman perched on his lap.

"Morning Sunshine," Tara says with a big goofy smile.

"Morning."

"Leave us for a minute, Butterfly." Ryker taps her thigh, and she gets up, kisses his throat, and steals my coffee right out of my hands before leaving the room.

Little brat. She's lucky I love her.

Ryker leans back in his chair, deadpanning me, and I match his energy, unfazed.

"We need to talk, D."

"I'll set things right with whoever I took the room from last night. I hadn't planned on my sub being here for so long. Things kind of snowballed."

"I don't give a fuck about who you took the room from. And neither do you."

That's true.

"But you're right," he continues. "Things have snowballed, and I want to know what's going on."

Fuck, I don't want to say. Rubbing the back of my neck, I look down at my boots. "I've just hit a wall, Ry."

"A wall?" Ryker stands up. "You haven't hit a wall, D. You've hit rock bottom."

My insides squirm because he's right.

"You're letting strangers who aren't vetted into

our club. You're meeting people from your past to do shit you know can get you killed. That's not a wall. Hell, that's not even rock bottom. You're dancing with death and you—" He bites back the rest of that sentence and scrubs his face. "Christ, man. What's happened?"

"My father's dead."

Those three words have my legs wobbling. This is the first time I've said them out loud.

Ryker freezes. "How? When?"

"Stabbed in the yard. A month ago."

"Jesus fucking Christ, D. I'm so sorry."

Bet he is. Ryker lost his mom over a decade ago, and though he's recently come to terms with it, the grief is still there. It's there for me, too. Losing Miss Ashley was a blow that leveled us both. But I still had my dad. Even if I didn't visit him in prison, he was still… *there*. Here. Alive. In some fucked up way, I'd coped with his life sentence by telling myself that all because I couldn't see him didn't mean he wasn't still living. He wasn't still laughing.

He wasn't still fighting…

"What are you doing here, son?" My dad drops his duffel on the bench and storms over to me with his dark brows digging down. I can't tell if he's angry or scared. Maybe both?

"I work here." The coach here trained my dad, so they can train me, too. All I have to do is show up and do what I'm told, stay respectful, and keep my mouth shut. Easy.

Dad's voice drops low and he looks pissed. "How long have you been doing this?"

"Two months."

It's finally summer, so I've been able to juggle my time here and my hours at the coffee shop with no problem. I just haven't seen my friends as much as I want to.

"This is your kid?" Silas asks from behind me.

Dad gawks, then nods, even though his mouth is in a tight line and eyes are hard as steel. I have my mom's eyes, but my dad's coloring. Olive skin, black hair, big build. I can't wait to pass him in height and muscle mass.

"Well, he's a helluva scrapper. Makes sense now, seeing that he's yours." Silas chuckles, patting my dad on the back before heading over to the two guys warming up in the ring.

I go back to cleaning some of the equipment off.

Dad grabs my shoulder, forcing me to stop working, and regards me with wary eyes. "You've been fighting in the ring?"

"Only practicing." I jerk away from him so I can finish wiping the weight bench down. "Silas is giving me lessons in exchange for me cleaning the place."

Dad wipes his mouth. "Your mother will have an aneurysm if she finds out you're here." When I don't say a word, he adds, "You really want to be a fighter, huh?"

"I always said so, didn't I?"

We glare at each other, and I silently dare him to tell me I can't do it.

"Okay, kiddo." He squeezes my shoulder, and I don't even flinch with pain, which is a testament to my tolerance. He's literally clutching a cut my mother carved into me two days ago. "But we're going to have to keep this from your mom."

"No problem." I'm already keeping what she's doing a secret from him. It seems fair to balance the scales and keep a secret from her, too.

Even as Dad stares at me with love and respect in his eyes, I want to knock his teeth out. I want to grab him by the throat and scream in his face, See me! *How can he be so motherfucking clueless? How can such a smart man be stupid enough to love a monster that abuses their child so badly all the time? Dad spoils her rotten. He lets her get away with disrespecting him. He gives her all the control in the house while he's the one paying the bills and busting his ass all the time. I don't get it. For that matter, how the hell is he even here right now when he's supposed to be working a double shift?*

Then I realize the truth. Oh my God. *Dad's been lying to us for forever. He says he's working until late every day when really, he's* here.

Cold anger pours over my body like a bucket of ice.

I hate him.

And yet… here I am, looking at my father like he's my idol.

Because he is.

Fuck my life.

Grinding my molars, I let a chilled calmness settle over me and clear my throat. "Silas says I can start in the ring, for real, soon."

"What? No. You need to train a lot before you go against an opponent."

I've trained my whole life; he just doesn't realize it. "I'm good, Dad. Real good."

He grins at me like I'm adorable for saying that. "Good isn't enough, son. You have to be ruthless."

That gets my attention.

"If you want to fight like me, like any of us in Silas's ring, you have to be cold. Cruel."

I can be cold and cruel. "How?"

He inhales slowly and exhales even slower. "The trick is to always fight against the bad guy. You're the hero in the cage, not the villain. You're going against the worst of the worst and can stop at nothing until they surrender."

Why does it sound like surrender *is code for something worse?*

"There's less guilt that way," he explains. "Fighting is just you serving justice. Silas only pits us against criminals and very bad men, Dmitri."

Is he trying to say all this to scare me off? It's not working. I'll gladly take my pound of flesh from anyone who swings their fists at me since I can't do it to the one who's ruined my life... and my body.

"I can handle that."

Dad's expression falls. "You're going to get hurt. Badly."

"I can handle that, too."

"This isn't like a fight on the playground, kid. Even if you take on one of the younger guys closer to your age and weight, they won't stop until you do. Understand me?"

"Yes." *I can't wait to show my dad what I can do. To prove to myself that I'm not a whimpering little pussy who cowers under his mommy's hateful hands. The kids I fight at school barely take the edge off my aggression and I need this more than I'll ever tell my dad. Or my friends.*

"I want to do this. With or without you, I'm going in the cage." *I hold his stare, which is nothing as heartless as my mothers, and wait for him to concede or drag me out of the gym.*

"Okay," he whispers, his shoulders falling. "Okay, Dmitri."

The triumph feels like a loss, but I don't know why. "I'll fight the bad guy and win every time. Just watch me."

Dad's cheeks mottle with redness that splotches down his neck. "Just remember one last thing." He presses his forehead to mine. "We're all bad guys, D. Some of us are just better at hiding it than others."

Crossing my arms, I keep staring at the floor. "Had to pick up his ashes and scatter them." I couldn't keep Dad's remains. It would have driven me insane having him so close. Even dumping them in the river had my mental health snapping into pieces.

Ryker's brow pinches. "You should have told me. I could have been there for you."

"It's not your place."

"It *is* my place, you asshole." Ry slams his hand on the desk. "We're fucking *family*, D."

He's right, but that doesn't mean I want to burden him with my past. Doing it while I was going through my Hell made me feel shitty enough. I've cried in his arms. I've hidden in his closet. I've beaten the shit out of him because I felt like it and he said I could.

We've been through too much already, and he's finally in a better place, thanks to Tara. She's been his Butterfly, and the love of his life, long enough for him to work through a lot of his demons and find closure with his past. I'm glad. Ryker deserves happiness because I might have had a rough upbringing, but Ryker's was fucking devastating and it ruined him for a very long time. Tara's changed a lot of that. She helped him find peace.

Can Daelyn do the same for me?

Holy shit. That I'd even consider that a possibility proves I've lost my ever-loving mind. I'm suddenly beyond grateful Daelyn ghosted me this morning. If she knows what's good for her, she'll stay away. If she doesn't, I'll fucking make her.

Time to move on and get back to what I'm best at. "So, what's on the list for today?"

Ryker lets out a long sigh. "A delivery should be

here shortly. Last night, we had an incident in the penthouse. Sophie was... tested."

My hackles raise. "Who am I killing?"

No one disrespects Sophie on my watch. *But you weren't on watch*, the angel on my shoulder reminds me. *You were balls deep in pussy, being a selfish coward.*

You mean getting grief out of your system so you could be a better member of society? The devil on my other shoulder argues.

"Vault took care of it," Ryker says, cautiously. "And as of right now, you're on leave."

I shoot out of my chair so fast it knocks over. "What?"

"I don't repeat myself." Ry walks towards the door. "You need to work on yourself, D. That's not going to happen if you're distracted with work and pussy."

"You motherfucking *hypocrite*." Rage has my vision hazing red. "You did the same thing I am when you made Tara the Butterfly."

"Then I'm speaking from experience."

I close the gap between us, shoving my forehead to his, my nostrils flaring as I keep my temper on a short leash.

"There it is," he says calmly. "The animal that's been caged too fucking long."

I reel back as if he's punched me in the throat. It's suddenly too tight with a swarm of emotions clogging it. "Fuck you," I croak.

"I love you, D, but you're too dangerous like this. Remember the last time you felt this way?"

My memory flips through the compartmentalized scenes of my past and yanks out one of many times I've blacked out with rage. I take another step back, suddenly grateful for the reminder. I am my father's son, after all, and I can never forget that.

"What am I supposed to do, Ry?"

"Grieve. Blow off some steam. Find your peace."

How the fuck do I do that? It's not like I'm having a shit day or rotten week. My entire existence has been absolute Hell. You don't find peace from that. You just keep burning.

"I'm here for you, Dmitri. Always. So are Knox and Vault. We're your family. And in case you haven't taken inventory, your family's grown over the years. Sophie… Tara. You're safe here. But you're not safe being here."

His meaning seeps into my black-fog brain. I'm dangerous to be around. It's not something I'm proud of. Not after all the work I've done to tame my demons. It only took the news of my dad, who I haven't seen in years, to derail a decade's worth of work.

One step forward, ten steps back.

"You're right." That I was so willing to kill someone for disrespecting Sophie is a dead ringer that I'm not okay anymore. It's one thing to say it. It's another to mean it.

Will killing someone finally feed the starved monster buried inside me?

Doubtful. That thing is insatiable.

"The woman you brought in last night…" Ryker cautiously says. "You seemed content with her."

Content isn't the words I'd use to describe what I feel around Daelyn. But what we have isn't real, so I'm not going to look closer at it. Especially now that she's gone.

"She was fun," I say nonchalantly, ignoring the pang in my heart. "But she's gone now. I doubt she'll return."

"Mmm."

Ryker folds his arms, and we stare at each other until I finally look away. "How long did you watch us?"

"Long enough."

The entire club is wired heavily with surveillance cameras. If I'm honest, it's one reason I brought her to the Monarch. Because if I went overboard and couldn't reel myself back in, someone else would. That, and I have nowhere else to take her besides a hotel.

I live at the club. It's never felt like an embarrassment until this moment. I have nothing to show for my life. All my money is divided up in other people's dreams, to better them. And what's left is a nest egg I have no clue what to do with. Having a house seems pointless. I'm always working at the Monarch, so I'd never be home to enjoy it. Investments outside my circle of friends aren't an option because I don't trust anyone else. I have nothing, and I am nothing.

And now I'm being forced out of the club and put on suspension. Lovely.

"Guess I'll go." My feet numbly take me to the door Ryker's holding open.

"You want my place for a while? Tara and I can stay at—"

"No." I'm not kicking him out of his house for any reason. Using Ryker's personal playroom to blow my load occasionally is one thing, but staying longer than one evening is way too much. "I'll figure something out."

Leaving Ryker to his club business, I pull my cell out and make a call while sauntering down the hall. "Hey. You around?"

"Yeah. What's up?"

"I'm coming over."

Chapter 19

Daelyn

Guilt for ghosting Dmitri grinds my conscience the entire way home. My pussy hurts, my head's banging, and there's a hollowness in my belly that feels a lot like regret.

But I couldn't stay with him a minute longer. Not with how good it felt. How safe it felt.

How right it felt.

We'd fucked until I finally tapped out. Then he cleaned me up, made me drink water, and peppered kisses all over my sweaty skin before holding me all night. He fell asleep first, his deep, even breathing lulling me to sleep too. When I woke, it was in a panic. I had no clue what time it was and needed to get back to Addie.

And back to reality.

I'm also no further at finding information out about Dmitri than I had been two days ago. Because the things he shared about his mom and fighting and stuff? I'm not telling Kaleb any of it. There's no point. The past is in the past.

It's not because I want to protect Dmitri. Or... well, that's what I'm sticking with, anyway. And it's definitely not because I'm falling for a guy I barely know. I'm not that stupid.

No. Kaleb wants *new* information. The past can be googled if it's that important to him. Though I have no clue why he hasn't looked Dmitri up already. In fact, why hasn't Kaleb joined the Monarch Club to get closer to him that way? He can afford the membership fees. Either he's letting everyone else do his dirty work again, or he doesn't know about the Monarch at all.

Or maybe he tried to get in and got denied?

Pulling my cell out, I check it for the hundredth time.

No notifications.

I'd taken a big gamble yesterday, not only by going to the Monarch Club and spending the night there, but I'd turned my cell off before I left my house. Kaleb tracks my location sometimes, and I didn't want to risk him seeing where I was. Stupid, really, because he could also have someone tailing me. It wouldn't be the first time.

My stomach clenches the instant I take the first step up to my front door. Something's off. I feel it. Digging out my key, I unlock the door in a hurry. Dread consumes me when I see the state of my living room. Furniture is knocked over, plates are shattered, picture frames lay on the floor broken to pieces. My TV is busted.

My home has been destroyed.

"Where the fuck have you been?" Kaleb steps down from the upstairs landing, each thud of his boots on my wooden steps collide with my rapid heartbeat. "Where." *Thud.* "The." *Thud.* "Fuck." *Thud.* "Have." *Thud.* "You." *Thud.* "Been?" *Thud.*

Hooking my thumb over my shoulder, I play it cool. "I was just—"

He punches me hard in the stomach.

Doubling over, I gasp for air, my mouth opening and closing like a fish.

Kaleb grabs me by the back of the neck and

pushes me into the kitchen. I stumble in a rush to keep up because I know damn well he'll drag me across the floor by my hair if I fall. He picks up a chair and shoves me into it.

"Let's play a game." He snags another chair and sets it next to me at the kitchen table before straddling it. Pulling out his knife, he grabs my arm and holds it down before slamming the point of the blade into the wood, nicking my thumb.

My eyes widen as terror floods my system. "Kaleb, why are you doing this?"

"That's not an answer." He yanks the blade out and thrusts it down again, not looking at where he's stabbing. He misses the tip of my middle finger by a hair this time.

"I went out to clear my head. That's all." Tears spill and the bees in my belly swarm. "I swear that's all."

"You had to clear your head *all fucking night*?" Kaleb frees the blade again, slaps his hand over mine to keep me locked in place, and glowers at me, waiting for my answer.

"Yes. I… I stayed at a hotel. I didn't realize my phone died."

Kaleb palms his knife tighter, holding it above his head. His expression is so dark, so fucked, that panic has me jumping out of my seat so I can try to wrench my hand out from his grasp. "Kaleb! Don't!"

He brings the blade down, cutting the side of my forearm. The more I fight his hold, the more the knife cuts into my skin. "Kaleb, stop!"

He pulls it out and I know this next strike will be a clean impalement. He's been toying with me so far. I'm going to lose a finger or have a hole in my hand or arm next. I've seen him do this before.

"Kaleb, please!" I piss my pants. Urine drips down my legs, puddling on the floor.

"That's a nice dress to clear your head in." His grip on me loosens just as he stabs down one final time. I rip my arm away just before the knife embeds into my wooden tabletop.

Sobs wrack me as I hug myself.

"You feel that fear pumping inside you?" Kaleb growls in my face. Ripping the blade out of the table, he holds it at the hem of my dress, between my legs, and seethes. "That's how I felt all night when I couldn't fucking find you, Dae."

My dress tears as he cuts the fabric clean up the middle. I'm so paralyzed with fear, I suck in big breaths and keep crying. "Kaleb, stop."

"Who did you fuck last night?" He shoves his hand between my thighs, cupping my pussy, and I cry out because it hurts. I was already sore from Dmitri, and Kaleb's brutal touch makes it worse.

"Myself," I say through sobs. "I fucked myself, okay?"

Not a lie. Figuratively speaking, the actions I've taken recently, and the consequences I'm now facing, I did indeed fuck myself.

He leans in and smells my neck and hair. "You smell different."

"It was lavender bath salts." My stomach's rolling. "I normally use jasmine."

Our faces are so close I can feel his breath on my lips. With an angry, twisted smile, he wraps his hand around my throat and squeezes. "You turn your fucking phone off again, or let it die, and I will not miss next time. Understand me, Dae?"

The point of his blade is suddenly next to my right eye, driving his message home.

"Yes. I'm sorry."

He drops the knife, the sound of it clanking on the floor shattering me. Relief floods my body like a dam's burst. I cry so hard and ugly that I can't feel my cheeks. My breaths wheeze out of my lungs. My legs give out.

"Shhhh." Kaleb squats down and holds me close. "I hate when you make me be a bad guy, Dae. But it's for your own good. You know that, right?" He gently tips my chin, so I'll look at him. "Fuck, babygirl, I love your tears." He drags a tongue up my cheek. "So sweet, just like you."

My entire body trembles. I cry even harder.

How did I get this low in the gutter? How did I ever think Kaleb was my hero? When did I become this trapped and far from safety?

Then again, I've never known safety a day in my life. He didn't drag me here; I was already waiting for him to find me in this Hell.

"Let's get you cleaned up," Kaleb says cheerily. "You go take a shower and wash the piss off. I'll take care of the mess down here."

I crawl away from him, still sobbing.

"Nuh uh. Get up, babygirl. You only crawl when I tell you to." He hoists me to my feet and slaps my ass. "Go on now. Addie will be home soon. You don't want her to see you like this, do you?"

My stomach plummets. More sobs tear out of me.

"Jesus Christ." Kaleb snatches me up and hugs me tight. "Come on, babygirl. It wasn't *that* bad. Calm the fuck down."

It's the *calm the fuck down* that's said in a darker tone. That's the only warning I'll get before he terrorizes me again if I don't listen. So, I pull myself together. Wrapping my arms around his middle, I inhale the scent of cigarettes, booze, cologne, and laundry detergent and I pull. Myself. The fuck. Together.

"Better?"

I nod against his chest.

"Give me a smile, Daelyn."

With all the bravado I can muster, I tip my head back and smile up at him.

He cups my face and kisses the tip of my dripping nose. "That's my good girl."

I finally break away and head upstairs to do what I'm told. I scrub myself raw in the shower. I bandage the cuts Kaleb just gave me. I tell myself I deserve everything I'm getting because I did this to myself.

Surprisingly, Kaleb hadn't destroyed the upstairs rooms, but he definitely slept in my bed last night. Cigarette smoke lingers in my room and there are burn holes in my bedding and cigarette butts have been stubbed out on my end table before getting flicked all over my floor.

Great.

Opening a window, I plug in my diffuser and fill it with a new floral scent before getting dressed. When I return downstairs, Kaleb's sweeping glass shards off my floor. "I'll have a new TV delivered this afternoon."

"It's fine."

His expression tells me I don't have a choice.

And as much as I want to reject his offer, I need

a TV and for my house to go back to normal because I can't let Addie see what a mess I've made of our lives. And there's no way I can afford a new TV right now.

"Want to grab breakfast?" he asks, pouring the broken glass into a trashcan.

"Umm. Sure." It's not like I have a choice. "Where do you want to go?"

"You'll see." His smile makes my insides squirm. "We'll wait for Addie to come home. I want her to go with us."

Oh, hell no. "She's got work all day." I'm not sure if that's true or not, so I pray I'm not caught in a lie. "And I'm starving. I haven't eaten in like two days."

"Okay." He tosses the broom and dustpan on the floor. "I'll have Ace clean up the rest. Let's go."

I don't want Ace in my house, especially if Addie might come home soon.

"Let me just grab a pair of shoes really quick." I take the steps two at a time, even though my lower half hurts from last night, and rush into my room. Grabbing a pair of Converse from my closet, I slip them on and sit on my bed. My heart races and hands shake as I text Addie.

Daelyn: Don't worry about coming home early. Stay at Tasha's and work on your tan!

I quickly hit the send button.

"Thought you said your cell was dead."

I gasp at Kaleb's voice. He eyes me from the doorway, his arms crossed over his chest.

Oh shit, oh shit, oh shit. "I charged it while I was in the shower."

He extends his hand out, expectantly.

Terrified, I hand him my cell and hold my

breath as he quickly checks my battery, then hands it back to me. "You can charge it more in my car. Let's go."

I stare at the screen, seeing that, by the grace of God, I was down to one sliver of battery power left, anyway.

Throwing my hair up in a ponytail, I follow him out of my house, and by the time I've buckled up in his passenger seat, I'm back to being detached and numb.

I can do anything in this state of mind.

I am, after all, a bad guy.

Chapter 20

Dmitri

"What's going on, bro?"

I lean against the long stainless-steel counter and cross my arms. Knox is beside me, sauteing veggies. "My dad's dead."

Not sure if the more I say it out loud, the better off I'll be, but it's worth a shot.

Knox turns to me. Without another word, he grabs the back of my neck and jerks me into his body for a hug. I'm taller than him by about three inches. So why does it feel like he's the giant here?

"Fucking Hell, D. I'm so sorry."

"Me too." I should have visited him more. Should have done better by him.

The night that sealed Dad's cage bars will always and forever haunt me and has been a recurring nightmare I've had for years.

"You speak to your mom?"

The mention of that woman has ice shooting through my veins. "No." I shove him back so I can breathe. It's like there's a bear trap wrapped around my goddamn ribs, puncturing my lungs.

"Figured she'd come crawling out of the gutter if she knew." Knox shifts his wok and shimmies the vegetables around, making them sizzle.

"Well, if she comes around me, I'll finish what my dad should have done a long time ago."

"And end up in prison, just like him? Naw.

Don't do it, bro. She's not worth it." He drizzles some kind of sauce onto the veggies. "Besides, maybe she's dead already."

"I'm not that fucking lucky."

It's weird that when I talk to Knox about my family, it doesn't sit the same on my chest as when I talk to Ryker or Vault about it. Of the three of them, I'm closer to Ryker, but Knox and I have a bond that's built on being similarly broken. His dad knocked him around back in the day and takes advantage of him financially now. That's on Knox to figure out. I'll help him handle his Pops when he's ready. *If* that day ever comes.

Until then, we talk about our trauma like an old movie where you discuss specific scenes. It's a lot of, "Hey remember when…" Well, you can fill in the blank. The point is, we see our pasts as old lives. Like we've been reborn, reincarnated, over and over with each step we've taken to better ourselves.

Knox no longer leans on drugs to get through the day.

And I'm not the frustrated, impatient kid suffering from malnutrition I used to be.

Be better. Clean. Wash my hair. Put on clean clothes.

I am better. I am clean. I wash my buzzed hair. And my clothing rack is crammed with the finest threads money can buy.

See? All good now.

"What is that you're making?"

"Chicken stir-fry. I'm starving." Knox sprinkles some kind of flakey seasoning into the pan.

Gotta hand it to the guy, he went from a junkie teen to a phenomenal chef who owns his own club and seeing him climb from the bottom to the top will forever be a highlight of our friendship. I'm really proud of him.

He also knows I love chicken stir-fry, so I'm touched. "What are you gonna eat?" I joke, as if I could eat the entire wok full of chicken and veggies myself. I mean, I *could*, but I won't.

He plates our food and hands mine over. We quietly walk out of the kitchen and go over to a booth in the back corner of his club. It's nine in the morning, so no one's here.

"How's business?"

"Getting there." Knox already has a pitcher of ice water and two glasses at our table. The man's prepared, like usual. "So, you're just visiting to tell me the news, or is there something else you want to share?"

I shove a forkful of veggies and chicken in my mouth and practically swallow without chewing. I'm fucking starving. "I need a place to stay for a while."

"You and Ryker in a fight or something?"

"No." I shove another bite in my mouth. And another. Damn, this is good. "I just need a break from the club for a bit."

"What's mine is yours, D. You still got a key?"

I nod, shoveling more food in.

"Christ, man. Slow down. My dishes should be savored, not inhaled."

He's right, but I can't stop. I'm not even sure when the last full meal I had was. Oh yeah… "I went to that place up by North Street. The one with the pink roof."

"Maggie's?"

"Yeah."

Knox takes a sip of his water. "Any good?"

"Had the steak hash with mushrooms." I shrug. "It was okay. I mean, I ate it."

"You'd eat a grilled flip flop if you were hungry enough."

True. "I'm not sure what it was missing or whatever, but you should go there one morning and figure it out."

"Want to go now?"

"We're already eating this." And I'm not about to let it go to waste. "Fucking delicious, by the way."

"I know." Knox stuffs a big bite into his mouth and chews.

I stab into another piece of tender chicken, but my mind wanders to breakfast with Daelyn.

"Hooya gowif."

"What?"

"Hooya gowif?"

"Jesus Christ, you animal. Chew your food before you talk."

Knox swallows hard, chokes, and chugs some water before he repeats, "Who did you go with?"

"Where?"

He slams his glass down. "Maggie's, asshat!"

"Oh." Her name is on the tip of my tongue, but I bite it, so she's stays there. "What makes you think I went with someone?"

"You just got this stupid dopey look on your ugly face, bro. Only a woman does that to a man."

"No one you know."

"Ohhh, so there *is* a woman. I was just bluffing. You always have that stupid dopey look on your face, man. I think it's because of all your concussions and broken noses."

The laugh that bubbles out of me feels so good.

I flip him the bird before taking another bite and finish my plate in half the time it takes Knox to polish off his.

"Maybe you should take her out more often," he finally says. "If that's when you'll eat an actual meal instead of thriving on your fancy espressos." He uses his fork like a conductor's wand. "Say it with me. Coffee is not water. You can't hydrate with lattes."

Speaking of hydration, I hope Daelyn's drinking water.

My hand instinctively goes to my cell. The urge to text her is so strong it churns the food in my belly. But I refrain. She ghosted me. I need to respect the boundary she's set, even though it hurts like hell. I think I scared her last night with how much we did together.

I must have read her wrong.

Last night she begged for things I was all too eager to give her. She came around my dick more times than I could count. She screamed my motherfucking name and I know damn well a lot of the club heard it, even with the music playing over the surround sound. I made her keep eye contact with me in the beginning. Halfway through our third scene, she had me tied up on the bed and was riding my dick like she was trying to win the Kentucky Derby. By the end, I was an animal searching for a place to burrow, and her pussy was my home. I fucked her until I couldn't feel anything other than her body giving way to mine, her cum coating my tongue, her legs quivering around my waist, her nails shredding my skin. The combo kicked me over the edge more than once. My balls are so drained, it's a shock they haven't shriveled into raisins.

I check my notifications, hoping she's called or

texted and maybe I didn't hear it.

There's nothing.

And why would there be? She dipped and I doubt I'll ever see her again.

It's best this way. Leaning on her or using her as a distraction is an insult to the spectacular woman she is. Daelyn deserves better than me.

Be better. Clean. Wash my hair. Put on clean clothes.

"Earth to Dmitri." Knox waves his hand in my face. "You in there?"

"Yeah." I clear my throat. "Sorry."

"You didn't hear anything I just said, did you?"

"No."

His expression falls. "It's okay." He grips my shoulder and squeezes it with sympathy in his eyes. He probably assumes I'm thinking about my dad which makes guilt flare in my gut.

"You got plans today?" he asks.

"Not really."

"Good. You can come with me." He waggles his eyebrows at me. "We're going noveling, loser."

Chapter 21

Daelyn

My heart sinks when we pull into the parking lot to the restaurant Dmitri and I had breakfast at yesterday morning.

Kaleb knows I was here with Dmitri.

Keeping my expression blank, I climb out of his car and slam the door shut. We're dead silent as we walk in and wait for the hostess to seat us. I'm under dressed again. My surroundings sound muffled, and I feel like I'm walking on uneven marshmallows as we follow the hostess to a table in the center of the restaurant.

"Welcome to Maggie's! I'm Rory and I'll be your server today. Can I start you off with a drink?"

Panic has sweat blooming down my back as I look away from her. *Please don't recognize me. Please don't say something about me coming back so soon.*

Kaleb orders our drinks because my tongue's tied. He also orders our food.

Did he tail me yesterday or just look up my location on the app?

Maybe I'm being paranoid. Only one way to find out. "What made you pick this place?" I ask with a light, cheerful tone.

"I know you've been wanting to try it."

That trips me up. "When did I say that?"

"That time we passed by after the switch off with Emmanuel."

Suddenly too stunned to speak, my mind races to connect the dots in this new game he's playing with me.

"Remember?" He cocks his brow.

No. I don't remember. I didn't know about this restaurant before Dmitri took me here. But I clearly remember the time I'd been sent, on Kaleb's behalf, with two duffel bags filled with cocaine that I had to hand over to a man named Emmanuel. Ace was with me that day. But it wasn't on this side of town, so I couldn't have said I wanted to come to this place to eat.

That... wait... no. I'm sure I didn't know this place existed. Or am I crazy?

They say when you've been through enough abuse, the chemicals in your system change and can actually cause some kind of brain damage. You don't remember things correctly, if at all. I think I'm suffering from something like that because nothing makes sense to me anymore.

"You look confused, babygirl. Here, let me refresh your memory." Kaleb pulls his phone out and taps the screen a few times before sliding it across the table.

These videos have nothing to do with me allegedly saying I wanted to come to this stupid restaurant. But they make terror spike in my system again because the first one playing is of me pulling bricks of coke out for someone to check the quality of. And I'm the only person in the video that can be identified...

"It's pure," I say to the headless man on camera. "We don't fuck with cutting."

My vision tunnels.

Kaleb casually swipes his finger across the screen, bringing up another video. And another. Photos come after that. All of them damning. All of them are evidence that would earn me major jail time.

"Why do you have those?" I whisper. The betrayal stings. How could he have had his men do this?

"Why do you think?" His jawline sharpens with his smile. "Relax, babygirl," he says with a chuckle. "I just like to make sure you understand the severity of your actions."

My. Actions.

Icy dread encases me. "You're blackmailing me."

"I'm reminding you of who you are, and who owns you." He points at my wrist. "Because branding you clearly isn't enough anymore."

"What's that even mean?"

"It's time to put you back on a short leash, Daelyn. Can't have you thinking you're allowed to hole up in a fucking hotel room all night when you have responsibilities at home." He cocks his head to the side. "We don't want CPS or the DEA or anyone else to see these things, do we? What will happen to Addie if you go to prison?"

It's a miracle I get my napkin up to my mouth in time to catch the vomit that flies out of me.

Kaleb sits back and looks disappointed. "Jesus Christ, you're turning into such a weak fucking kitten, Dae. Go clean yourself up."

Holding the napkin to my mouth, my vision blurs as I snake through the tables and bump the bathroom door open with my hip. Tossing my napkin in the trash, I barely make it to the toilet before I heave again.

I have to do something.

I need to get out of this.

I need to save Addie!

Dry heaves make the vessels in my eyes burst. I haven't had anything to eat since yesterday morning, beyond those few bites of hamburger and fruit I had with Dmitri at the Monarch.

Dmitri.

I pull out my cell, my instincts screaming that I should call him for help.

But I stop myself. I can't possibly run to the man I've been ordered to ruin with a sob story about the man who sent me to ruin him. That's fucked.

I don't think I've ever realized how very alone in the world I am until this moment.

I've spent my whole life leaning on the wrong people when I needed saving. Foster kids. Councilors. Kaleb. Even Addie.

No more.

No. More.

Flushing the toilet, I rise and roll my shoulders back. My emotions drain out of my head like sand in a sieve, landing in the open box at my feet. The lid slams shut. Calmly walking over to the sink, I wash my hands, rinse out my mouth, and splash cold water on my face.

Blotting dry, I toss the paper towels into the trash and leave the bathroom as a very different creature. I may be stuck between a lion and a wolf, but I'm not without my own claws and teeth.

Kaleb's right where I left him, only his plate is empty. He sits back, eyeing me like he's trying to get a read on my current state of mind.

He won't be able to. I've perfected my masks, and this one is my toughest to peel off.

Dropping back into my seat, I dig into my food like a ravenous animal. I've barely chewed before I swallow and stuff another spoonful in. Chugging my drink, I drain the glass and lift my finger to catch the server's attention. "Can I have more orange juice when you get a chance?"

Not waiting for a reply, I shove more food into my mouth and snag Kaleb's drink, sucking it down greedily. "I didn't realize I was this hungry."

"No food service at the hotel last night?"

"Didn't bother looking." I suck a piece of food out of my teeth. "I was too busy enjoying a self-care night."

"Self-care." Kaleb's smile is a real one. He's amused by me. Good. "Is that what it's called?"

"Sounds classier than finger-banging myself until I decide I'm ready to ride a massive dildo while I've got a vibrating butt plug stuffed in my ass, doesn't it?"

Rory, the stealthy server, grabs my glass and pours more OJ into it. Her cheeks are bright red. I don't care that she's heard. In fact, I hope lots of people do. It'll mess with Kaleb's head.

"That definitely explains your hobbling this morning, babygirl."

I salute him with a hushpuppy and eat it.

"Next time you need your holes stuffed…" Kaleb leans in with a devilish grin. "Call me. I'll send my boys to do the job. You remember how well that went before with Emmanuel's crew, right?"

My mask nearly slips.

Three years ago, Kaleb allowed Emmanuel's

men to run a train on me to "gain respect".

He also tried to have Ace fuck me once. Said it was another initiation thing. Ace refused to do it and ended up getting his ass beat so badly he was out of commission for weeks. I have no idea what he did to get back in Kaleb's good graces, but whatever it took, he's been Kaleb's right-hand man ever since.

I think his refusal is the only reason I tolerate the piece of shit.

After cleaning off my plate, I sit back and belch loudly. Kaleb laughs because a few people look over at me with disapproval. "Your manners are deplorable, Daelyn."

So is the fact that you're still breathing. "I don't have to impress anyone here. Their opinions of me don't matter."

"That's my girl."

I'm not your girl.

Smiling, he waves Rory back over to us. "Can we get the check, please?"

"Sure thing."

Less than five minutes later, Kaleb's paid the tab, and we're back in his car. "Got plans today?"

"Yes." I buckle in. "I've got a mountain of work to do."

"Why do you insist on working for that dumb company, Daelyn? They don't pay you what you're worth."

I lean back and close my eyes. "You know why."

I refuse to take handouts. I'm trying to be legit. It's ridiculous Kaleb would even ask such a question after he's just shown me all the incriminating evidence he has against me.

"I can take care of you, if you'd let me."

"No, thanks." I cross my arms and look out the window. "You've taken care of me enough."

Understatement of the century.

"You know everything I've done is for your own good, right?" He starts the engine. "The videos, the tracking app, the jobs I put you on. It's all to help you reach your potential."

My potential as a what? Drug runner? Whore? "I have zero interest in running some mafia club cartel circuit circus thing, Kaleb. I just want an honest, simple life."

"You still don't get it." He pulls out of the parking lot. "People like us don't get to have honest, simple lives. We're made different."

"Agree to disagree." Tears prick my eyes and I hold them back, reinforcing my mask. "I'm out. You said if I did this thing with that fighter that I'd be out."

"I did."

"Are you rescinding?"

"No." He sighs and puts his hand on my thigh. "I'm just really hoping you change your mind and want to stay with me." He side-eyes me. "You're all I have, Dae. You're the best thing in my life."

And yet you punched me in the gut, tried to stab me, and choked me this morning. "I have to do this for myself. If I mean that much to you, you'd want me to be happy, right?"

"I want you happy with *me*." His sudden burst of anger is punctuated by the heel of his hand smashing against the steering wheel. At least he's not touching my thigh anymore. Kaleb exhales loudly through his nose as he tries to calm back down. "I'm sorry I've been an asshole lately."

Lately? Try forever, psycho. "It's fine."

"You deserve better."

Yup. I do. "You're trying your best."

"See? That right there." He grabs my hand and lifts it to his mouth, pressing a kiss on my knuckles. "That's why I can't live without you. You're the only one who gets me. You love me."

I haven't said the words *I love you* to him in years. He's only fishing right now and I'm not taking the bait.

My silence makes him drop my hand like a hot potato. "I'm going out of town for a few days."

That perks me up, even though I don't show it. "Where to this time?"

"Miami."

Long ago, I would have begged him to take me with him. Not that he ever would. Now, when he goes on these trips, I never ask because I really don't care. Besides, the less I know, the better.

"When I get back," he warns, "I expect you to have done your job."

Saliva floods my mouth, and I swallow before answering. "Okay."

He looks over at me, once again trying to get a read on my state of mind. And once again, he fails.

"I leave tomorrow and will be back next Friday. Ace will stick around."

"Great," I say, annoyed.

Kaleb knocks the side of my head, making it smack the window. "Watch your fucking tone."

The rest of the drive is dead silent and when he pulls up to my house, I get out and slam the door shut. Ace steps out of my front door, watching me cautiously.

"Dae!" Addie says behind him, beaming a big

smile.

Fuck. My. Life.

Kaleb peels wheels, leaving without another insult or slap. Hurray for small mercies.

Ace's gaze roams my face, stopping at my throat before sailing down the rest of my body and landing on my bandaged hand. His brow pinches slightly as he grinds his molars.

With a big, fake smile in place, I slip past him and step inside my house to see it's good as new and there's a much larger TV mounted to my wall.

"Ace bought us a new TV."

Judging by Addie's tone, I can tell something's off with her.

"Yeah. I can see that." Turning to face him, I block him from coming inside. "Bye, Ace."

He doesn't budge from my doorway for a full count of ten, but eventually, he nods and leaves.

Dropping onto the sofa, I bury my face in my hands and sigh heavily.

"Dae?" Addie plops down next to me. "I want to talk to you about something, but I don't want you to get mad at me."

Chapter 22

Daelyn

My stomach plummets. This has already been a shitty day, and whatever Addie has to say will probably make it worse because she never says stuff like this. I'm never mad at her. I honestly can't imagine her doing anything that would truly make me angry.

"What is it?" I keep my face buried in my hands, waiting for Addie to speak up. When she doesn't, I glance over at her. "Addie, what is it?"

Her eyes widen, gaze sliding all over my face and then she does exactly what Ace had just done. She looks alarmed. "Holy shit, Dae."

Shit, I forgot that I'm a mess. I immediately go into defense. "It's nothing."

"It's not *nothing*." She gets up, her hands balling into fists. "Did Kaleb do that to you?"

"It's fine."

"It's not fine!" she yells. "He's such a fucking asshole, Daelyn. Why do you still hang around him?"

"It's complicated."

"Nothing can be that fucking complicated. He hurt you." She tosses her hands up. "Again!"

I shrink in on myself, very aware that out of the two of us, Addie has the most sense.

"Oh my god, that's why we got a new TV, isn't it? He fucking love bombed you with a flat screen."

I'm not about to correct her and say he only

replaced what he broke in a fit of rage. It'll further prove her point, which I don't need.

"You have to get away from him," she says. "Fuck that fucking dick. I'm gonna kill him."

"I'm working on a way to get him out of my life. But it's taking me time."

"Like *years*?"

I hate that she's entirely too accurate.

"It's complicated," I stress again.

"Well, it's a good thing he never comes into this house. I'll put a bullet in his head if he ever does."

I bite my tongue and let her carry on, because she's a stronger, better person than me. If one of us is going to die in the gutter, it will not be Addie.

"He's such a psychopath, Dae. Ace even told me that—"

"Do *not* talk to Ace about stuff, Addie." I stand up and jab my finger at her. "*Ever*. He's just as bad as Kaleb."

"He's nowhere near as crazy as that monster."

I once argued on behalf of Kaleb the same way she is for Ace. "Red flags are red flags, no matter what they're made of, Addie." She goes to open her mouth and argue but I cut her off before she has the chance. "Don't defend him. He does Kaleb's dirty work, and that makes him just as bad."

"And what does that make *you* then, huh?"

My heart collapses. "It makes me bad too," I admit quietly.

"No. It makes you stuck. Just like Ace is stuck." She fists her hair, frustrated and angry.

Holy crap, I wonder how much Ace has shared with her. "I don't want you involved in Ace or any of the other guys Kaleb runs with. Understand me?"

She clamps her mouth shut. Then she storms up the steps and slams her bedroom door closed.

Great. I don't know why I thought raising a teenager would be easy. And the hoops I jump through to keep her are eventually going to break my legs. But she's worth it. Even when she hates me, I love her with my whole heart.

Trudging up the steps, all my aches and pains roar to life and I'm so ashamed of myself for a million and one reasons. I know she can hear me knocking on her door, even with her music blasting. She has every right to be mad. Kaleb is dangerous, and I've had to keep him around. I haven't shared what I do for him because the less Addie knows, the safer she'll be.

Or so I thought.

But if Ace is confiding in her, that puts a big rip in my flimsy safety net.

Addie's right. Ace is as stuck as I am. It sucks. It's not fair. But I'll be damned if I let Addie fall into this hole with us, too.

Wanna hear one of my worst secrets? I sometimes wish Addie lived with Tasha's family permanently. They're well off and care about her enough to let her stay over all the time. She'd be safe and happy and loved there.

But I can't imagine asking them to do that.

In my desperate moments, I stare at the number to Addie's current case worker and almost call her and tell her to come get Addie and re-home her because I'm failing miserably at giving this beautiful soul the life she deserves. Except I know what would happen if I did that. Addie would fight it. She'd hate me. I'm not sure I could survive it.

Plus, I can't risk the chance that they'd re-home

her somewhere else, and that place might be a million times worse than her home here with me. She'd run. Get caught. Be sent to a group home until they found placement for her elsewhere. I can't stomach the thought of putting her in that position. I love her too much. I'd give my fucking life for her.

And I don't want to live without her.

Does keeping her make me no different than Kaleb? Because he keeps me for the same reason. For love. But is it love or something more toxic like… fuck, I don't even know. I'm so confused and hate myself for everything I'm doing.

"Addie?" I knock again.

She swings the door open, her eyes bright with tears. She looks so young like this, her upset expression reminding me of when she was little. Her freckles have popped out across her nose and cheeks from all the sun she's been getting, and her full face is rosy and flushed.

We stare at each other while her music screams from her little speaker. Then we wrap our arms around each other and squeeze hard.

"I'm so sorry," I cry against her shoulder. "I'm trying. Please know I'm trying my best to do right by you."

"You don't have to do right by *me*," she sobs. "Do right by *you*, Dae. You're worth more than this." We hold on tight for a long time until she says, "You're getting snot in my hair."

I back away, snorting, and wipe the tears off her cheeks. "I love you."

"I love you too."

Walking into her room, I plop down on the edge of her bed and sigh. Time for a conversation change.

"So, what is it you wanted to tell me before we got distracted?"

"Forget it. It's not even important."

"Everything about you is important to me. Spill it."

"It's not a big deal."

"Sounded like one downstairs."

"Yeah, well, that was before I saw your face. What the hell happened to your eyes?"

"I busted a few blood vessels puking."

"Eww. Why did you puke?" Her eyes blow wide. "Jesus, you're not pregnant, are you?"

I smack her arm playfully. "No, I just had an upset stomach and yacked my breakfast in the restaurant bathroom."

"My worst nightmare comes to life."

Addie doesn't deal with vomit. Hers, or anyone else's. She could have won an Oscar for the performance she put on when she had the flu last fall.

"So?" I push the subject.

"So what?"

"What is it you want to tell me?"

Her shoulders droop and she climbs onto the bed next to me, sitting with her legs crossed. "Okay, look, I know it's super last minute but…" Her cheeks pinken, but the look in her eyes is more excitement than fear.

"Just tell me, Ads."

"Tasha's parents have invited me to go to the beach with them," she says in a rush. Her brows pinch tightly together, and it looks like she's holding her breath, too.

"When?"

"Tomorrow." She chews on her bottom lip. "I

don't have to go. It's too last minute, anyway. And I have to work so—"

"You're going."

Addie gawks. "What?"

"Call off work. You are one hundred percent going to the beach."

She beams at me like a kid on Christmas morning. "Really? I can go?"

"Hells yes."

"Oh my God!" She squeals and tackle-hugs me. "You're the *best*!"

"I mean, I am pretty cool. I've got rizz and everything."

Addie pushes off me. "Please. For the love of God. Don't *ever* say those words again."

I giggle, feeling lighter than I have in weeks. "Why did you think I'd be mad about you going to the beach with Tasha's family?"

"Because I feel bad," she says, slumping. "You've never been to the beach and now I'm asking to go… without you."

"Addie." I choke back several emotions cramming up my throat. "Babe, I will *never* be mad about something like that. You should get to experience all the great things out there."

"But going to the beach is something you've always wanted to do, too."

"I'll get there someday."

Her brows pinch again.

"Hey." I shake her. "Don't wait for me to have *your* best experiences. If we share them, great. If we don't, I'll wait for you to come home and tell me all about them. I will never *ever* hold you back from living your best life, Addie."

She sniffles and wipes her nose with the back of her hand. "I still feel bad."

"Well don't. I'm happy to get you out of my hair. You're annoying and loud."

She flips me off, huffing a laugh.

"Seriously though, I'm glad you're getting an opportunity like this. That's really nice of them to include you in their family vacation."

"I was shocked they invited me. I think I gawked like a fish at them for like five whole minutes. It was embarrassing."

"How long is the trip for?"

"Just until Sunday." Addie blows out a sigh. "We'll drive most of the day tomorrow and come back late Sunday. Tasha's mom says I don't need to pay for anything."

Tasha's mom, Corrinne, is a saint.

"Well, I'll send you with money, anyway. And I want to talk with Corrinne first about all this, okay?"

"Yeah, sure." Her excitement has her vibrating.

"You're going to the beach."

"I'm going to the beach."

"*You're going to the beach!*" I squeal.

"*I'm going to the beeeeeaaacccchhh!*"

We scream and laugh and kick our feet.

Soon after, I go into my bedroom and call Corrinne, who confirms everything Addie's told me. Turns out they have a beach home they've rarely used and are thrilled Tasha will have a friend coming along for once.

I dig into my emergency fund and hand over an extra two-hundred dollars for Addie to blow on whatever she wants. If one of us is going to be happy, I'm glad it's her.

Peeking into her bedroom, I find my girl rummaging through piles of clothes all over her floor and bed. I think she's pulled her entire wardrobe out of the closet.

"I'll be back in about two hours," I say.

She looks up with a bikini in her hand. "Where are you going?"

"The hardware store."

Chapter 23

Dmitri

My first cage fight was on my sixteenth birthday, and I was so terrified and restless, I'd barely slept the night before. Tossing and turning, I remember thinking one thing: *Dad's gonna watch*.

One might assume I was stuck on that thought because I'd been nervous about my performance. Fuck that. My form was perfect. My agility, damn good. I'd blown Silas away with what I'd been able to accomplish in my short time training with him. Naw, it was something else that ate at me…

"You need to get your ass in the MMA for real, Dmitri. Don't waste your time here in this shithole."

"I like this shithole." Bob and weave. Pivot, kick. *"I'm happy here."*

"Kid, no one's happy here. I've built my empire on the misery of others."

I look around the gym that's falling apart and has a leaky roof. "Old man, if this is your empire, you need to upgrade."

Silas's raspy chuckle makes me grin. "You excited for tonight?"

"I'm ready to fight." I jab into the punching bag, practicing exactly what Dad and Silas have taught me for the past three months. I know it's probably too soon for me to go in the ring, but I can't wait anymore. I don't care if I get my ass handed to me. I just want to swing and hit something that'll bleed like I do.

"Your dad's coming, right?"

"Yeah." Dread hits my gut at the thought. I still have a hefty bruise on my torso from my mom hitting me with a chair last week. She's been off the booze lately and her mood swings are insane. If my dad sees the huge bruise, will he know it's not from a fight? Sounds unlikely, but any possibility of getting caught, and having what my mom does to me found out, has me freaking. So far, I've trained with a shirt on. Silas keeps telling me to take it off, but I refuse.

Even if I don't have a fresh bruise, I've got a collection of scars I don't need seen.

Christ, if Dad sees any of them, he's going to ask questions. I've spent years coming up with lies for each mark on my body, just in case they're seen, but I'm not confident I can say one of them to my dad's face...

I toss and turn on the couch. Knox's house is comfortable, but his sofa is too fucking soft. I'm used to my firm cot in the dungeon at the club. Not some squishy, plush shit like this. Punching my pillow, I readjust and sigh. Sleep evades me and I stare at my cell, desperate to text Daelyn and check up on her. It's stupid, I know.

Fuck, I'm exhausted. Wired. Annoyed.

Flicking the lamp on, I frown at the book I bought today while shopping with Knox. Fucker dragged me into the romance section of a huge bookstore like it's the secret passage to happiness. For all I know, he's right. What did I have to lose by at least checking them out? And with Daelyn on my mind, I'd headed right to the dark romance because I figured dark and dangerous love stories fit my mood best. Now here I am with a vampire book I never planned to read.

Turning to the prologue, I stare at the words on the page. Okay, well… that's actually kind of interesting.

Four hours later, I'm invested and can't put it down. Sleep can fuck right off. This guy's mate is in danger, and neither of them even realizes it.

About six more chapters later, I crash into a fitful dream…

"Happy Birthday to you. Happy birthday to you. Happy Birthday, dear Dmitri. Happy Birthday to you!"

Mom claps when I blow out the candles to my cake.

Dad sits across from me with this huge smile on his face and hands me a knife. "Cut it up, Son."

My mom makes me the same yellow cake with white icing every year for my birthday. I don't like it, but I'll never tell her that. I just eat it like a thankful son should and tell her what a great job she did on the decorations and lettering.

"I have a very special present for you," she says, her eyes beaming with delight.

I've never gotten presents on my birthday. On instinct, I look over at my dad.

Okay, he's just as surprised as I am. That's weird, right?

"It's for both of you." Mom gets up and heads over to her purse. She pulls out an envelope and places it in front of me. "Open it."

I tear the flap and pull out the slip inside. It's a black and white picture of a… "What is this?"

"You're going to be a big brother," Mom squeals. "Isn't that wonderful?"

I'm not sure what reaction she's looking for, but it's not the one she gets.

"What?" Dad stands up and snatches the sonogram picture from me. He scans the photo, brows furrowing, then

his jaw clenches tight, and he glares at my mom. "Anya."

She wraps her arms around his neck and kisses him.

He pries her off him and backs away. "I... I need a minute." He grabs his keys and leaves.

"Come on, silly." Mom squeezes my shoulders and kisses my cheek, unfazed that my dad's just bolted. "Cut the cake. I'm starving!"

Numbness spreads through me. I'm going to be a big brother. My mother will have another child to hurt. My dad's got another mouth to feed. I can't understand how this could have happened. The way my parents have been fighting lately, I find it hard to believe they would—

Okay, I'm not thinking about that. I'm nervous enough about tonight, I don't need one more thing to make me nauseous.

Eating birthday cake with my mom, seeing how happy she is, I latch onto the hope that this will be what turns her around. She's having a baby. That explains why she stopped drinking. If she can stop drinking, she can stop hitting. Right?

Later, at the fight, I go against a twenty-four-year-old that's my size and weight. I look older for my age, so no one raises issues about me as far as I know. Which is good, because I stare at my opponent and turn him into the bad guy, just like my dad said to do.

I turn him into my mom.

And I don't stop swinging until the bell rings and I'm ripped from his limp body by Silas and two other men.

My dad never shows up for the fight...

Knox is stupid loud in the bathroom, clearing the gunk out of his throat and brushing his teeth. He showers, dresses, and comes out in all his good morning glory. "You look like shit. Want breakfast?"

"No." I sit up and run a hand across my buzzed

hair. It's gotten a little longer since I haven't clipped it for a couple of weeks.

"I gotta go into the club today. A new stove is being installed and I want to make sure it goes smoothly."

"K."

"Wanna come?"

Yes, but in a different way than he's referring. "Naw, I'm staying back. I want to finish this book."

Knox's coffee mug clanks on the counter. "I knew it. You're a closet reader."

"That's not even a thing."

"Keep telling yourself that." He waggles his eyebrows at me. "You're sucked into the story, huh?"

"Seems like it."

"Don't be ashamed. Reading is a great form of escapism, bro. It's not cheap, but at least it's not drugs."

I scrub my face and head into the kitchen with my jeans slung low on my hips and no shirt on. "Get the fuck away from that machine before I break your face."

Knox throws his hands up and backs away from the espresso machine.

I make us both an acceptable drink and hand him his. One sip has Knox's eyes rolling in ecstasy. "Fucking marry me, D. This is so good."

He's the only person who can say shit like this to make me laugh. Around others, Knox is a very intense guy who's not easy to get along with. But it's an act. His armor. We've been through too much together for him to be hard around me. "Do *not* tell Ryker or Vault that I'm reading vampire porn. They'll never let me hear the end of it."

"Your secret's safe with me." Knox tips his mug and takes another sip. "Fuuuuck, I could come in my pants drinking this."

"TMI."

He shoves on his shoes and grabs a baseball hat, putting it on backwards. "I have no clue when I'll be back."

"It's fine." Not like I need a babysitter or anything. "Thanks for letting me crash last night."

Knox waves off my gratitude. "You know you're always welcome here." He pauses before heading out. "You going back to the Monarch tonight?"

"No."

I'm going back to Daelyn's house.

...

When Knox leaves, I feel off kilter. I enjoy being alone, but not in a space that isn't mine. Going back to the Monarch Club and hiding in my dungeon won't help yet. I think I'll just get pissed off that I don't have Daelyn there to play with.

Waiting until nightfall to see her is already proving to be near impossible.

She ghosted me. I'm in a headfuck. We need to stay away from each other.

At least for now.

Needing a distraction, I pick up the romance book again. Knox isn't wrong. Reading is a decent escape from real life, but unfortunately, these damaged characters on the page are a little too relatable. Figures I'd randomly pick a book that has a fucked-up hero I can identify with.

Christ, did I just compare myself to a *hero*?

I'm mental.

Hours pass and I finally finish the story. Spoiler Alert: They live happily ever after. They also have a lot of sex. I think I could have gone without that part because it just makes me want the same thing.

Tossing the book on the couch, I lean forward and bury my head in my hands. The scenes in the book were hot. The danger was intense. The heroine reminded me of Daelyn because she was an adorably hard-headed baddie.

Daelyn's words from the other night filter into my mind. *I'm a bad person who does bad things.*

Closing my eyes, I sit back and focus on her face, the trepidation in her ocean eyes, the frustration in her tightly knit brow… the way she pouts.

The way she screams my name.

The way she rides my cock.

The way she keeps eye contact with me while she orgasms.

I made her connect with me. It might have been brief, but it was the most erotic fucking thing I've ever seen in my life. Considering I'm an experienced Dom in an elite sex club, that's saying something.

She was just so *pure*. Daelyn's sweet and raw and perfectly made for a man like me to spoil.

She said she was bad.

I think I like her bad.

Fuuuuuck.

Unbuckling my jeans, I pull out my hard dick, spit in my palm and start stroking.

I'd give anything to have her ride me right now. I want her to wrap her hands around my throat and squeeze until black eats the fringes of my vision. I want her to sink her teeth into my skin and break it to taste my blood.

I stroke myself harder, squeezing tighter.

I want to bury my face in her cunt. Rim her tight little ass. Hold her down and fuck her into oblivion so she can't walk away from me again.

I want to tie her up and come all over her body. Hold her hostage and use her like a toy.

My balls draw up tight. Heat blooms down my back.

But I can't come like this. Not without more stimulation. Not without pain.

Grabbing my balls, I tug so hard it's a wonder I don't tear them out. My eyes cross as my orgasm barrels out of me, ropes of cum spurting from the pierced head. Hips jacking up, my shoulders digging into the back of the couch, I fuck my hand until the temporary high fades, and I'm left with a mess to clean.

After a quick shower, shave, and clothing change, I give up waiting any longer. Weaving through traffic, I make it to her house in about half an hour and park my bike between the two dumpsters again.

Already, my head is a little calmer. Scanning the street, I count the number of cars parked. Listen to music playing from someone's backyard. The smell of BBQ eventually wafts through the air. The sun finally sets.

I'm not even sure if Daelyn is home or not. Still, standing like a creepy watch dog lets me breathe a little easier. She said she does bad things. I can't imagine what they might be, but I'm sure she's not the only one in her circle of friends who does bad shit. At least that's the rule of thumb in my world.

And Daelyn is definitely in my world.

A tiny, blue light glows inside her home. I think it's from her computer. The house is otherwise dark, but I finally see her shadow pass the front window, and I'm suddenly like a puppy waiting for my owner to let me out of my cage to give me attention.

Heart galloping, I cross the street and sneak into her backyard where the sliding glass door awaits.

Without touching it, I look down and notice a four-by-two jamming the slider.

She doesn't want me to come inside.

My heart sinks into the abyss that swallows all my joy whenever I manage to find some.

"Okay." I step away, disappointment climbing up my body. "Okay."

I have to respect her wishes. I need to walk away and stay away for good.

Heading back to my bike, I swear it's like my limbs have turned to rubber. My legs can't operate right. My joints are too loose. Climbing on my bike, I take one last look at her house, preparing to let go for good when my cell goes off.

Whoever it is can fuck off.

Unless it's Ryker. Or Vault. Or Knox. Or Sophie.

Damnit.

Pulling it out, I blink at the notification, fully aware that I've likely lost my motherfucking mind and have started hallucinating because there's no way I'm seeing what I'm seeing on my screen.

Daelyn: Hey. Sorry for leaving like that. I didn't want to wake you and the entire day got away from me.

The air leaves my lungs in a ragged sigh.

Straddling my bike, I text back and stare at her living room window, waiting for her reply.

Chapter 24

Daelyn

With the house to myself, Addie at the beach, and Kaleb out of town, I can finally breathe. I've spent most of the day catching up on work and took a late shower. I haven't been able to get Dmitri out of my motherfucking head at all.

So, I finally texted him and lied to myself by saying that it was to get this shit for Kaleb over with. His response is almost immediate.

D: Want to play another game, Firefly?

This man and his games. I bite my lip to hide the smile he's not even around to catch.

Daelyn: What do you have in mind?

D: Two truths and a lie.

This is the second truth game we've played. It works well in my favor, so I'm down.

Daelyn: Okay. I'm hungry. I'm horny. I'm naked.

Little bubbles pop up while he types, and I clutch my cell tightly, eager for his response.

D: You're not naked.

Daelyn: Lucky guess. One point for you.

D: I'm hungry. I'm horny. I'm standing outside your house.

My heart lurches into my throat and I look out the sliding glass door. Disappointment smacks my heart when I see he's not there.

I bought a new lock for the front door last night

at the hardware store and will not be giving Kaleb a fucking key. I also put a wood beam on the sliding glass door because if Dmitri can get in that way, it's only a matter of time before Kaleb tries, too. I figure if Dmitri wants to see me again, we can just meet somewhere. I'll go to the Monarch or his house or whatever. There's no need for him to sneak inside my home again.

In fact, I'd rather he didn't, since Kaleb's likely watching me somehow.

Daelyn: You're not standing outside my house. Point for me.

Two seconds later, there's a knock on my front door.

Heart in my throat, I creep over and peek out the peephole.

Oh my god.

Wrenching the door open, I yank Dmitri by his t-shirt and rip him inside, slamming the door shut and locking it. "What the hell are you doing here?"

"Figured I'd use the front door like a gentleman, instead of sneaking in like a stalker."

A mixture of fear, anxiety, excitement, and joy swirls around my heart, making it lose a healthy rhythm.

Dmitri rushes towards me and kisses me hard. Our tongues swirl around each other. Rising on my toes, I cling to him tightly, and it's like we're suddenly making up for lost time.

He grabs my ass, lifting me off my feet. I wrap my legs around him as he stumbles through my living room and up the steps.

"I can't stop thinking about you," he says against my mouth. "You've ruined me."

Guilt swirls in my belly because that's exactly what I'm supposed to do. I was ordered to ruin him.

And I don't want to.

He kicks my bedroom door open and lays me on the bed. We separate long enough for him to pull his shirt off. I yank on my clothes, tearing them off me like they're on fire.

There's a chemistry between us that shouldn't exist. A connection that shouldn't be there. I'm not sure how I'm going to survive this, but it's not me I'm most worried about in this situation.

"What if I do ruin you?" I ask while he peppers hot kisses down my neck.

"Firefly, you could stab me in the heart while kissing me and I'd die a happy man." He tugs off his belt, slipping it effortlessly through the loops, and turns me over. Cracking my ass with it, he spanks me hard enough to make my cheeks clench.

"That's for being a bad girl and leaving the club without saying goodbye." He spanks me again. "That's for robbing me of the honor of taking care of you after I ravaged your sweet body for an entire night."

"I'm not even a little sorry," I lie, breathlessly.

"Brat." He spreads my legs wide and licks my pussy. "So, fucking wet already. Good, because bad girls need to learn their lessons." He grabs my hands, pulling them behind my back, then trails the belt down along my butt again. "Can I bind your wrists?"

"Yes."

I can't explain why him tying me up brings a calmness to my chaotic brain. But having some of my mobility impaired makes me focus on the trust I need to have in Dmitri.

Hold on. Trust? I *trust* him? Jesus, I'm fucked up.

Staying still while he makes quick work of wrapping the belt around my wrists, I let my body relax.

"Too tight?"

"No." Anticipation has my heart smashing against my ribs. Earlier in the shower, when I couldn't get Dmitri out of my head, I couldn't make myself come no matter how hard I tried. I felt too empty. Too numb. And I've been uncomfortably needy ever since.

I hear his pants slide down. Then he's suddenly looming over me, the bed dipping with his weight, springs squeaking and headboard knocking against the wall.

"Did you miss me?" he whispers against my ear while gently moving my hair over so he can kiss my neck.

"Not even a little."

"Liar."

He nips my earlobe hard enough to make me yip. My pussy clenches and I swear I'm so wet it's leaking out of me. Sliding his arm under my belly, Dmitri pulls up, so I'm arched and more open for him.

"I didn't miss you either," he growls along my sensitive skin. "Not when I jerked off at the image of you coming, not when I stood watch outside your house all fucking afternoon, and not even when I saw you blocked my way in through the back." He presses his dick against my pussy, sliding in so easily it's like my body's trying to swallow him whole.

And at this angle, he's so fucking deep I can't think straight.

Dmitri groans behind me, his thick arms

bracketing my head, trembling slightly. "Ffffuck." He keeps his thrust slow and deep. It's torture. "I've been dying to get inside you."

Scratch that.

It's amazing.

Something about a man like Dmitri, who can probably get any woman he wants, saying what he just did to me sends my lust into high gear. I clench around his dick, making him moan.

"Christ," he hisses. "Do that again."

I don't give him what he wants. Instead, I turn my head and bite his forearm. Hard. So hard I break his skin.

Dmitri rattles apart, roaring with a release that has my eyes crossing with pleasure. I didn't even come, and I don't care. The only thing hotter than a man dying to get inside you is for him to lose his mind the instant he gets what he wants.

He pulls out and quickly releases the belt around my wrists. I'm out of breath and haven't done anything but lie here and take a glorious dickdown. Tapping my thigh, he signals for me to roll over and I spread my legs wide so he can have easy access to whatever he wants next.

"Eyes on me." He slides down to lick my pussy and shoves two fingers inside me and hits my g-spot. Groaning, I keep my gaze locked on his, even if it's hard to see in the dark and I want nothing more than to close my eyes and let myself go.

But this connection we seem to have built is something I've never had before and is worth more to me than a release. I've always detached during sex because it either wasn't that good, or it was disgustingly miserable. Dmitri makes everything so much better.

I wish we had the lights on so I could see how hot he looks between my thighs. Right now, he's more like a shadow. A deliciously big, bad shadow.

I grip the bedding, my belly heating with a coil that tightens, tightens, tightens…

Clamping my thighs around his head, I hold his face against my pussy with both hands and gyrate against his mouth, coming hard enough to make my ears ring.

D hooks his arms under my legs and keeps tongue-fucking me long after I've let go and melted into a puddle on my bed. He makes me come two more times. The last one makes me cry because I can't handle how sensitive I suddenly am.

I can't stand that I'm letting him do this.

I can't stand myself.

"I can't feel my legs."

"Good." He rides up my body, laying hot kisses all over my sweaty skin until he finally reaches my mouth. "Now you won't be able to walk away from me so easily this time."

I shouldn't walk away from him. I should *run*.

Holding Dmitri against me, my mind swirls with ways to get out of this mess. To survive it. I need to look out for Addie and myself, but my instincts scream for me to look out for Dmitri too.

"What's the worst thing you've ever done?" I suddenly ask.

Dmitri lifts up and I can see his pearly white teeth in the darkness when he answers with, "You really want to know?"

I nod.

"I cried in front of my mother."

That's... not at all what I was expecting him to say.

But I've hit a nerve because he pulls away from me and there's a chill between us now. Dmitri sighs heavily and turns on the lamp by my bed and I blink against the sudden brightness of it.

"What the *fuck*?" Dmitri's tone is so harsh it makes me flinch. He's on me in a flash and my fight-or-flight response goes haywire. I freeze. "Daelyn, your throat."

I reach up, having no clue why he's looking at me with such terror. "What's wrong with it?"

His gaze goes to my hand. My bandaged hand.

That's holding my bruised throat.

Annnnd now he's seeing my broken blood-vessel eyes because the light is shining on me.

He grips the side of his head and steps back. "That's why you left. I went too far... I..." He doubles over and screams, "*Fuck*!"

"Dmitri—"

"Stay back." He puts his hand up like a shield to hold me off. "Seriously. Stay back from me, Daelyn. I don't want to hurt you again."

The crack in his voice has me scrambling off the bed to make this right. "Dmitri, it's fine."

"*Nothing* about this is fine." He grabs his clothing from the floor. "I'm leaving. I will not come to you again. It's over."

No. No, no, no, no.

"I'm so sorry, Daelyn. There's no excuse to have done that to you. I don't even remember when I could have—"

"It wasn't from you," I blurt out.

He goes so still I think he's a second away from

exploding. "What?"

It's too late to take it back now. And honestly, I don't want to lie to Dmitri. Of all the things I could let slide in my miserable life, Dmitri believing he hurt me when he absolutely didn't will not be one of them.

"It wasn't from you." My shoulders droop because I've just dug my grave deeper by admitting that.

"Who did it then?" Dmitri's tone is level. Too calm. "*Who*, Daelyn?"

"It's no one."

"Bullshit." He storms over to me and cups my face. "Give me a name."

Slipping away from him, I shake my head. "It's no one."

I'm not giving up Kaleb's name. Dmitri can glower all he wants, but I'm not giving him Kaleb's goddamn name. I'm too scared Dmitri will go after him and what will happen then?

In a desperate attempt to tell him something, I count on my fingers. *One.* "I'm a bad person." *Two.* "I was sent to ruin you." *Three.* "I like desserts."

His eyes widen.

Message received.

Chapter 25

Dmitri

I'm at a loss for words. I can honestly say that's never happened to me before. Daelyn just gave me two truths and a lie, and I know *exactly* what the lie is. She told me the other night that she hates desserts.

She's a bad person. She was sent to ruin me.

Daelyn succeeded in her mission because this cannot get any worse. And when I find out who's hurt her, I'm going to kill them.

Instead of walking out the door, I'm closing the space between us and crouching down so she sits taller than me. I want her to feel like she's got some power here, and I'll shrink myself to seem smaller if it'll help.

No words are said. She won't even look at me. It gives me a chance to really examine Daelyn and work shit out in my head. The little veins around her eyes are broken. Either she's cried or screamed too hard. There's also a blood vessel in her right eye that's busted, bleeding red towards her iris. Could have been caused by lack of oxygen or strenuous activity. Vomiting too hard can sometimes do that. Or asphyxiation. Which definitely relates to the handprint around her throat.

I close my eyes and count to ten. The fury flooding my system will not get an outlet here, so I need to control it for Daelyn's sake. The last thing I want to do is go off the rails and destroy her room in a fit of rage, because it'll only terrify her more. She's been through enough as it is.

There's a bandage on her finger and another on her arm.

I can't believe I was so lust-crazy for her when I came inside that I hadn't noticed those things. Even as I wrapped a belt around her wrists and fucked her from behind. Dark room be damned, I can't blame the lighting for this unforgivable mistake. I was too focused on getting my dick wet to notice her well-being before taking what I craved. That I've become a mindless monster is reason enough to walk away and never see this woman again.

Except that's not happening. From this night forward, I'm keeping her with me. If Daelyn won't tell me the name of the walking dead man who hurt her, I'll drag it out of her another way, because for her to get those marks means she went against orders somehow. They've used cruelty and pain to force her back in line. They tried to hurt and scare her.

I'm a bad person. I do bad things. She said those things the other day with guilt pouring from each word.

And she's protecting the monster that's sent her to ruin me.

I can't be mad about it, because I've protected enough monsters too and I know how sharp that double-edged sword feels…

"Dmitri, come eat," Mom orders from the other side of the door.

I can't move from toilet. "I'll be out in a minute."

I didn't hear her come home. How long have I even

been sitting in this bathroom?

The news I got today has me operating in a fog. One I need to get out of before my next fight. Swiping my tears away, I stand up and roll my shoulders back.

And cry all over again.

Fuck.

Fuck, fuck, fuck!

Rage controls me, and I throw my fist out, busting the vanity mirror over the sink. My knuckles sting. I use the pain to focus.

Splashing cold water on my face, I get my act together and finally open the door. Only when I see my mother standing in front of the freezer with a bottle of vodka in her hand, I lose my shit all over again.

"The fuck are you doing?" I never talk to my mom like this. But I'm mad. I'm mad and sad and scared. Miss Ashley is going to die of cancer. The only mom I've ever had. The sweetest woman in the whole wide world is refusing treatment and is going to die.

Why couldn't it have been Anya instead?

My gaze drags down to her round belly.

That's why.

Because God is cruel and gives rewards to devils while punishing angels.

"Dmitri," Mom chides, putting the bottle behind her back like I can't see it. "Why are you crying?"

"Why is there vodka in your hand, Mom?" My chin trembles because I have too many feelings slamming into me at once. I don't know how to control them. "Answer me!"

"Because I was moving it out of my way to reach the ice tray." Her hand rests protectively over her belly, but the other still holds the bottle behind her back. "Why are you crying?" she asks again.

Maybe I'm delusional, but it sounds like she genuinely cares. And I need someone to talk to about this, so I fall for it. "Miss Ashley is going to die of cancer."

Her eyebrows pinch. "Who?"

"My friend's mom."

In all this time, I've never told either of my parents my best friend's names. They've never come over when my parents were home, and I've never ever talked about Miss Ashley. Why share the only ounce of happiness I have in my dark world with two parents who don't give a shit about me?

It's clear that not even my dad cares anymore. He spends more time arguing with my mother than he does fighting in the ring. He doesn't come to any of my fights. He doesn't come home for dinner half the time anymore either.

"Oh well, why would you cry about that? She's not your mother."

My vision hazes red. "What?"

"You always were a crybaby," *she huffs.* "No matter how much I've tried to harden you, you're just like your father. Too soft. Too weak."

I'm on her in a blink, getting in her face so fast she doesn't have time to back up. "Fuck. You." *Hot tears flood my vision.* "Fuck you!"

"You do not disrespect me like that!" *Mom lifts the bottle of vodka and cracks me over the head with it.* "You do not cry over another woman!" *She hits me with it again and I fall onto the floor, blood pouring from my head.* "I am your mother!" *She screams like a deranged banshee.* "I am your fucking mother,* not her!"

I want to get her off me, but I'm too scared I'll hurt the baby if I push her back.

Screaming and crying, the heels of my combat boots scrape the carpet as I try to slide away while she sits on top of me, scratching and clawing, beating on me.

"Anya!"

We both freeze and look over to see my dad standing at the front door.

He storms over and tears her off me. She screams and kicks when he hauls her over to the couch. "What is wrong with you?"

She doesn't say a word.

Next, Dad turns to me. "Jesus fucking Christ, what the hell happened in here?"

He must be truly blind and stupid if he can't figure this out. Anger has me grinding my molars. "Look with your goddamn eyes for once."

Tearing off my shirt, I show him what he's failed to acknowledge for far too long.

And the worst part is...

My dad's eyes go wide and all the color drains from his face because he really never saw the signs that I've been abused for the better part of ten motherfucking years.

I turn around so he can get a good look at my destroyed back. All the cuts she's made with knives. All the burn marks. All the scars bruises can't hide to remind me exactly who and what my mother is.

Mom has never hit me above the neck or below the belt until today. She always aims at the places I can easily cover with clothes.

"You did this to him?" *Dad's voice is dead calm.* "Anya. Did you do this to my son?"

Mom shrugs with no remorse. "He's mine as much as he is yours."

Dad swipes his mouth with a shaky hand.

Our gazes meet and I hope he sees all the hate I have for him. All the resentment. All the pain. I hope it hurts to know he's failed me.

And even as I stand raw, exposed, and bleeding from a split skull, I only feel sadness for someone I'm not even related to. Miss Ashley. *It's so surreal, I can't grasp why*

I'm focusing on her when I can't do anything to make her better. Then again, I can't do anything to make my home life better either. I'm stuck in this Hell until I'm eighteen and can move out.

Then I'll never look back…

"Come on." I pull Daelyn up off the bed. "Pack a bag and come with me."

"What? No, I…"

"You what? Want to destroy my life? Do it. I'd love to see you try." I pull out the blade from my back pocket and flip it open. "Go ahead," I say, handing it to her.

She pales and won't take my knife. "Dmitri, no."

"Why not?" I must be certifiable at this point. "Here. I'll help." I hold the tip of my knife to my heart, piercing the skin easily. "Just push it."

I won't beg her to twist it, too. One can only hope for so much.

"Stop!" she cries. "I'm not going to do this!"

"Why not, Daelyn?"

"Because I don't want to hurt you!" she screams at me. "And I can't tell you anything more because I don't want anyone to fucking *die*, okay?"

She starts hyperventilating and backing away from me, only she can't get far because the bed is in the way.

Jesus. What am I doing?

Closing the knife, I shove it into her hand and curl her fingers around it. "Then keep it and shove it into the one that's got power over you."

She shakes her head. "It's not that easy."

"I assure you it is. I'll do it for you if you just

give me his name."

"It's more complicated than you think."

"I can't help if you won't tell me more."

"I can't!" she yells.

How did my life blow up like this?

Running a hand over my face, I'm still naked and obsessing over a woman who's just admitted she's here to "ruin" me, and my first line of defense was to let her drive a knife through my heart.

I would have let her kill me. Sounds crazy, but I would have.

I've played with death for a long time, and it's time to end the game. I'm sick of feeling the way I do. I'm tired of being lonely. I loathe my body. I'm terrified of what I'll do, even accidentally, to someone if I lose control. I'm done trying to find some semblance of joy where there is none. I want this to be over. I want to not feel anything anymore.

I want to tap out.

I need to surrender.

The realization that I've finally lost my will to fight has my knees buckling.

Chapter 26

Daelyn

When Dmitri collapses like a house of cards on my floor, my fate sets into motion.

"Teach me to fight." I drop to my knees in front of him. "Teach me to defend myself so I can get out of my mess."

His far-off gaze slowly focuses on me. "What?" he croaks.

"Teach me to fight," I repeat, clutching his shoulders. "*Please*, Dmitri. I'm tired of being the punching bag."

A sigh blows out of him, and he glances away.

He's not going to do it. Shame and guilt land heavy on my chest, making it hard to breathe because I've single handedly knocked this man to rock bottom. This mission started so easily. All I was supposed to do was fuck him the night of the fight. Spread my legs and let him rail me.

But in true Kaleb fashion, his simple job grew until it got too big to control.

Because I do *not* have control over this. Not really. Not without jeopardizing my life and inevitably Addie's, too.

I know how to shoot a gun. I know how to take a punch. I know how to detach and how to live in fear while pretending I'm brave. Kaleb taught me all of that. None of it has helped me.

"Please, Dmitri." His taut muscles are hard

under my sweaty hands. There's a terrible favor on the tip of my tongue, one I have absolutely no right to ask for, so I keep it inside because I can't ask him to save me.

I know he wants the name of my abuser, but I can't give it to him. My brain's hardwired to protect the guy who's been in my life too long. Kaleb might be a monster, but he's also been the only person who's never abandoned me. *Everything I've done is only to help you*, he'd say. He gaslights and stonewalls all the time, but I still don't always see it when he does. My brain's too muddled, too stuck in the fear of retaliation to examine his actions closer until it's too late.

This is my only chance to change that.

"I need to learn to fight, or to at least hit where it counts." I'll never be strong enough to take Kaleb down, but if I can land a punch that will knock him down a few pegs, it'll give me hope. I'd rather go down fighting than lay like a dog for him to kick.

I've tried online self-defense videos, but it's not the same as having a real partner. And I can't go to in-person classes because it'll raise a flag for Kaleb. He won't like it and will show me that by giving me his own lesson.

Trust me. Been there, done that.

"Please, Dmitri."

Why won't he look at me?

Because I just fucked him and then fucked *him. He owes me nothing*, I remind myself.

"I'll do it on one condition…" Dmitri reluctantly looks over at me with a coldness that makes me shiver. "I want to be there when you go after him."

Go after him? I'm not going after Kaleb. I just need to hold my ground for once when he comes after me. Because that's what will happen now. I will not let him hurt Dmitri any more than he already has. But finding a way around giving Kaleb more information about D is going to be hard. I just have to remember that I hold the power here. Kaleb has nothing on Dmitri if I keep my mouth shut.

"I'll protect you as much as I can." My whispered promise makes my confidence shift. I mean what I say. Here's hoping I can deliver with action.

"I don't need you to protect me, Daelyn. Just give me his name and I'll handle it on my own."

"I told you, it's not that simple."

"Life and death are always that simple. You either live, or you die."

Imagining Kaleb dead rips me in half. His dying would solve all my problems, but I can't imagine my life without him. I don't want this to get that far.

Is this what Stockholm syndrome is like? Because Kaleb might not have kidnapped me, but he sure as shit keeps me locked away for his own devices and I depend on him. Lean on him. Use him as a brace and safety net when I'm struggling.

It's got to stop. I can't go on living a life where the most toxic, dangerous, deranged man on the street is somehow, in my warped brain, the hidden hero who just happens to do very bad things and has a temper that's landed me in the hospital more than once.

I don't want to find the bigger, badder monster to save me. I want to save myself, and that starts with fighting back.

"Tell me his name," Dmitri begs again. "Don't protect him."

My silence is answer enough. I will not give him

Kaleb's name.

I'm still trying to figure out why Kaleb hasn't just gone after Dmitri himself. If he wants to ruin his life, fuck him over in every way possible, he's got the means to do it. Why send me instead? It makes no sense.

"I can't give you his name," I say again. "And I completely understand if you tell me no." My hope of learning from a skilled fighter starts to vanish like fog in the morning sun. "It's shitty of me to even ask, considering why I'm... why I was sent to you to begin with. You need to leave and never come back here, Dmitri."

He flinches at my words like they hurt to hear. "Firefly, I'm not leaving without you." He rests his hand on my leg. "We're in this together now. Understand me?"

Too many emotions hit me at once. Relief, fear, guilt, anger, sadness.

"Please understand..." I say with a trembling voice, "I'm not doing this for me. If that was the case, I'd just let him kill me and be done with it. But there's someone in my life that I *cannot* let him touch. And that means I'll do anything to get us out of the hole I'm in with him."

Dmitri's face softens even more. "Who?"

I can at least give him this much. "Addie. She's like a sister to me. There's nothing I will not do for her."

"She's the one who lives here with you?"

I nod. "I've been doing all I can to get out of this position, and you were supposed to be my last job." A choking sob bubbles out of me because I'm a horrible person to have done this and I'm furious I let Kaleb use my weaknesses to get me to this point.

"Okay," Dmitri says stiffly. Then he takes my hand and runs his thumb over the burn scar on my wrist as if he's silently letting me know he's putting two and two together. "I'll help you get your power back."

Chapter 27

Dmitri

Without having years to train Daelyn, I can't teach her to fight like I do, but a few good defense moves will at least buy her time until I can deliver the final blow.

Which is exactly what I plan to do.

You need to leave and never come back here, she'd said. Like that's going to fucking happen? I can't walk away from this woman. I couldn't before, and I damn sure won't after today. "Pack a bag."

"What?"

"You're going to stay with me. Addie is, too."

Daelyn shakes her head. "No."

"I'm not asking."

It's shitty to not give her a choice, but I refuse to let her deny what's right and practical. She and Addie are in danger. I can protect them both on my turf. "Tell Addie to get packing."

"She's not here." Daelyn's cheeks get a little splotchy. "She's away for the weekend and I don't have much time left either."

My heart slows to a stop. "How long do you have?"

"Until next Friday."

Wow. Didn't realize ruining my entire life came with a goddamn deadline. Wonder what's supposed to happen next Friday? I'll keep my questions limited for now. Daelyn's being selective and cautious with what she's willing to give me and the more I push, the less she's likely to share.

"I can't train you in a week, Dae."

"I know." She won't look at me. "But anything is better than nothing, right?"

Jesus Christ, why can't she just say his goddamn name?

The angel on my shoulder pokes my conscience. *Like you told your dad about your mom?*

Yeah, you kept that shit from him for a decade, asshole. Then look what happened, the Devil chimes in.

The day my father finally learned about everything, he left the house staggering like a zombie. I tried to follow him, but fell unconscious down the street, in a pile of vomit, thanks to the concussion my mom gave me with the vodka bottle.

I wasn't able to stop my dad from going into a blind rage.

He apparently stumbled through town, into a bar, and…

Beat a man to death.

The guy's name was Brent Calloway. He was a drug dealer on the south side who had a rap sheet a mile long. But my dad didn't know that. He just swung his fists at the first man his fury focused on and never stopped. Not even after Brent's face collapsed into pulp. No one tried to stop my father, either. Maybe they were too scared, or maybe they were grateful to have one more rat off the street. Who knows. My dad finally snapped out of it and climbed off the dead guy. Then he ordered a drink at the bar, called the cops, and turned himself in.

So, I know *exactly* how far rock bottom can take you.

If I can save Daelyn from anything close to that level of misery, I'll do it, even if it means treading carefully and scraping information out of her in other ways. I can't begrudge her from protecting this guy. She must have her reasons, whether they're logical or not doesn't matter, because she's the one who will suffer if things go south. Her and this chick named Addie.

I can handle anything that comes my way, I just don't want them caught in the crossfire when it comes to blows with my mystery enemy.

Who the fuck is this person coming after me?

Honestly, if I made a list of people who'd love to fuck up my life, I'd probably run out of ink. Lots of folks hold grudges. It's one more reason I keep my circle small and stay on my turf. My first reaction is suspecting a club member. As a Dom, I've pleasured plenty of people in those rooms, and some have very jealous other halves, but I can't imagine any of them would go this far. They're too high in society to fuck around and find out with me. They're too weak.

Which means it's someone lower. My long-awaited return to the Scrapyard may have opened the door for past fighters to come at me for revenge. Not everyone is a graceful loser. Your body isn't the only thing that gets busted in the cage. Your pride and ego take a beating too. I've heard about opponents retaliating but haven't had it happen to me before. Mostly because I've never given anyone a chance to try.

I live in a highly secure sex club. No one knows my full name. I don't carry an I.D. Hell, I don't even have social media. No one can find dirt on me because all my dealings are in the Monarch Club, where NDAs are signed in advance, or in the fight ring, where no one wants their identities known because the shit we do is illegal and no one's trying to get caught or have our fun spoiled.

Silas is the only one who knows all our true names, and he's so good at keeping secrets, nothing could crack him.

Bookies have tried.

Cops have tried.

Competition has tried.

He's also excellent at covering his tracks because he makes the most money from the fights he puts together. The man has serious pull and respect in all corners of this dark world and knows how to get rid of all evidence.

I often think about how life could have been different if my dad had gone to the cage that day instead of a bar. For a price, Silas would have covered the crime for him, and he wouldn't have gone to jail. But knowing my father, he would have felt too guilty for taking a man's life and turned himself in, anyway.

After my dad went away to prison, my mom left, and I was on my own. Ryker was dealing with his mom, and Vault and Knox had their own shit, so staying with any of them wasn't something I wanted to try. I stayed with Silas often, and he converted an old office on the second floor into a bedroom for me at the Scrapyard. Looking back, I guess you could say it was my first playroom. My first taste of freedom. We grew close, but never enough for him to tell me how to pull off what he could. Silas always said the less I knew, the safer I was.

Daelyn's doing the same thing now.

"I have to be back by Sunday," she claims,

standing up. "Addie comes home then, and I need to go back to our normal life. I don't want her to stay here alone, even for a night, and she can't be at the club."

That catches me off guard. I don't understand why Addie can't be at the club if it's safe there. But I'm going to follow Daelyn's lead for now because she needs this power more than me. I'm not happy about it, but I'll take what I can get, and give what I can to Daelyn in the meantime.

I think on some primal level, my instincts have scrambled. I want to protect her, but there's also a feral part of me that wants to possess her. If she's mine, no one will ever touch her again.

And make no motherfucking mistake…

Daelyn. Is. Mine.

…

Daelyn packs a bag so fast, it's like she's expecting her house to explode in t minus ten seconds. "There's another problem," she says, stuffing underwear inside her duffel. "He tracks my location on my cell. If I turn it off, he'll—"

"I see what he'll do," I growl, glancing at her throat.

Her cheeks blaze red. "I don't want him to know where you live or about the Monarch Club."

I appreciate her attempt to protect me, but it's a forgone conclusion. "I live at the Monarch Club." That takes her by surprise. "And it's fine if he sees you're there. No one can get in without being vetted, so there's no risk of someone slipping in who shouldn't be there."

"I got in," she counters, making it clear she

doesn't belong at the club.

"I fucking *vouched* for you." Does my tone sound harsh? Yeah. Do I care? No. I'm pissed the connection I thought we had, that felt so fucking real, was only an act. She's done all this not because she was interested in me, but on behalf of someone who forced her to do it.

But what should I expect? That some woman was going to drop into my life and be *the one*? That shit only happens in the books Knox reads. And for Ryker, apparently, because he's got Tara now.

This sucks. I thought I'd found a flicker of light in my darkness. It's why I've been calling her Firefly.

Damn, my head hurts.

"Let him see where you are. He'll think you're doing your job." Again, my voice is harsher than normal. "But you can't have your cell in the club. It goes back into the security center we have in the lobby."

"I need to be able to check in with Addie."

"You can call her from my phone."

Daelyn shakes her head. "She can't be involved. That includes having your cell number on hers. I don't want to explain or lie to her about why I'm not using my phone to call her."

She's either being way too paranoid or way too protective. The woman is living with Daelyn for Christ's sake, so Addie's semi-involved already, whether they realize it or not. The way Daelyn's acting, however, has me suddenly curious about Addie's age.

"I'll make sure you can use your cell during off hours at the club." It's a dick move. I could let her keep her cell in my room in the basement, since we'll be training down there, but I also want a goddamn power card here. If it's her cell phone, so be it. I need ways to make Daelyn give me more information and holding her cell phone for ransom may help with that. "Ready?"

She hoists her duffel bag over her shoulder and stops in front of me. "I'm so sorry, Dmitri."

I clench my molars and don't respond.

She *should* be sorry, but also, I don't blame her for what she's done. We've all been stuck between a rock and a hard place before. Doing what's right or what's easy aren't always options. And as she looks up at me with blood vessels busted in her face and a handprint bruised across her delicate throat, I know one thing is the truth between us: She protected me. That's how she earned those marks.

We make it back to the Monarch Club in no time, and I've used the bike ride to settle my nerves and come up with a new game plan. Parking in the back, I swipe my key card and hold the door for her. She handed over her phone before we even left her house.

Daelyn follows me through the club, passing Sophie and a guy she's got on a leash. I don't say a word and keep my focus on the doors that lead to my dungeon. When we get there, I let Daelyn inside first.

Her eyes sail around the nearly empty room. My cot is against one wall, a punching bag hangs in the center of the room, and there's a rack with all my clothes hanging neatly on the far wall.

"The bathroom's through there," I say, feeling suddenly awkward and ashamed.

I came from nothing. I'm used to nothing. And I've just let the enemy into my sacred space. No one comes down to this forbidden area except for a select few I allow. Yet I just let this little monster in and held the goddamn door for her.

"Put your things down over there and sit on the floor."

Daelyn's brow knits with confusion, but she does as I command.

"I'll be back in ten minutes," I say. "Don't fucking move."

The color drains from her face.

Leaving her alone in my room, unsupervised, is as ridiculous as it is necessary. Lie for a lie, truth for a truth. I'll use every tool in my possession to get her to be real with me. So, I'm being real with her.

Shutting the door, I lock it and head straight for Vault's security room. It's freezing in here because he always wants the equipment cooled down. We've got a lot of high-tech gear in this place.

He doesn't look surprised to see me. "What's up, man?"

"I need you to dig up some information for me." I brace my hands on his desk and let out a long exhale. "Daelyn's paperwork is in the temporary guest folder. Run a background check on her and her roommate, Addie. No last name known. I want to know who their parents are. Their friends. Jobs. Fucking blood type. Whatever you can get me."

Vault sits back, concern hardening his eyes. "What's going on?"

"Just do it, okay?" I turn to leave, but Vault stops me with another question.

"Are you in trouble, D?"

"It's nothing I can't handle."

He stands slowly. "It's not just you I'm worried

about."

Vault's reminding me that I'm bringing danger not just to my bed, but to the club. As if I'm not aware?

"Just get me the information and I'll decide from there." We stare at each other for a long moment, then I add, "I won't let Hell fall over the club. If it comes close to that, I'll leave. I won't put anyone here in the crosshairs. You have my word."

He knows I don't break promises.

But I *will* break the woman waiting for me in my room.

Chapter 28

Daelyn

Sitting in this dingy, dark room on the concrete floor makes me detach again. I'm so exhausted, so sick and tired of everything and of myself. If Dmitri leaves me here until I decay, I won't mind.

His room smells like him, which makes my body and brain clash because I feel both safe and trapped at the same time. I can't believe he lives down here. I'd call him a liar if it weren't for the rack of clothing hanging across from me. Each piece looks expensive and well taken care of. The blanket at the foot of his cot is also folded nice and neat. There isn't even a spec of dirt or dust bunny on his cold floor.

The punching bag hanging from a chain looks menacing and well-used. How many hours a day does he spend throttling that thing?

Dread seeps in as I realize what I've done. I'm locked in a dangerous man's room, in a basement of a club, with no way out or to call for help.

Suddenly, the door unlocks and swings open. Dmitri carries in a tray of food, though he still looks angry. "Thought you'd be hungry."

I don't move from the floor.

When he looks around as if he's trying to find a place to rest the tray, he blows out a quick sigh and lowers it to the floor in front of me. "I live simply, and I don't eat where I sleep, so I don't have a table or chairs."

But he's not going to let me out of this room, so he's breaking his housekeeping rules and letting me eat on the floor like a pet. I can't tell if I'm insulted or flattered.

My nerves are too shot for me to eat the food he's brought, but I don't want to piss him off by rejecting it. Pulling the lid off the first plate, I stare at a massive pile of hand cut fries.

"Wasn't sure what you'd like, but I know those are okay." He sits on the floor across from me. "The first thing you need to remember about fighting is that you're the hero in the cage, not the villain. You're going against the worst of the worst and can stop at nothing until they surrender."

The fry in my mouth is hard to swallow. "Okay."

"The second part to that is..." His gaze darkens. "We're all bad guys, Daelyn. Some of us are just better at hiding it than others."

I couldn't agree more. "I'm so sorry," I say again.

"Don't apologize for doing something you felt you had no choice of."

His response is more than I deserve. Everything Dmitri's giving me is more than I deserve. Tears spring out of me immediately, and I curl my legs up to hug my knees and tears well in my eyes.

This is awful.

"Fuck, come here." Dmitri shoves the tray of food away and drags me across the floor and into his lap. "Damnit, woman, I can't stand your tears. You've got to stop before I crack."

Fuck, babygirl, I love your tears.

I cry harder.

How can these two men be so opposite and the same all at once? It's driving me crazy. I think I've officially hit my breaking point and that's why my eyes keep leaking. I've never felt so raw and hollow in my life. Rock bottom is a scary place to be. I'm starting to wonder if there's any hope of climbing out of it.

"Can we just start teaching me how to defend myself?"

"After you calm down and eat, baby."

That's more than enough incentive to get my ass into gear. I polish off half the plate of fries and chug some water. I don't have it in me to touch the burger or fruit cup. "Now?"

He swallows hard and nods, unfolding his body and standing up. He's a giant in this space. Holding his hand out for me to take, we clasp hands, and he lifts me to my feet.

We go slow with my first lesson. My movements are sloppy because I'm seriously drained from the past few days, but Dmitri's patient with me.

"Good girl," he says after I block his kick. The smile he gives me shoots life into my heart. "Again."

I repeat the movements over and over. Each time he fake-attacks me and I go through the moves, feeling a little more confident each time. But Kaleb doesn't always punish me with his fists.

"What about when he has a knife?"

Dmitri's balanced on one leg, the other extended over my head, like a martial arts instructor. He slowly brings his foot back down. "A *knife*?"

My immediate instinct is to hide my bandaged arm, which is pointless, but I do it anyway.

"Okay," he says quietly. "Hold this." Calmly pulling out his own blade, he hands it over and shows me three simple ways to disarm him.

I know he's being easy on me, but he's also bigger than Kaleb, so my bravado lets me believe I can do this when the time comes. Maybe I'm being delusional. Or maybe it's the constant encouragement Dmitri keeps giving me. Either way, I can almost see a light flickering at the end of my dark tunnel.

"Again," I say, rejuvenated.

We practice for hours until Dmitri says we're done.

"I'll get mats for tomorrow." He swipes the sweat from his brow. "It's late. You should rest."

I'm too buzzed with adrenaline to rest, but I'm not defying the man who's helping me. I think if Dmitri told me to lick dog shit off his boot, I'd do it.

Anything to get the help I need to free myself from this constant torment.

"I'll sleep outside," he says, going for the door.

"Don't leave."

"My cot's not big enough for both of us."

"Then you take the cot. I'll sleep on the floor." Stepping closer to him, my hands ache to hold his arm and keep him close. "You make me feel safe," I blurt out. "And I know I don't deserve your help, but… please don't leave."

His eyebrows pinch together as he looks at the floor instead of at me. "I'm having a hard time trusting you, Daelyn."

"I understand."

"I'm not staying the night with you. If that's a problem, you can leave."

He's giving me a choice.

"I want to stay." My feelings are hurt, but I respect the boundary he's put between us. "Thank you for helping me."

On that note, he leaves.

But doesn't lock the door this time.

...

Dmitri

The club's finally winding down. It's almost four in the morning, and I'm too restless to sleep. It's too soon to expect Vault to have worked his magic, but I'm hoping there's a chance he's at least gotten started. Entering his office, it takes all of two seconds for that bubble to burst.

Vault is passed out at his desk with an energy drink in his hand. The man works entirely too much. We all do here. And I'm sure he's putting in double time because Ryker's taken me off duty.

After placing the drink can somewhere it won't get knocked over and ruin his equipment, I slip out, clicking the door closed quietly behind me. Guess I'll head into Ryker's office and tell him I'm coming back to work. I can't let my friends pick up the slack when I'm perfectly capable of handling my own responsibilities.

The doorknob doesn't budge when I touch it, and there's the distinct sound of bodies slapping together and Tara's moans on the other side of the locked mahogany door.

Pivoting once again, I head to the penthouse where Sophie usually lingers.

She's blowing out candles and has her shoes kicked off. "Hey you."

Her voice is a balm to my nerves. We've

connected in a lot of ways over the years, and she's become a dear friend of mine. "Got a minute?"

"For you? Always." She sits on the bench used to tie our subs. "What's up?"

I don't even know where to start. "Can you just... rub my back?"

Her features soften. "Sure, D." Sophie hops off the bench and escorts me to the bed while I pull my shirt off. Once I lie face down, she climbs on top of me, and skates her chilled hands along my skin.

We don't speak.

When I get like this, words don't help anyway and I'm not looking for advice. I just need comfort from someone I trust.

I wish it was from Daelyn.

"You ever want to turn back time and have a do over?"

Sophie digs her elbows into my lower back, working out the knots. "God no. I don't want to get my PhD ever again. Once was enough torture."

Fair. Sophie's a rocket scientist. How she has time to juggle the Monarch and still go to her day job is beyond me. The woman never sleeps.

"But..." She pours oil over my back and massages harder. "I guess if I could get a second crack at things, I'd do them the same. Even the awful shit."

"Why?" Wouldn't she want to skip those parts?

"They made me the delectable creature that I am." Her hands glide over my scars while she works out more of my tension. "I like who I am. Part of me was shaped by the bad stuff. Who knows what I would have turned into had my life been all rainbows and popsicles."

God love her.

"What about you?" She nonchalantly traces my triangular shaped scar.

"Sometimes I want to." Turning my head to the side, I sigh. "Sometimes I wish I was just fucking dead."

Her hands pause at my lower back. "Well," she says, moving slower. "I, for one, would be devastated if you weren't around anymore." She massages a little harder. "No one else makes coffee like you. I'd be forced to drink that disgusting mud Ryker makes. Or worse, have to switch to energy drinks like Vault. I swear that shit's got chemicals stronger than rocket fuel in them. His brain's going to melt out of his nose if he isn't careful."

Laughter bubbles out of me. "His brain's practically a computer circuit board. It would take straight acid to melt it."

"You're probably right." She rotates and works on my shoulders next, and her tone goes back to thoughtful and light. "I think it's important to remember that everything happens for a reason. And everyone in your life is there for a reason, too. It's all just to get us one step further on our journey."

"That's… very open-hearted of you."

"I saw it on a social media reel."

What do you know, I'm laughing again.

"Want to talk about the girl you played with the other night?"

I stop laughing. "Why?"

"Oh, I don't know. It's not like you to bring an outsider here. You've never made concessions like that before. She's very beautiful."

"She's very complicated."

"Wouldn't expect her to be any other way."

I try to look over my shoulder at her. "What's that supposed to mean?"

"D, you're not the type to go for a simple woman who will lie down at your feet and suck your toes when told to. You want a challenge. Someone who's a little unhinged. You'd be bored to tears in two seconds flat otherwise."

Sophie knows me too well. "What if I told you she was sent by someone to ruin me?"

"Then I guess the ruining better come with a lot of lube, whips, and a few choice tasers because it would take a lot to knock you down, big guy."

I lean up to look at her. "I'm dead serious, Soph. Someone sent her to come for me."

Her brow furrows with deep concern. "How did you find that out?"

"She told me."

Sophie's expression goes back to impassive, but her tone darkens. "And you trust her enough to believe she's telling the truth?"

That makes me pause. "Yeah," I say, surprising myself. "I do."

"Are you still in contact with her?"

"She's in my bedroom as we speak."

Sophie's brow arches. "Then, like I said, the ruining better come with a lot of lube, whips, and a few choice tasers." The right side of her mouth pulls up.

Lube, whips, tasers... I've got an arsenal in the club to ruin Daelyn with.

And four whole days and nights to do it.

Chapter 29

Daelyn

There aren't any windows in Dmitri's room, so I have no clue what time it is. I crashed on his cot after trying to stay up, silently willing him to come back and be with me. I need comfort, even if I don't deserve it. When he never returned, I curled into his bed and cocooned myself in his blanket.

His door creaks open and he slips in. "You awake yet?" he whispers.

"Yes." Sitting up, rubbing the sleep from my eyes, I immediately look for my cell because it's a habit to check it first thing in the morning. "What time is it?"

"Two in the afternoon."

Oh my God. "I'm so sorry." Leaping out of bed, I get tangled in the blanket and hop on one foot. Shaking myself free, I hurry and fold it nice and neat before fluffing his pillow and lining it up perfectly on the top of his bed. "Let me just—"

"Easy, Daelyn." He grips my shoulders. "Slow down."

"I took your bed. I've invaded your space. I'm a burden. And I—"

He smashes his mouth to mine.

I shove him back. "I haven't even brushed my teeth!"

He chuckles. "Your breath's not that bad."

His expression shows he's lying. "Ugh!" I storm

over to my bag and dig out my toothbrush. What gives? Last night he said he didn't trust me anymore and today he's kissing me first thing and laughing?

The man's got issues.

Flicking the bathroom light on, I scrub my teeth and stare at myself in the mirror. I've seen roadkill that's looked better than me. My eyes are swollen, the bruise on my throat looks ugly, and my face is pale.

Dmitri leans on the doorjamb, his arms crossed over his massive body as he stares at my reflection. "We're going to work on endurance today."

I spit my toothpaste out in the sink. "Okay."

He pulls his t-shirt off and unbuckles his belt. I freeze with the toothbrush hanging out of my mouth and gawk at him. He slips by and starts the shower.

Trying to remain respectful, I force my gaze back to the sink. It doesn't last long. The glass shower door lets me see Dmitri through the reflection in the mirror. Every glorious inch of that man makes my pussy swoon. The room steams. My heart races.

His voice cuts through the foggy silence when he says, "You can come in here if you want."

Is this a trick? Or is it a green light? A little olive branch, if you will.

More like an olive tree trunk by the size of him.

"Umm. Okay." Confused and excited, I strip out of my clothes and step into the shower with Dmitri. Hugging myself, I stand there like I have no clue what to do.

"Turn around." He pulls the showerhead down and sprays my hair, back, ass, and legs. "Face me." He does the same to my front side, then hangs it back up. "Don't have much," he says, pointing at the shelf of shampoo and soap. "But it's all yours."

My throat tightens. "Why are you being nice to me?"

"Do you want me to be mean to you?" Without warning, he pushes me against the tile and leans his body against my back, pinning me.

God help me, but my response is probably not what it should be. The gasp I give. My body melts and eyes flutter. Fuuuuck he's sexy when he's mad at me.

Dmitri caresses my ass. "You've been a bad..." *Smack*! "Bad..." *Smack*! "Bad girl." *Smack*!

My ass stings and legs turn to rubber. "Dmitri."

"Tell me to stop and I will." His hands glide up my wet skin and he kicks my legs wider while collaring my throat with one hand. The other braces against the tile in front of me. "What's your safe word, Daelyn?"

"Crocodile."

I brace for him to thrust inside me and take what he wants.

"I'm going to ruin you," he growls against my ear.

I nod my consent.

His hand doesn't squeeze my throat, but the way it feels on my neck is all I focus on as fear slides into place. He could do anything he wants to me down here. No one will help me. No one knows I'm in this place. If I scream, I doubt anyone will hear it through the thick concrete walls.

Damn if my body doesn't heat up.

He's not going to hurt me. I trust him completely.

"I want inside you," he says in a deep, rumbling voice. "I'll tear you apart to get in there if I have to."

My eyes roll back, and I bite my bottom lip.

He reaches between my legs and feels how ready I am. "So fucking wet. Dirty little slut."

I whimper.

"I'm going to fuck this pussy until it only remembers me." He shoves the tip of his pierced dick inside me. "*Only* me." He pushes in a little more. "Because this cunt in mine until I say otherwise." Dmitri bottoms out, making me gasp for air and rise on my tippytoes to accommodate his size.

"Yes, King."

He mumbles something that sounds like *fuck*, but I honestly can't be sure. He's railing me too hard and between that, my blood pressure spiking, and the rush of water over us, I can't hear clearly.

Our bodies slap together. I think I'm going to shatter.

My head tips back against his chest as he reaches around and rubs my clit. My climax starts crawling towards me, digging its hot nails into my belly and dragging itself towards my pussy.

Dmitri lets go and pushes me forward, so I have to hold the wall while he fucks me.

My orgasm retreats.

He plays with me like this, edging me over and over, until I'm so dizzy with need, I slap the tile in frustration.

He laughs and pulls out, jerking off until his orgasm swirls down the drain between my feet. Then he washes up and opens the shower door to step out. "I told you today's lesson is about endurance."

With that, the motherfucker ghosts me.

...

Dmitri

She's too easy. One quick session in the shower has her entirely riled up. The little monster couldn't get herself off after I left. I heard her try. Poor baby. Look, I may be willing to help her defend herself, but I'm still allowed to have some retaliation. She is, after all, here to fuck my life up.

Except feeling her tight, wet pussy fit so beautifully around my cock is a dance with the devil I should probably hold off on. We didn't use a condom last night or this morning. Daelyn's clean, per my requirements set on rewards with Silas, and I'm clean because I'm a Dom at the Monarch. But raw dogging is not something I do. Ever. Jesus, why do I keep slipping with this woman?

I don't even give a little foreplay with her. My addiction to her body brings out the primal side of me. I can't stop myself from getting inside her as fast as possible. I swear my vision goes white with the first thrust every time. All I want is to mount her, fuck her until she passes out, and then coax her awake so I can do it all over again.

Sophie was right, regular girls bore me. At least Daelyn keeps me on my toes, even if she's bad for me.

My girl comes out of the bathroom looking downright murderous. She thinks she's hiding her frustration behind a stoic expression, but I know the telltale signs of a sub in need. Her wet hair drips on the floor as she storms over to my cot and pulls an outfit from her bag.

If she's a good girl, and does what she's told, maybe I'll give her a reward later. For now, I give Daelyn her cell phone. The instant she sees it, her eyes light up, and she snags it from me.

A few seconds later, she's calling Addie. "Hey you!"

I hear a female's voice from the other end but can't make out what she's saying.

"That sounds so fun! Well, be careful. Don't get eaten by a shark or I'll be so mad at you."

Addie says something else and then Daelyn's phone buzzes in her hand.

"They just came through." Daelyn smiles again. "Okay, love you, babe. Have a blast. I'll call you later, okay?"

She hangs up and looks at the texts, her eyes shining bright, and I swear it looks like a completely different woman. She's happy. Relieved. Content. I don't think I realized that I've not seen her look like this before. Addie did this. Addie made Daelyn's mask fall effortlessly.

Curiosity gets the better of me and I step closer, hoping to catch a glimpse of a photo of the woman who can work such a miracle on Daelyn. Before I get the chance, Daelyn closes the app and locks her screen, handing it back to me. "Thanks."

"You're welcome." I slip the phone into my back pocket. "Time to stretch."

I've laid one of my mats out for her already.

Yanking her wet hair into a low pony, Daelyn gets on the floor and starts warming up. The smile is gone from her sweet face, and her mask is back on. She's bendy, I'll give her that. Once Daelyn's warmed up, we go over the combos I taught her yesterday. She's a little sloppy and slow, which is fine. I don't expect her to be a savant in the ring on day two.

We go at it for three hours before I allow her a

break.

"That felt better." Daelyn wipes the sweat from her brow. "Can we do it again?"

"As many times as it takes for you to feel confident, Firefly."

I've gone back to calling her that nickname. It keeps slipping out and honestly, I don't want to stop. She might be my enemy, but she's still mine.

Daelyn disarms me three more times but gets madder about it instead of happy. "Damnit!" She throws my knife on the ground. Fisting her hair, she walks in circles around me.

Maybe a short break is in order.

"What's the worst thing you've ever done?" I ask, picking up my knife and heading to my mini fridge to grab her a bottle of water.

"What?"

"You asked me, and I told you. Now I want to know yours." I keep my tone level and body disengaged.

She takes a long pull from the bottle, guzzling it down. After wiping her mouth with the back of her hand, she says, "I once had two slices of cake for breakfast when I was told I could only have one."

My anger flares. "Bullshit."

"Bullshit is you saying that crying in front of your mother is the worst thing *you've* ever fucking done."

It takes all I have to not punch a wall. Keeping my hands at my side, I suck in three calming breaths and sit on my cot. "The day I cried in front of her set a series of very bad things into motion directly afterwards."

"How?"

"I was upset about something and broke down in tears and screamed at my mother. She got mad and busted my skull open with a vodka bottle from the freezer. My dad walked in on us fighting and finally learned that she'd been abusing me for years. She was pregnant at the time too, so instead of going after her, he lost his head and took his anger out on someone else. That someone else died and my father went to prison, where he was recently murdered. So yeah, my showing vulnerability to my mother was the worst fucking thing I ever did because it cost me everything."

Daelyn drops her attitude immediately. "Jesus, Dmitri."

"Your turn." Sitting with my elbows on my knees and hands clasped, I keep my tone level and bored. "The suspense is killing me."

"Okay. Here it goes." Daelyn tosses her hands up. "I've done a lot, but the highlights probably include being an accomplice to robberies, a liaison for a drug cartel, facilitating seven hand offs for unregistered guns, I've committed arson by burning down a competitor's barn, and once, when I was eight, I stole a pack of pop rocks from a convenience store."

I don't think she's joking.

"Drug cartel?"

Daelyn nods. "And arson."

"And guns."

"Don't forget the pop rocks." She sighs as if the confession has lifted a weight off her chest. "I'll take full blame for the pop rocks, but the other shit I've done, I didn't have a choice. I mean, I guess I did. It was do it or suffer the consequences." Daelyn shrugs, shaking her head. "I didn't think I could survive too many more consequences."

I want to kill the man who owns her.

"He's got videos of everything," she says quietly. "Every bad deed I've done for him. He'll use it to get Addie taken away from me if I don't…"

"If you don't fuck my life up and ruin me."

"Yes."

Part of me wants to protect her, the other part of me wants to scream. I have no clue how much of what she's saying is even true. It could all be lies, a grand ploy to get me to trust her again. Why else would she admit to all that? One call to the cops with this information, and I could put her in prison. Hell, if the cartel she's involved with finds out she just ran her mouth, it could get her killed. How far down the rabbit hole is this woman?

And how deep am I willing to go with her?

Daelyn drains the rest of the water bottle and tosses it in the trash. "It was a slippery slope. Sometimes I try to pinpoint when the first big mistake was, but they all blur. I can excuse so much of it. He's… very persuasive."

"How old were you when you met him?"

"Twelve."

I'd bet my eyeteeth he's older than her. He groomed her. Brainwashed her. It doesn't make what she's done right, but it gives me a little more ammo. "What's the worst thing he did to you?"

Her brow pinches. "Probably this." She holds her hands out. "Sending me into your life."

Ouch. My heart deflates.

"I should have known better." Daelyn readjusts her ponytail. "After all this time, I should have known he wasn't going to let me off so easy. One fuck and I was supposed to be done. Out. And now…"

My dead heart turns to ash hearing her say all this. But I can't be pissed that she fucked me that first night as a way to get out of her bad situation. I didn't give two shits about her that night. I was a raging beast with a heat-seeking missile between my legs. I wanted to fight, fuck, and blow steam off. I didn't need anything but a warm hole. Still, it hurts on some base level of my black soul that she's only here to fulfill a job.

"Do you regret it?" I tilt my head and look at her again, desperate to read her facial cues and body language.

She blows out a shaky exhale. "No."

I'm not sure how to take that. No, because she likes me, no, because I'm helping her, or no, because she's almost done her mission and will be free of this guy.

Tell me who the fuck he is, goddamnit. Who owns you?

"Come here." I crook my finger at her. She crosses her arms, looking scared. "I'm not going to hurt you, Firefly."

Gulping, she comes a little closer and I grab a small silicone pad from under my pillow. I'd stashed it there while she was in the shower, not sure if I'd use it or not. But the hard work she's putting in calls for a reward.

I strap the pad to my thigh and cock my brow at her.

Daelyn's confusion is adorable. "What is that?"

"A grind pad. Take your shorts off and ride my thigh. You look like you need a release."

Her cheeks redden. "You can't be serious."

"Well, if you don't want a reward…" I start unfastening the strap.

"Wait."

I freeze, clenching my molars to keep from smiling.

"I'm not going to be able to come with that thing, Dmitri."

"Yes, you will." I'll make sure of it.

"If this is another endurance test, I've endured enough already, fuck you very much."

"Shut up and ride."

She slips out of her shorts and straddles my thigh. "I hate you for this."

"Hate me hard enough to cream all over my leg."

Daelyn whimpers as she positions herself against me. Her splotchy cheeks make me believe she's embarrassed, and I don't want shame to spoil the fun we're about to have.

"Take what you need from me." I stiffen as Daelyn clutches my shoulders to support herself while she mounts up. "And keep your eyes on me while you do it."

Daelyn squirms, seeking friction that makes her feel good. Locking eyes with me, she moves back and forth, her cheeks blazing red now. Gyrating against me for a few minutes only increases her frustration.

I pull out my knife and flick the blade open. My girl's eyes widen when she hears it, but she doesn't take them off me. Not even when I run the sharp tip across her chest, circling her hardened nipples. We work carefully with each other, playing a dangerous game.

Fisting the front of her sports bra, I cut it open,

freeing her tits. The swells fall in front of my face, making my mouth water while she rides my leg. I capture one with my mouth, grazing her nipple with my teeth, biting down hard enough to make her gasp. Daelyn's grip on my shoulders tightens, her nails digging into my skin while her speed picks up.

Grabbing a fist full of her hair, I tug it hard enough to make her back bow, which gives me easier access to her tits. She hisses through clenched teeth, her pace speeding up. Pinching one nipple hard, I make her cry out and her thighs shake. She grinds against me faster.

"Tell me who owns you."

Ignoring me, Daelyn closes her eyes.

I pinch her nipple again and twist it. "Eyes on me, Firefly."

Her eyelids fly open, her breaths quickening as she grinds on me harder, faster.

"That's my good girl."

She whimpers, swirling her hips for better friction.

"Tell me who owns you." I want the name of the man who put her in so many dangerous situations. "Say his name, Daelyn." I tuck the blade away but hold the handle against her throat. She's so far gone, chasing her release, that I don't think she notices. "*Say it.*"

"Mmmph." Her body shakes and I can hear the wet noises her pussy makes gliding along the textured pad. My girl is drenched.

"You want to be filled, Daelyn? Stuffed with cock, and stretched around my length until you can't feel anything else?" I shove the knife handle harder against her neck.

Her brows pinch. Eyes get glassy. Her pretty little mouth parts when she starts panting like a dog in heat.

"That's it, slut. Chase your release. Soak my thigh with your cum." I drop the blade on the cot and use both hands to hold her hips, helping her move faster on me. She's so fragile in my hands. So powerful. "Come on, baby."

Daelyn trembles so hard I think she's going to rattle apart. And then she stops. "I can't!"

Shoving off me, Daelyn storms over to the wall, and slaps it while she screams.

The girl's gone mad.

Chapter 30

Daelyn

Endurance test, my ass!

I was so close to an orgasm just now from Dmitri's words, his grip, the knife, the bites, the way he made me look at him, the friction of the textured pad on his thick fucking thigh... all to have it still not be enough for me to blow. He did this on purpose just to make me fail.

I hate him.

Slamming my palms against the concrete wall, I throw a complete hissy fit.

"Daelyn." The asshole has the audacity to come near me.

"Fuck you." I shove him back, wanting nothing more than to kick him in the balls, just like he taught me when we were training earlier when he said to always fight dirty if I'm in danger.

I'd put those skills to use right now if I could see straight.

This isn't a simple boohoo-I-want-to-come-and-can't meltdown. I'm seeing red. Unraveling at the seams. All my pieces that were sewn into a Frankenstein have come apart again and I can't pull myself together.

What the hell is wrong with me?

I'm not just confused anymore, I'm straight up stupid. Why did I tell Dmitri about every bad thing I did, and gave him ammo to use against me?

Because I trust him.

Oh hell no. I don't even *know* him. And my track record for picking men to confide in is abominable.

Maybe I told him those things because I'm self-sabotaging? The possibility makes me queasy because the repercussions are huge and would result in the very thing I'm trying to prevent.

"Daelyn." Dmitri grabs my arms and pins them behind my back. "Stop. You're going to break your hands hitting the wall like that."

So what? Punching concrete is better than punching his head. One will hurt me. The other will hurt him.

"I said stop!" He knocks my legs out and takes me to the floor on the mat. "Fucking hell, Dae."

I squirm and snarl under him, no longer certain of what my goal is. He keeps my wrists together in one big hand, his knee pressed against my lower back, and he spanks me once, twice, three times.

Damn me straight to hell, but my groin grinds into the mat and the noise I make is half moan, half sob. This is fucking humiliating.

"Tell me what you want," he says, sounding out of breath.

"I want…" Tears well because I cannot believe I'm acting this way. It's ridiculous. "I want you to fuck me until I black out."

I'm not even sure if that's possible, but, goddamnit, I need relief. I want to forget who I am, why I'm here, and what's at stake. For once, I just want someone to take care of me in the ways I need. A sex-induced coma might help.

"Fuck," Dmitri grunts.

He hauls me over his shoulder and fireman

carries me out of his bedroom.

"What are you doing?"

"Shut the fuck up." He spanks my ass so hard the sting makes my aching pussy clench. "I'm giving you what you want."

My stomach rolls as he takes me out of the basement, up the stairwell, and kicks open another door.

Oh my god. People are going to see me looking like a crazy mess. Embarrassment flares, making my cheeks feel sunburnt.

When I reach around to cover my bare ass with my hands, Dmitri knocks them away. "Let them see what's mine." His long gait brings us quickly into a room and he drops me unceremoniously onto a hard piece of furniture. "Bend over."

My eyes widen with shock as I stare at the long, thin, black leather covered bench. Heart racing, I look under it and see cuffs and a bar with straps. The rest of the room is just as intimidating. There's a huge X against the wall with cuffs at the top and bottom. There are enough riding crops and whips to tame a stampede of stallions hanging on the farthest wall.

Ball gags, dildos, chains… *spikes*.

The bed on the other side of the room has a hefty mahogany stained four-by-four mounted at the foot of it with cuffs and rope attached at the far ends of the wood.

Dmitri brings my attention back to him when he says, "I'm going to tie you down and fuck the frustration out of you."

His desire slowly penetrates my hazy, raged-filled brain. I blink. Nod. "Yes, please."

"Do you want the bench or the bed?"

I get a choice? "Both."

His chuckle makes the hair on my arms stand on end. "Let's start on the bed."

Making my way over there, I pass the selection of ball gags, wondering what it would be like to use one.

"Not this time," Dmitri says, as if reading my mind. "I'm gonna need you to use your words today."

I bite my lip and climb onto the bed while my stomach flip-flops. I've never done something like this before.

"What's your safe word?"

"Crocodile."

"Good girl." He stands in front of me in only a pair of gym shorts. When he flashes a smile, my heart sighs. "See the cameras?" Dmitri points up at the ceiling. "There are four in the room. Everything is being watched for our safety, okay?"

"Someone's watching us right now?"

"Always." His gaze intensifies. "Even when the club is closed, surveillance does not stop."

I swallow the lump in my throat. "Can they hear us?"

"Sometimes. If they turn the sound on for that room."

Panic hits my bloodstream.

"These cameras are *not* in my bedroom," he quickly adds, likely knowing my mind just went to the confessions of all the illegal shit I've been caught up in.

I look at one mounted in the far corner. The woman in the lobby told me, when I first arrived here and filled out the forms, that cameras were everywhere because safety is the Monarch's first priority. In a way, I like having the extra caution. Not that I think Dmitri would hurt me, but it's comforting to know I'm not completely alone and at the mercy of someone else.

Even if that's exactly what's about to happen.

"I can say crocodile if I don't like it."

"Absolutely. And the scene will stop immediately."

"Okay." I trust him. Damn my stupidity, but I trust him. I loathe how desperate I am for an escape and that it's turned me into this...

"Face me and spread your arms out wide."

Leaning forward by the foot of the bed, I feel like a criminal with her head on a chopping block while Dmitri goes over to another part of the room for something. Closing my eyes, I calm my racing heart and wait. My head hangs off the edge of the wooden four-by-four and my legs are bent under me, spread for balance.

Dmitri gently cuffs my wrists. "No way out..." He fastens a collar around my neck. "And so many ways in." Squatting down, he kisses me softly and adds, "You can also tap the wood if it's too much."

"Yes, King."

"God damn," he growls, standing up and sliding his shorts off. He kicks them to the side and pumps his length, giving me a great view of the piercing at the tip of his dick. Then he fists my hair. "Open."

My jaw drops, and he guides his cock slowly into my mouth.

"That's my good girl."

He fucks my face like he's got all the time in the world.

Locked in place, I can't escape him. Not that I want to. But what's going to happen when this is over? How is it going to end? What will Kal—

"Fuuuuck," Dmitri hits the back of my throat, making me gag. "Your mouth feels so good on me, Daelyn."

I focus on his words and grunts. My thoughts shift to making him feel good, until it's all I think about.

"You take me so well, baby. Fuuuck yeah."

I suck him harder and find a rhythm we both like.

"You're doing so good, Firefly." He grunts and fucks my face slowly. "But I need your pussy now." Dmitri pulls out and climbs onto the bed. The mattress dips from his weight as he positions himself behind me. I expect him to ram inside me. Take what he wants. Instead, he uses a vibrator on my clit and stuffs two fingers in my pussy. "You're soaked already, and we only just started."

We didn't just start. I've been trying to get myself off since I woke up, damnit. My pussy's so swollen and wet, it was a menace while we trained. And the more needy I got, the sloppier my moves became.

"Fuck me, King." Pressing my cheek against the wood, I feel a calmness settle over me. I'm a whore to want this as badly as I do. And I'm an asshole because I want it from Dmitri, the man I'm here to ruin. "Make it hurt."

I want him to punish me.

He nips and licks down my back, holding the vibrator against my clit. Then he pushes his way inside, robbing me of breath. The man's hung like an ox. And that piercing makes it even more enjoyable.

Keeping his thrusts slow and deep, he fucks me for forever like this. I'm strapped to the wood so I can't see him at all, and the vibrator against my clit is starting to make me numb.

"More," I mumble in a foggy haze. "I need it harder."

Ignoring me, Dmitri maintains his steady pace, making each deep thrust hit my cervix. Hooking his finger through the loop of my collar, he tugs it occasionally, calling me his good girl. His cock is huge. Movements deliberate.

"I want to see you," he growls, finally pulling out. Next thing I know, he's got me uncuffed and flipped onto my back. "Hang on." He shoves a wedge under my hips and then shoves his way back inside. "Eyes on me, Daelyn."

He moves over me like a big, dark wave. The intensity amplifies. I reach up and hold on to the footboard while he picks up speed. "Come for me," he says with a growl, "and I'll make sure you get what you want."

A breath shudders out of me because I'm not sure I can. My head is too mixed up. Being with this man feels too good and wrong at the same time.

Shoving into me harder, faster, he grunts. The vibrator shifts on my clit. My fingers dig into the wood.

"Look at me," he snaps, just as I feel my body coiling. "You break contact, and we *will* start all over again. And I'll go even slower."

I shake my head, silently pleading with him to not do that to me.

While secretly hoping he will.

This man acts like I'm the only creature in the world that exists. He takes his time... savoring, enjoying, pleasuring.

"That's my good girl. You're doing so good, taking what I give you." His brow pinches, gaze hardening. "I'm going to fill this needy pussy with my cum."

"Yes, King." I arch more so he can get deeper. The pain of him hitting my cervix makes my brain short circuit. I love it. "Fuck me like a whore."

He doesn't. He fucks me like I'm a new toy he doesn't want to break yet.

I pinch my nipples while he drives into me. We keep our connection. The room spins. The vibrator turns up to the highest setting. His hips become pistons. My eyes flutter.

"Don't you fucking dare." He lets the vibrator go and grabs my throat. "Stay with me," he barks. "Fucking stay right here with me, Dae. Don't look away."

My body locks.

His rhythm changes.

My release surges through me like lightning, making all my nerve endings fire off at once until the last shocks of my orgasm fade. Dmitri's eyes harden and he pulls out, jerking himself all over my belly and pussy. He grunts like an animal. Beads of sweat drip down his temple and I know it's not because he's over-exerted himself. It's because he worked hard to hold back.

"You good?"

"No." I swipe the hair from my face. "I want more. It wasn't enough."

He doesn't look surprised or insulted. "How

much more do you think you can handle?"

Rising to my knees so I can kiss him, I bite his bottom lip hard enough to make him gasp. "Give me everything you haven't yet, Dmitri."

"You sure you can take it?"

"Only one way to find out."

...

Dmitri's got me strapped to the bench, face down. My arms are cuffed beneath me, and my ankles are attached to a spreader bar. I wheeze with every thrust he makes while my tits smash on the leather bench.

He ruts me like a beast. His hands dig into my waist while he thrusts into me hard. He's smacked my ass so many times, the sting no longer registers. I've come twice, and both had my throat sore from screaming. I'm numb and alive at the same time.

This is what I needed. To surrender wholly to a monster who could tear me in two.

I hope whoever is watching on camera is taking notes. This is how you fuck a woman.

I want Dmitri to take my ass, but it feels too good the way he slams into my pussy to tell him I want something else. My body's a live wire—crackling and zapping. Sweat pours down my temples. My hair sticks to my back and face. I feel sick and dizzy and so happy I could die.

"Tell me who you belong to," he says, slamming into me.

Not a chance. If I say the name, he'll know who has power over me and I'm not about to give him that satisfaction.

Slap! Dmitri spanks my sore ass and rubs away the burn. "Fuck, you look so good with my handprints on you." He spanks me again.

I come on the bench. *Again*.

Choking out a half-sob, half-groan, I grind against the leather like a mindless animal while he rails me. I can't catch my breath. The world's so foggy. I wanted to be fucked into oblivion and Dmitri is delivering.

"I'm gonna fill this pussy up," he warns. "And you're going to take it all. You're going to squeeze and hold me in there. Isn't that right?"

"Yes, King."

He lifts one leg, balancing it next to my ribs, and fucks me so hard my vision goes white. Then he roars with his release, and I feel him jerk inside me, a heat blooming in my core as he unloads.

"Squeeze it," he orders.

I try to remember how to make my body work and clamp around him.

Dmitri hisses between clenched teeth and groans. "That's my good girl."

He pulls out slowly, and I lay like a limp noodle on the bench while he unties me. I'm exhausted. Spent. Boneless. I'm not even sure if I'm still human at this point.

"Up we go," he says, but he carries me over to the St. Andrew's cross instead of the bed like I assumed he would.

Oh my god, we're doing *more*?

"You better hold my cum inside you, Firefly." He lifts one of my arms and fastens it to the cuff. "Or I'll have to strap you back on the bench and fill you up all over again."

My knees almost give out. How does he even have any fluids left?

Lightly chuckling, Dmitri ties my other wrist up and then nudges my legs open. Reaching between my thighs, he runs his fingers along my pussy lips. "So wet." With his eyebrow arched, his tone deepens. "Is that you or me that's got you drenched?" He shoves his finger into his mouth, tasting it. "Mmmm. That's you."

I sag against the restraints.

"You're so beautiful when you're freshly fucked." Dmitri nips my neck and runs his hands all over my body. The contrast of gentle and rough, sweet and savage, does things to me.

"You're doing so well for me, Daelyn. Can you keep going?"

Yes. No. Maybe so. I nod. "Mmmph."

"Use your words."

"Yes, King." I don't even sound like me anymore.

"Good girl." He leaves me strapped and stranded while he plucks a few toys from the wall. I don't even care what they are, I just want to keep going until I collapse.

"Eyes on me," he says, suddenly in front of me again. "Let me see those ocean eyes, baby."

I flutter them open, swaying against the cross. My eyelids feel so heavy, and my legs are rubber.

He drags a riding crop along the sides of my breasts, tapping them with a sharp but light crack. My nipples harden instantly.

"Let's see if I'm still inside you." He shoves a finger between my pussy lips, and my hips buck against his palm, chasing friction already. "So.

Fucking. Needy."

"Yes, King." I don't care if it makes me pathetic. I am needy. I need Dmitri.

"Will you tell me who owns you now?"

Biting my lip, I shake my head. I want to be mad at him for constantly asking, but part of me knows that's why he's torturing me like this, and I won't tell him to stop because it feels so goddamn good.

He shoves two fingers inside my pussy and hits my g-spot. I groan, my head flopping back against the cross. The diabolical man drags me so close to the edge of another orgasm, only to deny me at the last possible second.

I scream and shake against the restraints.

I whimper.

I beg.

"Keep me inside you," he growls against my cheek.

Then he starts the process all over. Slapping my tits and clit with the crop. Biting my nipples. Hitting my g-spot with his thick fingers. And denies my orgasm again when I won't give him the name he thinks he needs to hear.

I'm so out of it, I almost slip with his third try.

But when Dmitri stuffs a vibrating butt plug in my ass, and gives me a nice hand necklace, I start cracking. The fissures of my barriers crumble to the ground between us. He mildly taps my clit over and over and over with the riding crop, so fast and precise, it makes my eyes cross.

"Please," I wheeze, my head falling forward. "I can't stand it anymore."

"If you want to stop, say your safe word."

I don't want to stop. I need to come.

"Give me what I want, and I'll give you want you want, Daelyn." He hooks his fingers against my inner walls, driving my lust up the charts. "Come on baby, say it."

"Say what?" I cry out.

"Who owns you? Say his motherfucking name." He drives into me harder, faster. Throwing the riding crop on the ground, he uses his now free hand to pinch my nipple while he bites on my neck.

I groan loudly, pulling on my cuffs, desperate to touch him.

"Better keep me inside you," he warns. "Or I will stuff this pussy with my cock and fuck you until you taste my cum on your goddamn tongue."

I explode.

The orgasm he's edged me towards finally rips out of me with his name on it.

"Dmitri!" I scream, convulsing around his fingers, my body thrashing against the cross. "His fucking name…" I sob, "is…" Liquid gushes from my cunt and my thighs shake uncontrollably. "*Dmitri.*"

That's the last thing I say before passing out.

Chapter 31

Dmitri

I think I broke her.

Scratch that. I *know* I broke her.

I asked Daelyn for the name of the man who owns her, and at her weakest, most desperate, vulnerable, rawest moment…

She said *my* name.

Hell, she didn't just say it. She fucking screamed it.

I'm not gullible enough to believe she meant I owned her. It was a fluke. Like I said, I broke her. Her brain no worky no more. Neither does her body, for that matter.

Grinding my molars, I carefully free her from the cross and catch her as she collapses against me. Fear and adrenaline have been coursing through her system for hours, along with enough endorphins to knock out an elephant. I pushed her right over the edge today, and she screamed *my* name at the end.

She's falling for you, sighed the angel on my shoulder.

Good, use that to your advantage, tipped the devil on my other side.

Cautiously placing her in the tub, I get water running and dump a bunch of bath salts in. Cocooning her between my legs, keeping her close to my chest, I hold her as the tub fills. Her body's been through a lot. Not just with me, but with whoever owns her.

Holding her hand, I lace our fingers together and study the burn scar on her wrist. It's ugly. The thought of someone bringing Daelyn pain, branding her like she's cattle, has me seeing red.

Squeezing my eyes shut, I count to ten and relax. She's safe with me. Always will be.

To make sure I don't add to her misery, I massage the parts of her I can reach. Rough sex can bring on some serious cramps afterwards, and if I can minimize them, I will.

Her body fits so perfectly with mine. So soft. So beautiful. So real. I think that's what I'm attracted to most about her. I'm not a fantasy for Daelyn like I am for the members of the Monarch. I'm an equal. She's a fighter, like me. She endures, like me. She hurts, like me.

When I make it to the joining of her thighs, I gently caress her pussy, feeling the slickness there as my cum finally leaks out of her. My girl lasted exactly seven hours and thirteen minutes in that playroom. She took everything I gave her.

I think I'm in love.

No, you're not, you're just in a nice headspace, the Devil says, poking my heart with his pitchfork.

Mmmm but it's so nice to be here finally. It's been a while, says the dipshit angel floating away on a cloud.

Ever since I was a kid, I always imagined having these two angels playing tug of war with my conscience. It makes me stay humble and aware.

"As long as I draw breath, I'll never let anything bad happen to you," I whisper against Daelyn's ear.

She's still out cold.

Keeping her against my chest, I cup my hands and pour warm water down her exposed skin. Then I snag a washcloth from the little basket to my right and use it to gently wash her face. Man, she's got a lot of hair. It's tangled and damp and sticking to everything. Gathering as much as I can in this position, I try to twist it, so it'll stay up. The whole knot unravels the instant I let it go and all her good smelling hair falls into my face.

Some of it tickles my nose and I sneeze.

We stay in the tub where I keep reheating the washcloth I've placed across her tits until I think the bath salts have done all they're going to do for her. Getting out is tricky, but I manage.

"Daelyn," I say, trying to wake her.

Her head flops back on my shoulder. "Don't go."

Sitting on the edge of the tub with her on my lap, my arm wrapped around her waist to keep her upright, I dry her off. "I'm not going anywhere, but you gotta wake up for me, baby."

"Stop."

I freeze, my brow furrowing. "Am I hurting you?"

"Don't do this."

She's lost me. "Don't do what? I'm just trying to dry you off, Dae."

"Please don't make me do this." Her breaths punch out in short bursts. "Stop, stop, stop!" Daelyn jerks herself upright, her eyes flying open in panic.

I let go immediately, and she slips off my lap and crashes onto the floor. "Oomph!"

Do I touch her or not? "Daelyn."

"I'm okay. I'm okay." She shakes her head, contradicting what she's saying. "I'm okay." My girl looks around like she doesn't know where she is.

"Easy, baby…" I slide onto the floor to be at her level. Nodding my head, I keep my tone soothing. "Breathe, Daelyn. You're safe. It's just me here with you."

Her chin trembles and she looks confused.

"You passed out on the cross. I gave you a bath and massaged your muscles. I was just drying you off."

Daelyn's exhale trembles from her lips. "I'm okay."

No, she's not, but she's going to be as soon as I find out who's terrorized her for so long.

I slowly inch closer. "Can I touch you?"

"I'm fine."

"Alright."

"I'm gonna be okay."

"Yes, you are." Especially if I have anything to do with it.

"I'm safe."

"One hundred percent." God… *damn*. What the fuck kind of monster has a chokehold on her like this?

Daelyn lets out a sigh and tries standing, but her legs wobble and give out. "I think I'm broken."

"Yeah… sorry about that."

"Don't be," she says, trying to stand again. My girl looks like a newborn fawn, all wobbly and frail. "I loved it." Daelyn fumbles with her first step and I catch her. "Jeez, you really know how to break your toys, man."

Her dark humor makes a laugh bubble out of me. "You're not my toy."

"Pity," she says, sighing when I cradle her in my arms and carry her out of the bathroom. "You're the one who owns me. If you won't play with me, who will?"

My heart stops in its tracks, and I freeze midway to the door. "What did you just say?"

She's already fallen asleep in my arms again.

…

I leave Daelyn in my bedroom, tucked in tight on my cot. I can't stay here and watch over her while she sleeps. Not with her last confession swinging fists in my brain.

"You're the one who owns me. If you won't play with me, who will?"

That was probably her subspace talking.

Yeah. Definitely.

So why do I feel like it's more than that? Why am I suddenly willing to do anything to make that true? If Daelyn was mine, and I could play with her whenever I wanted. Worship her day and night. Take care of her. I'd be the luckiest motherfucker in the world if she were mine.

Or the stupidest, considering she belongs to someone else, and is only here to ruin me.

I keep forgetting that crucial part. I've blurred a lot of lines between us. Made some big fuck ups. Am I so desperate for comfort and to belong to someone who might love me for exactly who and what I am that I've run straight into the arms of an enemy?

Yes.

Which is why I'm putting space between us and am currently in the kitchen making a late dinner.

"D, we need to talk."

I pop a grape in my mouth and turn to Ryker. "About?"

Oh fuck. It's not just Ryker. Vault's here too. The hairs on the back of my neck stand up. "What's going on?"

"I think you better sit down," Vault says.

"I think you better tell me what the fuck you two are doing coming at me like this." It makes me feel cornered and caged, and I don't appreciate it.

"I did some digging on your girl."

"Okay." I cross my arms and lean against the stainless-steel counter, giving Vault my full attention. "What did you find?"

"She's been in the foster system since she was seven. She was rehomed several times until she stuck with a family and turned eighteen. Has a degree in—"

"We already went over her AA degree and medical coding job."

Vault glances over at Ryker, then back at me. "She's fostering someone."

"Yeah. Addie."

Ryker's brow digs down. "You know about Addie already?"

I shrug. "Daelyn's gotten into something she's trying to work her way out of. Addie's a big reason for it."

They both look crest fallen. "Do you know who Addie is?"

"No." And I don't care. If she's important to Daelyn, that's all that matters.

Vault steps a little closer. "Addie's been in the foster system since she was two. She landed with Daelyn after her last foster's house burned to the ground."

"Okay." I don't get why they're acting like this

is terrible news. "Daelyn's busting her ass to take care of her." I'm not about to go into the details with these two yet. I'm still gathering my intel.

Vault's tone grows even more serious. "Addie's parents died in a murder suicide."

Ryker looks down. His jaw clenches and body language is too stiff. I don't like it.

"The dad beat the shit out of the mom a lot," Vault says cautiously. "The cops were called to their house often, but no charges were ever pressed."

That's awful. I feel sorry for the woman, but she's not my problem. "I'm not following what this has to do with Daelyn."

"Matthew Kenzel is Addie's father." Vault's brow pinches. "Annie was her mother."

"Okay." I fail to see the problem. I don't know a Matt or Annie Kenzel. "What's the issue?"

"Annie was short for Anya," Ryker says. "Anya Petrov."

I... I must be hearing things. Did he just say *Anya Petrov*? "What?"

"We found the paternity test she had taken, along with her medical records." Ryker steps closer, knowing what this news is doing to me. "Addie is your half-sister, D."

Chapter 32

Dmitri

I wait impatiently for the guards to bring my dad in for visitation. I'm so nervous, my knee won't stop bobbing under the table. It's been two years since he got locked up and I've been on my own. He refused to see me prior to now but called me yesterday and said a visit was needed.

I have a million questions, all of which die on my tongue when he enters the room.

His hair is long and has streaks of grey I never noticed when he'd kept it buzzed. His face sags a little and there's scruff on his jaw that never used to be there. Mom wanted him clean shaven all the time.

Dad approaches me cautiously, and I see he's got a limp, a busted mouth, and stitches on his temple. Guess he's still fighting, even in prison.

He sits down with a wince.

"Mom's gone," I blurt out, getting this over with. "She left the day of your trial."

I came home to an empty house and continued living my life like everything was normal. There was no way I was going to get dumped into the system.

Dad only nods and stares at the table between us. I'm not even sure he's listening to me.

"I stay at the gym a lot."

He nods.

"I graduated."

He nods again.

"I'm still fighting."

That makes him look up. "You need to stop."

I can't. I won't. He of all people should know what it's like to have this furious monster living inside you that needs an outlet before it eats you alive.

"That's not going to happen. Ever."

"Dmitri," Dad says in a warning tone. But that shit won't work on me anymore. *I don't have respect for him, or love for the woman who birthed me. They can both suck a fat dick.*

Whatever he's about to say next slides back down his throat and he chokes on it. *This is starting to feel like a waste of my time.*

"Why did you want to see me?"

Dad leans across the table. "I wanted to warn you."

"Of what?"

"Don't follow in my footsteps, son. I know you looked up to me. I know you thought I – "

"Looked up to you?" I rise from my chair. "You're not my idol. And you sure as shit were never my goddamn hero. You're a coward and a shit father who abandoned his son the instant your failures were right in your face."

Dad's eyes flash with hurt and rage.

I'm sure mine do too.

"I'm nothing like you," I seethe.

"You're worse. You're a combination of your mother and me." Dad's mouth quirks into a half smile that I'd love to punch off his face. "And she left you because she was finally rid of me, so she could go be with the man she'd been fucking behind my back for years. That child isn't mine. It's why we fought so much in the end."

"I don't care about her or that kid she squeezed out," I lie.

I've been worried sick about my baby brother or sister, but I haven't been able to find them. Not that I've looked too hard since I can't take them away from my mother. I have nothing. I sleep in an abandoned warehouse

Silas owns and uses for fights, then I help him tear it all down and wipe all the evidence of it away, preparing for the next time.

Between that and helping Ryker and my other friends with their shit, I don't have the time or the means to take care of a baby. Besides, for all I know, Mom gave it up for adoption, given that she said she had no intentions of keeping it for long. It wouldn't be a sacrifice if she did. It would be a fucking mercy to that child. She also said to not look for her. She disowned me. Abandoned me.

I tried looking Anya up once, but it was like she'd vanished off the planet. I wasn't all that invested in hunting her down either, so I left it alone. She cut the cord, and I've never been happier to be free of the bitch.

"Dmitri," Dad says again, and I'd knock him the fuck out if we didn't have so many cop eyes on us. "You need to watch your back."

"I'm fine on my own."

"You're not listening." Dad's anger leaks into his veins, making them pop out at his temples. His gaze flicks to the guards at the doorway before saying, "I fucked up."

I don't say a word. Saying he fucked up is an understatement. He ruined everything.

"The man I killed was dangerous."

"So was the man who killed him. Sounds like a fair match to me." I know I sound callous, but I can't help it. I didn't realize I had this much hate left in me until my dad opened his stupid mouth.

"Didn't you go to my trial?"

No. I didn't. I didn't read about, nor did I attend it, because I couldn't wrap my head around the fact that all of this happened...

Because of me.

I was a coward who hid while my dad was punished for a terrible crime he wouldn't have committed had I not been a little bitch who cried to his mommy that day and made our whole life blow up. And now here we are. Dad's suffering the consequences of my actions. Mom's moved on. I'm stuck and hungry and angry and tired and hate everything.

"His people are working me over. Tormenting me," Dad whispers angrily. "They've already come for me twice."

A buzzer goes off and a guard marches over to our table.

"They might come for you too," Dad rushes to say as he's lifted and manhandled away. "Eye for an eye, son."

They haul my dad away and I decide to never come back again…

It took him another eleven years to die in prison, and it seems with his death, my past is circling around me like vultures.

"You're sure it's the same woman?" I ask. Petrov is a very common Russian name. Anya is too. "It could be a coincidence."

Ryker huffs. "D, how many coincidences have to knock against your thick skull for you to see it's something worse than that?" He counts on his fingers. "Your dad is murdered in prison a month ago. You start fighting again and Silas magically has a woman ready for you to fuck on short notice. And oh, what do you know, that pussy belongs to the woman who just happens to be your half-sister's foster guardian. Are you kidding me here? This is a goddamn set up. And you better get away from all of it before we're spreading *your* motherfucking ashes in the river next."

I shake my head. "It's not like that with Daelyn."

"It is *exactly* like that. Someone's planned this. You're being set up. That woman needs to get out of my club."

I'm on Ryker in a blink. "She has a fucking name, and she's not going anywhere."

Ryker rolls his shoulders back, squaring up. "This isn't your club, D. It's not your call to make."

"She's my girl, and this is my home. It's just as much my call as it is yours."

"Listen to yourself," Ryker snaps. "You don't even know her and you're acting like you're ready to lay your life on the line… and for what? She's working for the fucking *enemy*, D!"

"*I know!*" I roar in his face. My heart smashes against my chest as I let it all sink in. "Fuck…I know." Leaning on the counter, I bury my face in my hands and try to calm the hell down. Ryker's snapping at me like this because he's scared for me.

"Wait." Vault steps closer. "You knew she was sent by the same people who killed your father?"

"That hasn't been verified," I argue, rubbing my tired eyes. "But she's been sent by someone who has her trapped in their game, just like me."

Ryker leans on the counter beside me. "Fucking hell."

"They're using Addie against her," I explain. "And they've got enough dirt on Daelyn to send her away to prison for a long time."

Vault runs a hand down his face. With a heavy sigh, he stares up at the ceiling. "Why is nothing ever easy with you motherfuckers?"

"How deep is she into this?" Ryker arches his brow. "We need to know exactly what we're dealing with."

I owe him this much. "I think she's been groomed since she was about twelve. She's very protective of him and won't give me his name. She's got a signet burned into her wrist, so—"

"Could be gang or mafia related."

I agree with Vault. "Daelyn said she's met with cartel before. Guns and drugs."

"Jesus fucking Christ, Dmitri." Ryker storms away, blowing out a long exhale. "Fuck!" He slams his fists on the counter. "So help me God—"

"Take Tara and go." I know that's what he's worried about. The Monarch can be remade, but Tara can't be replaced. There's every possibility that whoever this is will eventually get into the club somehow, and Tara should be far away from here if that happens. Her safety is paramount to Ryker. "As soon as I find out who this person is and handle it, we'll be fine."

Ry shakes his head. "We're not going to let you do this on your own. And you know Tara."

I quirk a smile because, yeah, I do. That woman's too spicy for her own good. She'd never run from danger.

Just like Daelyn.

"How much does Daelyn mean to you, Dmitri?"

Ryker's question catches me off guard. "What?"

"If it comes down to her or you…"

"Her," I say without hesitation. "We save her at all costs." Daelyn's been through Hell long enough. I, on the other hand, own the place. "I'll meet my fate head on. If this motherfucker wants a piece of me, he can have his fill. But she's not to be harmed. He's been brutal enough to her."

Ryker's eyes flash again because he's just like

me when he comes to putting hands on a woman. You do that, then you should have your arms cut off and shoved up your ass before getting tossed over a bridge with cement shoes.

"I thought you didn't believe in fate," Vault says, breaking the tension.

"Yeah, well, that was before I met Daelyn."

Chapter 33

Daelyn

I wake up to a weird buzzing sound. Holy crap, my body aches. Rolling over, I find the source of the vibration and sit up. *My cell.* Dmitri's left my cell phone for me!

Holding the blanket to my chest, I wipe the sleep from my eyes and check my notifications. It's seven in the morning. Or is it night? Shit, I have no clue.

Three missed calls. One text. None are from Addie.

First voicemail: *Where the fuck are you, Dae?*

It's Ace. I immediately delete and move on.

Second voicemail: *Hi Daelyn, is Josie. Have you logged into the system yet? It's down for me and I can't get in touch with IT. I was just wondering if it's a me problem or a hospital problem. Let me know. I want to get started on this new batch of charts before lunch. K, bye.*

Delete.

Third voicemail: *Hey babygirl, just calling to check on you.*

My blood freezes.

I feel shitty about the way we left things, and I can't get you off my mind.

My grip tightens on my phone.

Kaleb sighs before saying, *Bet you're having fun at the Monarch Club.*

I break out in a sweat.

See you soon.

He knows I'm here. The relief of having one less thing to hide is miniscule compared to the raging need I feel to protect Dmitri. The rest of me is squirming like a kid in big trouble.

See you soon.

That wasn't a goodbye. It was a warning.

I'm more grateful than ever that Addie is far, far away from all this right now.

My stomach cramps hard. The sex D and I had last night is catching up with me.

Bet you're having fun at the Monarch Club.

Kicking the blanket off me, I head into the bathroom to freshen up. Holding my belly, I double over and check Addie's location.

Location not found.

Worry slithers up my spine, but I tamp it down. She probably let her phone die. *She's fine. She's safe. She's far away from here.* I drop her a text anyway and start the shower. When I get out, Dmitri's in the bedroom, sitting on the cot with body language that screams Do Not Touch.

"I was wondering where you went." Holding the towel tightly around me, I slip past him and dig out a set of clothes for the day. "Thanks for giving me my cell. It's in the bathroom if you want it back."

D silently stands and retrieves it, sliding my cell into his back pocket.

My stomach won't stop cramping, and it's shooting pain down my thighs. I like it though. The pain grounds me, makes me feel alive when I'm usually so numb. I want to thank him for yesterday, but… he still hasn't looked at me. I'm scared I've done something wrong.

"Have you heard from Addie?" he suddenly

asks in a deep tone.

Why is he asking about her? My protective instincts flare because I don't want her brought up any more than necessary. I want her away from all this badness. But... Dmitri isn't the bad guy here. Is he?

Fuck. I'm so confused.

"No." Guess it's a good thing she didn't text because I don't want to lie to Dmitri if I don't have to.

"You worried?"

"Yes, but I'm always worried about her. Comes with being a guardian, I guess. I'm sure she's fine."

His Adam's apple bobs, and he still won't look at me. "How did you become her guardian?"

The question catches me off guard. "Why?"

"It's not common for a young woman to take on a foster kid in her teens. I'm just curious." He looks over at me then and the sincerity in his eyes makes me pause. "You said you're like sisters."

I nod. "I love her with my whole heart." Sitting on the cot, I fold my hands in my lap. "I already told you she was in the system with me."

He leans against the wall on the other side of the room, his arms crossed, eyes boring into me. "Mmm hmm."

"The foster home she was staying in was the same one I'd been in until I turned eighteen. The Brenner's. They weren't the best, but definitely not the worst. She bawled her eyes out when I left. I'd go to all her soccer games, meet her after school for ice cream or whatever, and have always kept my promise."

"What promise was that?"

"That I wouldn't leave her." My heart feels heavy. "Then the Brenner's house burned down, and they lost everything. They gave Addie up afterwards and I did everything I had to so she could be with me. I think that was the biggest miracle of all. She shouldn't have been able to stay with me, but I met the requirements and, let's face it, the system's overloaded and they just needed a temporary solution, which was me. I made sure temporary became permanent."

"What about her parents?"

Why is he being so fucking nosy? "What about them?"

"Just curious if you knew anything about her past."

I know everything about her past, but I'm not about to share it with Dmitri. It's not my story to tell. "They're dead."

"That's... tragic."

"Her whole life has been tragic," I say in a bitter tone. "And I'm just making it worse with the amount of shit I've gotten myself into."

"Then why not give her up? Cut her loose?"

My hands ball into fists. "I guess you don't know the meaning of a promise. I said I wouldn't abandon her."

"Letting her go doesn't mean you're abandoning her."

"It does to Addie. And I'd rather die than see her go off with someone else who doesn't love her like I do."

The words leave a sour taste in my mouth. Holy shit, how many times did Kaleb say the exact same thing to me whenever I said I wanted out of our relationship?

I'm so fucked up.

And suddenly I'm all too eager to tell Dmitri all the wonderful things about Addie. Because maybe if he can understand how much I love her, he'll forgive me for what I'm doing to him, so I can save us all from Kaleb.

"She's so bright," I say. "Honestly, she probably could skip a grade or two with how smart she is."

He keeps quiet.

"Addie's like this bubbly hurricane of joy. And she feels everything with her whole body, you know what I mean? Like she's crazy happy or roaring mad. There's no neutral in her and it all shows on her face. And her freckles... she has the prettiest smattering of freckles across her nose."

Dmitri swallows again.

"Her whole life has been Hell and she's just blazing through it like a little shooting star."

"Like you."

"No." I tuck my hair behind my ears. "She's a million times better than I am. She's good and pure and wonderful. I'm trash."

Dmitri pushes away from the wall and ends up squatting by my feet. "You're not trash, Daelyn."

"I'm a bad person. She's the opposite of me. She's so good, she's—"

"Worth going through Hell for?"

"She's worth *dying* for." Which is a very real possibility for me. "I just need to get her to graduation. She's brilliant. She'll have scholarships coming in left and right and will be able to go anywhere, do anything."

Escape. Be free. Live a better life than me.

"You really love her, don't you?"

Has he not been listening to what I'm saying? "If

love exists, then it's Addie."

I don't know love with Kaleb, even if he's the only other person in my life I've come close to dying for.

"Tell me his name," D begs on his knees. "Just give me his fucking name and I'll end this nightmare for you. I can keep both you and Addie safe."

My walls rebuild. I gave away too much, spoke about Addie in a way that let him see she's my only vulnerability, and now he's trying to use it against me to get what he wants. "No."

His jaw clenches. Eyes harden. The look on his face is sheer disappointment, and I hate it because he doesn't understand. He doesn't fucking get it.

"I'm trying to protect you!" I yell. "And I'm trying to save my ass while keeping Addie away from all of this."

"You don't need to protect me, Daelyn."

The hell I don't. Fuck, I'm so exhausted and my stomach won't stop cramping, which is now just frustrating and annoying. Doubling over, I squeeze my eyes shut and let all my thoughts, all my everything, fly out of me. "I've spent my whole life doing mental gymnastics, Dmitri. Always trying to make my superiors happy. Always walking the line so I don't get in trouble or kicked out or put someplace worse." I blow out a long exhale. "I'm tired of trying to keep everyone happy or neutral, because at the end of every day, I'm fucking spent. The world just takes, takes, takes until I have nothing left to give and then it asks for more. And I'm desperate enough… starved enough… to keep letting it take from me just so I can receive an ounce of kindness back, no matter how false it is."

To that point, I can't tell if Dmitri really cares about me, or if he's just like Kaleb, who feeds me breadcrumbs to keep me hooked. And the worst part is, I'm willing to die for this man, because that's the endgame here.

"Please, Daelyn." D's voice is calm and soft. "Let me help."

"No!" Fisting my hair, I pull it and scream. "I'm not dragging you down with me anymore than I already have. I'll figure a way out on my own. I'll lie and make up a bunch of shit about you and send him on a wild goose chase."

"And how long will that last, Dae? Listen to yourself. That makes zero sense."

"I'll go to the cops and tell them what he's done. I'll snitch."

"He'll take you down with him."

"I'll string him along. Say that you're evading me, and I need more time. Then you can leave for a while and—"

"Stop." He grips my shoulders and stuffs his face into mine. "You can't get out of this any more than I can. Any more than Addie can."

I shake my head. "Addie's not—"

"She is. You're just too blind to see it, but she's in it because *you're* in it. Everything you touch will reach her at some point."

My mind goes to Ace. Dmitri's right. I've already ruined Addie. If she's not being groomed yet, she will be. Kaleb's too clever to let her go because she's the only string he can pull to make me do his dirty work.

My stomach plummets. "I've ruined everything."

"Give me his name."

"He'll kill you." I grip Dmitri's shoulders, sinking my nails into his flesh like if I can get my claws in him deep enough, I'll keep him with me forever. "I can't let him kill you."

Tears spill down my cheeks because everything that's been in my face all this time, I haven't really seen. I allowed myself to be blinded with the hope that I can get us out of this nightmare unscathed.

"I'm so sorry," I sob. "I never meant for this to happen. I was just supposed to be there when you won the fight. I was just supposed to fuck you." My confessions blast out of me like cannon balls, each one landing with a blow that destroys more of my life. "He only wanted to know about you, he said. He just wanted to find things out about you."

"What kinds of things?"

"I don't even know! He never said specifics." I swipe my tears, panicked. "But *everything* I say is used as ammo. He's smart, Dmitri. He calculates everything and is always two steps ahead. He knew you would be at the fight. Who could have told him about that?"

Dmitri frowns. "Lots of people, I suppose. It's not a secret that I'm a cage fighter. And I'd put my name on the board weeks in advance to draw a crowd and make more money."

I clutch him harder. If Kaleb can drag intel out of simple actions, maybe Dmitri can, too. "He asked me a bunch of questions about what we did after the fight. He wanted to know if you tied me up, made me come." I reevaluate the entire conversation I had with Kaleb that day and tell Dmitri what Kaleb deduced from it: That D has a conscience. That he's not selfish.

That he's gentle even during brutality.

"Did he say why he's after me?"

"He said you killed his father."

Dmitri swipes a hand down his mouth. "That's why you asked if I ever murdered someone that day at breakfast."

I nod. "Did you lie to me?"

D meets my gaze and slowly shakes his head.

If Dmitri didn't lie to me…

Then Kaleb did.

"No." I can't feel my legs. "No, no. He doesn't lie to me, Dmitri. He's *never* lied to me." I slip past him so I can pace back and forth. "This doesn't make sense."

"You would believe him over me?"

I stop and toss my hands up. "I don't *know* you!"

"But you know him. Who's more likely to play you, Daelyn? The man who's terrorized you for half your life, or the guy he sent you to fuck over?"

I get what he's saying. I do. But my brain locks in on the fact that Kaleb has never lied to me. It's a wall I can't climb or knock down. It's the very foundation our relationship was built on. "He wouldn't lie to me."

"Then he's mistaken me for someone else."

"Yeah. Maybe." A tiny seed of hope sprouts in my chest. "I bet that's it. Yeah." Relief filters into my exhaustion. "I can work with that. I'll tell him he has the wrong guy. I'll convince him of it." Oh my god, this could work! "He'll have to believe me because it's true. And then my part of the mission is over. Me and Addie will be free, and so will you." I look up at him with a smile that doesn't feel right on my face. "This is going to be okay. We're going to be okay."

Dmitri's expression cuts me to the quick. "Daelyn."

"No." I poke a shaky finger at him. "This is going to work."

He's not convinced.

And neither am I.

Chapter 34

Dmitri

Daelyn's being irrational. She's lost her mind if she thinks she can convince this guy I'm not the one he's looking for. She's pulling on every little strand she can find to validate her line of thinking, which is fucking delusional, too. Deep down, she knows that and her desire to cling to the notion that this man has never once lied to her baffles me.

This mystery enemy of mine has altered her brain chemistry with how he's manipulated and used her over the years. It makes me want to skin him alive.

She's standing as the barrier between me, Addie, and the man who's terrorized her for a very long time. There isn't a doubt in my mind that Daelyn would set herself on fire to keep those she loves warm. It makes her being manipulated that much worse. Besides, I don't need her protection and it's frustrating that she won't back down with this. Maybe she's played the part of protector for so long, she's incapable of stepping out of the role.

"It's fine. Everything's going to be fine." Her limbs tremble as she falls apart at the seams. "Right? This is going to work, isn't it?"

Unwilling to lie to her, I shake my head and watch her crumble.

I catch her before she hits the floor and hold her close. "Shhh." I pet her hair and tuck her into my body for safekeeping. "I got you."

It's like a lifetime of misery pours out of my girl. Sobs wrack her. Snot and drool drip out of her face while she ugly cries against me. My heart cracks more and more with each agonizing sound she makes.

Swiping the hair from her face, I pepper her forehead with kisses. "It's going to be okay."

I'll finish this, one way or another, and make sure Daelyn and Addie come out unharmed.

"How can you be so good to me, when I've been bad?" She hiccups, hugging me tighter. "I deserve punishment, not... *this*."

Closing my eyes, I let that sink in. Bet she's punished every time she steps out of line with that guy. Christ, how did this piece of shit make Daelyn this fucking loyal to him when he treats her so horribly?

You were loyal to your mother, the angel on my shoulder chimes.

To a fault, the devil adds.

Fuck you both.

"I'm not like him," I say into her hair. She smells like my soap. I miss her floral scent. "I'm not going to hurt you for doing things I don't like, Firefly."

She wails against me, like pointing that out makes this all so much worse. I'm in over my head here and can't find leverage to help me stay afloat.

"You did what you had to in order to survive." I cup her face. "Don't be sorry for that."

Her nose is red and running. Her eyes are a puffy mess. Her chin trembles so much, her teeth chatter. She hooks her arms around my neck and hugs me tight again. "I'm so sorry I did this. I should have fought back harder. Told him no."

"And suffer his consequences?"

"I might have survived it." Daelyn pulls back and looks me dead in the eyes. "But I won't survive losing you or Addie."

My heart rips in half. I think my soul just left my fucking body.

Swiping the tears off her face, I clear my throat and try to remain steady. "You're not going to lose either of us. But it's time you put your sword down, Daelyn. For just one day, lay it down." I kiss her cheeks, nose, chin, eyes, and finally her mouth. "It's okay," I whisper.

"I don't want you to get hurt."

"I'm a big boy. I can handle it."

She starts closing up on me again. "No. I'm not willing to risk it."

"It's not your risk to take, Firefly." I tip her chin. "Your only priority should be taking care of yourself and Addie. Let me handle the rest."

Daelyn shakes her head. "My head is so messed up." Her nails dig into my shoulders while she clings to me. "I know it's far-fetched, but he's got to be wrong about you, which doesn't make sense, because Kaleb's never wrong."

Boom. I just got what I needed.

"Not ever?" I say, rolling with the convo, not giving any hints that she just dropped his name.

"No. He's way too calculating for it. He never makes a move without knowing the next three already. He sets things up way in advance. He says you're the killer."

"Did he say he saw me commit the murder?"

Daelyn shakes her head. "I didn't ask. His dad is a touchy subject." She runs her fingernails up and down my back, over some of my scars, like it soothes her. "Maybe his dad was in a cage fight with you and died of injuries later?"

"It's possible." My brain's going a mile a minute, grasping at straws. Although I'd like to think Silas would have told me if someone I fought in the cage died later from their injuries, he probably wouldn't have, just to spare me the guilt. Mentally tracking every opponent is a no go, considering I've blacked out more than once at the Scrapyard. I have no clue how many men I've knocked down. Now I feel sick. I could be a murderer. *Fuck me.*

No. I'd have found out if I killed someone. Right? Shit. Okay, I need to piece this together with some dates so I can at least narrow down my list of potential victims. "How old was he when his dad died?"

"Thirteen."

Whoa. Hold up. "How old is he now?"

"Twenty-nine."

Quick math says I definitely was not beating grown ass men to death when I was sixteen.

And this guy is older than Daelyn by four years. A little more math and it finally dawns on me why she's been protective of him. "He was your first love."

"Yes." She cautiously looks at me like a child in trouble. "He was my person. My safe space. But…" Her brow crinkles and she clamps her mouth shut.

"But what?"

It takes her forever to speak again. While my patience wears thin, I hold her and wait. Pushing Daelyn for answers will only make her close up more. She has to do this on her own.

"Sometimes I lay awake at night and pull out all the fragments of myself," she finally says, sinking into my embrace. "I look at each piece and try to remember why it's there. How it came to be that way." She sniffles and wipes her nose. "I look at the things he's done, the things he says, his reasons and logic for dragging me along, and I see why there are so many torn up parts of me. It's because he ripped them up that way." Daelyn blows out a long sigh. "I always owed him. That's what he'd say. I owed him because he'd helped me. I owed him because without him, I'd still be miserable. I owed him because he kept me safe. Then he'd send me out to do something that put my life in danger and would look me dead in the eyes and say, 'don't you trust me, Dae? Do you really think I'd send you out there if it wasn't safe? Come on, babygirl, you know me better than anyone.' And I'd trust him to have my back, and I'd do whatever he sent me out for. If I push back or question his orders, he stonewalls or gaslights me. Manipulates my words, fears, and feelings until I cave. Then he beats me for making him have to do that to me, just so I'll listen and obey."

My vision hazed red at the beginning of her story, and right now there's a terrible ringing in my ears. I'm locked onto each word, every motherfucking syllable, coming from her sweet mouth like it's a cliff I'm hanging onto for dear life and it's crumbling under my grip. If I fall, I'll undoubtably shatter.

Black out.

Tear the world apart.

"Deep down, I know he's not my safe space. He never was."

My heart's thudding too hard against my ribs. I can't take a full breath.

"Chaos is my comfort zone. I don't think I know

how to live in a calm, safe space. I don't trust it."

"Makes sense," I say, stroking her hair. "If you've always been in high stress environments, leaving it can make you feel lost and scared."

I remember how terrifying it was after my dad went to prison and my mom left. I stepped into my house and, with the threat of my mother's anger no longer present, a unique brand of fear grew in me because I didn't know how to function in my own home when I no longer had to tip-toe around. So, what did I do? I ran to the Scrapyard and moved in there because chaotic violence was my comfort zone.

"Every time we're together, I keep comparing you two." She pulls back to look at me. "You're nothing like him."

It takes great effort to swallow around my tightening throat. Focusing on the brilliance of Daelyn's blue-green eyes, I remind myself of what's important here. It's not revenge.

"If I say his name," she whispers. "If I give it up… does that make me a bad person?"

I hold my breath and grow still.

"Does that make me a traitor? A snitch? A disappointment?" Tears well in her bloodshot eyes again. "Does that make me worse than him because he did so much for me and now I'm turning against him?"

"Everything he did wasn't for you," I say cautiously. I've got one shot to make this clear, and my brain is short-circuiting already because I'm so goddamn angry. "He did it for *himself*. There are things going on that you don't know, Daelyn. Things with Addie."

The change in her is instant. She shoves away

from me like I've electrified her. "What?"

"You really don't know what Addie has to do with this?"

Fury and confusion dance on her face. "Addie has *nothing* to do with this, Dmitri. Other than being the string he uses to keep me in line, that girl has nothing to do with anything."

"She has to do with *me*." I swallow hard, feeling the change in the room we're in. It's darkening because I'm losing my fucking head. "She's my half-sister."

Daelyn stumbles back. "What? No. That's…" But even as she tries denying the possibility, gripping her head as if she can squeeze the information back out, she realizes I wouldn't lie about that.

"Remember when I said the worse thing I did was cry in front of my mother?" I make my way closer to her. "Remember, I said she was pregnant? The child wasn't my father's. She left soon after my dad went to prison, and I never saw her again. Her name is… *was*… Anya Petrov. She married a man named Matthew Kenzel, who was the father of her child. They had a little girl. I even have a copy of the paternity test."

There's no word to describe the way Daelyn takes this news.

The color drains from her face. Her knees buckle, and she slams onto my concrete floor. Her eyes lose focus. Her breaths drag out of her in rasps.

"He knew," she finally whispers in a low, steady voice. "*He fucking knew*."

I don't say another word for fear of shattering her. The way she just flipped from a trembling leaf to a crouching tiger is alarming.

Daelyn swipes her hand over her mouth, her eyes darting across the floor as if she's piecing things I don't know about together.

"Holy shit," she whispers. Then she nails me with a deadly gaze and all the fragility in her explodes, leaving cold, iron armor in its wake. "He said he was going to take everything from you like you did him."

Which means he's going to take Addie.

"Kaleb Calloway," she says. "His name is Kaleb Brent Calloway."

Jesus fucking Christ. "Brent Calloway is the man my father killed and went to prison for."

Chapter 35

Daelyn

Of all the things that Kaleb's done, using Addie as the linchpin all along has finally made me snap. I'll kill him before I let him touch her.

It's surreal to feel the switch flip inside me. For half my life, I've protected that bastard, lined his pockets with money, helped him get power and respect. All he did for me was pretend to care and throw me breadcrumbs of praise or manipulate me into doing the next thing on his agenda. I knew it was happening most of the time, and I never stopped it because I trusted him.

Kaleb might do me dirty, but he'd never completely fuck me over. And if he did, he'd make it up to me somehow, and I'd be right back in his pocket where he said I belonged.

Like a well-trained dog, I'd go right back in my cage.

He bought the house I live in and charges me low rent, so Addie has a stable home in a decent school district. He paid my college tuition so I could get a degree and job that lets me work from home... so I could be close to Addie. He sends Ace over all the time, who's always bringing us gifts and food. And who does Ace talk most to? *Addie*. Kaleb's given me stacks of money to buy her clothes and even helped me pay for her leg when she broke it skiing—a trip he also contributed funds to. Maybe not directly, but with the jobs he sent me on and paid me for.

I've been so blind and dumb. Beaten, forced, fucked, and blackmailed over and over by that monster. Fear is no excuse for the way I've let him use and abuse me. *No more*. He's not using my love for Addie to keep me as his pet ever again.

"We have to pretend we don't know," I say carefully. "We need to keep acting like it's business as usual. Give me my cell."

Dmitri hands it over without question.

Dialing Corrinne, I keep the nervousness hidden in my voice when she answers on the second ring. "Hey, Corrinne, just checking in. I tried calling Addie this morning, but her cell must be dead."

"Oh yes, she mentioned needing to charge it last night, but I bet she forgot. They're with Saul on a charter boat right now. If she charged it, she might not have reception where they are. Too far out from mainland."

"Oh wow!" I taste the fakeness on my tongue like sugary poison. "A charter boat, huh? That sounds fun."

"It sounds like seasickness waiting to happen to me. I wouldn't be caught dead on a boat in the ocean."

"Well now you get to kick back and relax on your own for a while, mama. Good for you."

"Living the dream. I'm currently staking out my spot on the beach for the day. I plan to read a spicy book, drink some chilled wine, and live my best life till they all come back later this afternoon."

"I wanna be you when I grow up."

Corrinne's laugh is beautiful. "Next time, we're going to kidnap you and bring you with us. Addie's so happy here, Dae. Beach life suits her. Bet it would suit you too."

I think I'm going to throw up. "Sounds like a plan. Hey, thanks for bringing her."

"Thanks for sharing her. We absolutely adore Addie."

"Same."

After we hang up, I dash into the bathroom and shut the door. I can't feel my cheeks. I'm not even sure if my feet are on the ground. Gripping the counter, I stare at myself in the mirror, nausea swirling in my belly. I feel like I'm in another dimension. I can hear Dmitri in the other room, talking to someone, and I hang onto his voice to keep myself semi-grounded.

"Hey, get me all you can on Kaleb Brent Calloway. And I mean everything, Vault. Address, how many shits he takes in a day, the color of his fucking toothbrush. I want all there is on that cocksucker."

I sink to the floor.

You wanted the bigger, badder monster, Daelyn. You did this to yourself.

I don't know what Dmitri is going to do to Kaleb, and it's terrifying. Betrayal swirls in my heart, infecting me with regret. How can I feel guilty about what I've just done? Kaleb deserves this. He's a bad, bad man.

He's also the only one who's stuck by my side all these years.

"*It's you and me forever, babygirl.*" I shut my eyes and try to block out Kaleb's voice. "*No one knows me like you do. You're the only one I trust.*" I clamp my hands over my ears, like that's going to help me not hear him. "*See you soon.*"

"Daelyn?" Dmitri knocks softly on the door.

"Can I come in?"

I'm too scared to tell him no. What if he just busts the door down if I do? That's what Kaleb would do. No, scratch that. Kaleb wouldn't even ask permission. He'd just barge in like it's his right to invade my privacy.

"Listen," D says from the other side. "For what it's worth, I'm really proud of you. Speaking out is an incredibly brave thing to do."

It's not brave. It's suicide. I climb to my feet and somehow make my way to the door and open it. Dmitri stands back a little, his expression guarded but soft.

"I'm a bad person," I say, letting more tears fall. "I can't turn off my guilt for this."

It's going to eat me alive.

"Then feel it, Firefly." He hugs me tight and kisses the top of my head. "Feel every emotion that bubbles up. It's okay."

It's *not* okay.

"I don't know why I ever loved him." I need to get all this shit out of me so I can hopefully think straight again. "I don't even know what love is. But… he was there for me when everyone else only hurt me. He was there when I needed someone."

Kaleb loves me, he just doesn't show it like other people. He's incapable of being soft because his life has always been hard.

Jesus, why am I grappling for some thread of an excuse to let Kaleb off the hook for what he's done to me? How fucked in the head have I become?

"You *do* know what love is, Daelyn, and what it's not." He leans back and cups my face. "Love is doing anything for someone, taking care of them and being there for them. It's what you do for Addie. What you have with Kaleb…" He stops for a moment, and a sigh rumbles out of him. "Maybe it started as love but grew toxic. Maybe it was never real to begin with. Maybe it's a combo. But it's *not* love now. No man should treat you the way he has."

I know. Even when I was sixteen and he took my virginity, I felt sick about it afterwards. But I attached myself to Kaleb because he was a scary dog who bit everyone but me. He made me feel special.

Until he sank his teeth into me, too.

"Love is supposed to be unconditional," I argue, more to myself than Dmitri.

"True, but not really. It's one thing to love someone who has imperfections, but love should never hurt like this," he argues, stroking his finger along the cut on my arm. "Or this." He kisses my bruised neck. "Or this." He lays a gentle peck by my bloodshot eye.

He's right, and it makes me so sad. "I don't know love-love. Not like the kind—"

I almost say *like the kind I feel for you*, but I hold that shit in and shut up. I'm not in love with Dmitri. At least I don't think I am. I can't be. I shouldn't be. What I feel for him is only the effects of some kind of hero worship caused by a terrible event gone wrong and I'm clinging to a sliver of bright light as if it'll save me from being devoured by the darkness of my miserable life.

Dmitri is that light. Even if I know, deep down, he can't save me.

Even if I know, deep down, that I'm attracted to him because he's just another version of comfortable chaos.

Love-love isn't something I deserve. I've never had it from anyone. My foster parents didn't love me. I was only a government check in the mail, which they spent on themselves. Teachers didn't love me. I was one more body in the classroom, struggling to memorize useless information. I didn't have friends. No one wanted to be near an unstable person like me. Any guy I tried to be with, Kaleb would interfere and ruin it. Hell, I don't even know what unconditional love means, outside of what I feel for Addie, and she doesn't count.

My whole existence is based on conditions. Be quiet. Be clean. And above all else, be obedient. If I didn't do those things, I was severely punished or rehomed. Kaleb only amplified that lifestyle. *Do as I say, or I won't love you. Do this job for me, or I'll be disappointed in you. Obey or I'll make you regret it.*

"I've never been in love," Dmitri confides, bringing me out of my thoughts. "I mean, I love my friends. Hell, I'd die for every one of them, but I've never love-loved a woman in my life. I've never seen one and thought… *There she is.*"

His icy eyes soften as he stares at me. Silence spreads between us like invisible strings are pulling us in opposite directions of time and space. Even though he's holding me in his arms, I feel like I'm floating miles and miles away from him.

I'm terrified of how this is going to end.

"I have an idea," he says suddenly. "How about we go for a bike ride and get some fresh air?"

I don't want to. In his concrete basement bedroom, I feel safe. Outside, I don't. I'll be looking over my shoulder for one of Kaleb's men. I'll be checking my phone, wondering if he's tracking me.

"Can't we just stay here and train more?" I'm on limited time. It feels like there's too much to do for us to stop now and go on a joy ride.

"Trust me." He pulls me along with him. "I'll make it worth it."

...

Dmitri might be right. Being a backpack on his motorcycle, with my arms wrapped around his body, the loud hum of his bike and the air whipping against my limbs makes me feel good. He takes us out of the city and onto a bunch of back roads. We stop and have lunch at this little joint that claims fame for their hand cut fries.

"Damn, that's good." He takes another big chomp of his smashburger. "I'm fucking starving."

I left my cell at the Monarch. It's better this way, and I don't have to worry about missing a call from Addie because she's in the middle of the ocean, fishing. "Can I ask you something?"

"Of course."

"How did you start working at the Monarch?" I pluck a fry and eat it.

Dmitri wipes his mouth with a napkin. "It's a long story, but the club is Ryker's, and we go way back. We've been through everything together. When he opened the Monarch, it was only natural I'd be his right-hand man."

"So, you've always been a Dom?"

"No. I trained and studied for years. It's not as easy as some think." He stuffs a wad of fries in his mouth and chews. "Some idiots think using the title grants them permission to do whatever they want in a scene. There are safety measures to consider, after care, psychology. It's not all whips and fun times."

"Do you like it?"

"I love it. Being trusted to make a woman feel good, to give her an outlet and watch her unfurl and explode is fucking phenomenal. Honestly, it's the most rewarding job I can think of."

I take a sip of my water and try to not let jealousy rear its ugly head. "How many subs have you—" I stop myself from finishing that question. "Will you always be a Dom, then?"

"I'm only a Dom when I'm interested in taking a sub," he says. "Or if I'm chosen by a Butterfly."

"What's a Butterfly?"

"Every year the Monarch holds a Butterfly Ceremony. A selection of our members is bid on, and the one with the highest offer becomes the Butterfly for a month. She stays in the club, has full access to everything, and can choose any Dom she wants."

"I bet they all choose you."

His smile makes me think I'm right. "I'm intimidating. Most like the idea of me, but when it comes down to selection time, they chicken out or see someone they like better."

I can't imagine anyone better than Dmitri.

"I like being head of security more than I like being a Butterfly's Dom, anyway. Training really isn't my thing."

"What do you train them in?"

"Sex." He shrugs like that's such an obvious answer. "A lot of them want to explore new kinks they're afraid to try on their own. We offer a safe space for them to do that. And they sign an extra NDA tailored for Butterflies, so no one knows what we do with them for the month."

"They live at the club the whole time?"

"Yeah. We've got a kitted-out suite dedicated to them. And whatever they want, they get."

"Sounds like heaven."

"It is... until it isn't."

"What's that mean?"

"Most times, the highest bidder is their partner, but sometimes it isn't. Either way, they will have shelled out a lot of money and they expect reimbursement."

The way he says *reimbursement* makes me believe he's not talking about paying them back with money. "Oh."

"Yeah. *Oh.*" Dmitri leans back. "So far, we haven't had too many issues with that in our club, but I have no clue what it's like outside of the Monarch for our Butterflies. Hard to say what goes on behind closed doors, you know what I'm saying? But I would hope that if a former Butterfly had an issue, they'd come to us. Our time with them is spent building an unbreakable bond. They trust us to keep them safe. And we let them know that bond remains intact long after their month in our beds is over."

A slow breath stutters out of me. Before I can ask anything else, Dmitri crumples up his trash and asks, "You ready to hit the road?"

I swipe my mouth with a napkin. "Yeah."

Dmitri grabs our trays and I run to the bathroom before we climb back onto his Ducati. He takes us down another long stretch of road, and we end up parking by a bunch of trees. There's a huge field behind us. We're probably on private property and I missed the sign.

When I take my helmet off, the rich scent of flowers tickles my nose and the warm summer breeze kisses my cheeks. Closing my eyes, I let the sun soak into me and for a moment I trick myself into believing I've transported to another realm where no one can touch me.

Then Dmitri's hand skates down my back. His mouth presses against my shoulder. Okay, *he* can touch me.

I lean into him and sigh. "I wish we could stay here forever."

His breath on my heated skin makes goosebumps erupt all over and my nipples harden when he asks, "Does that mean you want me to keep you, Firefly?"

"Do you want to keep me?"

He tugs off my shirt and palms my breasts through my bra. Without saying another word, he kisses me slowly while his hands roam my body as if he's putting every curve to memory.

"What do *you* want?" he asks against my lips.

I'm not certain what answer won't get me into trouble.

"Daelyn." He cups my jaw. "Don't overthink this. Whatever you want, just name it."

I'm not sure I should tell him. He'll think I'm a freak. He'll see how messed up in the head I am. "I want to…"

Oh my god, what am I doing?

"Just say it, Firefly. Whatever it is, it's okay to tell me."

Fine. Here it goes…

"I want to be punished."

Chapter 36

Dmitri

I'd braced for every answer imaginable but that one. Ironic, considering I should have known she'd say that. My girl is battling the good and evil in her conscience. The guilt of betrayal, the consequences of her actions, and the desire to survive with her heart, mind, and body intact has her conflicted in a lot of ways.

Punishment has become a form of adoration for her. Every time we've fucked, it's been rough. Daelyn says she's a bad girl all the time. She thinks she doesn't know love.

I can work with all of that.

"What's your safe word?"

"Crocodile." Her eyes have lit up already. The shame in her tone is gone, too.

Perfect.

"Bend over my bike."

My beautiful, tortured girl does what I say, and doesn't even flinch when I pull out my knife and flip the blade open. I'd like to think it's because she trusts me enough to never hurt her, but I'm not so sure that's it. I think if I cut her, she'd only say she deserved it.

She'd be dead wrong.

Sliding her shorts down to her ankles, I make her kick them off while she faces the flower field. Biting and kissing her pert ass cheeks, I run the blade along her sweet skin, careful to not nick her. Hooking her underwear with my fingers, I pull it away from her pussy, loving that the fabric's damp already, and I slice it with my knife, making them useless.

"I'm gonna fuck you, Daelyn. And you're going to take it until I say otherwise."

"Yes, King."

My hands tremble as I unbuckle my belt and pull it free from the loops on my jeans. Folding it in half, I crack her ass with it once… twice. Two beautiful red stripes bloom on her skin and my mouth waters.

She pants, already breathless with need. "Again."

"Shut your mouth." I run the belt over her backside and slip it between her thighs, rubbing her wet pussy. "Bend over more and give me a hole to fuck."

Daelyn leans so far over my bike, her feet almost lift off the ground. Obediently, she spreads her ass cheeks, giving me a choice of two perfectly fuckable holes.

"Take them both," she begs.

I don't have lube, so unless I plan to tear her open, her ass isn't an option this time. Not with my fat dick. And this isn't about my pleasure, it's about her punishment.

"You'd like that, wouldn't you," I growl from behind her. Sliding my hand between her legs, I shove two fingers in her cunt and press the handle of my knife to her asshole. Daelyn stills under me. "Still want me to take both holes?" I twist the handle, teasing her ass more.

"Y-y-es."

That makes me pull away. The little groan she makes could be mistaken for disappointment, but I know it's relief. She wants a painful punishment.

She's braced for me to give her that. But I'm not willing to go so far. Besides, there are better ways to punish her that don't include pain. "Turn around and get on your hands and knees."

She practically melts onto the ground and looks up at me like a puppy in training.

"Crawl." I walk backwards and make her follow me like an animal searching for scraps of food, attention… *kindness*. Unfastening my fly, I lean against the wooden fence separating the road from the field and snap my fingers. "Suck my dick."

Daelyn scurries over to me and opens her mouth, taking me in as far as she can. Her teeth graze my shaft. She gags every time my piercing slides against the back of her tongue. I fist her hair and rock into her slowly.

Very slowly.

My girl's eyes water. There's dirt all over her knees. She keeps trying to speed up, and each time, I pull her hair as a reminder of who's in charge. "Go slower."

She pouts with my dick in her mouth. It's so fucking beautiful.

"Rub yourself."

Daelyn shoves one hand between her thighs and does what I say. The other strokes my dick while she sucks the head harder. Eventually, her pace quickens again.

"Slower."

She doesn't listen. If anything, the brat goes faster.

I cram my dick down her throat once, making her gag, and then pull all the way out. "Stop touching yourself."

Daelyn's eyes glass over as she obeys. *Desperate, needy little thing.* Her tits spill out of her bra. Her cut panties barely cover her pussy and ass. We both know someone could drive through here at any time and see her being a dirty bitch on her knees for me.

I walk away from her again and climb onto my bike. She watches me in horror, likely afraid I'm going to leave her stranded here, humiliated.

"Saddle up." I stroke my dick again. When she's about to stand, I bark another command. "Crawl, Daelyn."

Her head falls as she slinks over to me on her hands and knees like a good girl.

"Mount me, Firefly."

Using the nickname washes some of the trepidation away from her expression. I lean back, spreading my thighs to hold the bike balanced and let her figure out how to climb on top of me.

I'm patient.

She's crafty.

We both have great balance.

Daelyn slides down on my waiting dick and groans.

"Ride me slowly."

Holding her hips, I reset the pace every time she tries to go faster than I want. I force her to go slow. Extremely slow. Her thighs start shaking in no time and I'm sure it's from muscle fatigue. I hold us both steady, never letting her waver.

"This is torture," she whimpers.

Tell me about it. I want nothing more than to make her come. Bend her over my bike and fuck her into oblivion. But she asked for punishment, and this is it. "Shut your mouth before I stuff it with something to keep you quiet."

She bites her lip, her brow crinkling with hurt even as she groans while grinding against my cock. Daelyn's so wet, I can feel it on my balls.

"Mmm. Just like that. You take me so well, baby." My grip tightens on her hips as I rock her back and forth. Her pussy clenches my cock, and I know she's close to coming.

"Slower," I growl, making her lose the momentum she's gained.

Daelyn cries out, her limbs shaking while she sags against my chest. "Please…"

She doesn't get to say anything else. I pull her hair, making her lean back and I shove two fingers in her mouth. "I told you to shut your mouth."

Her eyes flash with frustration that's quickly swallowed by lust again.

Daelyn's full lips wrap around my digits, and she sucks on them while maintaining the slow pace I've set for us. She feels amazing. Her pussy's swollen, wet, and so goddamn needy, I'm not sure how much longer I'll be able to keep this up.

I lose myself to the pleasure and close my eyes, enjoy the exquisite torture I've set on us. The pace of our thrusts, the heat on our skin, the effort it takes me to balance the bike, her tongue on my fingers, her hand around the back of my neck, the way she takes every fucking inch of my cock, the way my zipper cuts into my balls, the way her teeth dig into my fingers…

My eyes pop open as pain zips through me. Daelyn's smiling with her teeth as she bites down on my motherfucking fingers so hard it makes white dots burst in my vision.

Then she rides me faster.

My clever girl's turned the tables on me and has flipped the dynamic.

"Fuuuuuck." I let her do it because this feels so perfect. She bounces on my cock, making me come while biting me hard enough to make my toes curl. My orgasm pumps, sending waves of pleasure through me. My voice cracks when I groan her name. I fill her needy cunt with my cum, loving how her body squeezes me, milking me, taking it all so greedily.

After pulling my fingers out of her mouth, I glance at the impressive teeth marks embedded on my skin.

"Bad girl," I say with a smile.

"I don't think I know how to be any other way."

Fine by me. I want her just as she is.

Pulling her off, I make her turn around and face forward. "Bend over."

She practically tips herself over the handlebars, and I shove my cock inside her again. With my height, it's easy to fuck her like this while she's perched on my seat. But my jeans are tearing, and the zipper is still cutting into my nuts.

"Get up." I slap her ass and have her climb off. "Go over to the fence."

Damned if she doesn't look over her shoulder and ask, "Walk or crawl?"

"Neither." I pick her up and carry her myself.

The fence is made with three wooden boards, and I quickly figure out how to use them to our advantage. "Lean in through the higher gap and wrap your arms around the top board for me."

Daelyn obeys beautifully. "I feel like I'm about to be crucified."

"No one's getting saved here, Firefly." Spreading my legs, I angle my cock and impale her in one thrust. She grunts loudly, taking every inch I've shoved into her, and then I fuck her hard enough to make her scream my name.

It's brutal.

Divine.

Our bodies slap together, the sun burns, the wood cuts into my hands while I hold on and I know it's digging into her too. We don't care. I rut her like a fucking animal.

She takes it like a queen.

"You want to come, Firefly?"

"Yes, King. Please."

"Beg harder."

"Please!" she scream-cries. "I need… I… I need…"

Pulling out, I turn her around so her arms can have a break, and lift her up, thrusting into her again. "You need what? Say it. Use your words." I pound her, my fingers digging into her ass as I bounce Daelyn up and down on my cock. "Tell me what you need, Queen."

She makes the sweetest noise I've ever heard in my life. Her tits bounce and legs flop while I rail her.

"Tell me what you need and it's yours." I want her to come around my dick hard enough to choke out all the terror racing in my veins. "Tell me."

"I need…" She grunts. "Fuck I need…" I bang her faster… harder… "I need *you*, Dmitri."

Her nails cut into the back of my neck as she clings to me. Her pussy clamps down. Her thighs shake against my arms while I fuck her so violently it hurts us both. She comes hard and long. Fat tears sail down her cheeks while her body melts, gushes, and clenches around me.

"Crocodile," she gasps.

I yank out of her so fast, my dick's still spurting my orgasm all over the grass. "You okay?" Her raspy breaths make me panic. "Daelyn. Are you hurt?"

"I think… I'm stroking out." She holds her chest, her eyes wide with panic. "Oh my god, I can't feel my face."

I jerk my jeans up so I can move faster. "I got you." Setting her on the ground, I squat down and cup her face. "Can you feel your left side?"

She nods while breathing even harder. Her panic is setting in. "Slowly," I bark. "You gotta breathe deep and slow, baby." Swiping the hair from her face, I press my forehead to hers and keep my voice steady. "In and out with me, okay?"

Inhale… exhale…

Daelyn holds my forearms, her ocean eyes locking on mine like I'm some kind of raft that will keep her afloat.

Inhale, exhale.

"Can you feel your face now?"

"It's all tingly."

"How about the left side of your body, can you move your arm?"

She nods and lifts her hand, wiggling her fingers.

"Right side good too?"

She nods. "Yes."

"Smile."

She gives me a psychotic looking grin that shows all her teeth. Both sides of her mouth are working, which is all I care about.

"Good girl." I don't think she's having a stroke. She's having a panic attack and sub drop combo.

Shit, I definitely pushed her too hard. Right when I think I've got my Dom tricks perfected, something like this happens and it reminds me I still have a lot to learn. "I got you," I say, pulling her into my lap.

"I can't feel my body. I'm floating."

"It's a flood of chemicals in your brain, Firefly. We overdid it." Stroking her hair, I hold her close and feel like an asshole. I should have never done this. I thought I was giving her a distraction, but I've only made her worse. "I'm so sorry, Daelyn."

"For what? Giving me the best orgasm of my life or for making me feel like I'm dying by coming too hard?"

"I shouldn't have punished you like that without knowing your body's limits."

"I don't even know my limits, Dmitri. How are you supposed to know them?"

"By paying better attention," I growl, hugging her tight. "I let myself go and now look."

She sighs, her breaths no longer harsh and raspy. Now, she just sounds out of breath. "I'm glad you did."

"Says the woman who wanted punishment."

"Says the woman who knows what it's like to always have to toe the line." Daelyn leans back to look at me. "Sometimes it's good to just let go and say, 'fuck it, I'm getting what I want', for once."

"Until the consequences bite you in the ass."

"I didn't bite your ass. I bit your fingers." She smirks. "And you loved it."

We both look at her teeth indents still on my

skin. "I definitely loved that."

Giggling, she rests her head on my shoulder and runs her nails up and down my back again. Just then, the sound of a car coming up the road has me covering Daelyn with my body to shield her from view. The vehicle slows to a stop, and the driver lowers his window, frowning as he looks at us.

Daelyn waves for him to keep going. "We're all good!"

"Yeah, roll on." I fail to keep my posture neutral. My protective instincts have me baring my teeth and arms wrapping tighter around Daelyn. I don't want this guy seeing any part of her body.

The man doesn't budge. "You sure you're okay, Miss?"

"Oh yeah," she says, flashing him a huge smile. "We're doing great."

Me and the guy stare at each other for a heartbeat and I cock my brow. I've never been suspected of violating a woman before, and I can't help but want to explain myself to the man now. But I also don't like the way he looks at us. He's not concerned... he's intrigued.

"Really. I'm fine," Daelyn repeats. "You can leave."

"Mind if I stay and watch?"

"Only if you want to lose your eyeballs afterwards," Daelyn says with a psychotic grin.

On cue, I pull out my blade and flip it open. My smile matches my girl's.

"Got it. Never mind." The man rolls his window up and lays on the gas, speeding away.

"Come on." Daelyn stands on wobbly legs and holds her hand out for me. "Let's get out of here."

Chapter 37

Daelyn

We pull into the Monarch's back parking lot, there's a man standing at the backdoor, holding it open with a scowl on his face. It makes me feel like a child about to get yelled at for staying out past curfew.

Dmitri doesn't look fazed at all. With his arm on my lower back, he escorts me through the club and up to a large office. A guy decked out in a three-piece suit sits at a large desk with monitors spread across the length of it. I guess this is Ryker, the owner of the Monarch Club, and Dmitri's best friend. Suddenly, another guy appears behind us, who I assume is Vault. Dmitri had said they wanted to talk with us when we got back, and I'm now trapped and surrounded without even realizing it's happened.

"What did you find out?" Dmitri asks, pulling me onto his lap.

Ryker glances at Vault, then at me. "How much does he mean to you?"

The question confuses me. "Who?"

"You know who."

No, I don't. He could be referring to Kaleb or Dmitri, but my answer is the truth for both. "He means more than he probably should."

Ryker's brow creases. "Hungry dogs are never loyal, Daelyn."

My heart skips as he gets up and makes his way around the desk again. Ryker stops in front of me.

Terror spikes in my veins because I don't know what's about to happen. So, I stare directly at Ryker and hold my ground. "I don't bark. I bite."

He crouches down in front of me, and I think he looks impressed with my response. "Tell us your side of things, honey."

Dmitri wraps his arms around me, but they feel like armor instead of a cage and I use that strength to speak up. "First, I want to make it clear that I had no clue Kaleb's plan went this deep."

Dmitri runs his thumb lightly along my ribs. Ryker watches me like a predator about to pounce. Vault, however, doesn't move. He's still as a statue, leaning against the closed door with his arms crossed.

I can't get out.

No one says a word as I stare into Ryker's unforgiving, stormy grey eyes and wonder how I keep jumping from one fire into another. These men could kill me, and no one would know. I recognize a cutthroat crew when I see one, and I'm grateful Dmitri has his. He's not alone like he thinks.

Not like me.

"I don't even know where to begin." I get off of Dmitri's lap and start pacing. "I don't know how much to say."

"Our boy's life could be on the line," Vault growls. "Say *everything*. It doesn't matter if you think it's important or not, just tell us what you know."

Nodding, I mentally scramble to figure out where to start. "Kaleb's crew was recruited through the foster care system." I can't believe I'm doing this. It's only forgivable because this isn't about me and my safety. It's about Addie's and Dmitri's.

I'd die for them. The thought strikes me like

lightning, making goosebumps spread down my limbs. And I *will* die for them once Kaleb finds out I've snitched. At least I'll go to my grave knowing I did the right thing for once.

"His mom was our case worker."

"For all of you?" Ryker asks.

"Yes. There used to be more of us, but they've either died or gone to prison."

Dmitri swipes a hand over his mouth and leans back in his chair.

"When he was seventeen, Kaleb took over for his father, running product up here from Miami." My mouth dries up. "A few years later, he started sending me out to deal with mutuals who dealt in cartel stuff because I'd earned my position with them."

"What's that mean?" Ryker asks cautiously.

"It means Kaleb brought me in as his second-in-command and I had to get initiated." My heart jackhammers. "By letting them take turns on me."

Dmitri's chair creaks as he stands, but Ryker shoves him back down and holds him there. "Let her speak."

"It's okay," I say, numbly. "It was just one time." That single night of pain and humiliation, the terror beyond belief, is fuzzy in my mind now. I remember staring at Kaleb while it happened, clinging to him mentally until I somehow tricked my mind into imaging it was him touching me, taking me, and not the others. It made going back again and again, with a smile on my face and a gun in my hand, worth it. I could look them in the eyes with no fear. And within a couple years, it was no longer an act. They didn't intimidate me anymore. In some fucked up way, I'd earned their respect and they started to only deal with me.

See, babygirl? I told you to trust me. Do exactly what I say, and you'll climb to the top with me. Ride or die, right? It might hurt, but I won't let anything really bad happen to you. Shutting my eyes, I force Kaleb's voice out of my head.

"They didn't like working with Kaleb because he wasn't predictable enough and insisted I was the only one they met with because I could be trusted."

I once overheard Emmanuel say Kaleb was a necessary evil or he would have blown his brains out years ago. At the time, I would have done anything to save Kaleb from eating a bullet. Now, I'd love to feed him one myself. I suspect Kaleb's got something on them big enough to keep their relationship going, which is odd considering Kaleb's on the lower tier of the food chain in the cartel world. After a couple years of being the liaison, I stopped meeting with Emmanuel's men, on Kaleb's orders, and Corey took over the meetups. I also heard rumors that Emmanuel's crew got popped by the DEA and are either in prison, hiding, or dead. I keep all of this to myself though.

Ryker arches his brow. "Which cartel was this?"

I shake my head, unwilling to give them up. "They're not relevant to this. And it's safer if you don't know."

That takes Ryker aback. "Safer for who?"

"You." I'm not on Emmanuel's side, but I know limits, and that's definitely a hard line. "I'm not risking any of you unnecessarily."

Dmitri glances over at Ryker and they share a look I don't understand.

"So, like I was saying, Kaleb's mom is the one

who put us all in Kaleb's reach, which I've only just recently put together how calculated it truly was once Dmitri told me Addie is his half-sister."

Now that my eyes are wide open, it's easier to put all the pieces together. Nothing was a coincidence in my life.

A harsh laugh bubbles out of me thinking about how foolish I've been. "I remember feeling so special when me and Kaleb spent time together. He's a charmer. Elusive. Cruel and sweet. To a kid like me, he was a god."

I bet Ace and a few others would agree with me. No one likes Kaleb now, but it didn't start that way. He was a savior for us to latch onto. Now he's got so much dirt on all of us, we're stuck with him forever. And he's too unhinged for anyone to challenge and survive.

"In the beginning, he would have us do small jobs for him. If we failed or refused too many times, his mother would eventually show up at our houses and threaten to relocate us." A shiver runs through me. "The very real threat of being placed in a home that's worse than the one I was already in made me compliant fast. No sooner would she threaten me, Kaleb would sneak into my room that night or the next day, taking my side. He'd trash talk his mom and say how unfair and horrible she was. But then he'd somehow talk me into doing whatever it was I didn't want to do. He'd spin it as doing him this big favor and say he needed me and would promise that he'd never ask me to do something if it wasn't really important to him. He'd say he was scared his mom would take me away from him if I didn't do it and that he couldn't protect me if he couldn't reach me."

"How old were you when that started?" Vault asks.

"Almost thirteen."

"Christ," Ryker scrubs his face and starts pacing.

"They were small jobs at first. Scary and thrilling. And every time I finished one, Kaleb would come to me soon after praising me and saying that he's so proud of me."

"Positive reinforcement," Vault mutters.

"A couple years of getting attention like that and I would volunteer to do bigger, more dangerous things for him." They don't ask what those are, and I don't offer examples. "I moved out of my foster parent's house when I turned eighteen. There were nine of us in Kaleb's crew by then, and I was his favorite. I was his girl." Saying that makes my chest hurt. God, I've been so fucking stupid. "I caught him cheating on me and our relationship died a dozen more deaths before I was able to successfully put a wall up between him and me."

They don't ask for details and again, I don't offer any.

"I was in the process of moving across state and starting over by myself when he set fire to my former foster parent's house." I look at Dmitri. "Addie was still living with them at the time."

Ryker's brow furrows. "She lived with you in the foster house?"

"Yes. It's how we got so close. She truly is like a sister to me. And yes, Kaleb's mother placed her there."

Vault rubs the back of his neck and grunts.

I clear my throat, unsure if I've confused them

or not. Fuck it, I'll keep talking. "Addie wasn't home the night of the fire, so she wasn't in danger. The Brenner's barely got out alive and lost everything. Kaleb came to me asking if I wanted to take care of Addie." I lean against the desk and hug myself. "I didn't hesitate to say yes. The fear of her going to someone else... *anyone* else... terrified me. I couldn't risk losing her. But I didn't realize that taking her would tie me so tight to Kaleb until it was too late."

"How so?" Ryker asks.

"I needed a house, a good job, and a solid foundation for me to be approved as her guardian. Kaleb bought the house I currently live in, and charges me minimal rent so I can afford it. He funded my college degree so I could get a job working as a medical coder at home. That way I'm with her more. It took time to get all the paperwork in place, which was miraculously rushed and pushed through. Until recently, I thought that part was a miracle, but now I see his mother must have still had pull in the system to make that happen. And all those things came at a cost."

I look down at the scar on my wrist.

"He brands us. Once he does, you're in for life. That's the price I paid to keep Addie. And God, how I wish I hadn't done it. Letting Addie go, and keeping contact with her, would have been the better option. But I know Kaleb and I knew his mother. I couldn't risk Addie going into a worser Hell just because I wanted to run from Kaleb. His mother threatened me enough times over the years with my placement, and that bitch would have absolutely put Addie in an extremely abusive home just to punish me."

I can't even look at Dmitri now. I'm scared of

what I'll see if I do. Does he hate me yet?

"If you're branded," Ryker says, "why did you think doing this one last job for Kaleb would get you out?"

"Because he's never lied to me." I say it automatically, so easily. So stupidly. "I now realize how foolish I am to have believed it." My throat tightens and I want to cry. "But it's too late to run now. I'd rather face him head on, with no fucks left, than live one more day regretting not having done things differently all those years ago."

"How did he know about the Scrapyard and Dmitri fighting that night?" Ryker asks.

"No clue. But if there's a shady person in this city, I guarantee you Kaleb knows them. And that old man who runs the cage fights is shady as hell. When I stalked the building looking for Dmitri, he denied ever having seen me, or about there ever being a fight, and acted like he had no clue who Dmitri was. He had me feeling delusional, even when he was the one who brought me up to the room that night as D's prize."

Ryker glances at Dmitri, but his expression doesn't give away anything.

"Where's Kaleb's mother now?" Dmitri asks. His voice controlled. Scary.

"She died about three years ago."

Ryker and Vault look at each other for a quick second.

"You're sure?" Vault asks.

"Yeah." I remember it was about the same time the DEA took down Emmanuel's crew. I always suspected the cartel had her killed, but never dared to ask Kaleb about it. I look at Ryker and add, "Kaleb was devastated, which made his behavior worse for a while. He got more violent and obsessive."

"With you."

I nod. "After the drugs started running dry, Kaleb got involved with gun runs and he dragged me with him to the first meeting. They called me his lap dog and said they heard I was a bitch who liked getting fucked by animals, and for me to bend over. I refused. Kaleb lost his head. It got… really ugly."

It's hard to believe the guy who let Emmanuel's guys take turns on me is the same one who, when another crew wanted the same thing, killed every single one of them and set their bodies on fire in a warehouse. I wasn't there for any of it. Kaleb made me leave and told me what he did later on. *"I'll burn the whole world down for you, babygirl. That's how much I love you."*

I made Kaleb my hero that day, too.

Then he beat the shit out of me a week later because I didn't answer my phone when he called.

"I think everyone who works for Kaleb hates him. He's too unpredictable. Too vindictive. Like I said, he's earned respect through fear, not integrity. And I get there's a fine line when you're dealing with criminals, but he's only become more and more unhinged, so we all walk on eggshells around him. He's killed a few of us already and sent several to prison. I suspect he's used the footage he has on them as evidence to get them locked them up, just like he threatened to do with me if I didn't get him information about Dmitri."

"Who was the last one to go to prison?" Vault asks.

"Corey." Not like they know him. "He's Casey's brother." Not like they know him, either.

"Do they go to the same facility each time?"

"Yes, and I have no clue how that works."

Dmitri's brow furrows. "Do you know *why* they're sent in?"

"No clue. But several weeks ago, Kaleb was elated about a call he got from one of his connections in prison. I didn't ask about it because I was too scared to find out. If Kaleb's happy, it means something really sick and bad has happened."

Ryker looks over at Dmitri and again, I can't read the looks on their faces.

That's when the truth suddenly hits me like an anvil to the head. "Your dad died in prison," I say, turning to Dmitri. "Kaleb sent someone in there to do it." My belly twists thinking it's a good possibility that someone was Corey. I drop to my knees in front of him. "I'm so, so, so sorry."

The weight of Kaleb's actions crushes me.

Dmitri swallows hard and cups my cheek. "You have no reason to apologize, Daelyn."

Oh, but I do. "I helped him get too much power. I should have run, taken Addie, and hidden far away from here."

"Running wouldn't have stopped Kaleb from killing my father," he says quietly. "And it wouldn't stop him from chasing after you. There was never a chance of escape for you, Firefly."

He's right.

Dmitri runs his thumb across my cheek. It's so soft, so sweet. The opposite of what I'm used to. I pull away, undeserving of his tenderness.

D snatches my wrist and shakes his head. "Don't do that."

"I didn't do anything."

"Don't pull away from kindness, Daelyn." He tugs my arm slightly, bringing me closer. "Don't pull away from *me*."

Shaking my head, I wish I could tell him how horrible I feel. How sorry I am that Kaleb's twisted and has come after him like this. I wish I could say that these past few days with Dmitri have given me more joy than I've had in my entire life, because he kept me safe, he empowered me, he held and played with me. He cherished me.

Instead, I swallow all those useless confessions because they don't matter. My feelings don't matter. My life... doesn't matter.

"I have an idea," I say, going numb again. "It'll make him absolutely lose his shit, but I think it'll knock him down enough for you to take him."

Dmitri arches his brow. "We're all ears, baby."

I turn to Vault. "Can you clip surveillance footage and make a copy of it?"

"Sweetheart, I can do anything you need me to."

"Okay..." I straighten up. "I think I have a plan." Stepping away from Dmitri, I hug myself again. "He wanted to fuck you, take everything from you... so, we're going to give him a taste of his own medicine."

D tips his head to the side. "You want me to take everything away from him instead?"

"You already have." My smile feels cruel and cold. "You've taken *me*."

"That's not good enough," Dmitri argues, crushing my heart. "This doesn't end with you as a prize."

"It certainly started that way," I snap back. But he's right, I just don't want to see the truth about where this ending will lead us all. "I can't lose you," I whisper. "I refuse to lose you, Dmitri."

"We both know Kaleb won't stop until I'm dead."

"Once he discovers I've switched sides, he's going to kill me, too." It's amazing how calm I am saying that. I cup his face. The words *I love you* hang on the tip of my tongue, but I bite down on them and swallow. "I dug my grave a long time ago, D. If I can save you before I'm buried, I will."

"I'm not going to let you do that."

"You don't have a choice."

Chapter 38

Dmitri

I end up calling in Sophie to escort Daelyn back to my bedroom while I stay with Ryker and Vault. After everything Daelyn's told us, I need a goddamn minute.

"Your girl told us way more than I could find with my research methods," Vaults says. "Kaleb's not just elusive, he's practically non-existent online."

"Like me." With a heavy sigh, I scrub my face and lean over to rest my elbows on my knees. My entire life has spiraled down a deep rabbit hole in a matter of days.

"Don't even think of doing it," Ryker growls from across the room.

"I'm not thinking of doing anything."

"Don't lie. You want to take this on by yourself." Ryker stalks closer. "She's a dead woman walking, D. If this guy is as psychotic as she's painted him, he'll kill her for this."

My entire body locks as rage consumes my vision. "No, he won't."

"If he doesn't, someone else will... like a possible cartel connection. It's gotten too messy."

No one will touch her. I won't allow it. "I have to make sure she's some place safe when this goes down. Her and Addie both." I look over at Ryker and am once again struck with how empty my life truly is. How little I have to offer. Shit, I have nothing outside of this club, and bringing Daelyn and Addie here isn't an option. Addie's just a kid. I can't explain this place to her and I'm not about to roll a burning dumpster with a target on it into Ryker's house, either.

"They can stay with me," Vault offers.

"Or Knox," Ryker suggests. "Or me. Tara can help keep them comfortable until…" His voice trails off.

Until what? I die? I kill Kaleb? The cops come knocking on our door? Someone else comes to retaliate? No. I can't drag my friends into this.

"I'll put them up somewhere," I say, scrambling to think of where that might be. Maybe Silas can help me secure a place. He's got a lot of connections. And the man's a walking safe with no combo to his lock. What he knows, he never shares. He'd help me for the right price.

"I'm going to sleep on this for the night." When I stand, my knees pop and muscles ache. "Kaleb's not coming back from Miami for another few days, so there's still time."

"Don't do this on your own, D." Ryker shoves his finger at me. "We're *family*."

"I know." Which is exactly why I will do this my way. I'm not letting my friends, the only family I have left, get blood on their hands.

Heading out, it's like I've got one-hundred-pound weights strapped to my legs. Each stride I take is harder than the last. By the time I make it to my bedroom, I'm so exhausted I could sleep for a week. But I've now got a plan in mind and have made my peace with it.

Daelyn's sitting on my cot when I open the door and she quickly tucks her phone under her legs, looking guilty. "Hey."

"Where's Sophie?"

The toilet flushes, and Sophie comes out of my bathroom soon after. "If you're hungry, I can... Oh, hey D."

I give her a tight smile and nod towards the door. She takes my hint and leaves. There's no way I want her involved in any of this shit. Once we're alone, my room feels like a tomb. My safe space no longer feels like home.

Staring at Daelyn's lap, and the cell peeking out from under her thigh, I want to know who she texted or called. But I don't ask. It doesn't matter, anyway. If Daelyn's playing both sides, or is only on one, she's still going to lose somehow. Fucking hell, this is awful.

"How do you feel?"

"Terrified," she admits, her shoulders slumping. "I just texted Addie to see how her day was. She's sent me some pics. Want to see?"

"Y—" I cough to clear my dry throat. "Yeah." Sitting down next to her on my cot, I feel small and out of place in my room. Scratch being a tomb, my place feels like a prison cell on death row.

"Here." With trembling hands, Daelyn pulls up the text thread. "Look how big her smile is."

The girl in the photo is a striking image of my mother when she was younger. So much so, my heart gallops in my chest with panic. But there are noticeable differences. Addie's got a different shaped mouth, and her eyes are dark brown, not ice blue like mine. Her hair is dyed blue, and she's a healthy weight. My mother... *our* mother... always looked like a bony little bird on the brink of starvation.

Addie's throwing a peace sign with her freckled

cheek smashed against another girl's cheek. They've got matching bracelets on and look vibrant and happy. In the next picture, she's out in the ocean with her hands up in the air. The water isn't blue-green like the Caribbean, but it's still beautiful. She's surrounded by water and blue skies. The one after that is her name written with seashells in the sand. The one after that is her eating pizza and flipping the camera off.

"She comes home tomorrow," Daelyn says quietly.

"So do you," I remind her.

Our time is up.

Funny, when the club gets a Butterfly for a month, the days crawl by so slowly, it's downright painful. It might be fun, but it's always a lot of work. By the end, the Dom needs a long mental break, and the Butterfly is set free to live her best life with the experiences she's gained here.

Daelyn isn't a Butterfly. And I can't keep her, no matter how badly I want to.

"Are you hungry?"

She shakes her head.

"Tired?"

She nods.

Not giving a fuck about how we can't both fit, I lay down on my cot and tuck her next to me, holding her tight. My eyes burn from exhaustion, but there's no way I can fall asleep. Daelyn cries silently, facing away from me, and knowing she's trying to hide her misery, and that I'm pretending I don't see it, kills me.

Finally, exhaustion takes her under, and she passes out in my arms.

That's when I get to work.

...

The next morning, we head back to Daelyn's house. Every time I try to leave, she comes up with some excuse to make me stay. I don't like clingy women. But I love how Daelyn wraps her entire precious body around me when she begs me to stay a little longer.

"I take it back," I say, pretending to be annoyed. "You're not a firefly, you're a damn koala."

"I'm baaaack!" yells someone from the living room.

Daelyn and I break away from each other like we were just electrocuted.

"Yay!" Daelyn rushes out of the kitchen and straight to Addie. "You're home early."

"Yeah, too early by the looks of what I just cockblocked." Addie beams a big smile at me. "Hi. I'm Addie."

Daelyn's face loses some of its color as she gawks at me, not knowing what to say.

"I'm Dmitri. It's nice to meet you."

"Your eyes are crazy bright."

"Uhh, thanks."

"Sorry, that was random. Annnd awkward." Addie shakes her head, looking just like my mom would when she was embarrassed. "I'm gonna blame this on sitting in the car for way too long."

Daelyn grabs her bag from her. "What time did you leave this morning?"

"Saul wanted to drive most of the night so we wouldn't hit too much traffic. I couldn't sleep though, so I just watched a million hours of anime, and now my brain's mush." Addie slips past us and heads to the kitchen. "Ugh, I'm starving. Do we have stuff for pancakes?"

This is my chance to bow out. "I've gotta hit the road, Dae."

"Don't leave because I'm here," Addie calls out. "Have pancakes with us!"

"No, no, he's got stuff to do," Daelyn argues. "We can't hold him hostage with pancakes."

"A hostage situation would be so lucky to have my pancakes involved."

My feet won't budge. I need to leave, yet being in the presence of my long-lost baby sister has me pinned in place. This could be my only chance to get to know her.

"You look like a banana man to me," Addie says.

I *hate* bananas. "Yup, I sure am."

"See?" Addie slaps Daelyn on the shoulder with a spatula. "I'm so good at reading people. I just knew he was a banana pancake guy."

Daelyn rolls her eyes and then mouths, "*I'm so sorry*" at me when Addie turns her back to us.

Shaking my head, I keep my mouth shut, but there's no hiding the smile on my face.

"Come on, D. Help me set the table."

"Yeah, *D*." Addie cracks an egg, and pieces of the shell fall into the batter bowl. "Shit." She tries to pinch them with her fingertips, but the tiny pieces evade her.

"Use the broken shell in your hand to scoop them," I say. "They'll come right out."

Addie takes my advice. "Holy crap. That was crazy easy." She looks up at me and my chest tightens even as warmth spreads across it. "You're a genius."

"Nah, I can't take credit for it. My friend Knox gave me that tip."

Daelyn slams a bottle of maple syrup on the table behind us. "What else are we having with these hostage pancakes?"

"Ummm..." Addie purses her lips. "Chicken nuggets and ice cream."

Daelyn puts her hands on her hips. "What is wrong with you?"

"Ugh, I can't help it! They made me eat healthy stuff the whole time! I'm literally fifty percent smoothie now." She flips the burned pancakes in the pan. "My body is in withdrawal. I legit dreamed of a peanut butter sundae last night. With gummy bears on top."

Daelyn preheats the oven. "You're a pain in the ass. I don't even think we have chicken nuggets."

"I stuck an emergency stash behind the ice tray." Addie dumps three blackened pancakes onto a plate.

"Oh my god, you did." Daelyn pulls out a small, crumpled bag, and looks half annoyed, half impressed.

Addie pours more batter into the way too hot frying pan.

Watching them move around, picking on each other, laughing together, has me feeling like I've stepped into an alternate universe. One that's happy and warm and smells like flowers and burned breakfast.

Is this what my life could have been like if things had gone just a little differently?

Would I have lived in a house full of laughter

with the smoke alarm going off, and have ice cream for lunch?

"Oh my god!" Daelyn opens the sliding glass door and fans the smoke detector. "You've been home for two seconds and you're already causing chaos."

Addie laughs maniacally as she flips her pancakes. "Eat them while they're hot, Dmitri!"

I stuff my face with those burned, god awful banana pancakes.

It's the best meal I've ever had in my life.

...

"I'm gonna go," I say once again. We've cleaned all the dishes, and I looked at every seashell Addie's brought back for Daelyn, but it's seriously time to leave.

My girl walks me to the front door, looking awkward and nervous. "Thank you for…" She glances over her shoulder, even though Addie's gone upstairs to unpack and shower.

"Thank *you*. It was nice to meet her face-to-face." This is probably the only memory I'll ever make with my half-sister. "She's really happy," I say quietly, tucking Daelyn's hair behind her ear. "You've done a great job giving her all she needs."

Daelyn's expression falls.

"I'll have a car pick you up tomorrow."

"What? Why?"

"I want you both out of town before shit hits the fan with Kaleb, Firefly."

"*No*." She steps forward like she can stop me. "This is *my* fight, Dmitri."

"No, it's not." It never was. I bend down and

kiss her gently. "It's always been mine. And I'll do better if I know you and Addie are safe and untouchable."

"Dmitri."

"This isn't up for negotiation." I step outside, my palms sweating. "I can handle Kaleb, but I need you to make sure you and Addie are safe so I can stay focused."

It kills me that I'm basically manipulating Daelyn by using Addie as a reason for her to stay away. But I mean it. I'll fight stronger if I'm not worried about them getting hurt, too.

"Give me this. *Please*, Firefly."

She crosses her arms over her chest. "We'll discuss it later."

She's not going to back down. Not that I thought she would. After kissing me fiercely one more time, Daelyn shuts the door between us.

"Lock it!" I holler, relieved when the bolt clicks into place.

Stuffing my hands in my pockets, I head down the street to where I'd parked my bike in the alleyway like usual.

Kaleb stands by my Ducati, dressed in black jeans and a hoodie, with a gun in his hand. "It's about fucking time," he says, his gaze shifting to make sure we're alone.

"Yeah, Daelyn wouldn't let me leave any sooner." I stop right in front of him, and his expression hardens.

"Keep her name out of your fucking mouth."

"Oh, I've had more than her name in my mouth." I flash him a smile. "You know, she makes the best noises when she comes. And the way her pussy clenches my—"

He raises the gun and aims it at my forehead.

Footsteps close in from behind me, and I smile internally knowing everything I've planned is turning out perfectly so far.

Let the final game begin.

Chapter 39

Daelyn

By midnight, my stomach's a twisted mess and I'm panicking.

Daelyn: Call me.

Addie's asleep in her room. She crashed an hour ago, saying she was so happy to be back in her own bed.

Pacing my bedroom, I can't shake the feeling that something's wrong. My nerves are shot. I've just outed not only myself, but my family — because that's what Kaleb and the rest of his crew are to me, whether they're good or not.

And I gave them up to save the one I love most, and someone I barely know.

Staring at my cell, I'm positively seething because I've been left on delivered, just like the five other times I've texted this evening.

Daelyn: I'm scared.

Kaleb might not be home for another five days, but the time bomb I'm straddling is already ticking. *Fuck my life.* And Fuck Dmitri too, because he showed me what safety and peace felt like and then stripped me of both by taking me back to reality.

The best week of my life will cost me my entire future.

Rubbing my tired eyes, I creep downstairs, so I don't wake Addie, and head to my laptop. There's no way I can fall asleep, so I might as well stay busy and get work done and stay distracted. Opening the website to my bank account, I transfer all of it into Addie's. She doesn't know I've opened this one for her. All the money I get from the state to be her guardian goes into this account, so she'll have a nice chunk to start college with. If not college, then she can invest it or buy a house or something. No matter what, she won't have to depend on someone else to get ahead in life.

Unlike me.

My heart aches over Kaleb and I don't even understand why. He's awful. And yet...

My back sliding glass door creaking open makes me freeze. *Dmitri*. Relief flows through me, having him come back. I'm sure he's going to be mad that I forgot to put that wood slab back on it to keep it secure, but in my defense, I have a lot going on and those burnt pancakes kept setting the alarm off earlier.

"I've been calling and texting you all fucking night," I say, getting up from my desk and heading into the dark kitchen.

"I know."

My heart stops.

Ace stands in front of me, his gaze blazing with fury. He holds up a cell phone that's not his, and on it are the texts I've been sending Dmitri. How on earth does he have D's cell phone? "You fucked up, Dae."

I take a step back. "I... listen... I can explain—" I stumble over Addie's beach bag and crash onto the floor. Ace storms over and grabs me by the hair, his face inches from mine and I see his eyes are bloodshot. He drags me into the living room and shoves me against the wall.

"Dae?" Addie yells from upstairs. "You okay?"

My eyes widen with terror. *Oh my god. Oh my god.* Ace glowers at me and puts his finger to his lips, telling me to be quiet.

"Dae?" Addie calls out again. We hear her pad across her bedroom and open the door.

"I've got this one," the woman says behind Ace. "You take care of that little bitch upstairs. *Permanently.*"

"No problem, boss."

Panic races in my veins when Ace lets go of me to race up the steps. "Addie! *Run!*"

But it's too late. I hear her scream. A door slams. There's a bunch of banging and I try to fight off the person pinning me down so I can get help. But the woman on top of me has a gun to my head and something sharp in her hand that burns when it pricks me.

The last thing I see is that bitch's face in mine. Her blonde hair. Her piercing blue eyes. Her red mouth. It's *her*.

"You were supposed to be dead," I mumble, just as the drugs take me.

...

Dmitri

I'm cuffed to the wall of a familiar room.

Daelyn said Kaleb was unpredictable, but so far, I find that untrue. I'm right where I suspected he'd take me.

Groaning, I tip my head back, and try to stand so my shoulders are no longer bearing my weight. I was clocked in the head pretty fucking hard in that alley and I had to play sleeping beauty while Kaleb took my phone and my knife out of my pockets before him and his boy hauled my ass into the back of a truck and straight to here.

Now I'm tied to the wall, the same one I fucked Daelyn against that first night, and I feel like I deserve a prize for playing possum so well. It was a test on self-control I nearly failed.

I'll continue letting Kaleb think he has the upper hand for now. I work best when I'm being underestimated.

"Oh good, you're finally awake." Kaleb's so close to my face I could bite his nose off.

"Your breath wreaks."

He shoves my head back, slamming it against the wall.

Laughter bubbles out of me.

He paces back and forth, seething.

"You can't win this fight, Kaleb."

"I already have." He punches me hard in the belly next.

I wheeze, then laugh again. "Try harder, motherfucker. You hit like a little bitch."

Kaleb hits me in the head again, and my vision flashes black for a second.

I laugh some more.

At about five inches shorter, and probably fifty pounds of muscle lighter than me, he's still a force to be reckoned with. And I need to tread carefully so I don't accidentally die prematurely of a fractured skull or some shit.

"I fucked her here, you know." Looking around the room makes me feel slightly nostalgic. "Right here, against this wall, I had her wrists raw from these cuffs and cunt drenched around my fat dick."

Kaleb groans and covers his ears, but not well enough since he's still holding his Glock.

"You brought her right into my arms, Kaleb. I guess I should thank you. She's the best pussy I've had in a while."

He rears up and screams in my face.

"Kaleb, knock it off."

We both glance over at a blonde woman standing in the doorway.

"Mommy's home," I tease in a low voice.

Her heels click-clack against the floor as she saunters closer. "You look so much like your father," she says to me.

I swallow back my rebuttal. She's not worth wasting my breath on.

Gretchen Calloway trails a sharp, red fingernail down my torso, scraping my skin. "She chose this animal, Kaleb," she chides smoothly. "Your precious girl picked this monster over you. She turned on you in less than a fucking *week*."

His body language changes completely.

Where I merely pissed him off teasing him, his mother has actually triggered him.

Fucking hell, I hope Daelyn's got her doors locked like I told her to. I'm not sure what time it is, but I've got everything in place to keep her and Addie safe and a car will be on its way soon for them. Ryker, Vault, and Knox don't know what I've done and I'm hoping by the time they find out, this will all be over.

Gretchen runs her tongue along her pearly whites, eyeing me up just before she speaks to her son. "Daelyn's always been a disappointment. I don't know why you put so much effort into someone who doesn't deserve you."

"Shut up," Kaleb growls behind her. "Shut. The fuck. Up."

"I'm only telling you what you need to hear." Gretchen turns to him. "Dae's betrayed you with the man who killed your father. She fucked this man, over and over."

All the air blows out of Kaleb as the color drains from his face. "I told her to fuck him. You... you told me to do this. She followed *my* orders because it's what you wanted. Daelyn's a good girl."

"She's a whore."

Kaleb gets in her face. "Don't talk about her like that!"

"Or what? You'll do something about it?" Gretchen laughs. "Please. You're so fucking weak, Kaleb. I had such high hopes for you, but you've remained sloppy and pathetic. Your father was right. I should have aborted you."

Jesus Christ. This woman is horrible.

"You're pathetic. A weak little boy who could never do anything on his own. Even Daelyn is sick of your shit."

Kaleb's heavy breaths rattle out of him. His nostrils flare. His hand trembles when he raises his gun to her. "Shut up."

Gretchen laughs at him, just like I had. "Get that goddamn gun out of my face, Kaleb."

He pulls the motherfucking trigger.

...

Daelyn

"There she is."

My heart swells at those three words, my memory buzzing like a little honeybee bouncing across a flower field, bringing me back to Dmitri. *"I've never love-loved a woman in my life. I've never seen one and thought,* There she is.*"*

"Dmitri?" Groggy and disoriented, I blink a few times and his face comes into view. Except he's a lot thinner, and his hair is longer, and he's got facial piercings. Fury quickly sobers me when I realize who this is. "Ace."

"Wakey, wakey, Dae." He slaps the side of my head, making it pound harder.

"Addie."

"She's been taken care of," he spits out like she's trash. "About fucking time, too. I was sick of babysitting her."

Pure grief consumes me. Tremors takeover my body as a sob rips from my sore throat. "No." Drool dribbles from my mouth and I can't hold my head up. Sucking in a lungful of air, I scream and shake against my restraints. "*No!*"

"You did this to yourself," Ace sneers. "You fucking sealed her coffin when you sold Kaleb out." He holds a gun to my head and the look on his face is a mix of anger and resentment. "I should do us all a favor and blow your goddamn brains out right now."

I wish he would.

The guilt of Addie's death on my hands is unbearable.

She was all I had to live for.

And now she's *gone*.

Ace has scratches all over his face and arms. She must have tried to fight him off.

"How could you do this to her?" I scream.

Casey's holding me up, which I didn't realize until now.

"I didn't do this to Addie, Daelyn. *You* did," Ace claps back.

Pop! A gun goes off somewhere in the warehouse we're in.

"Shit." Ace pulls away from me and looks up.

"Get the fuck away from her." Kaleb marches down the steps with blood sprayed all over his face and chest.

Ace steps back and Casey lets me go, his hands raised in surrender.

The closer Kaleb gets, the more I shrink. *Oh God.* A familiar numbness creeps up my limbs and I welcome it. I detach completely. He can do whatever he wants to me, and I'd deserve it. No punishment would be severe enough for what I've caused Addie.

"The fuck?" Another of our crew steps up. "Kaleb, what did you—"

A bone-chilling scream tears out of Kaleb, and he spins around, firing off eight rounds, dropping our crew like flies. Then he storms straight towards me and raises his fist. "You stupid fucking cunt."

He breaks my nose.

I don't feel it.

He kicks my stomach.

I don't care.

Kaleb snatches my hair and pulls my head back. Whatever he's searching for in my eyes, he must not find. I've truly checked out.

"Kill me," I say calmly.

"You're not getting out of this so fucking easy, Daelyn." He yanks me forward, but I crumble to the floor. Whatever drug his mother shot into me has almost worn completely off, but I'm not going to let him figure that out. Especially considering my body doesn't seem to want to function after the news of Addie's d—

A fresh sob blows out of me. "She was a kid!" I scream on my hands and knees.

Kaleb kicks my ribs, sending me sprawling across the floor.

Everyone is here. Kaleb's entire crew. And most of them are dead on the ground.

He's lost his goddamn mind. I'm not going to be able to control or reason with him. And I've done this to myself. He knows I've betrayed him. He's taken everything away from me.

Dmitri...

I hope he stays away. Maybe he left my texts on delivered because he blocked me and has packed up and left town. I hope so. I hope—

"Casey, grab my girl a chair. The show's about to start."

Casey quickly follows orders and within a few heartbeats, Kaleb's slinging me into a folding chair. "You get the best seat in the house for this fight, babygirl." He pulls out my cell and takes a picture of me. I can only assume he's going to text it to Dmitri.

"He's not going to come," I say, taking shallow breaths. "If you think... Dmitri is... going to swoop in here... and save me... you've got him all wrong."

"The picture isn't for him, it's for me." Kaleb spits on my forehead, then caresses my cheek. "You look so beautiful, all busted and broken." His smile makes my stomach churn. "Sorry you lost Addie."

"Don't you dare say her name," I growl.

Kaleb cocks his gun and aims it at my head.

"Do it. Pull the trigger." I lean in with no fear. "Fucking do it, you sorry piece of shit!"

He hesitates, and I use the precious seconds to do exactly what Dmitri taught me. In three swift moves, I've disarmed Kaleb and have the gun pointed at him.

I pull the trigger.

Click.

I pull the trigger again, and again, and again. *Click, click, click*. My eyes widen with terror.

Kaleb's smile makes me back up. "You're adorable when you're stupid." He easily knocks the gun out of my hand, sending it sliding across the floor where Casey picks it up.

"You were really going to kill me," Kaleb seethes. "After everything we've been through, babygirl?"

"You mean after everything you've put me through."

"It was for your own good," he snaps. "Everything I did, I did out of love. You're my girl."

"No, I'm not."

His smile gets even worse. "You will be."

"Daelyn."

That voice.

My heart screams in horror when I see Ace escorting Dmitri down the steps at gun point. His face is busted and there's blood all over his clothing. When his gaze lands on me, they narrow viciously.

Ace kicks Dmitri in the back, sending him tumbling down the remaining flight of metal stairs.

"Daelyn," he grunts, staggering back to his feet. Blood pours from a fresh cut on his head.

"Your sister's dead, Dmitri." Kaleb whirls on him with that awful smile. "Daelyn killed your little Addie."

"*Addie.*" Dmitri stumbles forward, loses balance, and falls to his knees again. Vomit flies out of his mouth. I think he's concussed. Or drugged. Maybe both? Dmitri looks me dead in the eyes asks, "Is she dead?"

I don't know if I should lie or tell the truth. Which will help him more right now?

Before I can answer, Kaleb shoves me, tipping me and my chair over. I crack the side of my face onto the floor and cry out.

Then all the cell phones go off with this horrible noise and large projection screens slide down from their wall mounts.

Tick, tick, tick…

BOOM.

Chapter 40

Dmitri

The concussion I've got is bad, but I'm not surrendering anytime soon. Not when the show has finally started.

I owe Vault and Silas for this one.

With confusion plastered on his blood-splattered face, Kaleb looks around the dead bodies who have their cells going off. Then he glances at Ace and Casey, before he digs his cell phone out of his back pocket like they have theirs. The projection screens lower down in unison and an image appears on each of them.

Daelyn clumsily stands up and laughs when the video starts playing.

My girl's strapped to the St. Andrew's cross at the Monarch and I'm fingering her.

"Who owns you? Say his motherfucking name."

Daelyn's groan is loud on the speaker system.

"Better keep me inside you," I say. *"Or I will stuff this pussy with my cock and fuck you until you taste my cum on your goddamn tongue."*

Daelyn explodes, her orgasm loud in the warehouse.

"Dmitri!" she screams as she comes undone. *"His fucking name..."* she sobs through the surround sound, *"is... Dmitri."*

Her confession ricochets around the Scrapyard's concrete interior.

When Daelyn mentioned this clip from the surveillance videos would be Kaleb's downfall, I didn't believe her. But I did trust her. And seeing the glorious shades of red Kaleb's face has turned, I feel such pride for my girl coming up with this idea. I'm just sorry I wasn't able to save her from the consequences like I'd planned.

She's right about something else, too. Kaleb definitely thinks two steps ahead.

When I claimed I wanted to take everything away from him, Daelyn said I already had because I'd taken *her*. She wasn't wrong.

"You wanted this," Daelyn says, walks slowly towards him. "You asked for it. No... *demanded* it."

Kaleb's jaw ticks, his eyes are so fierce they could knock a grown man to his knees. But Daelyn's stronger than most men. Speaking of which...

Silas appears at the front entrance and nods. I'd worked with him while Daelyn slept during our last night together to create this nightmare for Kaleb. Silas's cooperation and expertise only cost me most of my savings. The rest of it I'd marked to go to Daelyn for her and Addie, in case I didn't make it out of this alive, which someone at the Monarch will find in my room.

My boys will be pissed that I didn't drag them into this Hell with me, but they can't do shit about it after I'm dead. I just hope they forgive me and understand that I'm willing to die, protecting them, too.

Kaleb grabs Ace's gun and shoots all four of the projector screens, like it'll stop the show, then he aims the gun at Daelyn. "You're out of the crew, just like you wanted, babygirl."

"No!" I lunge to shield Daelyn and knock her to the ground. The bullet pierces my shoulder instead of her head, the pain searing as I climb to my feet and barrel into Kaleb, taking him down. Except I go off kilter thanks to my head injuries fucking with my coordination, and Kaleb manages to roll on top of me.

We go blow for blow.

All the while, the surveillance footage plays around us on the big screens.

"Who owns you? Say his motherfucking name."

Daelyn groans.

"Better keep me inside you. Or I will stuff this pussy with my cock and fuck you until you taste my cum on your goddamn tongue."

"Dmitri!" Daelyn screams as she comes. "His fucking name… is… Dmitri."

The video loops again.

Kaleb's eyes widen because there's nowhere he can look that Daelyn won't be.

Smashing his head with mine, I knock him off me and we tumble across the concrete floor, tearing at each other. He's no match for my strength but makes up for it by being manic. Nothing causes him pain. He just swings, kicks, laughs, and screams.

The man's checked out.

"Who owns you? Say his motherfucking name."

Daelyn groans.

"Better keep me inside you. Or I will stuff this pussy with my cock and fuck you until you taste my cum on your goddamn tongue."

"Dmitri! His fucking name…is… Dmitri."

Kaleb clamps his ears with his hands. "Fuck!"

"Go!" I holler at her.

Daelyn doesn't move. Neither do Ace or Casey.

"It was supposed to be us!" Kaleb screams. "*Us*, Dae!"

She flinches when he screams her name.

Scrambling away from me, Kaleb bolts for her, and I tackle him to the ground once more. He's not getting his hands on her ever again, goddamnit.

Without a cage to keep us contained, we're like two wild animals off our leashes. And we're both fighting for the same thing.

If I kill Kaleb, Daelyn will likely resent me forever because she loved him first.

If I die, she'll hate Kaleb for taking away the man who showed her that love is safety, kindness, and support.

There's no winning this fight for either of us because we both stand to lose Daelyn.

It's hopeless.

So, I change the trajectory of my thoughts and block Daelyn out. I imagine everyone that's abused in some way. How they feel helpless and scared. How they have to bandage and hide their wounds. How they feel like no one in the world is on their side. How they blame themselves for doing something that makes them deserve to be treated so badly. How terrible things happen to good people and it's not fair. I think of bad people getting away with everything and that's not fair either. I think of Miss Ashley and Ryker and Vault. I think of Sophie and Knox. Of my dad. My mom. I think of Addie. Every time my fist connects with Kaleb, it's one more goodbye. One more door closing.

The more I swing, the better I feel. Pain sings through my body. My vision blurs. I can't move my left arm that much, thanks to the bullet hole, but it's okay. I still have my right arm, which works good enough.

Kaleb's jaw opens and closes.

I should break it.

His face is a swollen, bloody mess.

I should break that too.

"Dmitri!" Silas yells. "It's over."

Those words warble in my ears. "It's not fucking over," I growl. "Not if he's still breathing."

I lift Kaleb's head and see Daelyn's name tattooed on his bloody neck. Just when I'm about to slam his skull on the ground, something sharp pierces my side.

It happens again… and again.

Kaleb laughs, his arm jerking back and forth as he stabs me a fourth time.

My knife. I'd forgotten he took my knife earlier. The mistake costs me.

Daelyn screams. The terror of that sound races down my back and I hold my side, barely able to breathe. Blood pours from the open wounds.

Fffffuuuucccck. How could I be this stupid?

I'd gotten cocky thinking I would best this motherfucker and play with him, torture him, like he had me and my father. I tried to play a psychopath's game and I've lost.

"Dmitri!" Daelyn races forward, but Ace grabs and lifts her off the ground to keep her away.

I'm grateful.

My vision darkens as I fall onto my side, which gives Kaleb the upper hand. I'm cold and can't feel most of my body anymore. I think I'm going into shock.

"Keep her back," I slur, panting through the

pain.

Daelyn fights like a maniac to escape Ace's clutches. He ends up dropping her, and she does exactly what I taught her in a situation like this. My girl puts one leg behind his, crouches down, and straightens her back leg out, tripping Ace and knocking him down. She scrambles across the floor and heads straight towards—

Kaleb presses the blade against me again, bringing my focus back to him.

"You took *everything* from me," he says, blood pouring from his mouth. "You took her."

I hope I'm smiling, but I can't feel my face to tell. "You… gave her… to me…"

Lashing out, I grab his throat, covering Daelyn's name with my hand.

Kaleb slams his blade into me one last time.

Pop!

His expression stills, eyes lose focus. Blood drips down the side of his face, coating my fingers. I let go of his throat and he collapses with a bullet hole in his right temple and his brains splattered all over the left side of him. Leaning back, I fall on my ass, letting Kaleb go.

Daelyn's next to us, holding the gun. Eyes blown wide, she pops off every bullet in the clip at him until she's shooting blanks.

"That's my good girl," I say, collapsing with the blade still stuck in my side.

Daelyn's gun clatters to the floor and she falls to her knees. Tears pour down her beautiful face as she crawls to me. "No, no, no! Dmitri, *no!*" She hooks her arm under my neck and lifts my head. "Help us!" she screams. "Someone help!"

The strength it takes to touch her face is more than I have.

"There she is," I whisper as darkness consumes me.

I surrender and lose the fight.

Chapter 41

Daelyn

"There she is…" Dmitri strokes my cheek with the barest of touches and then his hand falls and he goes limp in my arms.

"No!" My heart shatters into a million pieces. I shake Dmitri, but he doesn't open his eyes again. This can't be real. This can't be happening. "Wake up, D." I shake him hard but he's lifeless. Blood creeps across the floor and it's a mix of mine, Kaleb's and Dmitri's. It stains everything red, red, red.

I can't think. I can't move.

I can't feel.

"Dmitri, don't go." I shake him harder. "Please." Why isn't he waking up? His body is still so warm. Sweat and blood have made his forehead sticky. "Please come back. Wake up. Don't die on me. I…"

This is a mistake. It was supposed to be me. I hug him tight and feel the wetness from his blood all over my hand covering his gunshot wound.

"It was supposed to be *meeee*!" I scream.

"Fucking hell," Silas says. "You gotta get out of here, sweetheart." The old man drags me away from Dmitri and I'm too stunned to fight him.

"I got her." Ace grabs me by the back of the neck and squeezes it. I'm still too shocked to realize I'm being shoved outside and into his car. The door slams shut. My pulse swishes loudly in my ears.

Dmitri is dead. *Swish.*

Addie is dead. *Swish.*

Kaleb is dead. *Swish... Swish... Swish.*

I scream until my voice breaks. This is all my fault. Dmitri was never supposed to get hurt. Addie was never supposed to be touched.

I can't live like this. I can't...

Ace shifts into gear and hightails it out of the Scrapyard's lot.

"Kill me," I whisper. "Or give me something to use and I'll do it myself."

Ace's eyes blow wide with terror. "Daelyn, no."

"Yes." My tone is as hollow as my heart, my eyes dead. "I can't live without them."

"Addie's okay," he lies, and reaches over and grabs my leg. "Dmitri will be too."

I shake my head and feebly smack his hand off me. "Fuck you." How dare he lie to me right now. "I was there. You took her. You..." I can't even say the rest. He knows what he's done.

Anguish cuts through me like a chainsaw.

This whole time, I thought for sure Ace cared about her. I was so terrified they were sneaking around behind my back, and to hear him say he...

"Look at me, Daelyn." Ace grips my chin and forces me to face him. "I didn't kill Addie. I swear. You know I'd never do something like that."

And I never thought I'd kill Kaleb, but here we are.

"She's alive." Ace grips my face harder. "I fucking swear, Dae. It only sounded like I hurt her because I needed Gretchen to believe I'd followed her orders. But I'd rather set myself on fire than lay a hand on Addie."

I want desperately to believe him, but…

Ace lets me go. "Dmitri came to me last night. He said he was setting something up to get Kaleb out of our lives for good and asked for my help."

My lungs collapse and all the air whooshes out of me. "What?"

"I don't know how he found out where I lived, but yeah. He came to me and said you told him everything about Gretchen from the beginning. Hell, he even said you told him all your crimes and started rattling those off, too."

I have no words because shame creeps into my chest, filling in the gaps my heartbreak hasn't touched. Why would Dmitri go behind my back and do this? "What else did he say?"

"He promised he'd get us out and asked if there was anyone else who needed help as badly as you."

I swallow the lump in my throat. Dmitri tried to save as many as he could and has paid the ultimate price for being a fucking hero. It makes me sick. "What did you tell him?"

Ace turns onto a long dark road. "I told him Casey needs help, too."

Casey, the brother of the man who murdered Dmitri's father. How could D have such forgiveness in him? Then again, it wasn't Casey who was sent, and Corey, like the rest of us, didn't have a choice with Kaleb.

The car stops and the backdoor opens.

"Come on, Dae." Casey's suddenly there, helping me out. "I got her from here, man."

"You sure?"

"Yeah. Go."

Suddenly, Casey has my arm slung around his

neck and he's walking me into a building, holding me up because my legs aren't working right. Ace takes off to who knows where, his tires kicking up dust and gravel as he disappears.

Casey voice is barely audible when he says, "You did good tonight, Dae."

I can't even respond. The reminder of what I've done sends me over the edge all over again and I bawl.

"Shhhh, I know, I know." Casey tucks me into his chest and holds me together. "He wasn't a good man. There was never any good in him, baby."

"There's nothing good in me either," I cry. "And Dmitri is now..." A fresh wave of grief steals the air from my lungs. I drop to my knees and scream out my sobs.

Lights flash in my face as a van pulls into wherever the fuck Ace has dumped me.

Casey hauls me to my feet. "Come on. We have to hurry."

Silas hops out of the van and rushes to the back, and a guy I've never seen before runs out of the building to meet him. They carefully pull someone out of the van.

It's Dmitri.

Hope is a dagger piercing my heart when Dmitri makes the most glorious, agonizing sound I've ever heard. *He's alive*! I try to break away from Casey to get to them, but his grip tightens. "Let them go in first, Dae."

The guy helping Silas get Dmitri inside grunts. "Fucking hell, bro, you're a mess."

D limps and can't walk without a lot of help. He screams out in pain, and my reaction is visceral to it. I escape Casey's hold on me, using the moves Dmitri taught me, and run across the gravel parking lot to get to him.

"He needs a hospital!" I shout.

"No cops. No hospitals. No evidence." Silas tips his head toward the door. "Everyone better get the fuck inside before we're seen."

Two motorcycles blaze up the road and fiercely turn into the lot with us. The first one sprays gravel as it skids to a stop, and the rider pulls off his helmet, tossing it on the ground as he lets his bike fall to it's side and he runs towards us. "What the fuck happened?"

It's Ryker.

And Vault isn't far behind.

"That's for him to say," Silas answers. "But he won the fight."

"Jesus Christ." Ryker helps Silas and the other guy carry Dmitri in. "You stupid motherfucker."

"Tried to... protect...y—" Dmitri's legs give out as he falls unconscious before they even get him inside.

"What the fuck happened, Knox?" Vault roars.

"I was brought in last minute to assist with a patch-up, which only meant one thing." The new guy, Knox, frowns. "That's why I called you guys."

Ryker, Vault, Silas, and the new guy all carry him into the building while I'm still standing in the parking lot, confused and unable to move again. I don't understand what's happening.

Vault pushes the door open and stalks towards me. One look at the blood all over me and he's pulling me into a hug. "Are you okay?"

"No." I don't want to be touched. I don't want to be here. I'm frozen. "He's been stabbed, shot, and beaten." My belly rolls imagining how much pain Dmitri must be in and I shove back from Vault. "He needs a hospital!"

Vault shakes his head. "The old man has a doctor on hand for shit like this." Vault looks at my face, and his brow furrows. "Your nose is broken."

"I'm fine."

"Here, let me set it."

"I'm fine! Fuck my nose. I don't care about me, fix Dmitri!"

Vault grabs my shoulders and says in an eerily calm tone, "Fixing you will help him."

I stall out and he nods his head. "On the count of three, okay?" He presses his thumbs against my sore nose, "Three... two... one."

Blinding pain almost makes me vomit, but I'm too disconnected for my brain and body to sync up.

"Atta girl."

"Get in here, Daelyn," Silas orders from the door. His fat belly stretches his blood-stained shirt out and he looks like he's about to keel over. I'm scared out of my mind. So many things have gone wrong, I can't process it, but I burst into movement.

Silas grabs my arm before I can make it past the door. "You're only job," he says sternly, "is to sit and talk with him, okay?"

My mouth runs dry when I hear Dmitri scream. Desperate to get to him, I push past Silas, racing towards that horrible sound.

Some guy in scrubs is already cutting D's shirt off. The stab wounds ooze blood, and his breathing is labored.

Silas shoves a fat finger in my face. "Just hold on to him and he'll hold on to you, understand me?"

I nod.

"Knox, start the IV," the scrub guy says.

"Talk to him, honey." Knox smiles, but it's not a nice one, as he gets to work. "Don't let all this be a fucking waste."

I gulp down all my pain and focus on what's important.

"Dmitri," I say against his ear. "You did so good." *There's so much blood...* "It's done."

"Happy thoughts, Daelyn." Knox runs the IV line and hangs a bag on a pole. "Happy sappy shit only."

I nod, trying to find something joyful worth saying. I'm not sure I can do this. There's too much blood. What if his organs have been punctured? What if his brain can't take one last concussion? What if...

"When you're all patched up, we're going to the beach." I place my hand in his, not liking how cold and clammy his skin feels. "How about that?"

Knox puts an oxygen mask on Dmitri's face.

There's a lot of fast movement. I can't bear to look at what they're doing to him. I can't stand to hear what the scrub guy is saying. Ryker stands in the doorway, his arms crossed as he glowers at me.

He blames me for Dmitri, as he should.

"Where should we go?" I run my hand down his arm. "Bahamas? Tahiti? Fiji?"

There's a lot of clanking and cursing from Knox and the scrubs guy.

I clear my throat and bend down to whisper in his ear, "Don't leave me. Please don't go. I'm sorry it took me so long to find you. I'm sorry you fought so hard... for so long. But I'm here. Me and you are *here*. The bad is over."

"She killed for you, bro," Knox chimes in from across the table. "Lucky motherfucker."

"She went to Hell just to drag you out," Ryker says.

"She's waiting for you to come back to her, D," Vault adds.

Tears silently slip down my cheeks while his family rallies around him.

I brush my mouth against Dmitri's temple and say, "Addie's going to be okay."

My heart breaks thinking of her. I don't know if Ace lied to me or not, but I'm desperate enough to believe that she's really okay. Even if it's not possible.

"She's probably making her horrible banana pancakes right now," I add, my throat closing up. "I'm so glad you got to meet her. Hug her."

I'm going to be sick.

Dmitri's eyes pop open and he tries to sit up like he just had a shot of adrenaline. His abs flex and several of the puncture wounds open and bleed more. He rips the oxygen mask off his face and screams.

"Fuck!" the scrub guy says. "Knox, get the—"

"On it!"

There's a lot of rushing around again and beeping noises go off loudly in the room.

Dmitri falls back, his head smacking the table he's on. Spittle flies from his mouth. "Fuck!" He hyperventilates. His face twists with agony, his eyes welling with tears. "This hurts." He groans with clenched teeth.

"Look at me," I say, panicking. "Dmitri, eyes on me."

He shakes violently, grunting as he tries to suck in a solid breath and can't. He slowly turns his head to me. "Dae…"

Eyes bloodshot and swollen, he goes to touch my face, but his shoulder is a wreck with that bullet hole, so it just flops and dangles off the table.

He cries out in agony again. "Fucking hell, get me something to bite on, damnit."

Ryker swiftly yanks his belt free and shoves past me to place it in his mouth. I grab his limp arm and rest it on his side, holding his bicep. Dmitri chomps down on the leather, his nostrils flaring as they sew him up.

It only takes a couple minutes for him to pass out again. I pull the belt out of his mouth and Knox puts the oxygen mask back on him.

"I hope he stays out for the rest of this," Vault says.

"Not with the massive concussion he's likely got," Knox argues.

Things grow frantic. Messy. When the scrub guy pulls the blade out of Dmitri's side, I nearly pass out.

"He's gonna be okay. He's gonna be okay." Knox works fast to staunch the bleeding. "He better fucking be okay."

I press my hand to Dmitri's chest. "Don't you dare leave me. I swear I'll crack into Hell to find you, Dmitri." The sweetness I tried to save him with evaporates. All I have is savagery left in me. "I'll drag your ass right back here with me. I don't care how long it takes. I don't care who I have to fight… who I have to kill… I *will* get to you." I dig my nails into his chilled skin. "I'm not letting you go. *Ever*. Do you hear me?"

Knox sighs. "We're good."

I'll take his word for it because I'm not looking

at the grotesque wounds on my man's body.

"Now listen to me." I scrape my nails along Dmitri's scalp. "You're going to buckle down and get right or I'm going to the beach without you."

His eyes flutter open, scaring the crap out of me. He slowly pulls the oxygen mask off again. "You… wouldn't… dare…"

"Try me."

His eyes glaze over for a few seconds before latching back onto me. "There she is," he says softly.

My heart soars.

"Keep your mask on, dipshit." Knox places it back over D's face.

Dmitri slowly raises his hand and flips him the bird.

Ryker and Vault chuckle from the doorway and I have no idea where Silas or Casey have gone.

Then Dmitri barks out in pain again, his body locking as a fresh wave of agony tears through him. "Fuuuuck!"

"Stay still," the scrub guy orders.

The pain he's in must be excruciating. "Hey, hey, look at me."

Dmitri's gaze swirls back to mine. His eyes are swollen and there's so much blood on him. It makes me want to kill Kaleb all over again. "Eyes on me," I order, taking the reins. "Stay with me, Dmitri."

He grunts and trembles while they work on the worst of his wounds. A tear falls from the corner of his less swollen eye. Our connection never breaks.

"You're doing so good."

His resolve hardens even though he keeps trembling in silent torment.

"Why can't you give him a painkiller or

something? Knock him out so he doesn't have to feel any of this."

"No!" Ryker and Vault yell at the same time.

"He doesn't allow that," Knox explains. "Stubborn masochistic fucker." He puts his hands up. "Not that I'm kink shaming, but damn, a little relief might do you some good, bro."

Dmitri clenches his teeth. "No."

I think I understand why he wants this pain, and it has nothing to do with sexual gratification.

If he can still hurt... then he's still living.

"I've got you," I say, lacing my hand with his. "You feel me?" I squeeze him. "You're still alive. You're still fighting."

His expression tenses as they finish closing the last puncture.

Finally, it's over.

"He's going to be okay," the scrub guy says. "I have no clue how he got this goddamn lucky, but the blade struck bone or soft tissues. Not a single vital organ was hit."

Relieved, I slump over, kissing his forehead. "Here that? You're stuck with me for life now."

"You had an angel on your shoulder tonight, D." The scrub guy pulls off his gloves and tosses them in the trash. "Either that, or the devil still isn't done with you."

Dmitri groans as his eyes flutter shut.

Chapter 42

Dmitri

"That's not necessary."

"First off, fuck you. Second off, yes, it is." Knox holds out some painkillers. "Shut up and take the damn things. It's over-the-counter shit, not Oxi."

I give in and swallow the stupid pills, chasing them with orange juice. "Where's Dae?"

"She'll be here soon."

I rub my forehead, wincing. My concussion has my head hurting more than the stab wounds on my torso, all of which are going to leave scars. I've got an extensive collection that seems to never end.

Knox tips his head to the ceiling and sighs dramatically. "I need a vacation away from you kids."

Ryker walks across the suite with a tray of grilled cheeses. "I think we've all earned a vacation."

"For real." Vault snatches a sandwich and takes a big bite.

"That could have gone so wrong," I say, too nauseous to eat.

"But it didn't," Knox claps back.

But it could have, I think again.

The last night Daelyn stayed with me at the Monarch, I waited for her to fall asleep, then I slipped out of the club and set my half-cocked plan into motion. I went for Ace, because he was the youngest member of Kaleb's gang, and it didn't take me long to realize he had a sweet spot for Daelyn and Addie. He was just as stuck as they were, too, which I used to my advantage.

I gave him a choice.

He picked Daelyn.

I think they all would have if I'd had the time to reach out to each member of Kaleb's crew. As it was, Ace only had a chance to contact Casey.

Two was better than none.

Kaleb never had their respect, but my girl sure as shit did, and I don't think Dae ever realized it. But to make my plan work, I had to make Kaleb come to me. His mother was just a bonus. Thanks to Vault's wizardry, I knew she was living in a condo in Miami. Why Kaleb told Daelyn his mother was dead is beyond me, unless it was one more thing to soften Daelyn with. Lord knows he wrung out her pity just to use her up however he saw fit.

Fucking hell, I'm glad he's dead.

Ace ratted Kaleb out once he knew Daelyn was on my side. He even said Kaleb never went to Miami but was letting Daelyn think she still had time to finish the job without him hovering over her.

Putting any amount of trust in Ace was a fool's move, but I did it anyway. He's only twenty, lost, angry, and scared because he's trapped in the same game as Daelyn.

I knew Kaleb was watching us the day Addie came home from the beach. I saw him across the street, staring at her house like he wanted nothing more than to burn it down because I was inside it. That's why I let him hit me first and allowed him to think he'd bested me so fast.

I also knew he'd want Addie dead because it would hurt Daelyn most. He'd save me for last so he could look like a god and show off his power to his crew.

I also gambled with the odds that he'd take me to the Scrapyard to end my life. Like Daelyn said, Kaleb knows every shady motherfucker in the city. And no one is more shady than Silas. Kaleb had the money to buy the old man's silence, but not his loyalty.

That belonged to me.

Silas played both sides of the fight and came out a rich man. As usual. Because of it, Daelyn's gotten away with murder.

My only regret was getting swept up in the desire for revenge. Daelyn and I planned to use the footage of us together in the club to throw it in Kaleb's face as payback. He might have sent her to me, but he never in a million years thought she'd leave him for me. We wanted to rub it in his face.

In hindsight, I wish I hadn't gone that far. He was tortured enough just having a mother like Gretchen. I think he was groomed the longest out of everyone, honestly.

Ace has left the city, and no one can reach him. I'm sure Casey's gone underground by now, too. Everyone else is dead and their bodies have been disposed of by Silas. We'll never know what he did with them.

Fucking hell, my shoulder hurts like a bitch. At least the bullet didn't destroy it. I'm sure I'll be back to swinging in no time.

I was lucky the other night. I could have died a dozen times and didn't. The image of Kaleb dying in my hands will be forever burned in my brain. I can't believe Daelyn killed him.

Does she regret it?

Does she hate herself for it?

Does she hate me?

We haven't talked since that night, and I'm scared for our future.

I know this is hard for her. Kaleb might have been a bad motherfucker, but he was her person for a very long time. I hope she finds peace with her newfound freedom. I hope she finds forgiveness for what I put her through that night.

Silas and his clean-up crew took care of everything at the Scrapyard. He might not be completely loyal to me, but he's one-hundred percent loyal to himself. As a former crime scene cleaner, he's an expert on getting rid of evidence.

Addie's safe too. Ace pretended to attack her that night, so Daelyn would believe Addie was dead, because Kaleb needed to believe it too. He'd be able to tell if she was faking something like that.

My girl's heartbreak was real and raw, and I used it to my advantage.

I hope she forgives me for not letting her in on all the aspects of my plan. I couldn't risk her hesitation and didn't want to jeopardize her any more than I already had.

Ryker's cell goes off and he frowns at the screen. "The girls have arrived. Sophie's letting them in."

I'm in the Butterfly suite, which feels awkward as fuck. It's been a week since the fight and every part of my body still hurts. I think I'm getting soft.

"Shit," I sit up and pull the covers off my lap. "I need a shirt."

"You need to lie back down before I tie you to the bed," Ryker snaps.

"Don't go threatening him with a good time," Vault argues. "He can't have physical activities for at least another week, or he'll bust his stitches."

I look like Frankenstein's twisted little brother. "She can't see me like this."

The door swings open and Daelyn comes in with Addie behind her.

I freeze, feeling insecure, awkward, and out of my depth. There are too many eyes on me, and I don't like it. I need a shirt, so my little sister doesn't see what a monster I am.

Addie carefully sits down next to me. Her gaze sails all over my face like she's searching for the hidden meaning of life behind my bruised eyes and bashed up mouth. Then her gaze drifts down my chest, landing on each scar, bruise, and dressing covering my bullet and stab wounds.

Without saying a word, she leans in and wraps her arms around me.

Yeah… I can't… fuck… this is…

My good arm encases her in a hug of its own accord. "Are you okay?"

"Shouldn't I be asking you that?" She sniffles in my ear. "Oh my god, I have a *brother*." Addie pulls back and I can't stand the tears in her lovely brown eyes.

"Please don't cry. I can't do tears."

"I'm not crying. I'm leaking. It's a piping issue." She quickly swipes her tears away. "See. All good."

"Damn, girl." I bring her in for another hug. This one hurts every part of me because it's tighter and I don't care if I pop a stitch. "I'm so glad you're okay."

She doesn't know about everything that went

down and it's going to stay that way, so help me God. But she knows I fought Kaleb, and that she and Daelyn won't be seeing him ever again.

She also knows, obviously, that Ace helped us and protected her, too.

"Thank you," she whispers in my ear while I hug her. "I owe you everything."

"Nah, baby sister. It's what family does for each other."

I look over at Daelyn, who's hugging herself. "Get over here, Firefly."

Addie moves so Daelyn can take her place.

God, she's so beautiful. My little killer.

My savior.

Cupping her cheek gently, I smile with my busted mouth. "There she is."

Daelyn's expression softens immediately. "Did you just tell me you're in love with me, Dmitri?"

Yeah, that's exactly what I did. I've never love-loved a woman in my life, and it's only because none of them have been Daelyn. The enemy of my enemy is my soul mate. Can you believe that?

My girl leans into me and tenderly traces my swollen face, one curve, one bruise, one cut at a time. "There he is."

She loves me too.

I grab her by the back of the neck and kiss her with all I've got in me.

After a lifetime of fighting, I finally get to claim my prize. My peace. My girl. My heart.

My everything.

Epilogue

Dmitri

Two years later…

I no longer live at the Monarch Club, even though I still work long ass hours there in security. Daelyn and I ended up buying a cute house out in the woods. We've got a king-sized bed to fuck in every night, a fully loaded fridge, and a walk-in closet. It always smells like flowers there too, thanks to whatever concoction Daelyn uses in her diffusers. It's amazing.

Addie's off to college. My smart little half-sister is officially a physics major. Can you believe that shit? I hooked her up with Sophie last year and Addie secured an internship for the summer with Sophie's company. That kid is going places. I'm so proud of her.

We have banana pancakes every Sunday morning, and I eat them like they're my favorite fucking meal. One of these days I'm going to actually like bananas. Don't kill my hope and say otherwise. The joy of having my little family around a table, laughing and teasing, talking about all kinds of shit, is such a gift. Winter break can't come soon enough because I want Addie back home. I'm looking forward to spending more time together.

Therapy's going well for me, too. I see the same

person Ryker does, so I trust them and have been able to work through a lot of my demons. Daelyn's done the same.

"Good morning," she chirps, joining me out on our private deck. The over-water villa we've rented has just about every luxury you can think of. I'm pissed we're only here for another week, but we both have responsibilities back home to return to.

"There she is," I say with a cheesy smile.

The blue-green ocean around us has nothing on the color of her eyes. I swear, every time Daelyn looks at me, I fall more madly in love with her.

My girl saunters over, wearing a silk kimono, and straddles me on the lounge chair. She kisses me like I'm what gives her life.

"Are you sore from last night, Firefly?"

"Only in the best of ways." Her stomach rumbles and she presses her hand to it. "Oh, for fuck's sake, shut up."

"I got you, baby." Snagging a piece of pineapple from the fruit plate I ordered for us, I feed it to her.

"Mmm." She closes her eyes and chews it. "Man, that's good."

While she eats another piece, I slip her kimono off and untie her bikini top. Then the bottoms. She giggles when I feed her another piece of fruit, a kiwi this time, and she bites my finger.

"Fuck, woman." My hard dick pushes against her. "Don't play."

"Oh, I'm playing." She runs her fingers over some of my scars and bites my bottom lip hard enough to break the skin.

My goddamn eyes cross.

"Bad girl." I smack her bare ass and grip it tight.

"I should punish you for that."

"You definitely should, King."

I love this woman so damn much.

Flipping her over, I bracket my arms above her shoulders, and she slips my swim shorts down over my ass. Kicking them off, I settle between her legs like it's my motherfucking throne.

"I should deny you orgasms, Firefly."

Her eyes widen. "Don't you dare!"

I shove the tip of my pierced dick into her pussy, teasing her. "Or maybe I'll take you so hard you won't be able to walk for a few days."

That makes her light up.

"Nah…" I lick my lips. "I'm fucking you slowly." I push into her a little at a time, relishing her torment. When I bottom out, her breath catches.

"Too deep?"

"Too *slow*."

Daelyn likes it most when I fuck her hard and fast. She loves it rough. I don't blame her. I do too. But when I move slowly, like this, it's a special kind of torture for us both. I feel her in every cell of my body when I take my time with her.

Rolling my hips, I move with expert precision, hitting her g-spot and grazing her inner walls with my piercing.

"Fuck," she whimpers. Her hips roll up to meet each of my thrusts.

"I need to taste you," I growl, sliding out and going down on her.

She comes on my tongue in no time. Twice.

Flipping her over, I spank her playfully. "On your knees, ass up, face down."

She squeals and gets into her favorite position,

wiggling her ass at me with excitement.

I can't punish her for long. Rewarding her is so much more fun, anyway. "Spread yourself for me."

Daelyn reaches back and pulls her cheeks apart. "Pick a hole, King."

I slam into her pussy in one harsh thrust that has her pitching forward on the double lounge we're on. "You take my cock so well, Firefly."

Our bodies slap together. The ocean swallows her screams, and that salty sea breeze whirls around my scarred-up body, soothing it like a balm.

We fuck until we both collapse. My heart's pounding so hard in my chest, I can't catch my breath. "I might be the one to stroke out with this one," I say, panting. "Shit, I'm seeing sounds."

Daelyn laughs and peppers kisses all over me. "What a way to die."

Laughter booms out of me. Grabbing her hand, I kiss her knuckles and lace our fingers together. "Marry me."

She stills.

I look over at her, shielding my eyes from the sun, and keep my expression neutral. "Marry me, Daelyn."

Ever since the day our lives changed, we've never discussed our future together. We bought a house, take care of Addie, work, play at the Monarch, and go on vacations. It's not enough for me. Honestly, I don't think anything will be enough for me when it comes to loving Daelyn.

"I wish I could do more, be more, offer more, but all I have is myself." My throat's getting tight. "If you want me, I'm yours."

"Dmitri." Her brow pinches as those blue-green

eyes search my face, like she's trying to read between the lines here.

"I love you," I say plainly. "But if you don't want to…"

"Shut up." She holds my cheeks and smashes her mouth on mine.

"Is that a yes?"

"I thought you didn't believe in marriage or family and all that."

"I also didn't believe in fate before, but here you are." I run my hands up her sides. "Is that a yes?"

"You really want to marry me?"

"And have a family with you."

Her eyes widen. "A *family*?"

"Kids. You know, the little versions of two people combined."

She sits up. "You've had too much sun. You're going mental."

I can tell she's joking. Propping up on my elbows, I cock an eyebrow at her. "I'm not saying I want to stuff you with babies today. But yeah, down the road, I definitely do."

"*Stuff me with babies*?" She holds the side of her head, gawking. "Did you swallow too much sea water?"

Flipping her over, I slightly press my body down to pin her and brush the hair out from her face so I can kiss her forehead. "I'm so happy. I want to be with you forever. I hate you."

Two truths and a lie.

Daelyn's pretty mouth curls into a smile. "I hate you too. I want to be with you forever, too. I'm all yours, King."

"Is that a yes?"

She bites her lip and nods.

"Use your words, Firefly."

"Yes."

I smash my mouth to hers, which makes her legs wrap around my waist, and…

"Do *not* stuff me with babies yet. I'm not ready."

"Well, I'm gonna stuff you with *something*." I thrust into her again and her eyes flutter as she takes all I give her. "Look at me, Firefly." Our gazes lock and I roll my hips slowly, sliding in and out of her in waves of pleasure. "Stay right here with me," I order, keeping our connection rock solid.

"I'm not going anywhere, King."

We make love three more times that day and she falls asleep in my arms, safely under a canopy of stars.

I feel like the king of the motherfucking world.

And Daelyn is my beautifully savage queen.

Other Books By This Author

For information on this book, other books in my backlist, and future releases,
please visit: **www.BrianaMichaels.com**

If you liked this book, please help spread the word by leaving a review on the site you purchased your copy, or on a reader site such as Goodreads.

I'd love to hear from readers too, so feel free to send me an email at: sinsofthesidhe@gmail.com or visit me on Facebook:
www.facebook.com/BrianaMichaelsAuthor

Thank you!

About the Author

Briana Michaels grew up and still lives on the East Coast. When taking a break from the crazy adventures in her head, she enjoys running around with her two children. If there is time to spare, she loves to read, cook, hike in the woods, and sit outside by a roaring fire. She does all of this with the love and support of her amazing husband who always has her back, encouraging her to go for her dreams. Aye, she's a lucky girl indeed.

Made in the USA
Middletown, DE
02 July 2025